ALPHA

A.D. ALIWAT

ALTAIR
PRESS

Published by Altair Press
New York, NY

ISBN: 978-0-692-86821-8

"We hold these truths to be self-evident, that all men are created equal, that they are endowed by their Creator with certain unalienable Rights, that among these are Life, Liberty and the pursuit of Happiness."

Thomas Jefferson et al.
United States Declaration of Independence

Part I
CLAWS

Me, Now

I hate pretty much everyone almost as much as I love myself. This is why life is for the most part easy for me. This is
why everyone loves or respects me, or most often, both.
This is why I'm an alpha.

I'm twenty-five years old. I work for Goldman Sachs, the
best investment bank in the world, in New York City, the
best city in the world. This means many things, the most
important of them being 1) I'm rich and 2) I work a lot.
When I'm not at work, I'm fucking. Seven days a week
I bang some of the most beautiful girls on the planet here.
This is because I know how people work, especially chicks,
and I'm good at getting them to do what I want. Being rich
and attractive enough doesn't hurt, but balls and brains are
really all I need, and what I have in spades. When I am at
work, I also fuck—I fuck people up, I fuck them over, here
in America and also all over the world. I love what I do. I
love fucking. Fuck is my favorite word.
I'm a part of the firm's Real Estate group, and though I
wish I could claim to be involved in the whole subprime

mortgage thing—which you probably know about unless you're an idiot—I was just starting out at the tail end of all that; I was an analyst, and a pretty junior one at that then. Now an associate, I've helped out on my fair share of devious deals, but nothing quite like that yet. The rules and loopholes that made that kind of thing possible are mostly still in place, though (as of me writing this in 2011—and while I can't predict the exact future, it's a safe bet that if they go away more will be discovered), so rest assured: I've been thinking up some comparably spectacular ways to fuck you up, fuck you over, to my sole benefit, and will do that shit as soon as humanly possible.

———— Origin Story ————

I was nine when I figured out it's better to be respected than liked. Prior to that, I was a nice boy. My mom used to dress me in sweaters sometimes when I was really little, and I had good manners and was polite and well behaved; adults loved me, and kids either liked me well enough or were indifferent. I was sitting in school when it first hit me.

My teacher, some hag who would always wear these loose dresses with little flowers on them (probably so she could look at pretty flowers in the mirror instead of her ugly self), had us watch a nature show. She told us it was a "rare treat." It was. We never got to watch videos because she was stupid and thought they didn't teach us well or something. I don't know what made her decide to put one on that day. Most likely she was just being lazy. If I had to guess, I'd say she spent that time sitting there eating chocolates in the dark.

The majority of kids slept or passed notes, but I watched with great interest. It was about a pack of gorillas, and it was then I learned the term "alpha male," its alpha being a gorilla named Gary. Whoever named him was either a jealous pussy-faggot or a dumb bitch who thought they had this great sense of humor and a name like that would just be *so cute*, but they didn't and it wasn't. "Gary" does not befit an alpha. I'm sure if he knew what they were doing, he and his 550 pounds of sheer muscle would have rushed over there and ripped their fucking heads off. Anyway, Gary was the man. Everybody followed him around and he got to fuck all the female gorillas he wanted when he wanted. This was because everyone respected him.

When another gorilla challenged Gary, he'd kick his ass. He did this until he was really, really old, and it took a young, huge, crazy gorilla to finally beat him then. This other gorilla (who was named "Loki") had spent a whole year eyeballing him before he actually picked the fight, and during it, Gary held his own. Only half the pack went with Loki, mostly because Gary, like I said, was the fucking man. I bet he fucked five of the female gorillas that night—the youngest, prettiest ones. Gary had ruled the pack with quiet authority, but Loki was loud and obnoxious; the one thing, though, is when Gary did get loud, he was the loudest.

In the middle of the next recess, I picked a fight with a kid from class, some little goober named Derek. "Hey Derek," I said.

"Yeah?"

"Fuck you." I could tell he was devastated. Derek liked me. We weren't good friends or anything, but sometimes we played kickball or foursquare or basketball or whatever at recess with other classmates, and we had gotten along well enough, I guess. That is up until that point.

"What?"

"Fuck you!" I said, pushing him. Two guys in the grade above us were passing by and stopped to watch.

"Hey, Frank! I'm telling!" he cried. I hadn't really felt bad about any of this, but when he said "I'm telling," I felt even better about it. Nine was a bit too old for anything like that.

He started running away, but I was faster and bigger than him so it wasn't hard to catch up and drag him to the ground. I hit him a few times before a playground monitor (another sloppy hag, probably went home to cats) pulled me off and brought me to the principal's office.

On the car ride home, after she met with the principal and that playground troll, my mom kept asking, "What happened?" over and over, shaking her head as she drove.

"I don't know," I would answer.

We pulled into our driveway. She parked the car and looked at me. "But you're such a nice boy."

"I just want to be cool."

"Well that wasn't cool. I'm disappointed, Francis." She shook her head once more. "It's not cool to pick fights, use language like that."

"It's not?"

She looked at me for a moment and then got out of the car. I sat for a minute.

That night, I spent some time in the mirror punching myself. Eventually I had a bruise on my stomach. I wanted to toughen myself up and my mom coddled me, me being an only son and she being a single mother. I never met my dad or knew too much about him, only that he was of Greek ancestry or something. My mom is almost all English and Welsh, which she'd often tell people to sound classier than she really is, and I still don't know exactly what I am . . . other than 100% Grade A, All-American, of course. She sent me to my room for a few hours that afternoon, but by dinner everything was normal. I kicked a kid's ass at school for what would seem like no reason; this didn't need to be glossed over. I needed tough love. I wanted to be hard, like a rottweiler whose owner beat it. So I beat myself, the genius boy I was.

I don't blame her completely for being the way she was with me, her codependence aside. I mean, I was pretty great (I always got good grades, even after this, and was fun to talk to), but also, I was born in the mid-eighties, and growing up, us Eighties Babies were all told we were the best, that we could be anything we wanted to be; it was normal to spoil kids and fill them with lofty expectations. The only difference between me and everybody else was that I really was the best and really could be anything I wanted to be. This was mostly because of the way I raised myself, though. She was also pretty passive with conflict resolution. My mom was a waitress, soft-spoken by nature, and used to getting shit from people all the time, so she didn't have much fight in her, especially at home. She mostly just hung out and drank tea or smoked cigarettes, reading the paper or magazines and watching TV or whatever. She had me kind of young, early twenties, and after getting fucked, pregnant, and left—her own real hopes and dreams dashed, replaced only by me—the weight of the world had more or less crushed her spirit. I'd exploit this fact most of my life. She was about as good a mom as a born and bred small-town waitress named Angie could be, which is to say not very, so again, I take most of the credit for the great way I turned out.

The next day at school people looked at me different. They stiffened up when I walked by or talked to them, even my best friends.

At lunch this kid in my class, Kingsley, who was athletic and who girls thought was good-looking, but since he was Mormon none of them could "go out" with him, approached me, flanked by his sidekick, another Mormon kid, shorter, named Earl. They were both blond and both assholes. My hair was (is still) dark and I was somewhere between their heights. "Hey Frank."

"Hey."

"So what was that yesterday, dude?"

"What was what?" I asked, effortlessly slipping into my role. It was still a role at that point.

"Why'd you pick on Derek like that?" I can't remember if Derek was Mormon too, but it wouldn't have mattered. Kingsley thought he was this moral compass or something. In addition to being the best athlete in our class and getting ranked first academically (I wouldn't say he was the smartest; that distinction would go to me, and we got the same grades, A's, he just got slightly higher marks because he'd do all the extra credit he could even though he didn't have to, the bitch), he also needed that. He needed to be the fucking sheriff.

"Fuck Derek," I said. I was sitting next to my two best friends, Peter and Kyle, who both turned to their food after I said this, stuffing their faces with tater tots.

"Watch it!" interjected Earl.

"Yeah, man," said Kingsley. "Not cool."

"Fuck you, too." I had the entire table's attention *and* the tables' around us.

"Hey, you know what, Parker, you're being really messed up. What's your deal?" asked Kingsley. Parker is my last name.

"I don't need your shit." My mom didn't argue or anything with her boyfriends at home because she was so weak-willed, but I had seen a few R-rated movies by sneaking tapes or at friends' houses that had HBO or whatever, so I knew cool phrases like this and had a pretty good idea about how to be badass. I was surprised how naturally it all came, but didn't let on.

"Frank!" pleaded Kyle. I shot him a do-not-fuck-with-me-right-now look. I think he just lowered his eyes back down to his tray and stuffed another tot in his cowardly mouth. I turned back to Kingsley and Earl, waiting.

"What a loser," said Kingsley.

"Yeah." They started walking away, shaking their heads.

"What did you call me?"

Kingsley turned around. "A loser. You're acting like one."

In a flash I picked up my tray, my lunch flying everywhere—onto my friends, other kids, tater tots and chicken nuggets here and there, a few globs of ketchup—and struck Kingsley over the head with it. When Earl grabbed me to try to restrain me, I punched him in the nose and made it bleed.

. . .

That afternoon in the principal's office, he, my teacher, and the school counselor were asking my mom all these questions about our home life, if anything had been upsetting me lately, stuff like that. The principal was bald, middle-aged. I don't know how he ever became principal. He spoke like a pussy, with this annoying, whiny voice, to the effect that he sounded almost British or something; for the head of our school, he was hardly an alpha. The counselor was in her late twenties probably. She was someone I wouldn't fuck at my age now because she would be way too old, but at the time I probably thought she was beautiful because there wasn't anything really too wrong with her face and she was blonde and wore lipstick. Kids respond to that kind of shit for whatever reason. So anyhow, they recommended I start counseling sessions with her, and when I refused (alphas never need counseling), they called it "strike two" and said if I had another outburst I would be suspended, maybe even kicked out, and then I'd have to go to the "alternative" school where the most screwed up kids from town went, kids who were like really, really stupid and ate glue all day or already arsonists.

There would be no other incident, though. The following day, I had it: respect. To pick on a little geek like Derek was one thing, but to stand up to a hero like Kingsley, fight him, and win, so fluidly, while taking out his stupid little deputy, was another. Within a week I was the most popular boy in class, within two, I was "going out" with the most popular and prettiest girl, Ashley. We would hold hands sometimes. This may be my most "intimate" "relationship" to date.

At home I had been grounded for two weeks but it didn't really matter; it was a little annoying, but I guess I still appreciated the semblance of tough love. I already had everything I wanted at school and that was the world that counted. Nobody really liked me, they liked Kingsley—but they *listened* to me. I picked what we'd all do at recess. I could persuade everyone in the class, even the boys that wore coats all year and just liked to read comic books or the weird girls that still played with dolls, to join in a class-wide game of Red Rover if I felt like it. My friends became cooler (though I'd soon ditch them). All my ideas were great, jokes hilarious. They were just afraid. But that was the point and it was easier for everyone; no one dared pick a fight, and I generally ruled with quiet authority like Gary. It worked.

They say your personality is formed by age five or whatever, but I'm proof that change is possible. You can be whoever you want to be. Sometimes all it takes is a little inspiration and effort. The beauty about choosing to be a dick is once you've made the choice and committed, you're unstoppable. Eventually everything becomes second nature or instinct, but you never forget what it's like to be nice, to be ineffective, so it keeps you hungry. And you always win.

——— My First Porno ———

I was eleven when I watched my first porno. I had seen a few *Playboys* and other magazines the previous year, and nudity in movies and stuff, but nothing that showed actual fucking until then. It was me and my friends Leon and Cole. They became my new best friends shortly after I beat up those Mormons because they naturally were cooler. They were both big, like me (big enough, that is, not freakish like some kids, just a little taller than most in our grade, with more muscle definition on their developing frames); they both came from families with some money, meaning a sense of entitlement came easy (I didn't, obviously, since my mom was just a fucking waitress, so another benefit of befriending them was being able to enjoy their nice things); and we were all considerably better at sports than most other kids. With girls, I typically went out with the hottest one in the grade, while second and third alternated between them. It was a good posse.

We were at Cole's house. He had a cool older brother in high school who was out for the night, so we decided to sneak into his room after his parents had gone to bed and snoop around. He had a pretty normal room for a high school kid I guess, except with a TV because they were rich enough for that sort of thing. Under his bed there was this porno stash, some magazines, tapes. I put the tape in that had the hottest chick on the cover—this blonde with big, fake tits. The first few minutes were story only, some stupid shit about a haunted hotel or whatever, so I fast-forwarded until I saw people naked. The blonde was getting finger-fucked by this kind of muscular guy with slicked back hair and a goatee. He was Italian, I think, but spoke in heavily accented English. "Yesssh, yesssh," he said. She moaned, her boobs wobbling (as much as fake ones can), nipples all pointy. "You like that, beeeeach?"

"Uh-huh!" she answered nodding, all into it.

"I am going to fockk you. I am going to fockk you in thee poooosy!" And then he did. First in missionary, then with her on top, then in doggy, then with her in reverse cowgirl, then sideways, before finally finishing up by getting a blowjob and giving her a wad to the face, which, after smearing around a bit, she swallowed.

I was in love. Not with her or porn or anything stupid like that, but with the idea it presented: dominance and power so direct and in such a physical and seemingly pleasurable way. Though my dick was hard then, I knew there would be a few years before I could really do anything with it. I could not fucking wait.

—————— **Moses Lake** ——————

The town I grew up in is this place called Moses Lake, in the middle of Washington State. I like being from Washington because it was named after our first president and was one of the last states that was made into a state. It makes you feel like a pioneer kind of still, like you can influence as much as George Washington and the other founders influenced America. In the area I'm from, especially, there's a lot of open space between the towns, and because it's technically a desert and there aren't many trees, there's a whole lot of sky, and it all seems rife with possibilities like our country used to be everywhere. You feel like you can fill up that space with something great. In my case, I wanted to fill it with myself, my greatness (and I did, in a way, in high school; you'll see how). Its vibe was something like Springfield on *The Simpsons:* an isolated Anytown, America where everybody knew everybody.

Whenever I tell people now I'm from Moses Lake, most, obviously, have never heard of it, and a lot of them ask if its name has something to do with the Bible. Its origins are less weird than that, but still interesting enough.

It was named after this American Indian leader named Chief Moses who liked to hang out in the area with his tribe before a bunch of settlers came and fucked his shit up in the late 1800s. The region it's in has 300 days of sunshine a year, which few people believe because practically everyone thinks all of Washington is Seattle. (And why wouldn't they in New York or anywhere else? They barely know the difference between it and Oregon, which, at least on the East Coast, they chronically, almost pridefully mispronounce "Oh-Re-Gone.") Since it was so nice and sunny, it was a natural place for some silly Indians to get pushed out of and also fucked in terms of forming a reservation anywhere close by. The lake itself is pretty big, though this is mostly because it was filled out by the guys who stole it, through damming and irrigation and shit. They made it better, like white people made all of America.

Apparently, one day while all this was happening, good ol' Chief Moses asked one of his tribesmen to count the grains of sand in a pile. His guy goes, "There are too many." Having set him up, the wise chief then replies, "It is the same with whites. There are too many." I imagine a single tear forming in his eye, like that famous seventies PSA of the Indian looking at all that garbage on the side of the road. Stupid asshole.

Anyway, the settlers named their new home "Neppel," taken from this place in Germany one prominent enough guy liked, and then during the 1930s, when it was incorporated into an actual town, the group responsible renamed it after the big chief, then long-dead. The residents also paid him tribute later on by naming one of the junior highs "Chief Moses Junior High" and by making the high school mascot "the chief," with students for many years yelling out "Home of the 'chiefs!' " instead of "brave!" during the national anthem at sporting events and assemblies. One year while I was there, this long-standing tradition was seen as un-American by a new teacher and the school put an end to it. It's kind of awesome that the school did that, because shouting out the wrong final lyric to America's most beautiful and important song is pretty obnoxious, but it's not as awesome as honoring the guy whose land we stole by patronizing him.

It's an okay place to live. The primary industries are agriculture and manufacturing, so there are a lot of blue-collar workers and Mexican immigrants. Most people buy everything at Wal-Mart, are sort of stupid, and like to keep things simple, never really questioning much of consequence; though there are a few smart winners around, too, your doctors, lawyers, and people with summer vacation homes from Seattle. They all live on the lake like multi-millionaires do in more affluent parts of the country. So, yeah, it's one of *those* towns, and that's fine because the people are the right type—easy to manipulate, easy to dominate. I'm proud to be from there.

—— Intro to Seventh Grade ——

Upon entering the seventh grade, I was faced with the challenge of ruling a much larger, more diverse group. There were a couple of tools I had at my disposal—my experience, of course, and the fact that my voice had dropped a bit in the summer preceding it. Still, gone were the same thirty faces in the same class all day and the same four or five classes making up each grade. This new school had 200 kids per grade with alternating class schedules. It's harder to maintain constant fear in an environment like that.

What's worse, the kids, instead of just being kids, began to define themselves, to split into factions—the skaters, thugs, preps, nerds, all that cliquey stuff. There would be leaders and subordinates among each crowd, but how do you reign supreme over them all? And what if, God forbid, the hottest girl happened to be a, say, goth? The answer was simple: be a prep. Male preps are typically jocks, but it being the late nineties, nobody really used that term anymore, and it was better to identify yourself in a group with girls, because otherwise it's gay. Everybody knew who preps were, and while mostly disliked by every other circle, they were still talked about, or respected, and this was all that mattered. In addition to acting sort of better than everyone and having some affiliation with a sport, all it really took to be a prep was to wear the right kind of name brand clothing: Abercrombie & Fitch, Ralph Lauren, Gap, with logos visible, but not too large (that would be trying too hard). The problem of the hottest girl being a goth wouldn't be one, not only because most thirteen-year-old goths are fucking fat freaks, but also, simply, if she were a goth she couldn't be the hottest girl. That's just how it worked. It wouldn't matter if she had the most beautiful face or whatever, or the biggest boobs, nicest ass, anything like that, because, by law, the hottest girls in the school were always preps. Fortunately for me, the seventh grader who actually had the most beautiful face, the biggest boobs, and nicest ass was a prep. Her name was Callie, she was in my second-period class, and after scouting the entire grade (cool and stealthily, of course) at lunch that first day to make sure there wasn't anyone hotter, I decided that bitch would be mine. (A caveat: In terms of traditional alpha principles, the thugs were really the most dominant at this age. Between their legitimate don't-give-a-fuck attitude, enthusiasm for violence, and advanced sexual activity, they commanded the most fear and were thus the most respected. However, they weren't really in the game. They played their own game, this weird fast-tracked life where the girls were pregnant at thirteen, fourteen, and the boys, in addition to maybe being fathers, had probably gone to juvie or been an accessory to a serious enough crime without getting caught. The rest of us, actually playing the game, followed them with distant awe, like they were Hollywood celebrities, but evil, poor, and 99% minorities (mostly Mexican). Having either dropped out, had babies, or gone to jail by high school, or all three, they were eventually forgotten.)

This meant I had to go out for the football team, which held tryouts the first week of school. And I also had to get a pretty good position, hopefully make captain. I tried out for quarterback.

In elementary school, after my transformation, I had always played quarterback during recess. This was not because I was the most qualified person for the job, at first, at least—after enough practice, I did get good—but mostly because I wouldn't let anybody else even try. As an alpha, this was my role. I was the leader. I was the fucking quarterback, always. And the quarterback on the other team was typically someone like Kingsley who knew better than to actually win, though I doubt they could have if they really tried. Like I said, I did get good, and I always had some top notch betas on my team like Leon or Cole to make the games barely even a contest, so that sometimes they weren't even fun. We would make them fun, though, by showboating and talking a lot of shit, loudly, too, with me being more a conduit for their volume, my style, again, being one of quiet authority. I could egg them on, however, with a single glance.

Here would be different. I actually had to prove myself, which was something I hadn't really had to do since I was nine. It was also around this time that I began to seriously consider what I wanted to do with my life, the start of seventh grade feeling pretty momentous in that "growing up" *Wonder Years* kind of way or whatever, and I decided then that the best job in the world was professional quarterback and naturally that should be my job when I was an adult, hopefully for a traditionally winning program like the Cowboys, Packers, or Broncos. The stakes were high. I mean, I was still confident . . . and I did believe I would be the starting quarterback, the team captain, and the guy to go out with Callie, to have her rockin' boobs, already budded—large B's, maybe even C's—in my palms when I wasn't gripping a football, to be the prince-in-waiting of the school (the king would obviously be an eighth grader, there was nothing I could do about that), and grow up to lead my team to win the most Super Bowls in football history, a record never to be broken for all time, but there was a chance I wouldn't. And I had never hated anything more than the idea of that chance.

The first day of tryouts were held on the second day of school. We all met in the gym, and there were many of us, forty, maybe fifty. I had Leon and Cole with me, a few other latchers-on from elementary school, even those shit-heads Kingsley and Earl, and there were similar groups clustered by their old schools, all of us talking loudly, some shouting even, vying for attention, trying to establish dominance already.

The coach came in—he was a big guy, fat really, but tall and with broad enough shoulders that he didn't look completely like a slob. His assistant coach was a bit smaller but looked pretty athletic. They lined us up along the bleachers, gave us a little introductory talk, had a look at us. We were told we'd play our crosstown rivals, the Warriors, in three weeks.

Afterwards, we went into the locker room, got our uniforms, learned each other's names as much as we could or cared to at that point, sized each other up. Then we went out to the fields, did some conditioning, some drills. There was competition, but nothing I felt I couldn't handle. Try-outs would go through the end of the week.

. . .

When all was said and done, I made second-string. That fucking fat idiot coach fucked me. There was this taller, slightly faster douchebag he thought was better than me, even though he wasn't (I was a way better passer), named Squanto. He was like half American Indian so he was abnormally tall and lean for a seventh grader. He actually looked Mexican, like a third of the kids in my town, but he wasn't short and troll-like like most of them were. Maybe the coach picked him because our team was "The Braves" and he thought it might have had some sort of advantageous psychological effect to be led by a real Indian, but probably not because he was too stupid for anything like that. I don't know; I guess I still can't really figure out why I wasn't first choice, so I'm reaching.

The situation was shitty but nothing I couldn't deal with. Squanto wasn't the type of guy that would get Callie regardless; his football skills aside, he was soft spoken and pleasant, not really an alpha. I had to make sure, though, and I also had to make sure I'd start seventh grade and for most intents and purposes my football career as a fucking winner, not a loser that rode the goddam pine watching someone else get all the glory.

Belt

Immediately after I learned I'd made second-string, I went home and beat myself with a belt. At first I held it by the buckle and just kind of whipped my back with it, and while it did hurt, it didn't feel like adequate punishment for making second-string. So I switched to holding it at the other end so that the buckle would crash against my back. The pain was deeper and longer lasting than the uneven stinging sensation I experienced before, and after hitting my left shoulder enough times and seeing more bruises forming than welts, I felt I had done the trick.

———— Bloodlust ————

The night before we faced the Warriors, who were also awesomely named out of fake-respect for subjugated Indians (their school was Frontier; I went to that other junior high, which we just called "Chief Mo"), I paid Squanto a visit. He came from this elementary school in the part of town that was next to mine, so his place wasn't too-too far from my own. I had found out where he lived the week before by asking a few peripheral questions to his friends ("Hey, so what school did you go to before here? Cool . . .") and looking up his last name in the phone book. It was easy math. I wore a black hoodie and pants, and carried a ski mask in my pocket for when the time came. I had ridden my bicycle, holding a crowbar with the handlebars. They were pretty similar in size and it didn't affect my steering all that much.

I rang the doorbell and hid behind a bush in his yard. Luckily, he answered the door. I hadn't really thought about what I'd do if he didn't. I sprang from behind the bush, wearing the ski mask, wielding the crowbar, and struck him on the left knee, his pivot knee. He screamed, screeched, yelped, whatever you'd like to call it—the point is, it wasn't masculine—and then I hit the other knee, too, for good measure, before that wimpy sound he made from the first strike had come to its natural end. The second sound was even worse, made him sound even more like a bitch. It was really inexcusable for a first-string quarterback, even if he was only twelve. I hopped on my bike and peddled madly away, never looking back.

The next day at school he showed up late with a cast on his left leg, moving around on crutches. I guess the strike to his right wasn't as effective, or else he probably would've been in a wheelchair or something. The rumor mill was in full swing, and fortunately, and as I had planned, the theory that stuck was that it was one of those cheating asshole Warriors that attacked him. This bonded my teammates even more and filled us with a burning hatred for our rivals that we didn't know we were capable of. When we took the field that afternoon, motivated by bloodlust, we were sharp and ready, more so than we ever could have been had I not done what I did, the brilliant kid I was. I would start and the team was fired up. It was a win-win.

Before the game, after the team locker room motivational speech, the coach pulled me aside and gave me my own little pep talk, told me I was a born leader, he knew it, offered other sports movie platitudes. Idiot. Anyway, I played amazingly well and we won 21-13. I of course dedicated our win and gave the game ball to Squanto, who had watched from the bench, presumably in the spot that would have been mine, his cast, signed by the entire team, digging into the turf. My signature was the largest.

———— A Good Reputation ————

Aside from Squanto, who became very well known throughout both grades as an object of sympathy—the worst form of popularity for a male—I was then the most popular seventh grader and, without a doubt, the alpha. The team was enjoying a winning season, having lost only once in five weeks, and I was its star.

Still, this was not enough to win Callie. She was so hot the eighth graders liked her too. I couldn't blame them; her knockers were bigger than most of their girls' and with all the attention, she seemed eager to please. Blonde-haired and blue-eyed, she epitomized the sweet faux-naiveté of a girl coming into her powers, excuse me, a female's only power: pussy. It's not that she would actually ever fuck anyone (we weren't thugs), she would just use a coy smile, a flutter of lashes, the acceptance of an arm around her shoulder or waist, stuff like that, to increase her popularity and drive the hormonal thirteen- and fourteen-year-olds of the eighth-grade class crazy. Seventh graders had no chance. But she liked me, as much as she could let herself, I could tell. I'd catch her glancing over in our social studies class from time to time, and she laughed at the jokes I'd occasionally make during class discussions, but everyone did, even the teacher, and even if they weren't really all that funny. I was, after all, the fucking quarterback, the prince-in-waiting.

I made it a point not to talk to her because I still planned on going out with her at some point, and if I struck up a conversation then, I'd risk entering into the friend-zone, a fucking stupid place for any guy to be. It's better to maintain mystery and attack when the time is right. So even though we shared some friends at the top of the seventh-grade strata, even sitting at the same lunch table, I ignored her completely. Instead, I coasted by dating the second-hottest girl in the grade, Virginia. Her boobs weren't like Callie's—no one's were—but she had a great ass and a pretty face framed nicely by shiny black hair. (Maybe you think it's been a little weird of me to describe all these seventh graders' boobs and asses and facial hotness and shit being that I'm a full-grown man now, but these were my exact thoughts at the time, and that's what this thing is about: truth; I obviously wouldn't try to fuck a twelve-year-old now or anything . . . this is just honesty—deal with it.) We would make out sometimes after school, before practice, in this secluded corner near the locker room and football field.

I had tongue kissed two girls before her. One was my girlfriend in the sixth grade, Brooke; the other some slut from camp over the summer. Brooke had been a shitty kisser. She just pushed her tongue in and out of my mouth, once in a while making wide, hard swoops. It felt like trying to eat a live goldfish or salamander or something. Also, somehow, invariably, the lower region of my face, from nose to chin, would end up covered with saliva. I tried to correct her, slow her down, to be more careful, use more control, but it was no use. She was just sloppy. When I broke up with her on the last day of school, telling her I thought we should be free for the summer, that we should go into junior high without any strings, to meet new people, do new things, she said, "That's fine. I was about to break up with you anyways."

"Yeah?" I asked. We were at this park next to the school where we'd always hang out before going home. I sat with her alone on a bench, our friends trying to listen in a few yards away.

"I didn't want you holding me down next year."

"Okay, even though that's basically what I just told you," I said.

"Well it's true."

"You know what else is true?"

"What?" she asked, her nostrils flaring.

"You're a shitty kisser."

"What?!?" She grabbed onto my arm.

"Really sloppy." I brushed her off and then got up. "Bye." I think she started crying, but I didn't look back. I just left with Leon and Cole and we went to Cole's house to play video games or eat grilled cheese sandwiches or something. I didn't talk to her for the rest of the summer, and when we saw each other the first week at our new school she smiled and tried to be friendly but I ignored her.

I can't remember the name of the slut from camp, but she was a good kisser. She must have practiced with another girl back home or something, 'cause she told me I was her first "real" kiss. Very soft and light, precise flicks. We exchanged addresses and she wrote me a letter a week after camp but I never wrote back. Only pussies write letters.

Virginia was a good kisser, too, but mostly because of me. She also told me I was her first kiss, except without the qualifier of "real," and I believed her because at first she seemed clueless, but not in the slobbery way of that force of nature Brooke. I said, "Don't worry about it, just follow my lead," and grabbing her and kissing her again, she followed well enough and we settled into a nice groove. A couple of sessions later and she was a pro, like me. She would tell her friends what a great kisser I was and it would be cake for the rest of junior high. I didn't really mind that she would spread this news just to talk herself up (she got to date the alpha and best kisser in the grade, so that must have meant she kissed well and was super cool, too). That's simply what chicks do because they're conniving bitches that hate each other almost as much as I hate them. But whatever. A reputation as a good kisser in junior high is invaluable.

——— On Reputation ———

Respect is created by one person for another; reputation is created by people for a person. Reputation, like respect, is one of the most important things there is. Yes, everybody should respect you, but what a good reputation ensures is that despite a person's real opinion of you, favorable or not, or with genuine respect or not, they'll still act in a way that seems favorable, that bends to your will, or as if they respect you. Your status on a plane above, or as alongside but on your way above, is maintained. Once a dynamic has been established for long enough, people are unlikely to change the way they behave with you.

Since humans are social animals, you're basically only as good as your reputation. I still have a great one. My reputation allows me to exercise power over co-workers. My reputation allows me to fuck beautiful girls. My reputation will soon allow me to rob clients blind, once I am made VP and get some of my own. It allows me to do pretty much whatever I want. It's my first and usually only needed line of defense. But it is a thing dependent on inertia, and as ridiculous as this may sound, I don't know if I'd be where I am now if not for my reputation as a really good kisser in junior high, as the cool seventh-grade quarterback, the guy that beat up the two Mormon kids before that. It's what brought me this far and will take me even further.

Tragedy

A couple of weeks after football ended, it was time for basketball. I made the "A" team. I wasn't the best player or captain or anything, but I did start, and that was cool.

Basketball was a lark compared to football, and the way I led our team to a winning record in that had more or less solidified my status for the year. I thought nothing could threaten my place on top. Then, during the second half of the season, tragedy struck: Virginia developed acne. A great ass is not enough to make up for a shitty complexion. So, after a week of noticeable bumps without signs of effective treatment, I broke up with her. "Can I talk to you for a minute, out in the hall?" I asked one day at lunch.

"Sure . . ." she said. We left the cafeteria and found a little nook in the hallway, near the bathrooms.

"Look—you're a great girl, and I like you a lot, but I don't think we should go out anymore."

Her eyes darted back and forth. "Wh—Why?"

"I just . . . It's not working for me anymore, okay? I like someone else."

"Wh—Who?" I apparently made her develop a stutter.

"Don't," I said. "Just don't." Then I walked back into the cafeteria and joined Leon and Cole in a conversation about what was on MTV the previous night or something. In the split-second before I left she had already started to cry. I had been actively looking for her reaction—to see how much I hurt her, how much not having me be her boyfriend anymore would wreck her—otherwise I probably wouldn't have noticed . . . it was really hard to pay attention to her eyes, anything, with all those fucking pimples.

I say this is a tragedy not because I actually cared about Virginia but because, before this, she was the hottest girl in the grade next to Callie. Now the hottest girl was Tiffany, who was dating Leon. In fact, all of the really attractive girls were dating someone on the team until there was no one even datable for a delta left. So what to do? I could poach Leon's girlfriend, but that wouldn't feel right. Not because Leon is my friend. There could be other Leons. Fuck him. But, rather, because it would feel like I'd just be getting his sloppy seconds, and he was a beta, and an alpha never takes a beta's sloppy seconds, that is unless there is a breakup and she then somehow becomes substantially more attractive, an alpha in her own right.

It wasn't really acceptable to be single for more than a week, two tops, if you were cool in junior high. So I came up with a plan—when I had to, I would make a girl up. Luckily for me, Christmas break was right around the corner, so that would buy me a little more time. But to maintain my status, I knew people would need to think I had another hot girlfriend soon. Also, I had told Virginia I liked someone else, and she would tell her friends this, swallowing her pride when pressed hard enough, so when it got back to me, there had to be someone to talk about, because what's the point of telling anybody you like someone unless you go out with them? You can't maintain top-dog status with any unrequited feelings out there. So who was she? She couldn't come from Frontier because people still knew people from there, cousins, friends that moved, etcetera. She would be from one of the next towns over. I'd date her until something else (real) materialized, a hot new transfer student, Callie realizing all the eighth graders were turds (they were), something like that.

—— Fake Girlfriend ——

During Christmas break, I was hanging out one day with Cole, who at the time was dating Paige, Virginia's best friend. He asked, "Hey, so who's the chick?"

"What do you mean?" We were in his bedroom, playing this new video game he got for Christmas, Mortal Kombat 4. It was super violent and awesome.

"Virginia told Paige you broke up with her for someone else."

"Oh, yeah. Just some chick."

"Yeah? Who?" Cole was kind of dumb, but he knew what he was doing. He was on the offensive. If I ever had to move, he probably would have been the next alpha.

"Some girl from Warden."

"What?" he snickered. "Warden?" Warden was this tiny farm town close by, and people from there had to come to Moses Lake for shit to do. While where we lived wasn't exactly bustling, it sure was compared to that fucking two-bit cow town.

"Even hotter than Callie."

"Bullshit. Where'd you meet her?"

"Lamonts. She was clothes shopping. Nicest boobs in the world. Coulda been D's. Seriously."

"Yeah?" I had him. The story worked. I probably wouldn't even have to give a name.

"Yeah. Got her number, we've been talking. She comes here at least once a week with her mom to shop and stuff. We're gonna go to a movie this weekend."

"Nice."

"But you know we won't actually be watching it." We high-fived and then got more into the game. He had come from behind and almost beat me but then I used a couple of cheap moves I knew from the previous version and won.

——— Bloody Nose ———

While I was pleased with how easy it was to get Cole to believe in my fake girlfriend, I also felt some level of shame afterwards. I mean, sure, everything about my plan and the way I executed it was genius and all, but really, I was the seventh-grade quarterback and pretty hot shit; I should have had a real girlfriend. It should have been Callie. It should have been Callie from the first day of school. Fuck the eighth graders—if I was going to be a professional quarterback, I should have been cooler than them by that point already. I should have been cooler than high schoolers.

These were my thoughts right before and as I started punching myself in the nose in my bedroom the evening after I went to Cole's. I did so cautiously because it was very important to me not to break it, not to make myself ugly, but to get it to bleed. It did, eventually, without any real disturbance to the cartilage or bone. I licked the blood when it reached my upper lip, but went to sleep that night without wiping off any of what lingered around my nose. It dried in the night and I washed it off of my face the next morning, the damage done, nothing left to see.

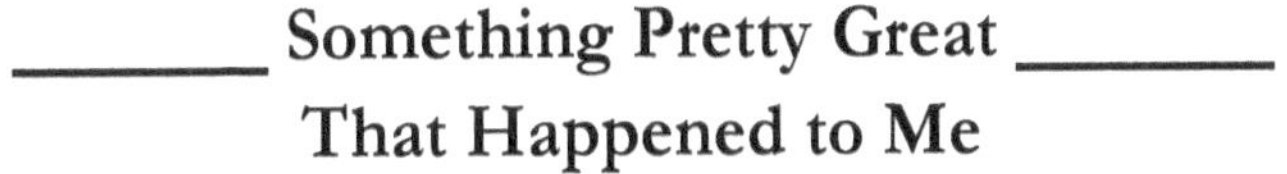

Something Pretty Great That Happened to Me

Two weeks after school resumed, things were going pretty well. Occasionally someone would ask me about my new girlfriend, and I'd say, "She's from Warden. You wouldn't know her, but she's hot." And that would be it . . . except twice. The first time was when this one guy, Ryan, who had been on the basketball team, was like, "Oh, hey, I got a cousin in Warden. What's her name?" And I responded with, "Your mom." That shut him up, mostly because it made everybody within earshot laugh. The second time, this girl, Shawna, one of Virginia and Paige's friends, goes, "Oh, hey, I lived in Warden when I was in the third grade. Maybe I know her." And I said, "Maybe you do, but I don't want you telling Virginia about her." Then she was all, "Come on. I won't tell!" And I go, "Yes you will. She's already been through enough," and left, just as she goes, "Is it Morgan?!?" This made me a little nervous at first. I didn't want her snooping around, asking questions to any of her old friends there. It was a pretty small town, so I think they'd know if anyone was going out with someone from Moses Lake, which was, by comparison, a booming metropolis. But then I thought about the way she said "I won't tell!" because she sounded a little in love with me, which I suspected anyway because most girls in seventh grade were, and I figured maybe she just wanted to know for her own purposes. Then it occurred to me that she probably never lived in Warden at all. This was probably the case, the bitch.

By the third week back, though, I began to feel a bit antsy. I hadn't made out with anyone in a little over a month. I liked making out. And seeing everybody else with their girlfriends pissed me off. I was the coolest guy in the fucking grade; I should have had a girlfriend. I didn't want to have to give myself another bloody nose, or worse. Something had to give, soon. And it did.

At the end of January the winter dance happened, and along with it, something pretty great for me. I was there in a group with Cole, Leon, Ryan, and these other kids Brady and Chris, who had also been on the basketball and football teams with me, and all of their dumb girlfriends, including my ex, Virginia, who was now dating Brady. It didn't irritate me or anything to be with the two of them holding hands or whatever; she was still ugly. I actually felt sorry for the guy. And I don't ever feel sorry for anybody.

The only time anyone actually danced was during slow songs. We mostly just stood around talking. Junior high was before it was acceptable to freak dance or grind (though the thugs did, before getting kicked out and probably just going home and fucking for real), so this made sense. Fast dancing without dry humping is fucking retarded and makes everyone who does it look like an idiot. Anyhow, I'd make everybody laugh, even Virginia, by making fun of fast dancers and ugly and unpopular kids at the school, and then, when a slow song started, hot off the heels of a hilarious joke, I'd steal one of my friends' girlfriends and dance with her. It was nice. We would move in very slow rotations, my hands on their hips, theirs on my shoulders, some space between us until I would pull them closer and we would more or less hug-dance. I was twelve at the time, and though I was on the taller end for a normal guy my age, around 5'5", the girls had already hit their first major growth spurts, so they too were tall, and it was easy to stare at their boobs, especially since their high heels made it so they might have only been an inch or two shorter than me, some even my height. But better than seeing their boobs was feeling them firm against my chest when I pulled them in. For the most part, it was a thrill for them, getting to dance with the super-cool, fun-loving seventh-grade alpha, getting a break from their lesser boyfriends to spend time with the best of the best.

Only Tiffany rejected me, and only the third time, after I had already danced with all of them twice—except

Virginia, who I refused to dance with at all—when I was cycling through the best ones (her and Paige) again. She was the first one I danced with, on the first slow song, because she was still the hottest girl in the grade next to Callie. I also did this so that Leon would have my sloppy seconds for the rest of the night. She wanted to dance with Leon, saying the song playing, Aerosmith's *I Don't Want to Miss a Thing*, was "their song," but I hardly believed that. Tiffany was a bitch.

Our territory in the gym had been near the cool eighth graders. This was mostly because of Callie, who would float between the two groups to say hello to the girls in ours, her lunch friends, and hang out with her boyfriend, Julio, an eighth-grade beta, and his friends. (The residual effect of the thugs actually being way cooler than everyone at that age was that all of the Mexicans were automatically a little cooler, including him, who, while a prep with good brand name clothes, wasn't that great at sports. He really had no business going out with Callie, despite his thirteen-year-old Mexican edginess.) So there I was, standing alone like a jackass while everyone started slow dancing around me, and just as I decided to make a break for the bathroom, to avoid further embarrassment, I felt a tap on the shoulder. I turned and it was this eighth-grade girl, Luanne, popular, with pretty nice boobs, mid-sized B's, brown hair, green eyes. I had seen her around school hanging out with the other eighth-grade preps. She grabbed onto my shoulders and I held her waist and we started to dance. In her heels she was a little taller than me, and even though it was a quarter of an inch at most, it was a little awkward. "I didn't have anyone to dance with either and I love this song," she said.

"It's not that I didn't have a partner, I was just gonna step out for a minute."

"Okay then." She let go, stepping back and breaking away. I grabbed onto her again. She smiled.

"So who'd you come here with?"

"Everybody."

"Okay."

"Everybody that matters, anyway."

"But no date?" I asked.

"You're my date now," she said, grinning. She had very nice teeth. She probably had braces the previous year. I was glad I missed that. I smiled back. But I couldn't tell if she was fucking with me or not. "You were the quarterback for the seventh graders, right?"

"Yeah," I said. "Led the team to a 5-1 seas—"

"Shut up. This is my favorite part." It was probably the chorus, since I remember her singing at this point, and girls rarely take it upon themselves to learn *all* the words to anything because they're stupid. If she were my age, I would've stopped dancing and walked away—nobody tells me to shut up—but since she was older and cooler, and because while looking around I could see how impressed everyone was with me, even the eighth graders, I let it slide. She pulled me closer and we hug-danced. Her boobs felt incredible pressed against my chest. I actually started getting a boner, so I backed away, which she loved (judging by her mock-angry expression, the crinkle of her little nose), and when the chorus came back and she pulled me in again, I had already made it die by thinking of Virginia's festering pimples. As the song was ending, she finished singing the last chorus, giggled, and said, "Thanks!" before letting go of my shoulders.

I, however, did not let go of her. "Can I call you some time?"

She laughed and broke away, rejoining her friends. Then she turned back. "Sure! I'm in the book!"

A week later we were going out. I guess this is as good a place as any to describe what I looked like then, and sort of look like now, because that does matter. I'm not the best-looking guy in the world or anything, but I could be a lot worse. While the most important thing in getting girls is confidence (and not looks like it is vice-versa), I do have physical features that help, and maybe I wouldn't have been able to land Luanne had I not looked the way I looked, though I probably would have. I was still not without some baby fat, but my face was forming nicely. Notably, I have: a strong jawline and chin, available eyes framed by a somewhat prominent brow, and an overall sense of symmetry. Chicks like symmetrical features because they subliminally think they're good for child rearing, and the others are indicative of masculinity and strength, without being ugly and broken like a real warrior's face (even though chicks kinda dig scars, not so much on the face). My least favorite features are my nose, which is a little too large, and my ears, which are the opposite. The biggest difference between now and then is that my eyes were really still those wide eyes of a child—now they are cooler, more mysterious and calculating, but in a way that somehow still seems inviting. Other attributes I have are a pretty long neck, a good ass, broad shoulders, and nice hands, with my ring finger a little longer than my index, another trait chicks like for some reason. Overall, my look works.

I found her number in the phonebook and called her on the Sunday following the dance, and we got along really well. A lot of girls were hard to talk to on the phone. Brooke, for example, from the sixth grade, talked way too fucking much. Spending any time on the phone with a high-pitched eleven-year-old who rattles on endlessly about nothing—shoes she wanted, how much she loved butter-flies—is a punishment, let alone ten to fifteen minutes a night. Virginia had talked too little. A typical conversation had me asking 75% of the questions, and getting next to nothing in response. This was unacceptable. First of all, asking too many questions makes you seem overeager, like a little bitch, and second, she should have had stories pre-pared for me. She should have been there to entertain me. I was, after all, the fucking quarterback.

The first was a case of being so pretty that she had li-cense to be as annoying as possible, the second a case of being so pretty she could be as boring as possible. I was sure the zits would change that for Virginia, make her de-velop a personality. Luanne, on the other hand, was pretty, but I suspected had had braces, which would have given her the character building necessary to become a decent conversationalist.

Through her I was reluctantly accepted into the eighth-grade social circle. I would go with her to their parties and nights out at the movie theater, which were fun because we'd make out and stuff, and she was a really great kisser, probably from the extra year of practice and tongue dexter-ity developed from having to kiss with braces (which was, in fact, confirmed when I eventually saw a yearbook from the previous year). At the movies we'd hold hands, and any of my old seventh-grade friends that happened by looked at me not only as their alpha, but a god. But there was a downside, too. The eighth-grade guys hated me and were vocal about it. This was weird for me, since I was used to everybody around me loving everything I did and said, or at least pretending to. I had to be tactful in the way I dealt with it. I would have liked to have just picked a fight with their alpha, the team quarterback, Nick, who the first time I went to a movie with them asked "What's this fag doing here?" but this wouldn't have worked for a number of reasons. First, Nick was considerably larger than me, and though I'm sure I could have beaten him by fighting dirty (aiming for the balls, biting, gouging his eyes, etc.; my hormones raging, I had that in me at that age), only a bitch like Loki the gorilla fights like that, and I was sure there would be witnesses who would discount my win. Also, even after I won, and even if this was somehow done legitimately, I still would not have assumed alpha status. Theirs was a bond formed over almost two years of dominating their grade and playing on sports teams. That kind of group dynamic for thirteen- and fourteen-year-olds is impenetrable. So what to do? I couldn't just take that shit. Well, the eighth-grade team had a worse record than us, so I used that. Whenever they'd talk shit, I'd remind them that I led my team to a "5-1" season while theirs had been just "3-3," the fucking losers. I knew they could trump me by alluding to my initial second-string status, but I figured they probably hadn't cared enough to learn this about me, and if they had, they would have done more damage to themselves by admitting they knew so much about a seventh grader than they would me.

And so it went. They hated me, but had to respect me to a degree, and any time they gave me shit, I used similar tactics and insults of pride to make them stop. I was cool about it though, un-clown-like. Frequently I made all the girls laugh with my comebacks, especially Callie, who I think identified with me as something of a fish out of water, having undoubtedly received similar attitudes from the girls in the circle at first, though in that passive-aggressive bitchy way chicks are wont to use. Luanne laughed hard also, but seemed only to really get into it after I'd make Callie burst out. I could hear the extra effort, which I found charming, though I also appreciated Callie's earnestness. I also appreciated the way her boobs bounced when she laughed. They seemed to get bigger every day, not that Luanne's were anything to thumb your nose at, either.

I was able to accept my role as an outcast and eventually parlay it into something of a "bad boy" thing, the misunderstood and distinct character within the group. In the end I felt comfortable with this niche, and actually, it was good practice for high school, which we'll get to later.

—————— **Stubbing Toe** ——————

It didn't bother me too much that the eighth graders would give me shit, since I knew exactly to expect it of them, but still, I kept a tally of how many times they called me a "fag" and would stub my right big toe accordingly. Getting called a "fag," while common enough in a small conservative town like mine, wasn't common for me, and it really was one of the worst insults you could receive since it meant you were the complete opposite of cool. I think by the seventh grade most guys that end up in the pros would never be called "fags" by anyone. Anyway, it never hurt for more than a moment or two, and I didn't have to do it as many times as you might think.

—— First Boobs I Saw and Felt ——

Once at a make-out party in early spring Luanne let me see and feel her boobs. It was one of the eighth-grade guys' birthdays, and because pretty much everyone was in a relationship, we all played "Seven Minutes in Heaven." We were in the game closet of his den, going at it pretty hard, with everyone else eating snacks and whatnot on the other side of the door, the bass of some rap and R&B mix CD rattling the boxes of Connect 4 and Battleship or whatever around us. There had been a rumor that somebody spiked the punch, and even though I eventually figured out nobody really had from my experience drinking later on, we all kind of played along and pretended we were getting drunk. And so: titties.

While kissing her against the door, I slid my hand up her flank, my thumb resting comfortably over her shirt between two ribs, just below her left boob. She lowered herself so my hand would cup it, and though I had already been hardening up a little, my dick then instantly sprang into a boner I had previously not known was possible. She took my shirt off, and I did the same to her. We stopped kissing for a moment, admiring each other's torsos before starting up again. I slid my hand up her back and undid her bra with my index, middle finger, and thumb—a technique I had practiced a few times with a bra I stole from Leon's older sister's room and a pillow. She held the bra, straps dangling, against her chest. "How did you do that?"

"I'm a natural, I guess." She smiled and let it fall to the floor. I looked at her boobs, which really were great B's, nice and round with small light-brown, pinkish nipples. I then pulled her in and kissed her again. I brought my other hand up to hold her right boob, softly at first and then with a light squeeze. She pulled me back so we were pressed against the door and kissed me harder.

"How long has it been?" she asked, breathing heavily. "Six minutes?"

"I don't know. Who cares?" I kissed down her neck, down her chest, then on her boob, and just before reaching the nipple, which I couldn't wait to engulf with my mouth and flick with my tongue, she grabbed my face.

"Don't," she said. I brought my head up and looked at her. "I want to . . . but we can't. Not yet."

I smiled at her. My hardon bulged inside my khakis. "I just want to make you feel good."

"I know," she said, kissing me and bringing my hand up to her left boob for one last squeeze. "But," pulling away again, "We're not thugs." She kissed me once more and then put her bra and shirt back on. I tucked my boner into the waist of my pants and then we walked back out to the party.

———— First Time Jerking Off ————

Later that night I jerked off for the first time. I stood in front of a full-length mirror in my bedroom, spit in my hand, and began stroking, thinking about Luanne's boobs. It felt good, strange but good. I had seen a lot of guys in pornos spit on their dicks before they stuck it in a chick, so I thought this would be best. When it dried out for the second time, though, I decided to use some lotion. Cole's brother swore by lotion. I thought of what her tit would have felt like in my mouth, then what having sex with her would actually feel like, how she'd move, how she'd look. It wasn't long before I felt this amazing burning feeling, a drop and hot rush in my pelvis, followed by a release. My cum splattered all over the mirror in front of me, dripping toward the floor, white and viscous. I admired it on the glass, then switched my gaze to myself, which I admired even more, especially my dick.

I jerked off five more times before going to sleep, alternating hands each time and making an effort to apply equal pressure. I wanted to make sure my dick would never get crooked. That shit always bugged me in pornos, and it seemed like the best fucking would be done with a dick that was strong and straight: undeniably powerful.

This was something of a concession for me as my first sexual experience. I had planned on coming for the first time (consciously; I had already had a few wet dreams, which were cool, but not like this) by a hot chick's mouth (or hand, I guess, if I had to). But I couldn't wait any longer, and I'm glad I didn't. To this day, nobody can really make me come like I can.

——— Jerking Off Now at Work ———

Now I really only masturbate at work. I have sex so often at home that it's unnecessary to do it on my own time, though I do once in a blue moon when I'm bored.

It's a lot of fun to rub one out at work. I don't get off on the thrill of getting caught or anything stupid like that (in fact I only do it in private bathrooms, not stalls); what I enjoy is synthesizing the type of metaphysical fucking I do all day—doing what I want with other people's money—with the physical sensation I'm supposed to feel from actual fucking. I jerk off probably a few times a week to this thought, really going all-out, maybe choking myself a little, or with a finger in the ass, when I'm contributing to something nefarious like a "short," the finer points of which would probably be over your head, but basically selling a thing that doesn't really exist yet or is mine to sell, or after I help close a lucrative deal where we made bets on an asset we sold fucking up when I or the firm knew for a fact it would fuck up because we had our hands in making it do just that, and I got paid a bonus for the fucked up thing in the first place and will again get paid now that the bet has come true because we knew the thing was fucked up because we made it that way . . . you know, that kind of thing. Sometimes this asset is a short, and that's even better.

I actually like to leave a little bit of semen residue on my fingertips afterwards so that pressing the keys while punching in numbers on Excel or whatever has an even more visceral effect for the rest of the day. Jerking off at work is fucking awesome.

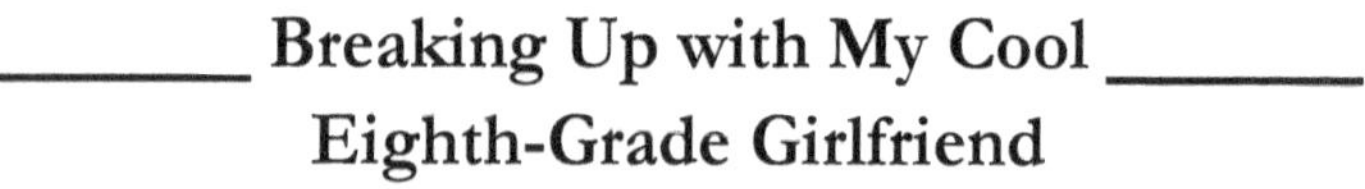

Breaking Up with My Cool Eighth-Grade Girlfriend

I broke up with Luanne three weeks before the end of seventh grade. She was still hot and hadn't done anything wrong, but I knew she would have no other choice but to break up with me the next week or the one after that, or if I were lucky, she'd do it a little bit into the summer. There was no way an attractive incoming high school freshman would hold on to her eighth-grade boyfriend. I also knew that by preempting her, I could achieve some form of legendary status as the guy that broke up with his hot eighth-grade girlfriend, a reputation that would follow me into the summer and next year, and maybe even high school, too. This was planning ahead. This was the type of cool a guy that grew up to be a pro football player would have at thirteen.

Luanne had done a lot for me I guess—unprecedented status, my first eye and handful of tits, not completely wasting my time when I talked to her on the phone—but she was also kind of a bitch, telling me to "shut up" all the time (though playful, it was still annoying) and often interrupting me while speaking. I hadn't understood at that point that that's what most girls consider proper conversation etiquette with their boyfriends. They think it's part of their charm or something, the shitbrains. Still though, I felt, for the first time, slightly indebted or loyal or something. Normally I did the girls I went out with a favor because I was so much cooler than them, than everybody, but it wasn't the same in this case. Luanne was actually cooler than me.

Understandably, she took it hard. "Wait . . ." She was frozen. I had brought her near the gym, where I could make a break to go to baseball practice after I was done and where enough witnesses would walk by to confirm that *I* had indeed broken up with *her* if she tried to report the opposite. "You're breaking up with me?" I just looked at her. "But I was going to break up with you next week." I smiled, in part because I knew this and also because I remembered Brooke saying the same thing last year around this time. I considered the disparity of truth in their statements, and how it didn't matter because in the end they were both affected the same way. "What the hell are you smiling about?!?"

"Well now you won't have to."

"You knew I was going to break up with you. Who told you? It was that little bitch, wasn't it? Always laughing at your crappy jokes."

"Nobody told me," I said. "I don't even actually believe you were gonna break up with me."

"Oh, I was," she seethed in that way only fourteen-year-old girls can. "I can't believe this! I started going out with you as a joke!"

"Oh, whatever." This was bullshit. Maybe she first danced with me as a joke (maybe) but she did not go out

with me as a joke. After the first time I called her, she was
in love with my ass. I started to walk away.

"Where are you going?"

I turned. "You liked me. A lot. I liked you too. Don't
do that to what we had."

"But I still like you," she said, sadly.

"I told you. We're done." And I left. Some of my
friends had walked by, some of her friends had walked by.
They all saw what happened . . . a legend was born.

—— Kissing Games ——

That summer I made out with eleven girls, in a lot of cases
more than once. They were all pretty, not necessarily the
hottest eleven girls I knew, but none of them were just cute
or even close to average-looking. Most of this was done at
parties, during games like "Spin the Bottle" or "Truth or
Dare?"; "Truth or Dare?" was great because everybody I
was with (all fellow incoming eighth graders) knew better
than to dare me to make out with an ugly girl or vice-versa.
This was mostly due to my reputation from school and
partly due to my behavior at the first party of the season,
where we played "Spin the Bottle."

I spun it and it landed on this ordinary-looking girl who
seemed to not even be out of her training bra and who had
thick arms, so I said, "Oops!" and spun again. This made
the girl, who had been blushing and smiling at the thought
of kissing me, get up and cry, her other average-at-best-
looking friends following and consoling her, shouting

"jerk!" at me as they took their mediocre parade out of the host's garage. I just kept spinning until it landed on a pretty girl, which made all of my popular friends in the circle laugh and the lucky, attractive-enough girl who got to kiss me, Caroline, who had decent boobs (marked overall by a sense of perkiness, with obviously something there, but in such a way that I couldn't tell if her bra was stuffed a little bit for shape) and big blue eyes, lick her lips eagerly before doing so. She was a decent kisser. This technique of spinning until I got my target or someone comparable became protocol when I played the game from then on, and after a while people came to expect it and would even help me cheat the bottle when they could tell who I was aiming for, just to get the game going again. Junior high kids are pretty desperate and, as a result, and thankfully for me then, pretty ruthless.

The decision to focus on quantity rather than just quality came after some thought at the beginning of the summer. I had enjoyed my streak of only going out with the hottest girls in whatever grade I was in since I was nine, but in junior high, when physical activity really came into play and I'd hear about other guys making out with more girls than I had, I got kind of pissed. I'm sure most of those girls were ugly, but still. Gary the gorilla fucked all kinds of attractive females, not just the hottest one or two. They don't have to all be 10s, some can be 9s. That's how you spread the seed. That's how you dominate. That's what makes you an alpha.

Eight of the girls were from my school, and included Tiffany and Paige, who were still the second- and third-hottest. Having broken up with their boyfriends (again, Leon and Cole, respectively), they were more than ready for some tongue action with me, the little king. I made out with Tiffany at three parties and Paige at four. It might be worth noting that Leon, who would also be in attendance, would get pretty mad when I'd kiss Tiffany, though he'd never do or say anything . . . you could just tell (Cole, on the other hand, didn't give a fuck, he had already moved on). Sometimes he'd even leave the room. I wouldn't mention this if it weren't sort of funny. I mean, he really got hung up on her. Really. Like a little bitch. Tiffany was hot, sure, but she was still just a fucking girl. He was an elite beta and simply by association with me could have gone out with his pick of any other girl in our grade. None of this strained my and Leon's friendship at the time in any way other than I lost some respect for him, though a bit later he did try to get back at me in some little passive-aggressive bitch move, which we'll get to in a minute.

The other three girls were just kind of random, one while I was out of town and two while they were out of town. In the former, I was visiting family in Oregon with my mom. We were there for Fourth of July weekend, at my aunt and uncle's annual barbecue. Their daughter and my cousin, Katie, who was a year younger than me, had a few friends over and I asked the hottest one—who actually was really hot for a twelve-year-old, boobs somewhat there already, great ass (if she were in my grade, in my town, she'd probably be second-hottest next to Callie)—to go for a walk with me in the woods by their house. We made out and I grabbed her butt cheeks over her jean shorts just 'cause I hadn't done that before and knew I could. It was fun.

In the latter it was these two friends visiting one of their families or just passing through my town or something.

They were at this big water park we had called the Aquatic Center, and were both pretty hot, one blonde, one brunette, maybe half Latino or something (that one had pretty good boobs, too), both wearing bikinis. They told me they were fourteen, and I told them I was fifteen. They were probably lying and were either a year younger than me or my age. The Aquatic Center wasn't really that cool to go to anymore because mostly just grade school kids went and stuff, and by that age cool people just swam in the lake or went boating with someone older they knew, but I didn't know anybody like that yet and it was really fucking hot, so I called up Cole and we went. I think the night before Leon had acted kinda like a bitch when I kissed Tiffany at a party so I didn't invite him.

Cole and I were on the diving boards in the deep end, doing some cool dives, throwing flips in here and there. There were two boards, one regular and one high dive, which was about nine or so feet in the air. I had done a front flip off both and a one-and-a-half off both, then a back flip off the low board, then, in an unprecedented move, a back flip off the high dive, which was actually kind of freaky, but I didn't let on. As I did it, a couple of people waiting behind me gasped, and when I came out of the water, as heroic as a Navy SEAL, they clapped.

Cole and I went back to where we left our towels, on this little patch of lawn in the shade. We were drying off when the two girls came up to us. "Hey, nice flips," the Latino-ish one said.

"Thanks." I knew it was more for me. Cole had not done any back flips.

"You're not leaving, are you?" asked the other one. We were still drying off.

Cole smiled. "Not now, we're not." Cole was just trying to be charming. We were never leaving; I hadn't said we were leaving yet. They smiled.

"Come swim with us!" said the half-breed. And so we did.

We were in the main part of the pool, swimming around, splashing each other a bit, talking. At one point, Cole and I both carried the girls on our shoulders, me the half-Hispanic one, him the other, and they had a chicken fight. Her legs, wet and smooth, felt amazing around my neck. The splashing and pushing annoyed pretty much everyone around us (it was packed), and all that was against the rules anyway, so the lifeguard, some bitch probably only two years older than me, blew her whistle and yelled at us.

"This is gay," I said. "You girls wanna go for a walk in the park?"

"Sure," said mine. So we left.

The Aquatic Center was situated in this park, McCosh, a bigger one for my town, bordered on one side by this little portion of the lake. There were large trees and little rolling hills of grass and cattails by the water. It was hot, so Cole and I were still shirtless, our impressive-for-thirteen, trim frames glistening as the sun dried the rest of the pool off of us. The girls had put on tank tops and shorts, which disappointed me.

They were blabbering on about themselves when, five minutes into the walk, at about the center of the park, I told mine I wanted to show her something down by the lake. I didn't really know what it would be when we got there, but knew it didn't matter and figured I could wing it pretty easily. Down by the water I saw a dandelion. It would do. I plucked it. "Here it is," I said, handing it to her.

"This is what you wanted to show me?" she asked, laughing.

"Yup."

She looked it over and smiled. Her teeth were nice and white, her half-Latino lips full. "Pretty."

"Not as pretty as you," I said, pulling her close. Then we made out.

When we walked back up to meet Cole and her friend, they were sitting on a bench, talking. "So what did he show you?" asked her friend.

"A pretty flower," said mine. She smiled at her friend, then at me. I was a good kisser and she knew it.

"I wanna see!"

Then mine asked, "Is there a bathroom anywhere around here?" Kissing her probably got her so excited she peed a little.

"Yeah, right down there," I said, pointing. "Cole takes a lot of dumps in this park. He'll show you."

"Hey, fuck you. I only take dumps on your mom."

"Ewww . . ." said both of the girls, though mine started first. She was the dominant one because she was hotter.

"Yeah, Cole. Gross. I mean, just 'cause I boned your mom doesn't mean you can take dumps on mine."

"You guys are crazy," said Cole's.

The half-breed hopped a little. "I have to pee."

"Cole, take her. I need to ask her friend something." I'm sure both of them would have preferred I use their names but I don't think I bothered to learn them. They both looked at me kind of funny.

"What do you need to ask her?" asked mine.

"It's about you." She smiled. I turned to Cole. "Come on, take her, man."

"Fine, whatever." Then Cole got up, the bitch, and led her toward the bathroom.

As soon as they were out of earshot, the other girl asked, "So what did you want to ask me?"

"Nothing. I wanted to show you the flower. Cole doesn't know where it is. It's my secret."

"Oh! Okay!"

We started making our way down to the lake. "Trust me, you're gonna love it. It's really pretty."

"Um, okay," she said. "It's really nice down here."

I saw another dandelion. "There it is." I plucked it and held it out to her. "Pretty, huh?"

She laughed. "It isn't pretty! It's a weed!"

"I see how it is. Well your friend thought it was pretty." I threw it on the ground.

"Well don't do that to it." She picked it up. "It's kinda pretty for a weed I guess."

"I think you're pretty too," I said.

She tilted her head suspiciously. "I thought you liked my friend."

"She's all right, but you, you're one of the prettiest girls I've ever seen."

"I am?" I pulled her in. "Wait, you didn't do the same thing with her, did you? You didn't kiss?"

"No. I brought her down here to ask about you. That's why she was smiling at you, because she knew I liked you. I showed her the dandelion but I didn't give it to her."

"What about Cole?"

"What about him?" I asked nonchalantly.

"Doesn't he like me?"

"He doesn't deserve you." She smiled. Then we made out.

—— **Intro to Eighth Grade** ——

The first week of eighth grade I started going out with Callie. At the end of the summer, she broke up with Julio, saying she wanted him to enjoy high school or something, but I know it was really because she wanted to go out with me. She had gone to some of the parties over the summer, but never played any of the games because she "had a boyfriend!" but I could tell she was jealous of all the other pretty girls that got kiss to me. Everybody knew what a good kisser I was. And whenever we'd just be hanging out and talking in groups or whatever, I'd always make her laugh with my jokes and antics. I asked if she wanted to go out on the first Friday, before football practice. We were outside, near the outdoor entrance to the gym. "So, Callie. I have something to tell you." I said. I looked at her. "I like you a lot."

"Yeah?"

"Yeah." I smiled. "Wanna go out?"

She hesitated, playfully, rocking back and forth, her t-shirt tight against her boobs, full C's for sure by now. She bit her lip. "Yeah," she said, finally.

I suggested we go to a movie the next day and she said okay and then we made out for a second when nobody was around. She deserved a little discretion at least since she was our school's golden goddess, almost as cool as me in her own way. The kissing was all right, but the best part of it was holding her close and feeling those amazing knockers pressed up against me. That almost gave me a boner, and I could tell she was into it too because when I told her I had to go she pulled me in for another quick kiss.

Everything was great throughout football season. I was starting quarterback and team captain. Squanto was my backup; I was almost as tall as him, having grown a couple of inches since last season (he hadn't grown much himself), and with the extra experience and established team chemistry from the previous year, it was really no contest. It also wasn't any sort of a contest with Leon, the little shit. He went out for quarterback, too, in what was his revenge: his silly attempt to get back at me for making out with Tiffany in front of him all those times. He thought he would be really good, but he sucked.

I basically laughed at him in his face afterwards. "Hey, so you made halfback, good for you," I said.

"Yeah."

I smiled. "Too bad about quarterback."

He just kind of shrugged. I was waiting with him for his mom to pick us up from practice. My house was roughly on the way to his, so she was my standard ride home when my mom worked the lunch and late afternoon shift. I never rode school busses growing up, unless, of course, it was for sports shit. Only losers ride school busses. "Hey, congrats," he said, finally.

"You don't need to congratulate me. I knew I'd get it." We continued to wait. He stood there doing nothing except, like, pretending to look at birds and cars driving by or whatever for what was probably a full minute. "You know why?" He turned back toward me, his face blank. Leon was of mostly French heritage, himself only like second- or third-generation American, and I think that explains a lot about why he was the way he was. At his house there was a picture of his grandpa wearing a beret. "Because that's my place. That's what I've always been. You've always been pretty good at receiving the ball, running with it. Halfback, wide receiver. That's you. I'm the quarterback."

"Hey man, look, I just wanted to try something different. You know? But I like running the ball. Should be a good season."

"I hear you, man," I said, laughing. Then, still smiling, "But here's what I'm saying: You take what I give you. I'm the quarterback. I have control. I have the ball, and I give it to you . . . if I feel like it. You take what I give. That's how it works. Got me?" He just stared at me dead-eyed throughout. At that point, his mom drove up in her fancy SUV and we got in. We never resumed the conversation; he simply went back to his position as my lackey, knowing his place. He'd never mention Tiffany or really challenge me in any way again, either, the pussy.

—————— First Boobs I Sucked ——————

The weekend after our last game of the season, I sucked on Callie's rockin' tits. I had again led the team to a winning record, 4-2 this time (good enough). She came over that next day, a Saturday. My mom had the lunch shift, and I stole some of her wine so Callie and I could celebrate. She was curious but reluctant at first. I told her as our school's power couple, we should be experienced in sophisticated practices like wine drinking. That sealed the deal. I thought it tasted kind of awful, and was a little disappointed that wine was my first drink because I knew it was mainly for women and pussies, but it was all we had, and I was ready to start experimenting with alcohol, especially in my house alone with my super fucking hot girlfriend.

I felt a little funny after my first glass, but pretty good after the second. I think it had the same effect on her. We started making out on my bed and within a minute I had my hand up her shirt and within a few seconds after that had undone her bra. I squeezed her left boob. It was firm and round, her skin very soft; her nipple already pointy. I couldn't wait to see. She moaned a little and then sat up and took her shirt off. Then there they were. "Let me look at you," I said. And I did, while she looked at me, expectantly. They were incredible—pinkish nipples with only slight brown undertones and a perfectly round shape. They looked almost like the fake boobs I'd seen in pornos, high and gravity defiant on account of our age. I dove on her with a playful grunt. She giggled. I kissed her again, feeling her boob, the other one this time. She started pulling at my shirt. I took it off. She kissed me hard and mounted me on the edge of my bed, grinding against my leg. We dry humped as we made out for a minute. I thought this was what a lap dance must feel like. It was cool. I didn't like being dominated for too long, though, especially after just having something pussy-ish like wine as my first drink, so I overpowered and mounted her, kissing her hard. She loved it. I started kissing her neck, first up near her ear, then, slowly, down to her clavicle, sucking lightly as I went along. I went down farther, kissed around her boob with the same technique, circling the nipple carefully (this took all the restraint I had; the second I saw her tits I wanted them in my mouth immediately, even more than I had with Luanne, but I knew it would be worth it to bring her to a proper boil). Finally, I descended on the areola and massaged the nipple lightly with my tongue in small circles. It was about as good as I thought it would be; that is to say: fucking amazing. I was actually glad Luanne hadn't let me suck on hers because Callie's were so much better and so much more fitting for the first tits I should suck. My dick raged against my jeans, then got even harder as we gyrated again. She moaned in this breathy way I had heard on pornos that weren't too over-the-top. I kissed back up her neck. We made out again for a little bit, and I waited for her to push me back down, which she did, of course. I then gave the other tit the treatment. Her breathing deepened. I started moving my hand down her side. When at her hip, the bone jutting out next to her flat, perfect stomach, I slid my fingers down and over until they were near the fly of her jeans. I figured no guts, no glory, and kept going.

She stopped me after less than an inch. "No," she moaned. "Not yet."

"Just let it happen," I said, kissing her, trying my hand down her pants again.

She pushed me away and sat up. "I'm not ready."

"You seem ready to me."

"Not 'til this summer." She gave me a quick kiss on the lips.

"Why this summer?"

"We're still too young," she said. "We're preps. Not thugs."

—— Grounded ——

That night, when my mom came home and noticed I drank half a bottle of her wine, she grounded me. I was in my room, doing curls with this little dumbbell set I got before the start of the season. Even though football had ended, I was already getting ready for the next season, in high school, when it would really count.

"Francis!" she yelled from the living room. I fucking hated it that she still called me that and refused to answer whenever she did. I told her from the time I was nine to call me Frank. She mostly only called me that stupid, effete fucking name when she was pissed at me. I hated it so much I once told her if, for whatever reason, I died young—got hit by a car, whatever—that I wanted my tombstone to read "Frank," and if it didn't, I would come back as a ghost and haunt her. She knocked loudly on my door, which was locked. "Francis, come out here!"

I finished a rep. "Who?"

"Open this door right now!"

"Who do you want?"

"Francis—Frank! Open up!" I put the dumbbells down and walked over. I unlocked the door and there she was, holding the half-empty bottle of wine. She said nothing, only held the bottle and looked at me with her brow all raised.

I smiled. "Yes?" My shirt was off and I'm sure I looked kind of buff and cool, and a little intimidating.

"What can you tell me about this?"

I acted all confused. "Nothing?"

"Frank, this was almost full last night."

"Hmmm . . . weird. You sure it wasn't another bottle?"

"I only had this one." She was right; I had looked all over for an alternative after I found it—I thought wine was one thing, but this one even had a somewhat feminine label. Her reminding me was just adding insult to injury.

"Well, I don't know! Did you get drunk and just forget last night?"

"That's it. You're grounded!"

What the fuck? I was almost fourteen and, for all intents and purposes, the man of the house. "Grounded?"

"Yeah. One week. You do not talk to me like that. I'm your mother." I smiled because I thought what she had just said was pretty funny, seeing that I could talk to anybody however I fucking felt like, and because she was trying to be all parental and shit, but I think she perceived the smile as embarrassment or recognition or something. "And come on, Frank. Don't drink . . . I'm very disappointed in you. I know teenagers want to experiment, but you're thirteen. Wait 'til you're at least eighteen, okay?"

"Are you sure Andy didn't come over and drink it?" Andy was her boyfriend at the time. "I wasn't here this afternoon. He probably needs to drink to think you're still attractive. You're getting kind of old."

Tears welled up in her eyes and then began to slowly stream down her face as she cried, quietly. "Two weeks, Frank. You're grounded for two weeks now. No friends. No Callie. No TV. Just your room." She walked away.

"Whatever!" I slammed my door.

She stuck to her guns and I did indeed spend that week and the next more or less in my room, but that was cool—I just worked out and listened to music and thought about how great it would be when I was playing pro football and jerked off and shit. A few times I punched myself hard around where my liver was almost to the point of throwing up to punish myself for getting caught. She'd never ground me again, no matter what I did or said. I hurt her so much with what I said to her then that I think she pretty much gave up on me in that moment, which was fine.

—— Stolen Pencil ——

Once in fifth period life science that year I stole a kid's pencil and sold it to another kid for a dollar. Sometimes it's nice to remember the little things.

It was a mechanical pencil, pretty nice, but used; hardly worth a dollar. When the first kid saw the other using his pencil, he accused him of stealing it. Up in arms, the second kid, Kory, this geek with freckles, said, "No I didn't. I bought it from Frank."

"Then he stole it!" The first one, Sam, fat, shouted, so goddam excited about his pencil that he forgot his place. Nobody called me out on anything.

"I did what now?"

At this point, the whole class was watching and the teacher, Mr. Hansen, this pussy who parted his hair (which was fluffy and stupid-looking) down the middle and probably didn't kiss a girl (another nerd, undoubtedly ugly) until college, intervened. "What's the problem over here?"

"Frank stole my pencil and sold it to Kory."

"No I didn't. I didn't steal or sell anything."

"But you just sold me this pencil! For a dollar!" cried Kory.

"Frank, did you steal Sam's pencil and sell it to Kory for a dollar?" Mr. Hansen asked.

"No," I said. "I did not." I stared at them both individually, my eyes icy. That shut them up. "Maybe they're just trying to get me in trouble for some reason. I have no idea what they're talking about."

I think they got detention or something, and the next day both of them apologized to me. It was great.

This was about as much as I ever bullied anyone, if you could even call it that. I don't think you can. Bullying is beneath alphas. Bullies are just pussies that are big enough to get away with exorcising their emotional problems. I was just amusing myself at their expense a little. It was just fucking funny.

—— Stolen Pension ——

At the time I obviously didn't know it, since I was still convinced I would be a superstar quarterback, but this episode was a pretty good indicator I'd do well in finance.

I basically stole a dollar from a kid, like my company more or less stole some pensions and tax payer money and other shit in that subprime mortgage thing, with zero accountability or consequences. This is going to get a little jargony, but I'm good at explaining things, so whatever: What Goldman did was take an asset, a collateralized debt obligation from mortgage-backed securities (like the pencil, except not outright stolen), from banks and other lenders (Sam, fat kid), that it knew would lose value, and then they short sold it to pensions and mutual funds and other institutions and whoever wanted it (Kory, geek), pretending it was valuable, for big profit because it was a recommendation from a trusted expert, the most trusted expert in the field (me). They also effectively placed a bet with an insurance company that the subprime market would lose value, since they knew it would because of what they were selling (this would be like if I had bet a kid in another class, like Leon or Cole, for example, that the pencil was not worth a dollar, and when the pencil was indeed found to not be worth a dollar, I would have then taken money from Leon or Cole as well, and been paid twice). Next, Goldman collected that insurance money, which was provided by tax payers, since the insurance company happened to be AIG, which couldn't pay its bills at the time of collection because it was collapsing, which it was, in part, because Goldman tricked them into taking that very same bad bet. This helped that really big collapse along, and later, as a result of it, when everything and everyone was tanking, more tax payer money was given to them directly from the Treasury in that TARP loan thing, but it had some pay caps and owed-interest and other strings attached to it that they weren't too happy about, so they got *more* money from tax payers through Federal Reserve loans, secretly, without Congress or really anyone knowing. These had, like, 0.01% interest and were just conditioned on Goldman selling them their shitty illiquid assets like some toxic mortgage-backed securities and corporate market instruments. In exchange, they got overnight liquidity, and this was used to pay back TARP and also buy up a shit-ton of great assets that would later stand to make them a fortune, none of which they'd have to share with anyone, ever, even though it wasn't really their money they bought them with and Goldman probably would've gone out of business like everyone else without it.

So, yeah, basically they sold some worthless shit to some idiots, made a bet that it was worthless to some other idiots, and everybody lost a bunch of money, including the American tax payers and their investments and pensions and retirement funds, since those were also all tied up in the markets they affected, but Goldman still got paid, as did the talent through bonuses, as did the execs, twice. And then they in essence got more free money on top of it from the Federal Reserve. In my case it's okay that I only got paid once; I still know I demonstrated preternatural ability, and besides, it was more badass to outright steal a pencil than buy it for like five or ten cents or acquire it against a pencil I would later trade back or whatever. The teacher in my analogy would be like Congress or the government, who eventually caught on but was powerless to do anything about it and didn't really care anyway because he liked me, since I was such a good student—kind of like how a lot of former Goldman execs are trusted to run or work for the Treasury Department. If instead of punishing Kory and Sam like he did, he punished, like, the whole class except us three, with all of them representing taxpayers or people that had retirement savings or some investments or pensions, or just the middle class or whatever, and also gave me, like, extra credit, the analogy would be perfect. Anyhow, I'm sure you get the point. This is the type of shit I do all week for a lot of money.

The more you fuck over, the bigger the bonus. Winners win, losers lose. I know the formula and am working on some stuff for when I get made VP and can really mix things up. I plan on adding at least another step, another payment. It's still possible since the Glass-Steagall Act hasn't been reenacted, not to mention the general lack of oversight and regulation we here at the firm enjoy. Anyway, you'll see. Or, more likely, you won't but I will, and I'll get paid, and get paid again, and paid again, and again, and again, and again . . .

—— First Time Fingerbanging ——

I fingerbanged Callie for the first time that spring. (If you were okay with me describing tits and asses and pretty faces or whatever before but think I'm crossing the line with this, I would say my sexual history is a big part of what's made me who I am and it will allow you to better understand me. Also, Romeo and Juliet were only, like, fourteen; I'm sure if Shakespeare could've gotten away with semi-graphic anecdotes about fingerbanging and shit, he would have; so, you know, it's cool.) I had tried a few more times since I first sucked on her boobs, but was never able to close. Once I got as far as her pubes. This was when girls still had hair, and that hair was fluffy; I appreciated how novel it all was at the time, but now a girl with anything more than a shortly cropped landing strip would creep me out and I probably wouldn't fuck them, even if they were a 10. All of these attempts were in private, at my house or hers. The time I closed was on a bus full of our classmates.

Instead of baseball that year, I opted to do track, mainly to see if I could make it cool. Should be impossible, but I did. Track was co-ed and Callie joined too so she could hang out with me, and also because she liked running to keep thin. This was before it was unacceptable for popular girls to play a sport (at a point, dance and cheerleading are as athletic as they should get). She wasn't very fast, but her boobs looked great when she ran, even in a sports bra. Some guys might be annoyed by the idea of their girlfriend running around, boobs bouncing all over the place in front of everyone, but for me it was a point of pride. It was like, "Hey, I know you see that, I know it gives you a boner, even you, girls, but it's all mine." I'd only get a little annoyed with Cole, because when we'd all be together, sometimes he'd stare, and he should have had more respect for me than to do that so openly in a smaller hang-out setting. To get him back, I'd always call him out on it, loudly, which would embarrass him, and Callie a little bit too, but would make me look super fucking cool and funny.

We had a meet over an hour away in this town called Pasco, which was a bigger one for Eastern Washington and part of something called the Tri-Cities. I did pretty well that day, got second in the pole vault and first in a race I ran. Even Callie got third in one of her events, a relay I think. After we were both all done with our events, we snuck over to a secluded part of the school grounds and made out for fifteen minutes.

The sun was setting by the time the team got together and on the bus, and it was dark as we rode the highway back home. We sat in the back, which we always did because it was coolest. Nobody else ever tried to sit there. A junior high sports bus was, in the same vein as some fancier modes of passenger transport—limousines, private jets, coaches, whatever—a place where the important people, the king and queen, sat in the back. Callie leaned on my shoulder and pretended to sleep, talking to me a little as I stared out the window. "My legs are cold," she whimpered. I was more than well aware at this point that the primary mode of conversation for a girl in a relationship was complaint; that never really did or would change.

She was wearing a sweatshirt, but her legs were bare because she had stayed in her track shorts. This probably had something to do with me telling her how good she looked in them all afternoon. I'd tell her her legs were sexy sometimes because she was used to all the attention being about her boobs, from everyone. Honestly, her legs were underrated, but I was happy I could effortlessly make her feel special. She might not have let me touch that glorious little thing between them had I not.

I took my sweatshirt out of my duffel bag and draped it over her legs. It was a nice little surprise. "Thanks," she said. She kissed me on the cheek. I rested my hand on her leg underneath it. She smiled at me and then closed her eyes again. After a minute, I started stroking her thigh, lightly. She giggled a little, her eyes remaining shut. I elongated the strokes one by one, making them slower and slower, until I had pushed her shorts up to the crease of her leg at the inner thigh. "You're being bad," she whispered, her breath soft. Then I went for it. It felt better than I could have imagined. Warm, already wet. Heaven. I pulled back out and slid her wetness around and then on the hood of her clit. I rubbed lightly, having watched enough porn to understand this is how to really do it at first. The position was a little awkward, which made it sort of tough. Her breathing intensified, and she pulled the hood of her sweatshirt over her head and chewed on the side to keep from moaning too loudly. There were people sitting across the aisle and in front of us, after all. I did this for a few minutes and then actually did go most of the way inside her, trying to imagine what my dick would feel like up there, but couldn't. It would be too much. It felt that good. This almost made me come, my dick popping the lap of my track pants up like a tent. I moved around between the clit and canal, occasionally sliding over the lips as I went. Then I concentrated mostly on the clit again, carefully, and after about ten minutes, her legs shook and she stopped me. She came.

I really was a natural talent, which I was proud of and excited about for the future. I also learned that day that girls are sluttier than I ever could have hoped. And they're dying to let it out . . . I had tried, like, five times prior to get her to let me fingerbang her, to let *me* make *her* feel good, all in the privacy of our own homes and under the guise of romance or intimacy or whatever, and it was on a bus, a goddam school bus, full of fucking friends and classmates and a few coaches, people, some, like two feet away, that the dumb bitch finally let me do it. What a fucking slut. That's what they get off on. It's never a guy. They may say they want romance and intimacy, and yeah, they can also come from that I guess (until they get sick of whatever idiot they suckered into staying with them for a prolonged period of time and dry up; chicks are fickle), but what really, really gets them off and makes them do shit they normally wouldn't do, the good shit, is a thrill. Something they can look back on and think, "Man, I'm crazy! How fun!" It's about them. God bless that little bitch for teaching me that. It made it all so simple later.

—————— First Handjob ——————

I got Callie to give me a handjob two weeks later. We were at the movies, watching this pretty violent action movie I picked out about aliens. I can't remember what it was, only that it was rated R and had been out for a few weeks and I snuck us in. She thought that was fun, but wasn't too into the movie itself. Violence made her squeamish, and when the aliens got shot their guts would explode everywhere. Same thing vice-versa with the humans. We sat in the back, and the next group of people were two rows ahead. About a third of the way in, she leaned into my ear and whispered, "This movie's kinda stupid, huh?" It was okay, not great, but fine. I was sort of into it, but thought maybe I could use her boredom as an opportunity to do something even more interesting.

I started the game. I had tried the last week to get her to give me a handjob, at my house while "studying," after sucking on her titties and rubbing her crotch over her pants a little (I didn't want to fingerbang her again until she had made me come), but still she wouldn't. Even after all I'd done for her the week before, the bitch. When, in my pitch,

I said, "Give good, get good," she left and didn't talk to me at all the next day at school. So, anyway, there we were. To get things going, I reached over and held her hand. "It's not so bad," I said, and squeezed. She rolled her eyes, so I leaned over and kissed her. We made out for thirty seconds or so. Then there was a loud explosion, which was as good a spot as any to stop and leave her wanting more. She leaned her head on my shoulder. I pulled her hand toward me.

"What are you doing?"

"Nothing." I put it on my lap, my dick already hard in my jeans from the making out. She pulled away after she realized what I had done. "Come on. I thought you were bored." I reached over again and she took my hand, tepidly. I brought it in and guided it over my dick in strokes grazing my head, and she, finally, took over. It felt nice but chaffed a little. I continued to usher her along. "That feels great," I whispered. Then, after a minute, she showed a little initiative, taking her hoodie off (she was always cold at the movies) and placing it on my lap. She unzipped my fly and took it out. She seemed surprised, and told me it felt really big. I'm sure it did. It was the first dick she had ever felt and the thought of it inside her probably boggled her mind, but honestly, I wasn't fully grown yet. Still, not a bad thing to hear your first time out the gate. Her jerking me off felt good, but it was obviously too dry. I kept stringing her along. "God, that's so hot Callie," I whispered, but in a cool, bassy whisper. She worked it for a minute. She was a little fast, overeager. It actually started to hurt, and I groaned a little, which I'm sure she perceived as pleasure, though I wouldn't have wanted her to hear it any other way. "Spit in your hand," I said.

"What?"

"Spit in your hand. It'll be hot." I wouldn't let her know she was hurting me. A girl shouldn't ever know she's capable of hurting you in any way, especially physically. It's weak and definitely non-alpha behavior. They should not be able to hurt you that bad regardless unless you're a real pussy, but whatever the case, it's never a good idea to show pain at all, even if it's just a little or as a joke. Also, had I let her know, she probably would have just stopped, embarrassed by her performance or something.

"That's gross," she whispered.

"It would feel amazing." Then she spit in her hand, worked it for about five minutes, spitting more as necessary, and I came all over the inside of her sweatshirt.

I was happy I finally got her to do it, even happier that it was in public because it proved my hypothesis about sluttiness, and most pleased I shot my jizz in her hoodie as a form of punishment for not talking to me that one day, but the actual handjob was only so-so. I guess I couldn't expect her to know exactly what to do with it. I doubt she had seen much porn, and we can't all be natural talents like me, but still. It was nothing compared to the way I could make me come.

She leaned her head on my shoulder for the rest of the movie, which she half-watched, spending the rest of the time gazing up at me, maybe looking away from the violence, but probably just looking at me in adoration. In the end I think the aliens won. It was pretty good.

—— Sack Tap ——

While it was cool getting a handjob at the movie theater and all, I still would have much preferred it if Callie had used her mouth. I'd been happy enough about everything sitting there in the theater, but soon afterwards, I grew more and more disappointed with myself—for not making her respect me enough to *want* to give me a blowjob, for me to have had to do as much prodding as I had just to get a simple handjob, for my first time coming with a girl being, ultimately, far less than what it could have been—so later on that night, I smacked myself really hard in the balls. It hurt a lot, and I slept like shit, and the next day I couldn't sit very comfortably.

—— Mexican Standoff ——

On the last day of junior high I knocked into a thug in the hallway just to see what would happen. While they continued to play their own game for both years, the thugs were still aware of me—everyone was—and I wanted to see if they also respected me.

His name was Anthony Lopez and he had been on the football team with me that year until he got kicked off for insubordination right before our first game. He was supposed to be starting fullback, I think. I'm pretty sure he was a year older than all of us, fifteen or maybe an old fourteen at the time, and sometimes he would drive to practice, alone, not with someone as part of a learner's permit, which I doubted he had, and couldn't have had if he were only fourteen, anyway. This was pretty fucking nuts considering practice took place right after school and he should have just come from class, and because there'd be a cop or two around, it being a school and all. Goddam, the thugs were respectable.

He was a big kid, two or so inches taller than me; built, Mexican. He must've been around 5'9", so there was probably a dash of American Indian or white in him somewhere to give him the extra height, but besides that, everything about him was very Mexican. He had brown skin, a little ratstache; he wore flannel shirts with only the top button buttoned. I knocked into his back with my shoulder as he was leaning against a locker, talking to another thug. I was alone and looking down. "Oops," I said.

"Yo, what the fuck?!?!"

I had passed him after the knock and, having turned, was now standing in front of him and his friend, a small, wiry thug, also with a ratstache, who was giving me the evil-eye. "I was looking down. Didn't see you."

"What? Is that supposed to be like an excoose?" He spoke with kind of a funny Mexican accent.

"Naw, it's just what happened."

"I think you fulla sheeet," said his friend, who spoke with a similar funny accent.

"I'm not." I just stood there and looked them both in the eye.

Anthony was pissed. "Lucky I don't knock you out."

"Ain't you gonna apologize?" asked his friend. Notice upon bumping him I never apologized. Alphadom means never having to say you're sorry. Had I, he wouldn't have respected me. A small crowd began to gather.

"I'd apologize if it wasn't an accident. But it was."

"What, you think you smart or somethin'? Shit's disrespectful," said the goblin-like friend. "Apologize."

"It was an accident, that's all I gotta say."

"What, whetto, you think you tough sheeet?" asked Anthony.

"I know you couldn't knock me out."

Anthony smiled. We sized each other up for a moment. "Hey ain't you the guy with the girlfriend with them big titties?" Of course he knew who I was, who my girlfriend was. We had actually gotten along decently in the two weeks or so he practiced with us, but he was a thug and that was the fall and this was the spring, and I had just disrespected him—all of these things made his pretend memory loss natural.

"You mean Callie? Yeah, she's my girlfriend."

"I'mma fuck her."

I laughed. "In your wildest dreams maybe."

"No, more like tonight. Keep runnin' your mouth, I'll be your worst nightmare, bitch. Now apologize."

I smiled. "Fuck you." He cocked his hand back like he was about to hit me. He jutted forward quickly but only slightly, just trying to fake me out. I didn't flinch. He was expecting me to and I could see it threw him for a loop. I smiled again. "You wanna go outside?"

Since a substantial crowd had grown and some expletives were exchanged, a security guard came to the scene—this pudgy asshole that was probably a delta growing up but was now an epsilon at life. "All right, all right. Break it up, knuckleheads! On the last day of school! Geesh!" He separated us and I walked through the crowd. I would've fought Anthony. I probably would've won, too, even though he was bigger than me. That is, if he didn't stab me.

"Aeey, watchya back whetto!" he shouted.

I just raised my hand and flipped him off, not looking back. Nothing would ever result from any of this, and despite him calling me names and saying things about my girlfriend that would normally make me plan some form of reprisal, I decided to let bygones be bygones as well. I knew things would sort themselves out for Anthony without me having to expend any energy. (In fact, this would be his last year of school and I think from then on he spent much of the remainder of his teens in-and-out of jail before he probably got shot and died or something.)

So, in the end, I guess they did respect me. Had they not, he probably would've tried to really hit me instead of just make me flinch. And after I said "fuck you," I should have been gunned down in a drive-by a week or two later, but wasn't. Maybe they didn't fuck with me also because they couldn't *prove* I meant to knock into him, making the exchange in general more gray than black and white, and their tone with me inappropriate considering how respectable I really was for having a hot girlfriend and being the coolest non-thug in school. They probably realized the error of their ways.

An important part of being an alpha is to be hateful and calculating, but to appear just inconsiderate. You need to put in effort to get what you want, but people will push back if they think you're doing something maliciously. If they believe you just don't know any better, are just kind of a selfish dick and they got in the way of that, rather than thinking they were a target, then you can get away with a lot more, and from then on they either avoid you or accept you as a force of nature.

—— Fun in the Sun ——

Moving into the summer, my goal was to get Callie to give me a blowjob before high school. I anticipated her breaking up with me within the first two weeks or so of freshman year because she was too hot and there would probably be some seventeen-year-old with a car who would want to take her out. That's just how the shit worked. Breaking up with her before the year started wouldn't do me any favors; I'd still be going in as a freshman. Granted, I'd have some sort of a reputation—everybody knew who I was in my grade, including at the crosstown school, which would merge with our class in high school, and some knew and respected me in the incoming sophomore class from my going out with and subsequently dumping Luanne, who I was sure was already established there and dating a cool seventeen-year-old with a car herself—but that aside, being a freshman is inherently shitty. My reputation and cache could only be enhanced by walking into school with the hottest freshman girl. To ensure that she wouldn't break up with me prematurely, I planned on treating her more and more poorly in the weeks leading up to school starting. Girls need some kind of drama in their lives and love to be treated poorly. Being a selfish asshole is obviously the easiest and most efficient way to deal with them and also get what you want. I was already pretty selfish anyway, but I knew if I really turned up the heat then, she would still be interested in me and probably wouldn't break up with me until after whatever cool guy asked her to take a ride in his cool car. I also planned on using the time I had left to cheat on her at least once so that when it came, I would still win.

The summer started out with promise because I had the house to myself a lot. My mom was busy, often staying at Jim's, her then boyfriend's, or working, so I could have Callie over pretty much whenever. Most days she'd come by in the early afternoon and we'd spend a couple of hours in my bedroom, which was decked out with tokens of young masculinity: a bed and curtains in earth tones, sports trophies and memorabilia here and there, a few posters on the walls featuring rappers and rock bands . . . Eminem, Tupac, Sublime. Any traces of childhood—action figures, comic books, gay shit like that—had been tucked away for over a year at that point. It was a young man's room, in every sense, tidy and organized but not *clean*. Organization is a masculine trait, cleanliness a feminine one. Cleanliness is next to godliness because manliness is godliness.

We'd make out every day, most of the time while I also sucked on her tits, and I'd finger her and she'd give me a handjob at least four times a week, doing so completely naked usually two or three. Getting naked with her was fun physically and awesome visually. Nothing was hidden in the bright afternoon sun, the details of our young unblemished bodies vivid even through drawn curtains—her figure, skin, everything, was spectacular. But in the grand scheme of things all the naked time was not the best idea, for one reason only: she wouldn't let me go any further. While a blowjob was the goal, and a realistic and reasonable one at that, I'd have fucked her if she let me. But she wouldn't. She said she "loved the way I made her feel" and she wanted to "do more," that her body was "going nuts" over it, "it really was," but she couldn't. She said she felt guilty enough for what we were already doing, that she didn't think she'd be this sexually active until at least the tenth grade (again, she "wasn't a thug" after all), and that while she wouldn't "trade what we had and what we were doing for the world," we couldn't move on to anything else. And so I had plateaued, which was beyond frustrating, especially considering the progress I had made that spring. The whole thing was at once amazing and awful.

—— Head Banging ——

Since Callie, at the very least, could have given me just a little bit of head during one of these sessions, but didn't, a handful of times after she went home, when I was really aggravated, I banged my head against this open spot on one of my bedroom walls. I'd mostly do it with the top of my head, battering ram style. The wall wasn't too-too hard—just drywall—so it never really hurt that much. But the last time, in addition to leaving a dent when I hit it, I fell down and was sort of asleep for a couple of seconds afterwards, and then saw stars for a few more when I came to. I felt that was sufficient punishment, even though I still didn't feel very much pain. Yes, Callie should have sucked my dick when I told her to, should have given me what I had honestly-earned by going out with her as long as I had then, but at the end of the day, I also knew she was just kind of a miserly bitch and that was her problem, really, not mine.

—— First Blowjob ——

Once, toward the end of summer, while Callie and I were lying in bed together making out and simultaneously getting each other off, I quickly positioned my dick at her inner lips during one of her down strokes. I was working her clit, making her buckle, and she momentarily forgot to pull back up. My plan was to try and play "just the tip" a bit and see what happened. What happened was the second she felt my dick touch her down there, she smacked me in the face, yelled at me, got up, dressed quickly, left, and didn't talk to me for three days. I used one of them to cheat on her.

I had pulled my stunt on a Thursday, and that Saturday there was a party at Cole's house. Cole's parents were out of town for the weekend and his older brother, Tyler, the guy whose room I watched my first porno in, had graduated from high school that year and wanted to throw a party to celebrate with his friends before going off to college. He let Cole have me and Leon over, partly because he liked us and trusted us not to be annoying, but mostly because he thought it would be funny to see us drunk before he left.

At the party's peak there were twenty-five or so kids there, mainly recent graduates but some cooler ones still going to the high school too. Cole's house was big and nice and accommodated us all well. I made up a backstory that I was Cole and Tyler's cousin, a junior from Warden, which Tyler went along with because I looked absolutely nothing like them and he thought it was hilarious. They were blond and oval faced, mostly looking Nordic, which they were, though they were also half "Spanish" according to Cole, a distinction he was quick to make since they had a Mexican-sounding last name and he wanted to seem better than that—"Some of the first Mexicans had blue eyes 'cause a lot of the Spaniards that conquered Central America were all blond and shit" he once told me. And he also claimed to be named "Cole" after "Columbus," which didn't make any sense at all, the actual name difference itself notwithstanding, that guy wasn't even fucking Spanish and only sailed for them. But that's neither here nor there. I think he just told everybody that shit to seem more exotic and fuckable than the blond guy with the weird Mexican last name that he really was. Anyway, Tyler also thought my story "might get me laid by one of the dumber sophomore sluts," and he figured that would be pretty funny, too. Cole was less enthusiastic about it because he felt it was his turf, and if anyone should be getting laid by a dumb sophomore slut, it should be him, but everybody already knew he was Tyler's brother—they looked pretty much exactly the same—so his was a lost cause. I had the same thought in conceiving the plan, except maybe not laid (I wanted to make sure the first girl I fucked was at least as hot as Callie, if it wasn't her herself in the next few weeks, fingers crossed); a blowjob from a pretty girl with nice lips would do.

Tyler had succeeded in getting us very, very drunk. Up until then, all Leon, Cole, and I had had was beer, and in my case, wine that one time, though I told this to no one.

He had us drinking screwdrivers, rum-and-cokes. My story was playing, and Cole thankfully kept his mouth shut. He'd have girls come up to him and go, "Oh, look at the little Tyler! How cute!" but no serious prospects. That shit was hilarious. There's nothing worse than being "cute" or "adorable" or a "little" anybody. I, on the other hand, had a pretty girl who seemed kinda into me.

Her name was Reagan. She was going into her sophomore year (she must have gone to Frontier or transferred in, because I had never seen her before) and she had dewy hazel green eyes and, more importantly, nice, full, dick-sucking lips. I was talking to her and her friend Dakota, who was also good-looking, but not as good-looking, making up stories about what it was like to live in Warden. I had only been there I think twice in my entire life, and really only knew that it was smaller than our town and had a strong agricultural bent. So I played up the folksy bullshit: I worked on my parents' farm, liked it better than Moses Lake 'cause you could see more stars at night, shit like that. It worked. When Dakota became distracted by one of their friends passing by, I asked Reagan if she wanted to step outside for a minute to look at some constellations with me, since I knew a lot of them from my stargazing childhood. She agreed.

We stood in Cole's backyard, which was big, dark, and on the lake. "What's that one?" she asked.

"Copernicus," I said. I meant "Capricorn," but it came out "Copernicus" because I was drunk. We had studied a little astronomy in science that year, and I immediately remembered Copernicus was an astronomer and not a constellation, and became a little embarrassed. I hoped she was stupid and wouldn't know the difference. Thankfully, she was and didn't.

"What's a Copernicus?"

"It's like a crab." Nope, that was Cancer, but I was on a roll with my C's and knew she wouldn't know the difference, the dumb bitch. "See?" I pointed at some random stars.

"Yeah, I think so." Then I grabbed her by the waist and we made out.

"Follow me," I said.

"Okay." I led her, hand in hand, back to the house, then through it, upstairs, to what I knew was Cole's guest room. Unfortunately, it was occupied. It was here I first heard the sounds of actual fucking, I'm sure. It made my dick a little hard. Down the hall was Cole's room, which was fortunately unoccupied. I knew it would drive Cole up the wall, and further assert my alpha status going into high school, where he had the leverage of being known by name through an older, cool sibling, a legacy, that I would hook up with this girl in his room, so I became happy that the first one was occupied, though I guess it would have been even more alpha-like to kick the people in it out (especially if they were like four years older) or go to his parents' bedroom.

I pulled her into the room and we started making out. I mounted her on Cole's bed. "This is crazy," she said. "I never do stuff like this." Sure she didn't. We continued kissing. I put my hand up her shirt, undid her bra, and lightly massaged her boob. "What are we doing?" she asked. I pulled her shirt off and mine too. I sucked on her tits a little; they were nice enough, B's. She moaned. I kissed her again and moved my hand down her leg, stroking the inner thigh, and then pulled at the top button of her pants. "Don't," she said, in between two kisses so rough they were nearly savage. I had been kissing her pretty hard throughout to try to inflame her lips, so they'd be even bigger for the blowjob I was now sure would happen if I played my cards right.

"Why?" I asked, sucking on her neck.

"It's—" another moan. "My time."

I had no idea what the fuck she was talking about. "What do you mean?" I kissed around her nipple then flicked it with my tongue.

"Don't tease me," she said with a light gasp. "You know. My time. My period."

I popped up and shot her a look. She smiled, embarrassed. But crisis breeds opportunity. "You got me so hard."

"Sorry."

"It's okay. You're one of the prettiest girls I've ever met." I kissed her again, on the lips, slowly this time.

She smiled. "Thank you." She closed her eyes, expecting another kiss.

I rolled away. "I can't. I'm too uncomfortable." I looked down toward my dick.

"Well . . . I guess I can do something about that." She grabbed my hardon over my shorts and started pulling while she kissed me. It chaffed so I quickly unzipped them, pulled them down, and took my dick out. She spit in her palm, the pro, and had at it. It felt good, but not as good as usual because I was actually really drunk and desensitized. This only helped me do what I came to do, though. After about five minutes, and twice as many spits, I said, "I don't know if I'll be able to come this way. Can you use your mouth?"

"What?"

"Can you use your mouth?"

"Really? I don't know. I've never done that before."

"If I could go down on you, I would." I wouldn't have. "I think you'd make me come like crazy."

She smiled and started sucking my dick. It felt awesome. And if she hadn't done it before, which I doubted but didn't care, she was a natural. Drunkenness aside, after only two or three minutes, perhaps because of the novelty, her amazing lips, the buildup from the handjob, or my own intense satisfaction for having a plan come together so beautifully, I came like crazy. I did this in her mouth, without warning. I thought it would be super badass to do it like that the first time. It was. She didn't appreciate it very much, the unsuspecting slut, the sucker in more ways than one, but whatever. It would've been great if she had swallowed, but you know, sometimes you can't have everything. You just get almost everything.

——— On Cheating ———

This incident would qualify as my first time cheating I guess, a practice I'd continue with every "relationship" I'd have afterwards. I like cheating. It makes me feel good about myself. It's a very easy way to win, since all relationships, especially more "serious" ones, are, in a way, wars.

Every little conflict is a battle . . . picking what movie to watch, where to eat, who to see, what to do. Now and again you see eye-to-eye, but often you get a little shit, or at the very least some indecision, from a chick. Sometimes you might have to compromise. That isn't really winning.

When you cheat on someone, you've already won, automatically. Those battles throughout the relationship are then made moot. Sure, I've still done basically everything I wanted to do in terms of picking activities and food and stuff, since girls respect you more if you don't do what they want, and generally are just looking for you to assert your leadership qualities and alphadom when they argue about that kind of dumb shit, but it was still nice to know that those battles were, in effect, just games, just a fun way to pass the time by meeting a little resistance and still getting what I wanted.

The most important thing for a man to do in whatever relationship he's in is to cheat, as often and as devastatingly as possible, since when it ends (which most do, and in the case of an alpha, should, and always on your terms), you then win by that much more. Everybody that breaks up has a little tally of their victories which they count after the relationship to see how they did; cheating gives you a million tallies and more or less makes the entire relationship a lie. The incidents are giant bombs that eradicate your opponent, and what's best, they also, in the end, make her respect you even more since you cared so very little about her.

I bring this same idea into work with me, with the deals I help out on for my boss's clients. I'm supposed to be working for their best interests as long as those are in keeping with the firm's, but I chronically cheat on them with others' when those better align with mine or the firm's. It makes me win in the end, either way.

We do these things called pitch books, and I tell one client one thing about an asset, another the other, and just take commissions as I go. The only thing that's missing is the look on their faces when they realize I've screwed them, but 1) They probably can't figure out I've done that at all, the stupid fucks, and 2) I'd never admit to it even if they were able to. Still, that look would be nice. If a complaint ever gets back to me, I play like everything's circumstantial; if something goes wrong, I had no idea it would. Deny, deny, deny. Feel for them, feel with them. Then they come back to us. We know them, they think, and they know us. Fucking shitbrained fucks.

—————— **Beginning of High School** ——————

The first week of freshman year wasn't too bad. Due to my reputation and the fact that my group from junior high was better at sports than the preps coming in from Frontier, we were automatically at the top of the freshman strata, which might not make that much sense—it's a little like saying you're at the top of a shit pile. But there was a difference. Our peers all respected us and none of the upperclassmen tried anything funny, while other kids would have their books knocked down and stuff like that. I'm sure Cole's role as a legacy, and the fear of Tyler coming back on a long weekend and kicking someone's ass for messing with his little brother, contributed to our immunity too, or might have even been the sole cause for it, though I would have never conceded this to him. Also, everybody saw me with Callie all the time, who was still, by far, the hottest girl in the grade. Nobody from the other school came close; the hot transfer girl from out of town was nowhere to be found. Just Callie. This made me look super fucking cool for a freshman. She was the goddess still, and while I was the grade's alpha, freshman year is a time for females to shine. I was okay with this, not happy, but smart enough not to be bitter or weird about it; I knew I'd have my sophomore, junior, and senior years, and really the rest of my life to reign supreme. The bitches can have their year I guess.

On the second day, while walking down the halls, I ran into Reagan, who saw me with a couple of my friends. "What are you doing here?" she asked.

"I go to school here now."

"You moved here?"

"Something like that." She looked me over, then my friends, and, realizing I was a freshman, became stricken with horror. Her face twisted with pain; those great dick-sucking lips curling in an almost unimaginable way. She turned around and stormed back in the other direction. It was hilarious.

I also ran into Luanne, who pretended not to know me, which was cool I guess. I mean, I know I fucked her up pretty hard. She was dating a cool sixteen-year-old with a car I think, and I wondered if she had had sex yet, and smiled at the idea of a cool sixteen-year-old getting my sloppy seconds, boob-wise at least. I know I was the first guy to get at those completely decent tits.

That week was also technically my and Callie's one-year anniversary. I had never gone out with a girl for that long before. It was kind of weird to think of myself with one person for an entire fourteenth of my life, but she had been the best option, so that made it feel less weird. I got her some flowers I stole from someone's yard and she let me titty-fuck her, which she hadn't let me do before. I lobbied for actual sex, or at least that overdue blowjob, it being a special occasion and all. No dice, but the titty-fucking was still good and I was happy about having some form of progress.

———— Getting Broken Up With ————

The second week of school was when Callie broke up with me for a cool seventeen-year-old with a car. Though I knew to expect it, I was hoping she'd give me another week, let me ride my reputation as the only truly cool freshman guy into the third week of football season.

This was the most important time of the year, maybe all of high school, first impressions and all. Football practices had been going well. There was, however, admittedly and disappointingly, a better quarterback there—this transfer kid that actually seemed to live and breathe the sport, fully, instead of just using it as part of a grander scheme like me. I wanted to be a pro quarterback and had played and trained for years really for power and pussy; he seemed to want it for its own sake. His name was Jamal and he was, obviously, black, which meant he was naturally, unfairly, genetically more predisposed to athleticism of professional potential. It seemed pretty odd at the time that he was such a good quarterback since there weren't many black ones (this was before Michael Vick). His family had moved from somewhere in the South; he had an older brother by a year that was already playing for varsity, Keith, and they both spoke with very thick accents. Anyhow, partly because Moses Lake was somewhat racist (we were geographically and culturally close enough to Idaho, where a lot of skinheads live) and partly because of the respect I had garnered off the field by having such a hot girlfriend, I was picked for starting quarterback. Besides Jamal, most people were afraid to tackle or really challenge me because of how fucking cool they thought I was, and as a result, the impression was that I owned Jamal during tryouts—racism made them all the more aggressive with him, and their restraint with me made me seem untouchable. This would change after Callie broke up with me, but we'll get there. First: the event itself . . .

While we walked together in the halls and even had a class together, biology, Callie and I didn't share the same lunch period. The school had divided it in two forty-five-minute increments since it had an open campus and wanted to keep lunchroom and parking lot traffic manageable. Otherwise, I probably could have gotten another week out of her. But whatever. So, she had P.E. fourth period, the last of the day, a class just for girls called "Figure Sculpting" (though maybe a fag could have tried to get in if he threatened a lawsuit; there weren't any out gay kids at that age in my town, not that it matters). There were several other P.E. classes held in the same area at the same time—our school having three gymnasiums, a weight room, and all types of outdoor sports fields—including weight training, which was attended by many of the upperclassman preps and football players. One of them, Danny, a cool junior beta with a car who was also the heir apparent to the starting varsity safety position, approached Callie on the first Friday as she walked with Tiffany from the locker room to her class's gym. This encounter was reported to me after the breakup by one of my many dedicated underlings, and I note it only for context here, because, again, I saw it coming. The goober that told me said he didn't know what they talked about, just that they talked and she seemed very smiley. During the next week, Danny invited her and Tiffany out to lunch with him and another guy on varsity, which she accepted, as a friend, of course, she would tell me on the phone that night, but not two days later she asked if she could come over to my house some time in the evening "to talk."

She came over at 7:30. It was a Thursday and I had just finished dinner, which I generally ate in front of the TV. My mom probably had made chicken that night. I think I was watching *Wheel of Fortune* or *Jeopardy!* or something when the doorbell rang. I liked those shows.

I told my mom we were going to study for a biology quiz and we went to my room. Now, I could have just preemptively broken up with the bitch, like I did Luanne, but I knew I had already won by cheating on her and I was curious about the production. I wanted Callie to edify me as to how a girl would try to break up with a guy like me. I mean, aside from being a freshman, I was still super cool, and I had probably made her come at least fifty times in the five or so months we had been kind of sexually active.

But first I wanted to try one last time to get that blow-job out of her. I planned to come in her mouth and all over her face as my parting gift. She was acting all quiet and weird because she knew she was about to break up with me, just sort of sitting there on the bed. I kissed her and shot my hand up her thigh. She stopped me quickly. "Hold on, Frank." I looked at her. She looked away.

"What's up?" I tried to kiss her neck. She moved so I couldn't.

"Look . . ." She sat up. Her hair was all pretty, with new highlights. She was wearing some makeup and this purple long-sleeved shirt that her boobs always looked perfect in. I'm sure she thought, "Hey, this'll be a nice thing to wear when I break up with Frank. I want him to remember me looking nice." Really, though, it just pissed me off. The decent thing would've been to come without any makeup, wearing one of those big ugly sweatshirts she was so fond of at the movies or whatever, so I wouldn't feel such a sense of loss. Instead, she was rubbing in my face the fact that those big, gorgeous fun-bags would no longer be rubbed in my face. She continued, "I'm in a weird place right now." I nodded, then just kind of stared at her. Maybe thirty seconds passed. "Aren't you going to say anything?"

"I'm listening." I waited. Nothing. She looked at me, probably hoping I'd repeat back what she had just said or ask her what's wrong or whatever, but that would have been me doing the work, and I had no interest in that. This was her show, not mine. I was having fun studying.

"It's just, high school is different."

"It's been pretty fun so far." I smiled. That fucked up her flow, made her squirm a little.

"Frank . . ." Her eyes welled up. "I don't know." She shook her head. I looked at her cockeyed. "You're making this hard for me." I wasn't really; I just refused to play her stupid fucking game. When I had broken up with girls I did it quick, clean. She was trying to get me to break up with myself, the fucking cunt. I don't know where she got that shit from—probably some bullshit chick flick at the end of the second act. This was obviously my cue to ask, "Making what?" but again, I was having too much fun.

"That's okay." I grabbed my package and jiggled it. "You make this hard for me all the time, Callie."

"Don't be gross. This is serious."

"This is *seriously boring*. When are you finally gonna give me a blowjob?"

"Oh my God . . . Stop!" She actually yelled. What a bitch. I'm sure my mom heard. "I need to talk to you. Be serious!"

"I am!" Louder than her!!! I lowered my voice to indicate gravity, almost to a whisper, "I really want to know when I'm going to get that blowjob."

"Never! Okay?" Fucking finally. "I'm breaking up with you!" I just smiled and stared at her. She stared back. Almost a minute passed. "Aren't you gonna say anything?" I remained silent, just continued to sit there grinning. "Why are you smiling?"

"It's cool, Callie. No biggie."

"No biggie?" I shrugged. "We've been together for a year and all you say is 'no biggie?' " What a fucking cunt. I'm sure she went into the conversation thinking, "We've been together for so long, we've done so much together, this will probably be hard for him . . ." But I demonstrated it wasn't, so she was asking for me to be hurt? I'm glad I never actually cared about a girl. For such silly and ineffectual creatures they're capable of downright evil. Sure, I'd broken up with girls and enjoyed the looks on their faces, but that wasn't this, she wasn't like me. It wasn't that game, it was just weird. I knew she had actually cared about me a lot, and in a tender way. While of course I didn't really care about *her*, I had liked her for what she had done for me: it was fun being in a power couple and having everyone think I was cooler because of that, and parlaying that power into more power. The system worked. Yes, the making out and getting naked and each other off was a lot of fun. And sure, I bonded with her over it, but not in any emotional way. It was more about shared experience. Those experiences were fun and she and her perfect boobs and body were a part of that fun. The fun and easy access to power were now coming to an end and that sucked, especially because the beginning of high school would be the best time to exploit that power. That was the extent of it. No biggie. There was more fun to be had, other ways to earn respect. Her callousness was surprising, but I'm sure she felt mine was even more so; "no biggie" was just the start of what I had to say.

"Yeah, no biggie. There are other girls. Ones that give blowjobs."

"Screw you, Frank. This is part of the reason I'm breaking up with you." It wasn't. There could have been other reasons besides Danny, but they, too, would all be cool seventeen-year-olds with cars. "Is that all you think about?"

"It was until I got one."

Her face turned red instantly. "What?"

"Now I think about sex a lot, too. I think I'm ready."

"You cheated on me?" I shrugged. She shook her head. "You're lying."

"Why would it matter to you anyway?" Pride. It's always just pride. "You're breaking up with me."

"But . . ." Callie was many things, bright was not one of them. "I . . . I can't believe you would do that." She didn't seem angry, just very, very sad. "No. You're lying."

"Ask Cole or Leon. Or maybe some of your new friends. It was at Cole's brother's party a month ago. There were upperclassmen there that probably heard about it." She started bawling. It was great. "I'm confused by the way you're reacting."

Choking, "How am I supposed to?"

"You don't like me any more. What do you care?"

"I liked you then! And I still like you. We've been through so much. It's just different . . ."

"Well you wouldn't give me one. I found a pretty girl who would." Even though the real reason I did it was because of this very moment, I knew just leaving it at that would fuck her up more. Especially the "pretty girl" part.

"I wasn't ready! Why couldn't you just respect that?"

"Does it really matter now, Callie?"

She dried her eyes. "No, I guess not."

"All right then." I stood up. "Guess I'll see you in biology."

She sat still. "Aren't you at least going to try to kiss me goodbye?" I stared at her. Girls are fucking weird when they break up with someone. What the fuck?

"No. But you can give me a blowjob if you want I guess." And she did, the stupid self-hating bitch! While also titty-fucking me! She almost let me fuck her, too (we actually played "just the tip"; she quickly slid her lips over my head before changing her mind (if we were on a school bus filled with people we knew, I'd have probably been in, the slut))! And I came in her mouth and on her face! And hair a little bit, too! And I smacked her in the face with my dick a couple of times! And it was awesome! And I did this all without kissing her goodbye! That probably drove her up the wall considering what a great kisser I was. Then we were broken up, which sucked, but still. Short of actually having sex with her, that went about as well as it could have.

———— First and Last Time Cutting ————

I cut myself a little bit after Callie broke up with me. Yes, I knew it was inevitable . . . but still. I was Frank Fuckin' Parker, and nobody broke up with me. And also, if I was going to grow up to be a superstar athlete, I should have been so fucking cool by high school, even freshman year, that she already should have, like, been super in love with me and wanting to grow up and marry me or something. Though, obviously, I would have never done anything like that and would've dumped her the second I found someone hotter.

I used a pocket knife and cut the top of my left bicep, since it wasn't my throwing arm. I only cut it a little bit; didn't hit my vein, which took some effort because it was all bulgy and big from working out. I was really happy with the way the breakup itself had been handled, particularly when I thought about that little bit of jizz glistening against the highlights in her hair, so I almost didn't do it at all, but in the end I had to. It only hurt for a second, but it was pretty messy. Afterwards, I mostly just felt kind of like a pussy for doing it. I don't know. It seemed appropriate at the time (I did it right after she left), but I instantly regretted it because deep down I knew that only senseless fucking pussies are the types that cut themselves, especially over something as insignificant as a girl.

Freshman Football Season

The next week was our first game. I started. We lost. It wasn't my fault or anything—my blocking arm was only a little sore from that cut wound and I otherwise played well—it was mainly because of our fat, shitty defensive line. But still, being the quarterback, I had to take some of the blame. I wasn't captain; Jamal, who started as halfback, was. This was a little weird for me, but at least he got some of the blame too because of that. I had lost games before, but never first games.

The guys on the team had heard about me and Callie the week before, and while they were all pretty cool about it ("Aren't you already getting blowjobs from older girls?"; "Cool, bro, who needs a girlfriend?"; "Girls don't fuck when they're freshmen, anyway"; etc.), on the field there was a palpable difference in the way they treated me. They actually starting going for it—trash talking during scrimmages and tackling hard and all that shit. Their support was artificial; even if only subliminally, I could tell they had lost respect for me. My reputation took a major hit.

After we lost our second game—this time thanks to our fat, shitty offensive line, whose incompetence forced me to throw two interceptions—I was moved to halfback, and Jamal assumed my position. In that game, the coach had had us switch in the fourth quarter, and he ran the ball for what would be our only touchdown, though I had got us into position for our two field goals earlier in the game. So that was that. I spent the rest of the season as a halfback. I was a pretty good runner and scored some touchdowns for us in what would end up being a winning season, which was cool and all, but it wasn't the same. And fuck if it didn't throw a wrench in my plans for becoming a pro. Before the start of the year, I saw myself having an amazing season as quarterback, and with a growth spurt likely at that age, and further experience and bulking up, I thought by the next I might make varsity, probably play second-string, and then I'd be the starting quarterback both junior and senior years, leading our team to two state championships probably. Then it would be a college scholarship at a school with a top program and on to the pros. When that shit happened, I had to remind myself of Michael Jordan and how he didn't make his high school team when he first tried out. I felt blacker than Jamal.

While I was the primary halfback, Leon was the other when he wasn't playing wide receiver. It was weird to be on his level, and even weirder because of that speech I gave him after he lost out to me for eighth-grade quarterback. I hoped he didn't remember it. I was doing my best not to.

It was really strange. I mean, I was the fucking quarterback, always, in life, in everything, so to not be the fucking quarterback where it literally mattered most to be quarterback fucked me up pretty bad. And I couldn't go and, say, bust Jamal's knee cap with a crowbar or make him fall victim to some other seemingly tragic event, since it would look all too suspicious to the half of the team that was there the first time around; and also, I hate to admit this, but we kind of needed the kid. He was really fucking good at football. And worse than getting kicked out of your slot to go on to a winning season is to lead during a losing one. Nobody wants to be king of the losers. Still, getting broken up with by the hottest girl in the grade and losing my niche on the football team was not the way to start high school.

——— Cleats ———

The night after the second game of the season—after my coach swapped me and Jamal and he scored a touchdown—before I went to bed, I placed my cleats on the floor in my room, spikes up, and fell backwards onto them. Upon impact one shoe sort of pressed into my back, the other turning over on its side. Since they were football cleats, they were only plastic or whatever, but they were still fucking sharp and the force of my fall was pretty hard, so it hurt like hell and I yelled pretty loudly. I had the house to myself because my mom was working the dinner shift, so it didn't really matter, but any neighbors that happened to be outside at the time probably thought that someone was being murdered. The shoe was pressed in there so well that it stayed with me when I sat up, falling off only after a few seconds, when gravity did its trick. My back had multiple contusions for the rest of the week. A few really bad spikes broke the skin, resulting in little open gashes that took the rest of the season to fully heal, and by heal I mean leave only the faintest of small round scars.

———— Rest of Freshman Year ————

Overall, I made ninth grade work, of course, because I'm a genius, but there isn't a whole lot else I have to say about it. Being a freshman just kind of sucked. But I knew it would. Sure, I still made out with, like, twenty-five hot girls at parties or whatever, four of them, including a sophomore, going on to become regulars or semi-regulars in my room (I decidedly remained single but had friends with benefits, or "play pals," so I never went more than a day or two without some action), and I got a few blowjobs and titty-fucked one of these girls whose boobs were big enough and was super cool and the most popular freshman despite the fact that I wasn't quarterback (Jamal, while starting quarterback, respected, and thought of as cool, was still a little too *exotic*, and by that I mean *black*, for the girls of my little conservative town to want to hook up with him; junior high is the time to mess with exotics for them, and Mexican was as dark as they went—they wanted to annoy their dads, not make them disown them) and generally I was left alone by upperclassmen unless at Class Olympics, assemblies, or other competitive venues where it was appropriate and expected, and always executed with a light heart; and I know I had a life that 99% of the other freshman guys would kill for (the remaining 1% comprised of Leon and Cole, whose lives weren't quite as good, but not dissimilar) . . . but still, freshman year of high school was the worst year of my life.

—— First Time Fucking ——

Going into that summer, I had one goal: get laid. Granted, this was the same goal I had had for almost a year (though last summer was The Summer of the Blowjob, I *had* felt ready for sex), but there was an important requirement that kept me from fulfilling it . . . whoever the lucky bitch was, she had to be at least as hot as Callie. Almost fucking her when we broke up was awesome, but the minor, fleeting feel of dick to pussy gave me just enough of a taste to demand no less from my actual first time. Also, if I fucked someone that was even a 9 ½ to her 10, she would win. And I always win.

It finally happened on the Fourth of July, which I felt was appropriate considering I'm pretty much the definition of an American Hero. I was again at my cousin Katie's annual barbecue, and her friend from a couple of years back, the one whose butt cheeks I grabbed while we made out in the woods, was there too. Her name was Cher. She was apparently a fourth Cherokee Indian, and I guess her parents, unlike reasonable people, hadn't found the popular entertainer by the same name obnoxious enough to warrant not naming their daughter that in the mid-to-late eighties. All the same, she went by Cherry, pronounced like "Sherry." She was going into her freshman year of high school, and her boobs had caught up with her ass. They seemed to be

D's, but maybe were just large C's; what mattered was, they were even bigger than Callie's. Her face was really pretty too—nice lips, cheekbones, eyes—with dark hair and olive skin. She also possessed an interesting genetic gift among the rest that made her even hotter: her arms were naturally very thin. There's nothing quite like the big-boob-to-thin-arm ratio.

My mom, aunt and uncle, and their friends, about twenty or more, were all hanging out, getting a little drunk, listening to classic rock, laughing, having a good ol' adult time while us kids did our own thing on the other side of my aunt and uncle's huge yard, which was over an acre I think. This mainly consisted of me telling them what high school and driver's ed, which I had just enrolled in, were like and lighting off the occasional firecracker. Katie's boyfriend had also come over, this guy named Dave, who seemed all right. He was quiet. That was the main reason I liked him. He listened, laughed at my jokes, and was more like a part of the scenery than a person. That, and I knew he'd eventually distract my cousin enough so that I could make a move on Cherry.

I made my freshman year sound really cool and didn't even have to lie that much because, again, my experience had been a lot more interesting than most kids'. They were all impressed that I was a starting athlete in two sports in a class of around 400, that upperclassmen pretty much left me alone, that I had had older girlfriends (only a half-lie, as I *had*, even though I hadn't *that year*, and one of my play pals then, who I guess could qualify as girlfriend-ish, *was* a sophomore), and that I had led our class to victory in the tug-of-war at the Class Olympics (this was an outright lie; we got last in that event).

At around sundown, we started a little bonfire and I snuck some beers away from one of the adults' coolers, which were all so full I knew nobody would notice. I had taken some blankets from the house beforehand, asking my aunt if we could use them since it was starting to cool down and all, and hid the bottles under those. Everyone thought that was super cool and badass. Katie and her boyfriend had never drank before, though Cherry said she had. She probably hadn't and was just trying to impress me because she was totally into me and I'm sure remembered what a great kisser I was.

After I had gone back for a third round, everybody was operating on a pretty nice buzz, though mine was a little less so because I had more experience drinking and had stuffed myself earlier on hot dogs and hamburgers. Nobody was really drunk, however, which I'd like to specify to frame the following events. It would not be alpha-like behavior to get someone drunk and have sex with them—that would be pathetic omega behavior, without any real sense of conquest—and this is not what I did. It was actually Katie's idea to get the third round. I guess it was my idea to get the fourth, but everyone was happy with this decision. We were all just buzzed and having fun.

Katie and Dave were halfway through their fourth when they left so Dave could help her "look for more firecrackers in the house." The bonfire was dying out and Cherry said she was getting cold. She was only wearing shorts and a small t-shirt, which made her boobs look insane. I invited her to share my blanket with me. She accepted.

"It's good to see you again this year," I said. She

scooted her foldout chair next to mine and I draped the blanket over our laps.

"Good to see you too."

"I kinda missed you last year." I put my arm around her. She rested her head on my shoulder.

"Really?" she asked, looking up at me.

"Yeah."

"Me and my family went camping."

"Fun?"

"Kinda. But I think I'd've rather been here."

"You were one of the first girls I ever kissed." She was more like the tenth. I guess now as an adult, having kissed hundreds of girls, this could be considered true, relatively speaking. At the time I wouldn't have considered her that, though.

"You *were* the first boy I ever kissed."

"Guess you'll always remember it, then."

She smiled. "Guess so."

I leaned in and kissed her. We both had beer breath, but whatever. She slid her tongue in my mouth. We massaged each other's tongues lightly with graceful strokes. While the only thing I could distinctly remember about the first time we made out was squeezing her bangin' butt cheeks, she was for sure a good kisser now. But that would only make sense since she started off with the master. "Figured you might want a reminder, anyway."

She smiled, reached in her pocket, and pulled out a piece of gum. She popped it in her mouth. We made out some more. After a while, I stole the gum with my tongue and then my breath was good too. I spit it out, reached under the blanket, and slid my hand up her thigh. She moaned lightly. I kissed her neck. She moaned hard.

"Wait!" She pushed me away. "Let's go into the woods. Where we were when we kissed the first time." It was dark and I was sure there would be a lot of bugs and maybe animals and weird shit, but the path through the woods to where we kissed before was pretty easy to navigate and I looked forward to finding out what she had in mind and, more importantly, seeing if she'd go for what I had in mind. So I took her by the hand, the blanket in the other, and off into the woods we went. It only took a few minutes to get to the clearing. "This is it!" she said, then we had at it. I tossed the blanket to the ground and kissed her hard but still in a controlled way. She responded with even more aggression, running her fingers through my hair and squeezing the back of my neck firmly as we kissed. I knew I might be getting into something interesting when I felt her nails a little bit. In a more advanced re-creation of our first kiss, I pulled her up by the back of her thighs, making her wrap her legs around me, and held her up in the air by the ass as we made out. She pulled my shirt off and gripped my back hard, scratching it. I let myself get a little sloppy with my tongue because that's what she seemed to want. Then she bit my shoulder briefly in this very strange way, and I tugged at her lip very hard with mine and sucked on her neck almost violently. I'm sure it left one hell of a hickey. Hickeys were never really my style. Some wore them as a badge of honor in junior high, but I likened them to wearing a name-brand shirt with too large a logo: it was like you were trying way too hard. Real skill came in kissing someone's neck or chest or whatever hard, and almost to the point of making a hickey, maybe leaving a little red mark that would fade in a few minutes, but never something purple that would be there the next day. But Cherry was a different breed of girl with all the scratching and biting and everything, actions more characteristic of dominance than submission, stuff I wasn't really used to, and I had to show her who was boss. And that I did. I pulled her shirt off, undid her bra, and began sucking on her luscious tits as I guided her down to the ground, quickly and forcefully but still gracefully, mounting her and then kissing her like I usually kiss, like I did the first time, the way I did when she fell in love with me. Then, sucking her neck again, hard as she scratched my back, I slid my hand up her thigh, stroking it in a couple of passes before reaching for the top button of her shorts. "What are you doing?" she asked.

I separated the button from the fabric. I kissed her again. "Just going with it." She kissed me. I tugged at her shorts and she pulled away, then them off.

She breathed heavily. "Are you gonna fuck me?" Whoa! They really did not make girls like this where I was from. I thought I just might tell my mom the next day that I was staying in Oregon. This is not to say I didn't enjoy the normal dance of having a girl *let* me do something to her. This was the natural and intuitive way to do it, classic dominance and submission, and I was good at it. But to have a girl basically ask me to do something to her, something dirty and great and very much what I wanted to do, well that just kind of blew my mind. Between that and all the aggressive physicality, I actually had respect for Cherry. I had never respected a girl before. There was something I had to clear first, though.

"Have you done this before?"

"What?"

"Had sex."

"Well . . ." She went quiet. My heart was racing, way more than it ever had in a hookup situation, and for a moment all I could hear were crickets and rustling trees and other weird noises in the woods all around us. There were also some firecrackers going off somewhere. She was taking a pretty long time to answer a pretty simple question, but one that was very, very important. I would not be having anyone's sloppy seconds. I didn't care if he lived in another state and that I'd never met him or would meet him. Yes, she was fucking amazing-looking and had already demonstrated that sex with her would probably be better than with a super hot girl from home like Callie, but this would be a deal breaker. Finally, "No. But I still think I'd be good at it."

A wave of relief passed through me. I kissed her. "Show me." She took so long because she was afraid I'd judge her for being a novice! And what an answer . . . what confidence. It was weird to respect a girl. But there it was. I heard strains of The Steve Miller Band or whatever the adults were listening to in the distance. Before that night, I hadn't really liked classic rock because my mom did a lot and that made it uncool, but the more buzzed I got and then the closer I felt to getting laid, the more and more I appreciated it. I started pulling at Cherry's panties.

"Wait." Was she going to ask the same thing? Or change her mind? Questions like this had never occurred to me before, really. Normally hooking up was this Zen thing I just did. But her style had thrown me for a loop. I was freaked out she wouldn't let me fuck her. She was the one. I wanted it that bad. She got up and grabbed me by the shoulders, pushing me on my back. She mounted me. She kissed my neck, hard, leaving a hickey that was there afterwards for about five days, then kissed all the way down my torso until arriving at my shorts. She undid my belt, unzipped my fly, pulled my shorts and boxers down, and proceeded to give me the best blowjob I had had to date. She was so fucking good at it that I began to question her experience level and whether or not she was actually a virgin, but soon realized there was such a thing as natural talent (to wit, me) and she wouldn't lie like that to the guy that was her first kiss, a guy she had obviously been a little in love with for the last two years—she was just extremely sexual, and that was great. I actually had to stop her after only about five minutes to keep myself from coming. I could've just come and then come again during sex, and maybe this would have helped me last even longer (we'll get there, I don't state this because I was quick), but that would have shown weakness.

I consider this my introduction to a special kind of girl, a favorite of mine ever since: one who really loves to suck a dick. I thought about all the time and effort I'd spent trying to convince Callie to give me head, and though it paid off in the end, fuck was it a chore. Here I had to convince Cherry to *stop*. When I did, she rose up to her knees and touched herself briefly before starting to lower down onto my dick, all in a matter of seconds, in what seemed like one fluid move. I was baffled that she didn't want me to get her off too, but it seemed like blowing me had gotten her hot enough and that stroke was merely to check how much.

It felt amazing at the tip, moist, tight. As appealing as it seemed to let this crazy little minx lower herself down all the way and ride it out, though, this is not how it would be done. I would not be fucked; I would do the fucking. I would dominate. So as she was taking me in, I grabbed her by the hips and pulled a reversal, positioning myself on top of her. She made this sort of yelping sound, half pleasure, half pain, as the mechanics of this were a little awkward. I executed the move while pulling my dick out slightly so I wouldn't break her hymen, but with it still somewhat in, which was good. She smiled, kissed me, and bit my lower lip lightly when she realized what I had done—when she felt me pressed over her and saw me there, poised, ready, her master. I moved in, slowly. It was really tight. She moved toward me too. I felt it get really, really tight and then not so much, which I guessed was the hymen tearing. It was weird. She gasped. But then I was in all the way, and then it was on.

I went in and out, slowly at first. I couldn't believe how good it felt. It was phenomenal. It was different than I thought it would be (more like jerking off or a blowjob, not this unique sensation unimaginable, really, before experiencing it, with wetness understated, friction overstated, but something else beyond these components too; indescribable, really). I was all the way inside of her and it felt pretty tight still, I picked up on every movement she made from the inside out. And after a while, after a few minutes of seeing her look sort of pained, and me still going very, very slow (which I didn't mind at the time because in addition to letting me truly understand this new sensation, it also kept me from coming), move she did. Like she had something to prove—which I guess she did, to me, the tiger. I was really glad I didn't wear a condom, not that I had one. I knew I was good in terms of not getting diseases because she was a virgin, but getting her pregnant did freak me out slightly. I figured I could pull out, though, and also, I wanted to make sure I felt sex the first time as it actually is. The rationale was, "If I die on the car ride home tomorrow, at least I'll know what it really feels like." One of the best decisions I ever made. I didn't know what her reasoning was for getting fucked unprotected, but also didn't care.

A minute or two after she had gotten used to it and me, she grabbed onto my neck and pulled herself up, so we were both kind of sitting and fucking. She was able to let me go really deep in this position and it felt great, and by the look on her face, for her too. This was also a nice one because I could see her boobs bounce and press up against them better too. I felt like I might come soon and to stop myself I thought of weird stuff (death and disease and my grandma and Virginia from the seventh grade's open pimple sores and things like that), but then I thought I might develop some sort of sexual fetish as a result of associating these things with the loss of my virginity, so instead I started doing complicated math problems in my head. Next I shimmied my legs out from under myself and moved onto my back, letting her ride me while I relaxed. I enjoyed that, but after a while it occurred to me that in our first position I was dominant, the second we were equals, and in this, she was dominant. That meant if this were a contest we would be more or less tied—the exquisite blowjob aside—and that would be giving her way too much. I grabbed onto her hips again and, rising, went back into that sitting position. I then pulled out, flipped her over, and fucked her doggy style. She fucking loved it, probably because she was part Cherokee, and the reason that they called it the "missionary position" in the first place was that Indians and other savages didn't fuck in ways other than doggy before white people came along; they took their cues only from the animal kingdom, Indians, the way they were, being really into nature and all that shit. Anyhow, I loved it too. It was great to bounce against that marvelous ass of hers. After about two or three minutes of this, I felt that amazing tingle, pulled out, and came all over her round, awesome butt cheeks, right there at the spot where I first grabbed them two years ago to the day. (Something worth noting is I stayed hard after I came—I thought that was natural, didn't know how special it was at the time. I'd learn about a year later that it wasn't normal, after a random hookup was impressed by how long it took me to soften up after fucking her so well and coming so hard. I found out I'm a part of only 10% or so of the male population that can stay hard after ejaculating. I am literally made for fucking.)

So that was that. I lost my virginity at age fifteen, which was young, but not too young, to a girl who was maybe a little young, but certainly had the body and libido of someone who wasn't. I lasted about seven or eight minutes and got through four positions, which seemed pretty good. I was happy enough with my performance. In addition to the hickey and some scratch marks, the next day I discovered I had been bitten all over my back, ass, and legs by mosquitoes. That was shitty, but at the time I felt nothing. I felt only power, pussy, and the most important awakening of my life.

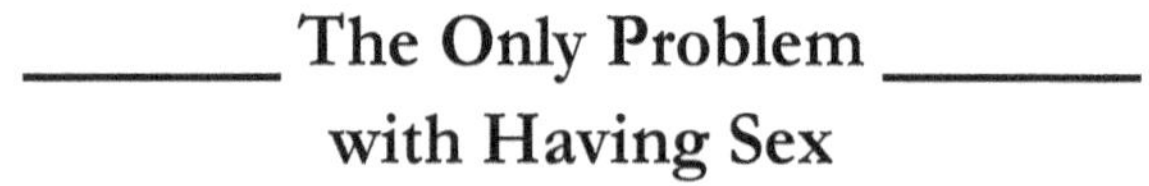 The Only Problem with Having Sex

The only problem with having sex was that almost right afterwards I felt like I needed more. When I got home, my goal of fucking someone as hot as Callie now achieved and actually surpassed, I bought some condoms and immediately began pushing for sex with those little friends that would frequent my bedroom. To find themselves in a situation like the one they were in—casually getting with a guy who was only a short time ago a freshman, starting while I was just that—they obviously had some self-esteem issues, even if I was as cool as I was. Pretty girls with low self-esteem, while incredibly common, the most common type of pretty girl, actually, still inspire joy in me like almost nothing else. Any one of them could have been dating a varsity athlete with a cool car, but there they were with me, in my bedroom, my mom watching primetime dramas in the living room outside sometimes while we listened to music and made each other moan.

I started with Britney, the one who was a year older and who was a really good-looking beta minus among her class (our arrangement very covert because of this), figuring the extra year she had on the others would make her all the more ready, though I knew by then that age wasn't everything. She wouldn't let me, saying she wanted to "save her first time for a real boyfriend." That I was not, certainly, and had no interest in becoming, and in all honesty, I doubt she wanted that either, not at least until I had my license and a cool car. I got it. I wasn't happy about it, but I got it. Silly sentimental bitch. So we just continued to get each other off with our hands and, on my end, with a little convincing, her mouth.

Afton (weird name, I know) was the hottest of the other girls, the ones in my class (despite her name, which itself brought her from a 9.6 to a 9.4). She was the one whose boobs were big enough to titty-fuck. When I brought it up to her, after having just made her come with my magic fingers, she cited the same reason as Britney. "Well," I lobbied. "I don't know, Afton. I like you a lot. I've been thinking about making things exclusive with you." This was not true, but with that type of romantic sentiment, I thought for sure I would be in. While I was against getting a girl drunk to take advantage of her, I had no problem exploiting one using purely her emotions. The first was a drug, and cheap, the other a game, and fun, requiring skill and entirely characteristic of dominance.

"I don't know . . ." she said. This was not good. I leaned over and gave her one of my amazing kisses. "That's not fair." I was that great a kisser.

"It's not fair that you don't know."

"When do you get your license again?"

"March."

She thought for a few seconds. "Let's just keep it casual. I'll let you know if I'm ready for anything more." And that was the end of that discussion. No sex. Cunt. She'd still come over sometimes and let me titty-fuck her, though, which was cool.

The next one, Erin (who I had also made out with a few times while playing "Spin the Bottle" after seventh grade), was probably the sluttiest of the three. It wasn't that she got around, it was more in the sense that she took the least amount of prodding to give me head and when she did, she'd get pretty into it, though not as much as Cherry had been. She was sort of a weird girl, spacey and quiet, with this habit of snapping her fingers randomly and just kind of staring at me after I'd make her come. It was creepy. When her eyes were normal they were pretty, though—had an alluring almond shape, a light green color. She also had nice long strawberry blonde hair and large B's. I think she might have had ADD and some mood disorders or something like that; I know she was on a number of prescription medications at the time (so I guess she was drugged up on something, but that had nothing to do with me). Whatever, though, she was hot.

We fucked. I didn't really even try. I had just made her come, reached into my nightstand, and pulled out a condom. "I got something for us." This approach would not have worked with any of the other girls, but I figured it might with her.

"Goodie," is all she said. Then we started. I didn't care if she had done it before (though she hadn't, as her later testimony and the slight blood stain left on my bed would confirm), so I didn't bother asking. I had had sex and got no one's sloppy seconds my first time. This was all that really mattered. While I thought it would be fun to de-virginize girls and make them be in love with me for the rest of their lives, it was no longer a requirement; it was now open season. Obviously virgins were still a preference, however. In high school, you still undervalue what a pro can do. It's definitely mind over matter when it comes to virgins.

Wearing a condom was both good and bad. I liked that it made me last longer, probably around twelve minutes this time, but the feeling was not the same. Still incredible, though. We got through three positions—missionary, cowgirl, and, oddly, reverse cowgirl (her idea). Reverse cowgirl was the most fun, and not just because I hadn't done it yet. It was a position that I could relax during while maintaining dominance. There's nothing like not having to look at someone's face while you fuck them to make you feel like you're the boss, especially while you're just kind of kicking back. She also moved pretty well. This was probably because she was a little off her rocker. Sex became a regular activity for us for the remainder of the summer, until she gave me an ultimatum and tried to make me her boyfriend right before school started, when I didn't really need her for sex anymore because I was also getting it at random house parties.

I still tried to fuck the fourth girl, Heidi, because hey, why not, but she wouldn't let me, saying she wasn't ready, blah, blah, blah, and actually stopped taking my calls and coming over. Whatever, though.

Despite my failure with three of these girls, I didn't end up punishing myself. I might have if I were still thirteen or fourteen, but at fifteen, I had the maturity and intelligence to know that not every girl would want to fuck me for various somewhat credible reasons and there wouldn't be much that I could do about it. Sure, two or three out of four would have been nice, but Erin was still a damn good lay. She kept me happy. Mostly, though, at the time I was just relieved to be fucking again so soon (only about a week) after losing my virginity and experiencing sex's amazing singular qualities, and the fact that I could do it now so regularly was pretty fucking great.

Clients

The way I tried to talk those chicks into fucking me is not unlike the way I communicate with clients in my current role, and is very much the way I plan on selling them shit when I'm made a VP. It's all in the talk. People love smooth talk, especially chicks. They like to be sold on things, like to think there's something better they can have that will make their little lives more complete. Clients are basically all a bunch of stupid chicks.

What you have, an asset, is like your dick. You're trying to give it to someone first and foremost so you can feel good and unload. What they have, money or business or whatever, is like a pussy. They guard that. They don't give it to just anyone. You have to prove yourself. But when you show them that your dick is the answer to their pussy's prayers, and they let you in and surround that asset with all their amazing money, there's really nothing like it.

Obviously any benefit they receive from the exchange is secondary. The way you fuck them determines what they get from it, and that's like the content of the asset. If you fuck them the way they want to be fucked, in mutually ben-eficial positions, maybe putting forth a little effort, going slow, working their clit or whatever, then hey, good for them. But you don't have to. Your dick can be selfish, you can fuck them hard, just for yourself; no foreplay. Pull their hair. Smack their ass. They'll still get something from it, even if they happen to lose a bit of money in the process. If that something is just more respect for you, so that they'll come back and let you fuck them again, only the way you want again, even better.

Also like with those chicks, it's a numbers game. But once you get one to take you in, like Erin did with me, and you have their business, you're pretty much set. You're good to fuck. Then it's time to find other clients to cheat on them and their interests with.

——— Truck ———

Toward the end of the summer, Cole turned sixteen and got his license. His parents bought him a new lifted truck. This was something of an issue for me.

He had always been my sidekick of sorts, the heir apparent. While Leon was definitely essential to the overall dynamic—just two guys all the time is pretty gay—he was less aggressive than Cole and actually seemed to care about his girlfriends and stuff, making him less cool. I had remained pretty untouchable up to that point, always dating and hooking up with better-looking chicks, having better positions on the football team (Cole was a linebacker, respectable and in keeping with his personality, but not so much alpha material), but this was because, generally speaking, we had a level playing field. I succeeded because of brains, charm, and hard work (we were similar in the looks department, I guess), but the whole car thing was a game changer. Had I been dating the hottest girl in the grade or the hottest from another class, or had I been guaranteed the slot as starting quarterback, it would've been an open and shut case, but as it stood, there was room for some deliberation. Cole had never had sex, and a number of people knew I had, but he had gotten blowjobs. I was worried the lifted truck could possibly give him the edge.

The entire thing was out of my control. I couldn't help that he was born in August (I think he actually should have been in the grade ahead of ours, but his parents opted to make him start school later for whatever reason). I also couldn't help that he was rich. My birthday would not be until the spring, and when it came, I knew there would be no lifted truck waiting for me. So what to do?

Cole would be doing a lot of driving me around, I was sure of this, and though I knew, really, the driver's seat would be the best and most masculine place to be, I thought the smartest way to handle the whole situation would be to treat it like a master-chauffer type thing. So, to swiftly try to establish dominance, I called him, to his face, in front of other people, "my chauffer" on the first weekend he had his license.

He had just picked me and these two girls up to go to a party. His truck had seating for four, and the two chicks sat in the back, where they were a little cramped. One of them, Amanda, who was pretty hot and among the girls who gave Cole head from time to time, kept complimenting him on his "sweet ride" with its "nice leather seats" and "awesome bass," etcetera, etcetera, and so, after a while, I said, "You know, it's not even Cole's truck. He's just my chauffer."

"Fuck you," said Cole. I laughed and so did the girls. "You'll never have a ride as nice as Texas." Cole named his truck "Texas" because it was so big. "Next time I'm gonna make you ride bitch in the back. Amanda, you can sit up here with me."

"That's where I should be right now, anyways."

"That's cool, Cole. The guy that gets driven around usually sits in the back," I countered. The other girl, Liz, started cracking up and then went "Oooooh!" Jesus, I was good. Really, though, I would have never sat back there all cramped up like that.

And so we went to the party, which was at this incoming junior's place, Brandon, a gamma plus, who had warmed to us a little over the summer at other parties, it now being acceptable for him to do this since we were no longer freshmen. Cole and I were getting along fine as usual, but then, without warning, he left me there about two-and-a-half hours into the night, and I am certain the exchange in the truck was why. I can't blame him. He learned from the best and I would have done the same thing.

I made the most of it, though. I had sex with some girl from Ephrata, this other town nearby (four positions, fifteen or so minutes), and just got a ride home from someone's older sister.

Two weeks later I keyed Cole's truck. It was the weekend following our first week back at school, which was a good week, marked mainly by an attractive freshman class and pretty good junior varsity football practices. These had actually started the Monday after Brandon's party, and in a twist, I was starting quarterback again, though that twist was that Jamal was second-string varsity quarterback. The fucker had the position that I always thought would be mine, that *should* have *still* been mine, even if he was better. All the same, I was happy to have my niche back. I again thought of myself like Michael Jordan, and the coming year would be the year I'd prove myself, and then I'd rise, meteorically, like he did. At any rate, we were at some other party, one of Brandon's friends', this guy who went by RJ. After my third beer, when everyone seemed to settle into the groove of the party, I asked Cole for the keys to his truck to retrieve my hat. I had intentionally left it there earlier so I could do just that. Cole was also fond of wearing hats (baseball or football, always), in fact he was wearing one at the time, a Seahawks hat, and this seemed like a perfectly good reason to ask him for his keys. He handed them over with a half-drunk smile and a nod.

I made sure the coast was clear. It was kind of hard for it not to be, considering the party was held a few miles outside of city limits in a remote agricultural stretch known simply as "the country." After taking my lap, I decided I'd advance on the truck from behind. I took out his keys and, using the very same one needed to access and drive it, carved a few nice wavy lines from the truck's driver side bed to its headlight. Then I went around to the other side, opened the door, and found and put on my hat. Once I had locked up the truck, I checked myself briefly in the passenger side mirror. I looked good in my hat.

When I got back inside, I approached Cole, who was hanging out with Leon. "There's something I think you should see."

"What?"

"Your truck."

His eyes bulged, nostrils flared. It was something like an angry twitch, but sustained, remaining on his face for around five seconds before he said anything. "What?!? What happened?"

"I don't even want to say it, dude."

"If anybody fuckin' messed with Texas . . ." He grunted and we, with Leon, went outside. We hurried down the long gravel driveway to where the truck was parked. He quickly inspected the front, which was closest, then, guessing right, moved toward the driver side. Under stars big and bright, he saw the damage. "What the fuck?!?! Fuck! Fuck! What the fuck?!?! I'm gonna kill someone! Fuck!" It was great.

"Holy shit," is all Leon said.

We went back to the party, a collective of about thirty or so kids hanging out, some inside, some outside in the back yard, and Cole went straight for the stereo, which was blasting rap music, Mystikal or something, throughout the house and yard from a centrally located den. He shut it off. There was a resounding "Boooo!" from people both inside and out. "What the hell?" asked RJ.

"Who the fuck keyed my truck?!?!" shouted Cole. There was a loud, unified "Ooooooooooooooh!" from all who had gathered around close. Many people knew how nice Cole's truck was. "Huh?!?! Come on! What fucking bitchass piece of shit had the fuckin' balls to mess with goddam Texas?!?!"

"Calm down," said Brandon.

"Texas?" asked RJ.

"I'm not gonna calm down. I need to know! Now!" Cole looked around. The room went silent. Nobody moved. After a few seconds, Wyatt, this beta senior who was a wide receiver or tight end or something on the varsity team, snickered. Cole immediately leapt across the room and punched him in the nose. A dog pile ensued, a bunch of the seniors jumping on Cole, then Leon and I joined in, followed by some of the other sophomores who weren't pussies and were cool enough to be at this party. Jamal was there, as some of the upperclassmen and his varsity teammates enjoyed hanging out with him for the novelty and whatever edge he could bring to their posses; he helped us instead of them. Some juniors helped both sides. Furniture was knocked over. There was some shouting. It all happened very fast.

We got kicked out, the party was over, and we weren't invited to many more for a while. It was cool, though, we would just show up anyway. Sometimes we would bring Jamal with us, too, and we all sort of became friends, though we more used him for his ability to perpetuate our mythos than enjoyed his company. I think he mostly used us to try to fuck white girls, which he might've a couple of times, ones that really hated their dads, I don't know. Nobody bothered us because they respected us more and were kind of afraid we'd ruin their parties, too. We were the untamed young bucks, testosterone and beer fueling our charge, fear alone left in the wake. Everybody thought we were a little dangerous, and that was cool.

I was very happy with my decision to fuck with Cole's truck. Nobody leaves me at a party or even suggests I ride bitch, especially in front of girls. I almost punished myself because Cole should have respected me more than to ever even dream of doing something like that, but then I realized that receiving that truck was the best his life would probably get and his only opportunity to one-up me, and that my energy would be better invested in only getting revenge on him. In the end, Cole's parents had to pay a little to get the scratch marks fixed and maybe the insurance on it went up a little bit. Deep down, I think Cole knew Wyatt had nothing to do with what happened, that it was all me, and I did it to get him back. But nothing was ever mentioned. Instead, I got my vengeance and we were all a lot cooler for causing such a scene. If I told him now, he'd probably thank me. It was a win for everyone involved (with the exception of Cole's parents), especially me, who it was actually a win-win for.

——— Sophomore Football Season ———

With my place as starting quarterback secure, I felt I was definitively the sophomore alpha again, Cole's truck aside. No, I wasn't on varsity, and yes, there were a handful of sophomores that were, but none of them started or were otherwise cool, and besides Jamal, they were mostly just the fat kids useful for second- and third-string offensive lines or the small, really fast ones for special teams. The important thing was to shine, and I could do that on junior varsity, and that would set me up for success the next year and beyond. My life was pretty good. School was fine. I got good grades still. We were having a winning season. On weekends I enjoyed fun times and easy pussy. There were only a few parties where I struck out and didn't at least get a blowjob in someone's guest room or home office or whatever. I had sex with three new girls during football season, two of these hookups becoming regulars in my bedroom by the end of the season, fucking each on average about twice a week. All of these conquests were very attractive; I made sure never to compromise my selectivity by getting too drunk or anything at parties.

Hooking up wasn't exactly too difficult a process: it simply involved acting kinda cool at first, then making people around me laugh or doing something else that was interesting, then focusing my attention mostly on just one girl. I proved I was special, so when I focused my attention on her, it made her feel special too. This attention didn't have to be entirely positive; in fact, in the beginning, it's best to tease a little, make fun, but touch a little, her arms, something. Then you withdraw some, either become conversationally remote or maybe you go talk to another girl for a minute, make her want you more . . . and after that you come back, talk to her like you have some sort of a connection, and, in the end, say something nice or sweet, see if she wants to go somewhere quieter to "talk," and voila, you're in Blowjob City or it's fucktime. It was kind of a numbers game still—I wouldn't always hook up with my first target, but I figured I'd get to whoever that girl was at some point in the future, and again, they were all hot.

None of these girls were as attractive as Callie, however, and I still for the most part viewed her as the prize hen in terms of my school. If word got out that I had fucked her, it would do a lot to further my status among the interclass prep elite. That was the main reason I wanted to do it, but also because she was, you know, pretty fucking hot. And spite, I guess . . . it would be fun to fuck her and leave her somewhere, since she dumped me and all. I wondered if she had had sex yet. She spent part of the last year dating that guy Danny and then the other half another guy from the varsity football team, Matt, a junior beta plus, who was actually better at basketball and starting point guard for that varsity team. That's when they started going out, I think, during basketball season, when he shined brightest. They broke up during the summer, though, with her remaining "single by choice" since. Maybe this was because she was sick of her boyfriends trying to fuck her after she told them she wasn't ready for that yet, or maybe one of them was actually successful in devirginizing her and now she wanted to start fucking casually. A lot of things can change over the course of a summer, as I well knew.

—— Jumping off Roof ——

When football was over, I decided not to go out for the tenth grade basketball team. The main reason for this, and the one I cited to friends when asked, was that I needed to get a part-time job to buy a car. Secondly, in terms of the big picture, basketball didn't really matter, not compared to football, anyway. I also wasn't terribly good at it, though I would have admitted this to no one. I was a little nervous I wouldn't make the team. It could only have twelve or so players, and I knew half of them would be "faux-thugs," the tall enough half-Mexicans and few black kids (excluding Jamal, who made varsity as a fucking freshman) that had good enough grades. Real thugs, of course, had already dropped out by then or, if they were miraculously still in school, would be full Mexican or close and likely no taller than 5'5". The faux-thugs were really, really good and started for the A-Team the previous year, a year when I was a benchwarmer for them, which really, really sucked. I was a hair shy of 5'10" at the time, and other benchwarmers and a few starters for the B-Team had grown considerably taller over the last year, and I realized that enough of them could possibly inch me out for one of those slots. That would have been humiliating. So, instead, I focused on the car thing and a scheme to get Callie to fuck me.

I had to punish myself for not being good enough at basketball, though, so one afternoon while tryouts were taking place, I jumped off of my roof. Guys that grow up to be pro athletes should be high school stars in pretty much all sports. I knew I was damn good at baseball, which was better than basketball, but still. To do something in keeping with the acrobatic nature of the sport, and my deficiency, I jumped from a point that seemed high, maybe thirteen or fourteen feet in the air, without being too-too crazy, and landed in a bush that lined the side of my house. It padded my fall more than, say, the hard, cold November ground, but it was still all scratchy and full of pokey branches and stuff that sucked to land on. When I got up, I walked with a limp through the next day and felt a little sore all over, my right side especially, for a few days after. Anything further to risk real injury would've been stupid . . . I had more important games to play.

—— After-School Job ——

Since I needed a car and wanted Callie to fuck me, the best solution, obviously, was to get a cool one. My mom had set aside about a thousand bucks for me, which was nice of her

I guess, but wouldn't really get me too far in that department. And, while it isn't really characteristic of an alpha to have to get a job at fifteen-and-a-half instead of just hanging out and playing sports, I was going to do everything within my power to be the coolest sixteen-year-old I could be. I knew that would be an important age for me. If I had to sacrifice a little in the meantime, so be it.

I started looking around and came to an important conclusion very quickly: the kinds of jobs a fifteen-and-a-half-year-old can get are not worth doing. They pay shit and suck. I could have been a bagger at a grocery store, busboy, movie concession retard, or some other embarrassing and degrading thing for minimum wage that only a complete fucking idiot would ever entertain becoming and that was about it.

So instead, I sold prescription drugs. Cole and Leon both thought it was hilarious that I had to get a job, and when they found out (a week after basketball tryouts, I was in the clear) that that was it, I had the last laugh. I had parlayed my fun weekend partying into an exciting business venture by stealing pills from my hosts. Since pretty much all of these parties were thrown by the richer kids in town, who were more popular and had larger houses to hold more people, there was easy access to expensive drugs—cabinets full of painkillers, antidepressants, anxiety medication, stimulants, shit common among people with too much time and money to worry about themselves. Stealing was the easy part. The houses were already full of teenagers who kept the hosts busy, and because most of them were just acquaintances and not really friends, everyone was therefore a potential suspect, if the host even noticed at all.

Selling them took a bit more tact. As a precaution, I packaged most in individual baggies at least a week after I stole them, even though everyone pretty much had the same shit. It would have been kind of dumb to try and move the very pills I had just stolen at the same party without doing anything to make it seem like they were from elsewhere. Badass and fun and funny, sure, but dumb. I charged between five and ten bucks a pop, depending on the drug, with bulk discounts. Anything more than ten pills only went to a few choice pill fiends, all rich kids, one of whom I know I stole from at a party of *his*. I think I actually sold him some of his own parents' Xanax, the moron. Anyway, when asked where I got my great stash from—a question that always seemed more like a curiosity than a press—I told people I had a connection, a cousin who worked at a pharmacy near Spokane, and that seemed to be more than enough to satisfy them.

It never really became common knowledge or anything that I was a drug dealer—if you'd even call me that—it was more on a need-to-know basis. But enough people did know that I was able to make some pretty decent money at it. Alphas, like Scarface, *can* be drug dealers, but it's still a little grimy. It was my only option, though, and it was easy, and I was happy to do it, though I slowed down a bit after saving up enough to get the car I wanted (which I'll describe in just a second), something I was able to do after about five months, between November and my birthday, really only selling to that handful of fiends and not at parties anymore. This was still more than enough to pay for gas and have beer money on the weekends after the main purchase was made.

The fact that this was my first "job" is another good indicator that I'm a natural for what I do now. It was smart work, not hard, and risky—but in such a way that I knew I wouldn't ever really get caught—and highly profitable.

———— My Cool Car ————

That winter, Leon turned sixteen and his parents bought him a new Lexus. This was less of an issue for me than Cole's lifted truck had been; that thing was just so damn powerful and demanding of respect. A Lexus was cool and fancy, and it did get Leon laid (by one girl who he didn't even make his girlfriend!), and of course I'd have taken one if it were offered for free, but still, it wasn't really me. It worked for him, he being kind of a pussy and all. It did get me critically thinking about the type of car I would get, though, still a little up in the air about it at the time. It had to be cool, tried and true masculine, like me.

In the end, I got a '78 'Vette. It was fucking beautiful—black, with gray leather seats—a dominant, muscular vision, worthy of me and carrying me through high school. It was the classic rock of cars, and since classic rock was in the air the first time I fucked, I knew it would drive me to insane amounts of pussy. I got it with my mom for about five grand at a police auction. I think it formerly belonged to another drug dealer or something, which I thought was pretty great. It needed about another two thousand in work, being a little well worn, but in a cool way.

My mom asked where I got all my money from, and I told her I had taken my birthday and Christmas checks from the past few years and invested them in the stock market, where I did pretty well (though I didn't know much about the greater financial industry at the time, I knew a little about the stock market, especially that it could make you rich, and that just saying you invested made you smart and impressive, a winner). She thought it was weird but believed me I guess. She knew I was good with numbers. I'm pretty sure parents would have had to sign off on something like that, but whatever. I think she just didn't really care. She thought it was a cool car, too. Everyone did.

We were a few weeks into baseball season when all the work had been done and it was ready. I had to skip practice to pick it up, and instead of going on any sort of a crazy joyride first, I decided to show it off back at school. I pulled up to the field as my team, JV—I was so good at baseball I made JV instead of just the sophomore team— was wrapping things up. I revved the engine and they all freaked out. We practiced next to the varsity players, some of which were my friends at that point from parties and stuff, and they freaked out too. My birthday had been that weekend, and I hadn't told anyone what kind of car I was getting. No one knew what to expect. (I never made too huge a fuss over my birthday; that's a feminine trait. Leon and Cole celebrated with me most years to some degree, but that year I really only planned anything with the two girls I was regularly having sex with so they'd fuck my brains out that day, which they did, in shifts. It was a Saturday. I had one come early afternoon, the other evening, and it all went off without a hitch—*that* was the way to start sixteen.) After revving the engine again, I drove off, all cool and screechy and badass. Even the coaches seemed impressed.

In addition to its classic and effortless cool, I also liked the car because it only had two seats. This meant I wouldn't really have to drive anyone around. I could just be alone most of the time, which made sense since nobody was really on my level. My only passengers would be girls. This would be nice because, as it was only a two-seater, it would make them feel more special, make it a little easier to get in their pants, not that it should be too hard anyway, but hey, why try harder at anything than you have to?

With the car, too, came another element of my style. Before, people knew me—or had an idea in their heads of me—based on how I dressed and, in a way, how I looked in my friends' cars, which I was always careful about associating myself with, really only riding around with people who had nice ones, mostly just Cole and Leon. I had worn pretty much the same stuff as everyone else up until that point, the same name brand prep uniform from junior high. The only thing that ever really changed was that some brands became a little more popular while others fell out of fashion a little, or maybe something new would emerge like American Eagle or whatever. Also, one season jeans would be a little cooler than khakis or vice-versa, or in the spring and summer we wore more hats. That was about it. Dressing like everyone else had worked then because nothing could've been worse than being different, than not fitting in. I could make uncool shit like track cool in junior high because of who I was, but it would have been tougher to make something like, say, tight pants cool. The line was drawn at fashion. Everyone was way too insecure, so uniformity was necessary. I didn't mind at the time; it made it all the more fair and easy for the cream, me, to rise to the top and stay there. But by that point in high school, I was ready for change, to look as different as I felt, to look better than everyone. And now with cars in the mix, standing out had become cooler than blending in; it would be smarter to dress as my own individual. So, my beautiful car and I then became one. This is not to say I appropriated the style of my car; I got my car because it was the classic and cool masculine I already knew I was—we just met at the way I subsequently dressed.

I started mainly wearing jeans and solid t-shirts—white, gray, black—and, when weather appropriate, leather jackets, one in brown, one in black. I had other clothes, of course, but in a nutshell, I dressed simply, in what could be considered timeless looks. I took most cues from James Dean (even though I hear he was half-a-fag), including wearing my hair a little like his, and some others from Steve McQueen. The expressions they wore on their faces also seemed effective, so I tried to carry mine more like theirs, too. I was serious, sometimes brooding, but not like a downer, and always capable of laughter and life—girls love that, especially when it seems like a surprise. Because they have minds like infants, girls absolutely love surprises. I was already pretty fit from doing all the sports and frequenting the school weight room and all that, but I worked out even harder, ate better, and at that point whatever baby fat I still had on my face melted off for good. Some people didn't get it at first, Cole especially, who started calling me "the Fonz," and while maybe my look was a little above him, I think mostly he was just jealous that people seemed to like my car better than his. Other guys at our school had lifted trucks. Nobody had a '78 'Vette. Girls prefer to be seen with a guy that's interesting and unique, generally because they're neither and want to be a part of the glow of someone who is. Soon thereafter it got so I would never strike out at a weekend party, usually fucking someone (often, admittedly, the same girls at different parties—but all really hot), and my regular bedroom fuck buddies—none pressuring me to be their boyfriend—grew from two to three, the third being an experienced graduating senior who brought my fuck game up to a whole 'nother level (typically six to seven positions, including the pile driver, twenty minutes at least). I would secretly tape them sometimes with this little video camera my aunt in Oregon got me for my birthday the previous year and show my close friends (and though I haven't shown anyone else footage since I was seventeen, this is a practice I've kept to this day). That shut Cole the fuck up. Anyway, baseball season went pretty well and by the end of sophomore year, I was not only one of the coolest guys in my class, I was one of the coolest in the school.

——— Fucking Ex-Girlfriend ———

I fucked Callie at the beginning of that summer. It didn't take an elaborate plan or anything . . . I didn't even have to drive her around in my cool car. It was at a party. We were both a little drunk and had been flirting for most of the night. It happened like pretty much every other party hookup I ever had; it was cheap and fun, and people knew about it immediately afterwards. The only difference was, it was Callie, known by then as the hottest girl in school, and a girl I had at a time spent four or so months trying to get head from and maybe fuck, unsuccessfully, the naïve, hopeful guy I was—or, rather, the fucking bitch she was—so that also made it awesome. In addition to winning the war that was our relationship, I had now also won the only battle I thought had eluded me.

We had been out of school for about two weeks then. While girls have always looked at me with somewhat doe eyes, after my car and style transformation, most that I walked by in the hallways, including seniors, would do that and smile, or even better, I'd catch some staring with mouths slightly agape, the wanton sluts. Callie did that once, on the last week of school. Her "decidedly single" status came to an end a few weeks after football season, when she started going out with the guy who had been the varsity quarterback, Brad, the senior alpha, who she dated until he dumped her toward the end of the year, probably so he could get as much pointless pussy as possible before going to college. So, anyhow, she was back on the market and when she looked at me I could tell she must've seen me as a new Frank.

The party was at this recently graduated senior's place, this girl named Kim. There were only about fifteen or twenty kids there; it had a pretty laid-back vibe. She lived in a big house out in the country, and her parents were gone for the weekend. All of the decor was classy, with dark brown full-grain leather couches and chairs in the living room and den, and there was nice, warm lighting everywhere, a fireplace, that kind of stuff. It was a fancy house, on a remote part of the lake, and the weather was perfect. Everything was right to put an alpha female like Callie in the mood to fuck.

Now that the stage has been set, I won't describe the scene. She doesn't deserve that. I spent enough time here on that bitch, and while she was somewhat important in previous stages of my life, a detailed account would be too much. By then, already, pussy was pretty much just pussy. It's like snowflakes. Yes, every one is different; every encounter, every episode, even with the regulars in my room, somewhat unique, but when you get down to it, it all adds up to the same shit: dick goes in, dick goes out, repeat as necessary, I come. Individual snowflakes eventually just form piles, and piles of snow are all the same, fucking cold and white. From here on in, only truly interesting encounters will be offered in detail. Callie was just number nine. What I will give is this: she wasn't a virgin (she lost it to Brad earlier that year, which I figured had happened otherwise he would have dumped her after only a couple of weeks), she wasn't the best I ever had, or the worst, and I didn't wear a condom. She was reluctant about that but had told me she was on the pill earlier in the night, so I pressed raw sex on the grounds of our history and the fact that we had already played just-the-tip that once, and I did this purely out of spite. I lasted around eighteen minutes and got through five positions. I would've liked to have lasted a bit longer, but her tits, which had grown to full D's, where they stayed, did me in. They really were something. I came inside her. And that was the time I fucked Callie.

—— First Time Fucking in the Ass ——

Fourth of July that year was the sequel to what it had been the previous year. I fucked Cher again, who had only gotten better-looking, a little taller, her hips flaring ever so slightly. We did it at our spot, and I say the sequel rather than a repeat because I brought my next level fuck skills, mainly honed with my senior friend, Cheyenne, making it bigger, faster, stronger, louder. And she brought hers, too. At about the sixteen-minute mark, after fucking her in missionary, modified missionary with her legs pulled over her head, in sitting position, standing up with her in the air, and with her on her side while I worked her clit (she came), I started fucking her in doggy, then in the wheelbarrow, where I moved my thumb closer and closer to her asshole until pressing on it, lightly. She moaned. I brought her back down to doggy, then fucked her harder and pressed a little more. She moaned louder, backed up so my thumb was in her asshole, and blurted out, "I want you to fuck me in the ass!"

So I did. My dick, condomless, was wet from her cum (of the nine girls I had had sex with at that point, I wore condoms with all but her, Callie, and one of my bedroom regulars, Hope, who was a virgin when she met me, then went on the pill, and, more importantly, had a very weak will, the weakest I'd ever seen, so I was certain I could make her get an abortion if push ever came to shove). I started slowly inching it in. She rested her head on the blanket beneath us. It was tight. It made her pussy seem loose by comparison, and you know how I described that. And kind of dry. It was also pretty weird. Like a grittier, ribbed pussy . . . It still felt good, but a different kind of good. She was tense at first and made a few pained breathy noises.

I had been interested in anal for a few months by then. I'd seen it so often in porn that the idea of my dick going in the same passage shit came out of didn't bother me, it actually seemed natural, and I had gotten to the stage where fucking pussy, though always great and amazing and fun, became as Zen to me as making out had once been (snow piles). I was a young man used to progress and conquest, and felt again like I had hit a plateau. Now, anal isn't one of those things where girls tread lightly, and from what I could tell, the types of girls that would be into it back home, around my age, would be one of two things: a complete slut or a girlfriend. I didn't know any real sluts, I mean I knew of them, but didn't know them personally. Some of them were actually pretty hot, though typically with over-tweezed eyebrows. The girls I had sex with were usually nice ones from good families relatively new to sex, who thought the idea of an object as large as my dick entering anything as teensy-weensy as their pussies was a miracle in and of itself, so forget about something even smaller, tighter, like an asshole. My one shot was Cheyenne. I took it just the week prior. She wouldn't let me, saying she tried it with an ex-boyfriend (she had the tact and intelligence not to say who) and it "hurt like hell." This was the same girl who actually enjoyed positions like the brute, reverse pile driver, and scissors, so this was really saying something.

But Cherry was down, so I had at it. After I was in about halfway, she relaxed, and my dick, still wet from her orgasm, moved a little easier. We took it slow. She seemed to get a little more into it, especially after her ass produced what felt like its own lubricant too; so we started to move faster. Before long, those great butt cheeks of hers were clapping against my lower abdomen, though it was a shallower variation of fucking. I came inside of her about five minutes later, around what I thought was the twenty-two-minute mark.

Fourth of July was then, unequivocally, my favorite holiday. Christmas had been number one, because getting free shit and money is pretty great, then Halloween, because it's so much damn fun and there had been great opportunities as a kid for mischief and getting candy and stuff, and in recent years it was nice because girls dressed like skanks, but now, having had two monumental Fourth of July's in a row, where I lost my virginity, then lost my dick-to-ass virginity, well, nothing can really compare to that. I had never felt prouder to be an American.

As Cherry pulled her skirt and panties back up, I laid there, nude, under the stars, contemplating this, how lucky I was to be an American. I never really felt fortunate about anything, since I basically invented myself and worked hard (well, as hard as I had to) for all that I'd ever gotten, but it occurred to me that none of that would've been possible had I not been from where I was from. Yeah, sure, probably if I were born in Sudan or Siberia or North Korea or some other shithole I would have made the best of that situation, too. But, really, the best way to handle something like that would be to move to fucking America. And here I was, a born and bred citizen, a cool sixteen-year-old guy with a badass car who got to fuck hot chicks all the time, now in the ass, too. You can't spell American without "I can." It really is the greatest country on Earth.

________ The Only Problem with ________
Having Anal Sex

Like in the summer that preceded it, my new experience developed in me an instant desire for further exploration. Fucking Cherry in the ass was hot and depraved, making it so it took me even longer to come through vaginal intercourse, which was kind of cool and all, but not really for my fuck buddies, excluding Cheyenne, who dug it. Hope and the other one, Suzy, started to complain. While before I could get myself to come with them after about fifteen or twenty minutes—really, out of consideration more than anything—I would now go for up to a half-hour and they would get pretty sore. And a lot of the time I could only come in doggy style or with them on their sides while imagining I was fucking their asses. It became sort of an obsession, so much so that I began to loathe Cherry for being so damn good at sex but not living closer. I'm sure the feeling was mutual.

Something had to be done about this, but as I knew, only a slut or girlfriend would let me do anal in Moses Lake. This was something of a catch-22.

I wasn't necessarily above having sex with a slut; there were a few in my school I thought were attractive enough and even more at the "alternative" high school, and if done discreetly, it could work. But it couldn't be done discreetly. People knew me at school and they also knew me in town, mostly as the guy with the really cool car, and I'm sure she would want to tell someone afterwards to be associated with me, and while obviously I could and would deny it, even having it exist as rumor would do untold damage to my reputation. In addition to this, there was a shot of me getting a disease. I didn't know if I'd really feel safe fucking those types of girls up there even with a condom. I mean, these were chicks who were having sex at twelve, thirteen (some, now, with a kid or two already), looking for a dangerous thrill with the thugs, who probably also fucked them in the ass, likely condomless, a type of sex where it's easier to spread STDs. I'd probably also have to use a whole bunch of lube and the idea of using lube kind of bothered me. I knew going into this whole anal thing that I'd probably end up using it (and I did, lots), but for purposes other than anal, lube is a crutch only used by people bad at sex.

I didn't want a girlfriend, though. I liked fucking around, a lot, and the thought of pretending to be committed to just one chick was fucking stupid. But I needed anal sex. So, instead, I got *girlfriends*.

Both let me fuck them in the ass and by having two, I wouldn't feel lame for having just one girl over all the time. And if one ever wanted to break up for some stupid reason, I'd still have the other to fall back on. Or in (the behind). It took a lot of careful planning. I never let either of them drive to my house, for example, in case one should be in the neighborhood and see the other's car. Instead, I always told them I'd pick them up when they wanted to come over—or, really, when *I* wanted them to come over—and this worked because I had such a great car and everyone wanted to be seen in it with me. While there was still a chance the other could see us together if we were out and about for too long, it wasn't all that likely because they lived on opposite sides of town—a fact that did inform my choosing them. They were Hope, the weak-willed one, and Erin, the girl who tried to make me her boyfriend at the end of the last summer.

With Hope, it went like this: I had just finished fucking her (twenty-five minutes, six positions) and she was lying on my chest, which was nice and tan and chiseled, running her fingers over it, feeling how hard and amazing it was. "That was nice, Hopi," I said. I liked to call her "Hopi" most of the time because "Hope" was sort of a weird name and I didn't like the way it sounded coming out of my mouth.

"It was. I think I'm starting to get used to going a little longer, too."

"That's good." She started tapping her fingers on my chest, individually and in order, pinky first, ending at the thumb. "What's up?"

"There is one thing, though."

"Yeah?"

"I wish you could come while looking at me again. In my eyes, I mean." For a weak-willed girl, this might sound like something of a complaint. It wasn't. Hope did complain sometimes—all chicks do—but this wasn't one of them. There was no reading between the lines with this dumb little dove. She liked me. A lot. I knew she secretly wished I would make things exclusive with her; she was just too non-confrontational to take a stand. Hope was completely sweet and earnest, all the time, and aside from her being hot—nice ass, pretty brown eyes, full lips and B's—and enjoying sex with me, this was what I liked best about her. She was easy to deal with.

"It's not your fault. It's me." This was not the type of thing I'd normally say.

"No?"

I kissed her forehead. This was not the type of thing I'd normally do. "I like you a lot, Hope." Or say, again. "I'm just having a few issues with intimacy at the moment." Or that.

"What do you mean?"

"Well, I don't know," I looked her in the eyes. "I think I'm kind of falling for you." She smiled. "But that's a problem."

"No it's not."

"Yes it is. I can't get too attached."

She withdrew a little. "Because of your other girls?"

"No, because . . . I don't know."

"What?"

I kissed her forehead again and held her close to me. "What would you think about making things exclusive?"

She was beaming. She ran her fingers through her hair. "I think that would be great."

I leaned over and gave her one of my trademark amazing kisses. I stroked her face. "So you're my girlfriend then."

She wrapped her arms around me, giggling. "I'm your girlfriend!"

And after that I fucked little Hopi in the ass for the first time. I told her I wanted to do something neither of us had done before, since I wished I had lost my virginity to her, and with a little prodding, she went for it. She was fairly sore in that entire region from the sex we had just had, but I used lube and with the return of that hot, dirty, depraved sensation, I was able to come in only seven or so minutes. She seemed to appreciate that. I held her for a while afterwards, something I also wouldn't normally ever do. All things considered, I think I actually sacrificed more in that exchange.

With Erin, it went like this: We were at a party taking place at this incoming senior Jason's, who was one of the cooler skaters at the school, a gamma, and while I had spent the last year avoiding her at parties in light of our history, I knew she could be the second. She was sexually adventurous and I was sure still had a thing for me.

"Hey," I said. We were in the kitchen. There were twenty or so kids scattered around the house.

"Hey Frank."

"How've you been?"

"Good. Yourself?"

"Can't complain." I took a sip. She nodded and took one from her drink. "I think about you sometimes."

She smiled. "Do you, now?"

"I kinda miss you."

"Can't say the same." She offered a tight, close-mouthed grin that let me know she actually could. I told her I needed to talk to her about something kind of serious, and since the party was pretty loud, asked if she would find a quieter room with me. I turned one knob, but it was locked and I heard some light moaning noises. This was probably a guest room or Jason's. We walked to the end of that hallway and there was another door with a sign that read "Do not enter" taped to it, which usually meant it was the parents' room. We went inside and I locked the door. As it clicked, she asked, "Why'd you do that?"

"So no one bothers us."

"I'm not going to have sex with you."

"I just wanna talk." It was a big room, nicely decorated. I guided her over to the bed. "Let's sit." We sat down. She looked at me skeptically. "Hey, don't look at me. I don't know what you had in mind. For me, just words."

She fell back and stared at the ceiling. "Why am I here?"

"Huh?"

"I know about you, Frank. Everyone does. You're sort of a man-whore."

I laughed. "You mean pimp."

"Whatever. Double standards."

"Well anyway, Erin, that was the old me. I'm more interested in intimacy these days. I'm over all that. It got boring."

"Oh, are you?" she said, rolling onto her side, propping her head up. She looked pretty good.

"I am. And of all the girls, I only really ever think about you."

She smiled and cocked her head. "Goodie for me I guess."

"You guess?"

"I don't know, Frank. You get a nice car and put your hair in a little pompadour and all I ever hear about you is Frank hooked up with this girl at that party or that girl was in Frank's car the other day, and now you what? Suddenly want a girlfriend? Doesn't really add up."

I leaned over her. "That's the thing, though, Erin. I've done all that already. It's out of my system. The more I did it, the emptier I felt. The only person I feel I ever connected with in any real meaningful way was you." She was smiling and covered her face. "I was just too dumb to get it at the time." I had absently watched enough romantic comedies on cable to know that this is how most feckless assholes get girls to enter into relationships with them, or at least it's a girl's little dream of how it should be done ("Oh, yeah, I'm confident and a real man, but I have one weakness, one thing that brings me to my knees, and it's you, Nicole, oh, you, it's always been you, blah, blah, blah . . ." or some other fucking ridiculous nonsense). Even Erin, smart enough to be suspicious of me and all my brilliant bullshit up to that point, wasn't immune to it.

"You're serious?"

"Dead."

She pulled me on top of her by the shirt and started making out with me. She ran her fingers through the very pompadour she had called into question. We got really into it. She took my pants off and blew me. I licked her pussy a little, something I only did maybe once or twice for her before. We started fucking.

About five minutes into it, I said, "Hey."

"Hi."

We spoke in breathy fragments while keeping a steady pace in missionary position. "You know what would make this special?"

"What?"

"If we did something we haven't done before."

"Like?"

"I don't know. Have you ever tried anal?"

"Tried it." This didn't really bother me. In fact, I thought it would make it easier, better. "You haven't?"

"Nope."

"Well, I've never done this!" At that point she stuck her finger in my ass. After I overcame the shock and realized what she had done, I was pretty pissed off, but then as she moved it farther and over my prostate, it actually felt pretty fucking good. I wasn't ashamed. It didn't feel gay. It felt weird, sure, but also kind of amazing. "How do you like it?!" She sounded almost angry.

"I do."

"I would have never thought in a million years . . . You really have changed."

"So you have done that before then?"

"Only in my dreams. I want you to fuck me in my ass now, Frank-o."

And then I took my condom off, had her slobber on my dick a little, and did. Of all the girls, she got the most into it. And she didn't even need lube, her asshole its own natural tap and a bit wetter one than Cherry's had been (this wouldn't be the case in most other sessions—nothing like a first-time-with-me thrill, especially in a bedroom we weren't supposed to be in). I wasn't sure how much experience she had had with anal, but it was enough to make it go smoothly, and it was awesome. I came inside her and then wiped my dick off on Jason's parents' comforter. Then I think I stole some OxyContin from their medicine cabinet.

In acquiring my girlfriends, I only had to make minimal sacrifices. I basically just stopped calling Suzy and when she called I wouldn't answer. Eventually she got the hint. I did this without any warning or conversation or anything, and

I'm sure being ignored like that made her fall even more in love with me, which was nice because she would be in my pocket for later, possibly when she could fuck longer without complaint. Also, being ignored like that after months of pretty great sex would make her feel like she had something to prove, and maybe she'd let me fuck her in the ass at a party or something down the line. I considered trying under the arrangement we had had, but I just didn't catch that vibe from her (not really slutty enough). I also briefly thought about making her a third girlfriend but felt like it would be too much to juggle. I'd still have Cheyenne come over because the marathon fuck sessions with her were always pretty great, lack of anal aside, and she would be gone in a few weeks for college anyway. I'd cheat on them, too, with whoever at various summer parties, which I'd never let them attend with me, and where I'd make an effort to conduct my business discreetly in case any of their friends were around, though they still managed to hear about a few of my hookups. They'd also heard about each other, meaning they disobeyed my orders—I had told both we should keep it quiet, that our relationships would be more intimate that way—which irritated me. But, anyway, I just denied all of these accusations. Though Erin was kind of smart for a girl, I was smarter than both of them put together, so I was usually able to flip those conversations back on them and make it seem like I was mad at them for not trusting me, the dumb bitches.

—— Steroids ——

That summer wasn't all good times and anal, though. A couple of problems did present themselves. First, it seemed I stopped growing. I was 5'10"-and-a-quarter and had been for the last four or five months. I measured myself frequently against the inside of my bedroom door, something I had done for years, and there had always been at least a centimeter or two of progress from the last measure, even in my mostly stagnant stages before hitting major spurts. With shoes, this was brought up to about 5'11", maybe 6' in a boot. My hair also helped, making me appear around 6'½" most of the time, but it was little consolation. I was an alpha. I needed to be at least 6' naturally.

I knew I could possibly grow a little more, that guys could until they hit eighteen, in some weird cases even twenty, but Cole was already 6'2" and Leon was at least 6' and it bothered me that I was shorter than them now. Also, there was no guarantee I would. It was an adjustment. I never thought of myself as the Napoleonic type of alpha—in fact, short guys with attitudes always just kind of made me laugh, like small, yippy dogs (I realize it's an exaggeration to call 5'10" Napoleonic; Christ, at least I wasn't an absurd height like 5'6" or 5'7", but this is how I felt, it was a major issue for me). Many of the other guys on the football team were also over 6', a few freaks even around 6'6", and this was less than ideal going into the next season, my first on varsity, with tryouts and practices set to begin at the end of the summer. I knew that the starting quarterback would be goddam Jamal (6'3") and he would also probably be the year after that, so I had to start seriously thinking about what to do to realize my dreams of professional stardom.

I'm happy with what I do now, happier than if I had become a pro athlete, and consider myself an alpha among alphas. These days, I think of most pro athletes as these creatures that are just there for my amusement, like animals in a zoo, or gladiators fighting for me, their king. But at the time I had a goal, and it was to dedicate my life to football. I had a few reluctant ideas about what a plausible backup might be, but it still wasn't finance yet. My thinking was only this: Athletes are at the top of American society. They are the alphas. I had been telling people this was what I wanted to be when I grew up for years, and had a lot riding on it—not only for my future but also at the immediate level of retaining the respect of my classmates and a good reputation. They were assuredly monitoring my trajectory since I was so cool and interesting and so much better than them, all looking at me like I was some sort of celebrity, a fountain of inspiration. Athletes are cooler and more impressive and inspirational than all other celebrities and the president even; that was me to them, and that's what I wanted to be to all of America, the world.

When you're a professional athlete, you get paid millions of dollars for doing something that's not only fun, but also physical and badass. You have fans: pathetic people without their own lives or hopes or dreams that measure their happiness on your weekly performance (this still boggles my mind, but in the best way possible—however, *my* role as a fan now is quite detached). You get to travel around to different cities and fuck their most beautiful women. You are given license to do pretty much whatever you want all the time, and are forgiven easily and often instantly when caught doing anything illegal. Professional athletes can literally get away with murder.

Under them would be rock stars (including rappers, other recording artists), something that, on the off chance I suffered a career-ending injury or something in the next couple of years, I could see myself becoming too, if necessary. I knew, at the very least, I'd be some kind of celebrity when I was older. Rock stars have many of the same qualities as athletes—millions for doing what they love, fans, easy pussy, fame, status, the ability to do whatever they want when they want. While what they do is still cool, the main difference is that it's less masculine. You connect with your fans in this intense, intimate, emotional way that is less about you and more about them, how you make them feel. When you're an athlete, it's all about you. They cheer *you* on. When you make music, you cheer *them* on, provide the soundtrack to their little lives, and all they do is cheer you back to say "Thanks." You need them. You don't need anybody when you're an athlete—you just need the game, which fans watch so they can see you at your best and show you how much they love you (or hate you if they're fans of a rival team; either way, you are respected). Still, I thought maybe I would learn the guitar or bass or something and join a cool band in college if the whole sports thing didn't work out. I lost my virginity with classic rock wafting through the woods, it informed the way I dressed and presented myself; this was saying something.

Next would be actors, which, while perhaps the most celebrated and the richest, are also the gayest type of celebrity. I mean, fuck, I love movies and all, but I could never imagine standing around saying lines and playing make believe all day. It's too fucking ridiculous. Also, even children and animals can technically be actors. It's not a job for a man. And, again, it's really gay.

Then there are politicians. I wouldn't like the work or the level of accountability associated with that. Yes, the president is the most powerful man in the world, and it would be great to be him because of that, but really, I could only see myself doing it under my own terms. I think I'd make a better dictator. I wouldn't enjoy having to deal with problems all the time and being busy and doing something not all that fun and trying to keep people happy and being scrutinized while trying to fuck a lot of chicks, which was something I couldn't ever see myself not doing. Fuck being president. The only thing nice about it would be the total, utter, absolute power, but that still wasn't enough for me. No, sports was where it was at.

The best sport, obviously, is football, and that's why I always saw my career in that. There's a reason why the Super Bowl is watched way more than the NBA Finals and World Series. I thought if I began to really care about the game in my junior and senior years, really applied myself to it like Jamal had his entire life, I'd succeed. Gone was the time of being just good enough for today. I now had to start seriously training on a constant schedule; this was when the dream was supposed to turn into reality. I had to be good enough to get a college scholarship—then it would be on to the pros, and then I'd have chicks and respect and stuff for the rest of my life.

Up until that point, I always, obviously, saw myself as a star quarterback. That had been my niche most of my years playing and also the role I played in the other parts of my life. But most pro quarterbacks stand around 6'3", 6'4", so because I was sixteen and only 5'10", and since this was the time to take it all as seriously as possible, begrudgingly, at first, I set my sights on halfback. It would work; it was a completely respectable and essential position, and most importantly, it was still glamorous. There were many celebrity halfbacks, and they were around my height. It sucked that I was only 5'10", but I would make the best of it. Even though I had been a halfback before, I really only understood it as this kind of fun position, like quarterback except just running and catching occasionally. Not having to strategize as much and throw took a lot of the thinking out of it, which was nice. Freshman year I got good enough yards for the season without trying too-too hard, but this was not the foundation for professional level play. I needed to learn how to really do it and then I needed to do it too.

I started looking at tapes from the video store and library as well as clips I'd download off the Internet (which was just starting to get some downloadable video options other than porn) and reading a lot, too, about great halfbacks and what made them great. Normally I didn't read unless for classes, since that's not at all cool in high school, so it was weird, especially in the summer. I was more of what they call a "power back," a larger halfback. This was nice, obviously because it's best to be on the larger end of anything, but also because the other type of halfback, the smaller, faster type, is called a "scat back," which sounds sort of silly and less masculine. I knew I was just sixteen and all, but I was significantly thinner than a professional or college power back, and slower than a professional or college scat back, so both of these things would need work. And other help, like supplements. And steroids.

I of course knew the health risks involved with steroid use, how it was bad for the heart and all that, and that was okay, but what kind of made me second guess my decision was that it makes your balls shrink a bit and boners harder to get and maintain. But then I learned this was only after prolonged use, and I really only intended to use them over the next few months, until football season ended. I got them through one of my prescription clients, this rich kid Alex, a delta plus, who, in addition to being into pills, was into just about everything else. I think his coke dealer had the hookup. It was a pretty fair trade, for Percocet, though I know I got the better of him a little. My other three steady clients at the time were also these rich kids pretty much into everything, and sometimes I wondered why they all still bought from me. I mean, I was pretty sure they could get the same shit from the guys that had access to cocaine and steroids and horse tranquilizers or whatever for a better price . . . I figured maybe it was loyalty at first, since I'd been selling to the majority of them for almost a year at that point, but settled on the idea that they just liked buying from me because I was so fucking cool.

Also in doing my research, I learned about Human Growth Hormones, and I became filled with happiness. Prior to this I thought God might be punishing me, that He was keeping me from growing for kind of fucking over so many girls and other people. But then I knew He loved me after all. If I could get to 6', I would be happy. I decided I'd shoot for 6'2" or so, since I would be tall without being too tall (anything above 6'4", 6'5" can look grotesque, like an oddity) and it was still a height at which I could enjoy a career as a halfback. I was committed then, thinking quarterback was a little too ambitious. Besides, halfback was only slightly less cool than quarterback, with a lot less work, which made it a better deal overall. Problem one seemed solved. But then my fucking shithead doctor wouldn't write me a prescription. The pussy-faggot, who had graying hair even though he wasn't that old, and a stupid-looking moustache, told me I was tall and healthy enough, and there wasn't a whole lot known about HGH's long-term effects since they were only invented in the eighties. Asshole. Also, none of my clients or other people I knew peripherally in the drug game could seem to get their hands on them. So I was fucked. For then, anyway.

They were anabolic steroids. I started using them in July, and by mid-August, when tryouts were about to start, I could see something of a difference. I was also taking creatine and whey protein, and had my mom cook me a lot of lean chicken. To get the most out of everything, I'd been going to the gym almost every day too, of course—or rather, four gyms. I did weekly trials at all three of our town's membership-only gyms until the high school's weight room opened for football prep. I also bought a jump rope that I used at home for various quick cardio exercises; it was black, so I named it "Jamal II" for motivation, since I wanted it to push me like the idea of the actual Jamal did. He would be starting quarterback; I wanted to not only be starting halfback, but a better player of the game than him.

The only thing that sucked about the steroids was using the needle. I stuck it in my shoulder and the top part of my ass. Needles freak me out a little. It's not really the pain, though it is a little bit I guess, but more the fact that they're kind of . . . phallic. I'd always thought of my dick as this strong, perfectly straight thing, capable of fixing someone, of delivering a type of antidote or medicine to whatever chick was lucky enough to get it stuck in her. My seed and life essence are amazing things. That's sorta what the needle did—it delivered this amazing thing to me. It was a little gay to stick in my ass, even if it was just the top of it and in a very fleshy area. (Perhaps this sounds a little strange coming from a guy who's confessed to not minding a girl sticking a finger in his actual asshole, but fingers are different . . . they bend, twist, curl . . . I was always very aware of it as a finger and feeling like a finger. Nothing dick-like about it, really.)

The funny thing about my body after it started to show more muscle mass was Erin liked it less. She said she preferred me trim, and complained soon it would look like I didn't have a neck. Weird bitch. While I agree bulking up to the level of a WWF wrestler or body builder would've been too much, my neck was long enough that that wouldn't have ever happened. Also, I looked fucking great, some slight bacne aside, like a Greek god. After that I started fucking her harder—pulling her hair most of the time, going for at least thirty minutes, demanding anal twice a week—mostly to show her who was boss and that I was too powerful for her to say things like that to me, but she seemed to enjoy it. Maybe rougher sex was her goal all along and she never really meant it. Probably.

Hope loved all my new muscles. While, yes, little Hopi loved everything about me, she'd especially like to tell me how big and strong I was, how safe she felt with me. She started calling me "He-Man," which might have sounded sarcastic coming from anyone else, but not that dumb, sweet thing, the peach, never. She also started having anal with me at least twice a week, but it was her idea. She knew I liked it and she was completely fucking in love with me. Hers was the opinion shared by universally everyone else: they all thought I looked great.

I could tell Leon and Cole were super jealous, and they started working out like crazy, too. Still, neither of them came close to looking half as ripped and awesome as me.

—— **Dumbbells** ——

The week before tryouts, I was lifting in the high school weight room when these two girls, Tara and Emma, both incoming sophomores, saw me doing curls with two fifty pound dumbbells. Tara was all giggles and Emma's mouth was exaggeratedly open when they approached. Tara had a brother that had been on the team the last year who must've been around somewhere; I'm sure that's what they were doing there. Otherwise the only girls that would come by were the volleyball players, who might lift or work out a little themselves, all of them too athletic to really be attractive.

"Oh my goodness . . ." said Emma. Her mouth immediately resumed its oval.

"Are those real?" asked Tara, staring at my arms. They were big and cut, several veins bulging from and crisscrossing each bicep.

I smiled, nodded, and did two more reps. I put the dumbbells down. "You tell me." I held out my arm. They felt it.

"Wow . . ." they basically said in unison. They were both pretty enough to make me pause my workout. Some guys wouldn't have done that, but those guys are idiots. You work out to get pussy. You basically do everything to get pussy. Yes, I was goal-driven and working hard, but that was for future pussy. Here it was right in front of me, ripe for the taking, and it seemed easy enough if I just put the weights down. And it was. That weekend I fucked Tara at a party. I'd fuck Emma a little over a month later, that time in the privacy of my home. This would be after another big event, and after another big transformation, which we'll get to very soon, but first it would bear mentioning my second problem that summer, as the event and my transformation also factored into solving that: I started running out of new hot girls to have sex with.

Right before tryouts, excluding Tara, I had fucked a total of eleven girls since becoming sexually active. Five of them were virgins when I got to them. The balance was made up of others like me, already on the scene and simply wanting someone else that was young and attractive to have sex with. Most of these girls, at least for the first time, I fucked at a party. As I saw it, there were about four girls per grade that would be both hot enough to fuck and themselves willing to have casual sex. I had already fucked those four that were going to be seniors. I had already fucked those four in my grade. I had the four that were incoming sophomores to look forward to, but this was not enough. Barring a magical influx of hot, ready-to-fuck girls from neighboring towns coming in for parties or whatever, it meant another impending sexual plateau for me, and I fucking hated those more than anything.

Here's the thing about Emma, though: she was a Mormon. Mormon girls were this great forbidden fruit. Many of them were hot as hell, what with their selective breeding, proclivity to some form of exercise, and good nutritional habits, but none of them fucked, not just when they were freshmen, but ever. They didn't have sex until they got married, which they would usually do at eighteen or something ridiculous like that and *just so* they could start having sex. They're not even supposed to have caffeine, for Christ's sake, so a dick in them is out of the question. I think it goes without saying that there's a great seductive quality to doing what you're not supposed to, though, and as somebody who knows people very well and how they work, I was able to tap into this. How? First, because it's pretty funny and interesting, but also necessary to frame that . . .

———— Varsity Tryouts ————

The first day was a Monday. We all reported in the early afternoon. It was pretty hot, it being mid-August and all—Moses Lake, which really is a desert, sometimes could get up past 100 degrees in the latter part of the summer. After going through the regular first-day bullshit, gearing up and getting a little pep talk from the coaches, we hit the field. I had known the coaching staff since I was a freshman—they were all mostly the P.E. teachers and whatnot—but this was a different dynamic here. You could tell this is what they lived for, that their places as teachers were just so they could run the football program, their real shit. They were basically the same, in fact all guys involved in high school athletics are more or less the same—former athletes themselves, big guys, maybe played a little college ball at some shitty school in some shitty program, charismatic for teachers, a little goofy and dim, their lives outside of their sport's season barely worth living, their once kinda hot wives having grown old-looking and probably fat. They were like my seventh-grade coach, except maybe with five or so more I.Q. points. Anyway, I liked them well enough. They seemed to like me, too—knew me from the weight room, had watched me a bit on JV, knew I was cool and had a cool car. One of them, Coach Beauregard, even had a nickname for me, "Hollywood." I know it was a little tongue-in-cheek, but not completely. He, they knew how badass I was.

I liked how seriously they were taking things. It matched my approach, though I actually had something to gain: a professional career. I know they had something to gain, too—their only true (though absurd) measure of self-worth, something I couldn't help but find pretty fucking ridiculous all things considered, but whatever. So there we were. I had this new body, this ready mind, and I was all set to test them out. This was supposed to be the easy part. It was winning games, hopefully state, and impressing scouts that I actually cared about. The first day we mostly did drills and conditioning, which bored me and wasn't at all challenging since I was already in such incredible shape. In the last twenty or so minutes, though, we did get to break off and have some mini-scrimmages, and that was nice. They were small groups and my team wanted me to play quarterback. I refused. It was no longer a temptation, I was totally committed. The guy that did play quarterback, who wasn't at all qualified (I think he ended up a backup on special teams, the loser), just handed me the ball the whole time. I owned the other team. Yes, I, not we. The coaches walked by each little scrimmage and I know noted my performance. It was my first impression and it was stellar. "Nice work, Hollywood," Beauregard said with a pat on the butt on the way out.

I did well that week. I was actually bigger than my main competition, this incoming senior Lyle, who was more of a scat back. He was only a little faster than me. I could take hits better, and my time as a quarterback helped me visualize the plays from a broader perspective, understand the big picture more. Halfbacks occasionally (blue moon, really, but still) have to pass, so I was all set for that, too. I was running with the ball better than him. I was, simply, better.

Lyle had been backup halfback the previous year. He might have even started a game or two. Experience and speed weren't the biggest things he had going for him, though: His main asset was that he was the nephew or something of one of the other coaches, Coach Lee. He was the defensive coach, had nothing to do with us, but it still mattered. All the coaches, Beauregard, who ran offense, him, and Davis, the head coach, were chums, and they all treated Lyle like he was twice as good as he really was. Another thing was that Lyle and Coach Lee were both Mormons. While Mormons are typically fair and have more morals and shit than most people, they're also very cliquey.

So add that on top of being related, and it's a one-two punch.

This is why, at the end of the second week, after spending ten days kicking ass in the hot August sun, on the Friday before the start of my junior year, when we were notified about who would be starting, my name was not on that list as halfback.

I was to start as a wide receiver. It was a fucking joke! There are some famous wide receivers but, you know, come on! It didn't make any sense! Lyle was smaller, a little faster; if anybody should have been a wide receiver, it should have been that faggy little scat back. His relation to Lee and their religion were the only fucking reasons. Normally, nepotism doesn't bother me. If you personally can use it, great, and if you can't and you're smart enough, you can work around it, you can still win, but there was little I could actually do about it in this situation. It felt like it was Groundhog's Day, seventh grade all over again, except this time it was really, actually unfair. To make matters even worse, Cole was going to be starting linebacker. I didn't feel threatened that he would usurp my role as the alpha or coolest guy in the grade or anything—my car, sexual history, and unique persona had solidified that—but I was furious that people might think he was a better football player or tougher than me. Linebacker's such a badass position. I'm pretty sure he started hitting roids also when he saw how beefed up I was getting. Leon was only a backup wide receiver or maybe a safety or something. I can't remember. At any rate, if I wanted a shot at the pros, I needed to start, then, as halfback. I needed to lead us to and win the state tournament. Scouts do not watch wide receivers that should be halfbacks. So what to do? Well, that wasn't a

question I asked. Had I, I probably would've come to a ra-
tional conclusion: If this was Groundhog's Day, treat it as
such. Bash Lyle's knees or whatever. Maybe it would have
raised a few eyebrows, but so what? I knew I could do it so
nobody could prove anything. That's all that would matter.
No, I didn't ask any questions. I didn't think. The steroids
did that for me.

I had hit them a little harder during tryouts. I was an
animal. I was a force. I was young, focused, edgy, and angry. All id. For those two weeks, to keep all of my testosterone where I needed it most, I even stopped having sex,
which was really weird and a huge fucking sacrifice for
me—to date, it's the longest I've gone without any action
since becoming sexually active, even when I was just getting
handjobs and stuff as a fourteen-year-old. When I found
out I was to start as a wide fucking receiver, I needed it
most to fucking kill someone. I actually felt capable of it. It
wasn't Lyle I was angry with. The idea of him annoyed me,
and I did wish him evil, but really, he was just a pawn, I
could see that through the roid-fog at least; it was Coach
Lee who needed to die.

Of course I didn't kill him. But I did fuck him up. And
here's how . . .

Upon reading my role on the team roster, first I stood
there in disbelief, then I quickly found Cole's name,
checked for Leon's, and, finally, settled on Lyle's, though I
already knew what it would read. I then realized I had been
standing there for more than the few seconds that would
seem normal and that other people were behind me, checking for their names, and that my continued presence would
cause them to wonder what my deal was, and that they
might read my name, too, and all of the embarrassment that

went with its placement. This is what first sparked my anger, which then became all-consuming, instantly. I was a bull. Lee was red. I walked from the locker room, through the weight room, and into the coaches' office, this long room with all of their desks that looked out through a window onto the weight room, where all three of them were sitting around guffawing about whatever stupid, loser ex-community or fourth-tier college athletes guffaw about, probably country music or jet skis or whatever. Before they really even knew I was there, I had punched Lee in the nose.

Everything that happened after then happened very quickly, but in my memory seems slow, lucid, each second its own separate thing. Lee fell back onto a desk against the window. I felt Davis grab the back of my shirt, which he then pulled hard. Beauregard got all excited and shouted, "What the hell?! Holly—Parker! Frank Parker!" He knew my name. Wow, I thought. I know he probably couldn't believe what had just happened, but I didn't understand what he thought simply identifying me in that moment was supposed to accomplish. Fucking idiot. I pulled forward, punching Lee in the right eye with my left fist, his hands too busy holding his nose, which was bleeding, to block me, then the left eye with my right fist. I did this fast and hard.

"Oh no you don't!" Davis tried pulling me up, back, ripping my shirt in the process. This was all that was left in his hands as I leveled into Lee's solar plexus, his fat gut. One, two. My fists little battering rams. I was all muscle and hate. A crowd was building, watching on the other side of the glass and near the doorway to the office. Beauregard—who was at least 6'2", and fat—tackled me, pushing me against the desk. Papers, binders fell to the floor. I crunched against a keyboard, knocked into a computer, moving it but not enough to make it fall over. I felt nothing. I squirmed away. I kicked Beauregard in the stomach. Someone went "Oooooh" in the doorway. Lee managed to squeeze himself out of the room. He told the crowd that had gathered to disperse. They didn't. I imagined he was on his way to the bathroom; he was bleeding badly. Beauregard grabbed me and I pulled away, leaping back, facing the coaches and the doorway. I was in the corner, but I was the monster in the corner. Davis assumed a ready, fighting pose. I did likewise. "I don't think you know what you're doing, son," he said.

"Wide receiver!?!" I screamed.

Beauregard held his stomach. "That's what this is about? You were gonna start, goddammit!"

"Everybody knows I'm better than that pussy! Wide fucking receiver!?!"

"Whoa! Calm down now," said Davis. "He's better for the position, plain and simple." Bullshit. I jutted forward like I was going to hit him. He flinched. I laughed.

"You're a bunch of washed up, sad fucking bastards playing favorites and fucking up your team's chances of success."

"Holy shit," said someone out in the weight room who knew I was right.

"What did you just say?" asked Davis.

"I didn't stutter. Fat retard." Coach Davis then lunged toward me. Up until this point, I was more or less fucked. It hadn't occurred to me in the heat of the moment, but my behavior was leading up to expulsion and an arrest for assault and battery, with Lee also probably entitled to some civil damages. That shit doesn't matter when you're fucked up on roids and just had your life's dream shattered. It also didn't matter that I had only taken it really seriously for about a month-and-a-half or so. It could have only been my dream for a week and I would've probably reacted the same way in the state I was in. But after Coach Davis lunged toward me; when he actually punched me, a punch that connected, well, that made the coming paperwork a bit more interesting. It was a good thing he was such a washed up, sad fucking bastard. Ex-jocks, like all jocks, never back down from a good fight. Jocks are alphas (or betas, aspiring) and animals. It's the appropriate way to react to someone coming in and fucking up your shit . . . and I not only beat up his assistant coach and kicked another one, but I also wrecked his office, knocked into some equipment, made a mess . . . in *his* little cave, *his* territory where *he* ruled the roost. Then, to top it off, I told him off to his face, something terrible and penetrating, something he undoubtedly woke up knowing every day: that in the grand scheme of things, he was a nobody, and what's worse, I accused him of being a nobody bent on sabotaging his own nobody pursuits. What self-respecting guy wouldn't punch a beautiful shithead like me, full of youth, life, and potential, for all that?

Of course after he hit me, I hit back, and back, and back. He was bigger than me, but I was younger, stronger, and angrier. Some on the team cheered after he attacked me—mostly Mormons, seniors that were Lyle's friends, and douchebags. Beauregard soon dove in, trying to break us up, and I hit him too. Then I hear, "You know what? Frank's right! Fuck this shit!" and see two black legs in the mix, followed by two black fists working Beauregard's ribs.

I didn't notice when I checked the roster, but apparently Jamal was passed up for starting quarterback in favor of Nick, that asshole I had to hang out with when I was dating Luanne back in the seventh grade—that eighth-grade quarterback guy. He wasn't as athletic or talented as Jamal, and that selection would indeed seem surprising to an objective third party. But Nick was another blond, good ol' boy country-type, and while not Mormon, he was enough like the other coaches in the ways they could better live vicariously through him that they ended up fucking over Jamal. He must've been standing there, fuming, looking at me like I was a hero for actually doing something about it before he got the balls to, too. Davis broke away from me and moved toward Jamal, who Beuregard was trying to restrain with limited success. Keith, ever the loyal older brother, then muscled in and put Beauregard in a full nelson. A senior at the time and both a starting offensive and defensive lineman since the last year, he was massive: 300 pounds, 6'6", maybe even 6'7". I dragged Davis back so I could beat up on him some more, and Jamal, freed up, again took to punching Beuregard. Gasps were heard from all around, which could only be expected. In the end, it took nine of our teammates to pull us all off each other. A computer monitor was also broken in the hubbub. The police arrived shortly thereafter.

———— My Defense ————

When the investigations by the cops and school had wrapped up, all I got was two weeks suspension. I more or less beat up the entire varsity coaching staff and that was it. Lee missed the first week of school and when he returned still had black eyes and a bandaged nose (or so I was told; when I came back, his eyes were only a little discolored and the bandage was gone, but I did get to see his beautiful new crooked nose). Beauregard was okay for the most part, maybe minor bruising around his torso, mostly just injured pride, I'm sure, though he could have also been a little banged up from wherever Jamal hit him. I doubt Jamal could hit as hard as me while I was roid-raging, and I was easiest on ol' Beauregard. And Davis was suspended without pay for two weeks or something like that, and also had some bruising on his face and body from all my punches. I kind of fucked up the entire football team, retarding the development of their season at its start—they had to bring up the pretty clueless JV coaches, running both squads simultaneously—but I didn't care. I thought it was funny.

If Davis hadn't hit me, it would have been an open and shut case, which it was for Jamal and Keith, who were both kicked off the team and expelled. (This was another reason why the football team had no chance that year, since they were probably its best two players aside from what I would've become. Jamal ended up moving back to the South with relatives while Keith stayed in town and maybe got a GED, having, in a strange turn of events, gotten my ex Luanne pregnant, but that's neither here nor there—it's mostly just hilarious.) But he did, so it wasn't, God bless him, and in the end we both sort of got the same sentence since neither of our stories could really be proven.

When pressed by authorities, I would just go on about my excellent track record at the school and in athletics, about how the coaches had it in for me because they were jealous of me and my potential for professional play, the religious nepotism involved, separation of church and state, those kinds of things. I'd talk about how I should feel safe and protected at school, how I didn't appreciate being called into question when I was the "child" who had been hit, that Davis, a respected educator and local athletic institution, should have known far, far better. I even mentioned how Beuregard patted my buttocks, and though maybe he intended to say "good job," it had made me very uncomfortable, that he'd done it to other "children" too, and that it was inappropriate, and that we could all sue. I wasn't particularly proud of these arguments; they were more characteristic of how a female would get her way—vindictive, petty, borderline ridiculous—but they worked because they were hard to get around, especially with my age and the slight bruise Davis left on my cheek. It was what the situation demanded, and I only used them when absolutely necessary. With friends and anyone else who asked, I'd just say, "Everyone's getting the facts straight," and leave it at that.

—— The New Me ——

Beating the coaches up was one of the best things I ever did. I wish I could take all the credit for it. By that, I'm not talking about the involvement of Jamal and Keith, which was understood as superfluous and separate; witnesses saw exactly what I did on my own. What I mean is, I wish that it was another one of my genius schemes instead of something impulsive and chemical . . . but whatever, I still did it. And it still made me 100 times as cool.

Before, I was only cool-light, I just didn't know it. Sure, I had the car, fucked a good amount of chicks, had a bit of an edge because I ruined a party that one time and a few people knew I sold some pharms, but really, at the end of the day, I was still just sort of one of the preps. Now half the preps hated me because I ruined the football team. Some people didn't like me before, but I don't think anyone really hated me other than a handful of jealous goths and a few girls I had fucked over a little. The other half of the preps, the people that didn't really care about football and were kind of smart and knew how stupid it was to make a big emotional investment in sports if you weren't actually playing them, loved me even more and thought what I did was badass and funny. Basically everyone else in the school that wasn't a prep loved me too, also for ruining the football team. The point is: polarization breeds respect. And, again, respect is one of the most important things there is. I was no longer just cool for a prep. I wasn't really even a prep anymore. I ran with them, but I was my own thing, complete, singular. The transformation I thought I made with the car and clothes wasn't in truth fully realized until then. I had only looked the part, now there was no part: just me. I was fucking cool for anyone—that *real* timeless, classic cool; an outlaw of sorts, masculine in its purest sense, a rebel playing by his own rules, cool incarnate.

Admittedly, those first few days right after the incident were a little weird for me, however. I didn't get that I was as cool as I was for a while. Since I had put a lot of stock into the whole football thing, when it became clear it wouldn't be happening, I was a bit fucked up over it. I knew I could try and walk on a team or something in college, but that seemed like a lot of work and pretty fucking far-fetched, and besides, walk-ons, even ones that "got heart," like little "Rudy" or whatever, are losers. Those people don't go pro, and especially don't become superstars. No, a college scholarship after an exciting high school career was the trajectory necessary to make it to where I needed to be. I was fucked. The investigations were also annoying and my mom was good and fucking pissed at me, but whatever. She didn't try to do anything about it.

Mainly, I had lost sense of who I was. I had been Frank Parker, cool guy, prep, athlete, in that order, since the seventh grade, fourth really, even though I was more just "popular" then instead of a "prep" (the strict dress code involved with prepdom doesn't start until the seventh grade; what matters is, I'd always been a member of the most exclusive club in school). I had been trying to become Frank Parker, cool guy, athlete, prep, in that order, I guess, with my sights on eventually becoming Frank Parker, cool guy, celebrity, athlete. Now, with half of the preps hating me, I had the feeling I'd only be welcome at half the parties I'd go to. The fear created from wrecking a party with Cole was different from the hatred created by more or less guaranteeing a losing football season before it could begin. While I still felt elite, I believed I no longer belonged to a tribe—a tribe, at least for my grade, I had led. Then I realized I was *just* Frank Parker. I could be described, sure, with words like cool guy or, again, cool incarnate, rebel, badass, whatever, but I viewed these as just descriptive words . . . they serviced me; I no longer was defined by any of them, and I no longer sought to become the definition of anything other than myself.

——— Noose ———

In those first days of confusion before I came into my new skin, I took my jump rope, tied a noose, secured it around the garage door track when my mom wasn't home . . . and jerked off like there was no tomorrow. Maybe you thought I would end that sentence with "tried to kill myself" or something. While I was, again, fucked up over having my childhood dreams squashed, only pussies try to kill themselves, and only a real bitch would try to do it with a fucking jump rope, even if it did have a badass name like Jamal II. Fuck that. I was usually pretty stern with myself in addressing failure, but I wouldn't give myself that much of a raw deal.

That isn't to say I didn't kind of feel like dying, though. I was youngish and coming off of roids, unsure of myself, with, once again, dead dreams, etcetera, etcetera, and thought, at the time, that if I couldn't be a pro football player, that maybe life wasn't worth living. My backup plan, becoming a rock star, didn't seem right since I hadn't ever picked up a guitar and I had an athlete's body and no musicians really have that. Even guys like in Metallica or really hardcore bands or whatever didn't have biceps like mine. I didn't think music was me or could be me, and I didn't know what else I could do with my life. I was lost. And so, when I say I "jerked off like there was no tomorrow," I literally mean I went into this whole autoerotic asphyxiation experiment knowing just how dangerous it was and not really caring if I died doing it. In fact, I tried to do it almost as hard as possible while still feeling some sort of pleasure. I thought, hey, assuming the risk alone was good enough punishment, and if I died, at least I'd die happy.

Of course, obviously, nothing that bad happened. Yes, it was weird and frantic and scary, but ultimately, all I ended up with was a stress mark around my Adam's apple and a truly fucking amazing orgasm. I kept the noose and occasionally used it throughout the rest of high school, but never half as hard as that first time, then only for fun.

——— First Mormon Girl I Fucked ———

I had sex with Emma the weekend after returning to school. I was bad. Everyone knew it and everyone treated me differently, accordingly. People looked at me the same way they did following my very first transformation when I was nine, except more intensely, and I looked at them the same way I looked at those eighth graders I had to hang out with when I started dating Luanne. They were weird, tense, some sycophantic, some remote, all afraid; I was confident and poised, knowing I was different now, embracing it, knowing I was not really wanted there by everyone, but acting like I didn't want them twice as hard. It divided people. Repelled some, brought others closer to me, including Emma.

Girls that have been forced to be good, but ones with hormones and curiosity, girls like her, have a little devil inside that can't wait to get fucked by a bad boy, but that boy must truly be bad. You can't be cool-light or bad-light. I wasn't a thug or Jamal; I was nontoxic in that regard, but that was it. Otherwise, I was the baddest person she probably knew.

I picked her up that Saturday night. Luckily her parents didn't try to meet me or anything like that. I expected a proper Mormon girl's might. But when I pulled up to her house, she just popped out, trotted to my car, and let me step on the gas so I could drive her into adulthood or whatever.

We had planned to watch a movie together at my place. I didn't even have to turn on the television, a small one I bought for my room with some leftover pill money. She came in, sat on my bed, and said, "Cool room."

"It's all right." I turned on the radio. It was some rap song.

"Do you have surround sound?"

"No."

"Oh, I thought you were turning on the stereo for surround sound. We only watch movies with surround sound at my house."

I sat on the bed and leaned back against the wall, my arms resting behind my head. "Might get it installed soon."

She turned toward me. "Is this 107.3?"

"You know it." 107.3 was this cool station out of Yakima that played rap and edgier R&B and stuff.

"I'm still not allowed to listen to this. I have to sneak it with headphones." She laughed nervously.

I brought my arms down and shifted my weight onto one side, my body oriented toward her. "So how'd you get your parents to let you come out with *me* then?"

She laughed again. "Well . . . they don't really know I'm with you."

"That old trick."

"So," she said, leaning forward, closer. "What are we gonna watch?"

"We're not gonna watch anything."

"Huh?"

"I had something more interesting in mind." I sat up. I was the bad one and she knew what she was getting into by hanging out with me. I leaned in and kissed her. We started making out. Up goes the hand, down goes her shirt, up go her nipples, out goes the hand onto her inner thigh, down go her pants, up goes the dick, down go her panties, on goes the finger, in goes the finger, out goes her hand onto the dick, on goes the condom, in goes the dick, then out, as repeated 'til orgasm, just like that, just like how it's done with pretty much everyone their first time.

What made fucking her different, though, was the level of wrongness involved. It was better than anal. She wasn't any good, really (she did try I guess, got into it a little; Mormons are overachievers), but that didn't matter, not when I knew how much I shouldn't have been fucking her. I mean, I really, really shouldn't have been fucking her. It made it extra hot and made me come after only about fifteen minutes. Sure, I had fucked virgins before, but never while completely sober and never someone who was a Mormon, and beyond being a Mormon by name or a Jack Mormon (cool Mormons who still partied and shit) or anything like that, this was a good girl with good morals who actually believed in her religion; she just happened to have a misplaced curiosity that I was able to take advantage of. The next day she would probably regret it to her core and think she was going to hell. The other virgins, the simple Protestant or Catholic by name preps, were all like me, looking for a thrill, a good time, and fucking them, while big for them I'm sure, didn't compromise everything they stood for, really; they were, at most, culturally religious, even if they didn't know it. What I did with this one had the potential to ruin her life from the inside out, and that made it amazing. I felt so much fucking power.

I blasted 107.3 as loud as my speakers could handle without ruining them as I drove her home. After I dropped her off, she never spoke to me again, would barely even look at me, which I loved.

_______ The Time I Literally Fucked _______ the Shit Out of Someone

The second Mormon girl I fucked was Lyle's sister, which I did purely out of spite a couple of weeks later. She should have hated me for what I did to her family and whatnot. Instead, she must've hated her uncle, or maybe her brother, or self (more than most girls), I don't know. It wasn't hard at all. It happened almost exactly like it happened with Emma—movie plans, a little ride back to my place, then bam. We met in one of my electives, art class. She, like Emma, was a sophomore. My experience with her was interesting for a number of reasons.

It was pretty weird. She was attractive, of course, but she kind of looked like Lyle, and that was a double-edged sword. The nice thing was it made it easier for me to focus on the reason I was fucking her: again, spite. It was a constant reminder of him. I tried to concentrate and get myself off on the idea that this was his sister, that it would kill him to know I was doing this, and I started formulating a plan to do just that—a "Hey, Lyle, I fucked your sister, ask her about it" would suffice, but it was the timing that would be crucial in order to inflict maximum damage. After he scored a touchdown? During the SATs? Prom? Graduation? Right before he went off to college or his mission or whatever? After he scored a touchdown, preferably winning a big game, definitely. Anyhow, the resemblance was overwhelming, and after a while, I felt less like I was fucking his sister than him. This was the other side. It grossed me out and made me feel kind of like a fag. She didn't look exactly like him or anything, but they had similar features and coloring, and their faces moved in the same ways. I'd often see Lyle as concerned, confused, or pained during practice, since he could see how much better I was than him, and she made similar expressions while fucking, it being her first time and all. In the end, and though this is gay, I mean, really, really, gay . . . I started getting myself off by thinking I was fucking the two of them at once. I hated him, and it feels nice to fuck what you hate. I mean, yeah, it was totally gay, but no gayer than using your own hand to jerk off, you know what I mean? It was only mental, and fuck it, it got me hot. Though this wasn't my first real threesome, it was my first threesome in spirit, and it was beautiful, despite it in a way involving another guy.

I hate fucked her/him intensely, almost as hard as I did Erin when I was on roids. (While I felt like it, to surpass that would've been too much. I'm not a good person, obviously, but even I have my limits; it was her/his first time, after all.) (S)he was loud. Eventually, it made her/him fart and actually shit a little, which was gross, but also pretty funny, and made me understand that the expression "I fucked the shit out of her" had a literal root beneath its magnificent poetry. Despite stinking up my room and fucking up my sheets, I forgave her/him in the end because it was a high point of pride that I literally fucked the shit out of someone (or, what's more, two people, simultaneously). It was this, in fact, that finally got me to come. I couldn't wait to tell people, mainly Cole and, especially, Lyle. (Now it would be "Hey, Lyle, I fucked the shit out of your sister. Literally! Ask her about it.")

In addition to bragging rights and getting back at someone who had pissed me off, this was a productive fuck in other ways. I had been a little worried I would simply transfer my anal fetish to a Mormon girl fetish, that I was just addicted to depravity and getting worse, that I would eventually only be able to come through evil, and I was on this slippery slope that would end in me trying to give a ten-year-old relative a Cleveland Steamer in church during Easter service or something. She cured me of all that. Her being Mormon hadn't been all that hot, I didn't really notice at the time; it wasn't what got me off like it was with Emma. It was all about the Lyle thing. Also, though I viewed her shitting in my bed as a good thing ultimately (pride overrides all), it was so gross in the moment that it turned me off to the whole ass area in general for a while (working together with the slight gay-related shame I felt afterwards for imagining I was fucking Lyle, as amazing as it was at the time). After that, I could come easily enough with just pussy again, and a few months later, when I'd give anal another go, there was no resulting obsession. It was just another interesting sensation, which is all it should be.

I told Lyle I fucked his sister a week later, immediately after he ran the winning touchdown in a game against Wenatchee, who we liked to call "Wetsnatchee." Their colors were purple and white because they were faggots (how someone could simultaneously be a wet snatch and a fag is something only a person from Wenatchee could answer). I wasn't really supposed to go near the fields anymore, especially during games, but I'd sneak in anyway. The team was celebrating, facing the crowd, exchanging back and forth cheers and "number one" signs and all that. Lyle was making the rounds, getting high-fives, hugs. Then he faced the crowd, a proud fist pointed toward the sky. "Hey, Lyle! I fucked the shit out of your sister. Literally! Ask her about it!" I shouted. He heard me. People on the team looked pissed. He just gave me this dismissive wave and went on celebrating, and he probably didn't believe me, but whatever, that didn't change the fact that it happened. At least a seed of doubt was planted, for sure. Maybe it grew into something nice and bothersome and she let it bloom one day in a big reveal. Regardless, I got what I wanted, and that's all that matters.

Breaking Up with One of My Girlfriends

I broke up with one of my girlfriends a few days later. Having been cured of my anal fixation, I didn't really have a good reason to keep both around.

When I started things up with them, they both tried to see me, like, three times a week, which was fine in the summer, but now with school, kind of tough for me to still go to parties on the weekends, fuck other girls I'd meet, or even—as nerdy as it sounds—just do some goddam homework once in a while. School added another element, too, in that both would want to hang out with me in public and could attempt to do so easily. To try to make it as uncomplicated as possible, right before the year started, I reminded them that I wanted to keep our relationships private, that we couldn't be all lovey-dovey in the halls or anything. With some time having passed since starting our respective "relationships," both suggested I was either ashamed of them or hiding something. I argued again that it was better to stay secretive, that our home life was ours, and we should keep it just between us, the way a lot of celebrity couples do. "Since you're with me, we are, after all, a celebrity couple," I'd add, and it worked.

After I got suspended, I thought when I actually started junior year classes, I'd have an even easier time with this because they wouldn't *want* to be seen with me. Kind of the opposite happened. Erin thought what I had done was "just great" because "football's stupid and you'll get your neck back," and Hope felt like she had to "be there to support" me, so they'd always try to walk around the school with me and stuff. I'd tell them that it was a weird time and I wanted to be by myself, and then later I'd have to hear about it for twenty minutes at home before fucking them—how I needed to share more, not be so distant. Having a girlfriend sucks, but having two, when you hear the same fucking complaints at length, twice, is fucking horrible.

I let Erin go in the end. After having the talk with her, I said we could still hang out, have sex and stuff like we used to, casually. She didn't accept, which sucked. I would miss fucking her. A lot. She could take a dick, which is invaluable for a sixteen-year-old with a lot of testosterone. But I knew it wasn't worth all the energy, and my new persona was already opening up doors for me that weren't there before. There would be other girls that liked to fuck, different flavors, variations to explore. She took the news fairly well, saying, "I get it. You were never really the boyfriend type." She asked if I had really tried. I lied and said I did. That was enough. So she let me fuck her one last time, and when I was about to come I gave her "The Bronco"—shouting Hope's name in doggy and riding her as she tried with all her might to buck me off. I knew she had always been sort of wise to what was going on and that it would make her pretty mad, and that would make me feel better about her making fun of my neck those two times. Anyway, I successfully came inside her before she could get away, with maybe just a little bit of after-jizz landing on her ass cheeks or something when she finally got me out. I then brought her home while she cursed at me and that was that.

I only kept Hope around so I could continue to have sex without wearing a condom. I figured she would probably never leave me because of how in love with me she was, and her will was so malleable that I was sure, if I wanted, I would only have to see her once a week—though I figured I'd want condomless sex at least twice. It just felt too fucking good. Also, if I broke up with her, it would piss me off to know that other guys, guys with "serious" girlfriends or whatever, like Leon, would get to feel something I couldn't. Fuck that.

—— Fucking Girls in Other Cliques ——

So there I was, fully formed, free of fetishes and juggling girlfriends. Ready, willing, able. It was halfway through football season. By that point, except for the Mormons on the team itself, everyone who had been upset with me had either forgotten what I did, forgiven me for it, or joined those who celebrated it. That's the great thing about people: they're stupid and have short memories. Because the team was having a losing season (only 1-4, the one win against Wetsnatchee), a lot of kids thought they were bringing our school and subsequently them shame. And since they looked at me as being in polar opposition to the team, because I and my fists had literally been that with its coaches, I was a winner. It didn't matter that I was the reason they were having a losing season in the first place, but whatever, it's a circular argument and I was happy to be on the sweet side of it.

Besides those Mormons, the only other people that still hated me, really, were some of the girls I'd fucked at parties that fell in love with me, or their friends. But that was cool. It was just "I can't believe he did that to her!" hate, which, despite their best efforts, tends to get girls a little wet. Some people were still afraid of me, too, but I was happy about it because that meant they were in awe of me. Otherwise, though, there wasn't enough of me to go around. Nerds, art fags, drama geeks, skaters, druggies, any remaining thugs, most preps, the few black kids that all thought I was on the right side of the good fight fought by Jamal and Keith, the blatant racists that were happy I put into motion the thing that got Jamal and Keith kicked out of school, all wanted to talk to me, to be my friend. Even goth kids would strike up conversations. It was nice being appreciated by others. Feeling completely comfortable and self-assured, and it no longer being the brutal environment of junior high and early high school, I was more open to receiving them, though mainly just to get the people that really mattered talking. All the preps would think it was weird, and that was a good thing. It would be news. Another reason was some of the skater chicks and a few drama geeks were actually pretty attractive and I thought it might be fun to fuck them.

I did, of course. Pussy flung itself at me like never before. I was welcomed at whatever party I went to, whether it was a standard prep party, where being feared and loved gave me free rein, or a weird skater or art fag party, where just being loved gave me free rein. I was a celebrity, a rare creature able to pass through any social group and tap it for its hottest chicks. I knew no bounds. It was thrilling to be around me, and like I said before, girls get off pretty easily on a good thrill.

My fuck tally for the year was thirteen (counting Lyle's sister as only one person). Thirteen. A lot of them more than once. There was one other Mormon (who was just one of Emma's friends that had hated me); the other three sophomore preps besides Tara; Lindsey, who was from out of town and visiting this big ORV state park close by called the Sand Dunes, and who I fucked in some bushes in broad day light; two drama geeks; a skater; and a goth. Also, there was a teacher.

Two of these are interesting enough to describe further: the teacher, obviously, and the skater. We'll get to them in just a minute.

——— New York City ———

I fucking love New York. It's the capital of the planet. We control everything . . . money, media, and also, it's a playground for the world's richest people. I've eaten basically every type of food there is (a lot of ethnic food sucks, I'll take a steak over anything, always), done all kinds of other cool shit. And what's best, girls of every variety are here.

Fucking girls in other cliques was the precursor to this thing I dubbed "Pussy Bingo" in college, my favorite game ever since. In short, it's about fucking chicks of different races and desirable body types. By now I've fucked ones of every color and creed, and am on to fucking diverse mixtures of nationalities to keep sex interesting. A bingo is never really achieved, it's more about checking off as many of the nearly infinite combinations of ethnic backgrounds and attractive physical features as possible. Now I'm mostly on to fourths—I swear, one of the last chicks was part Icelandic, part Namibian, part Swedish, part Unicorn; big tits, natural blue eyes, dark skin. Amazing.

New York's traditionally been a place where immigrants can come to try to make their dreams come true. It's my dream now that unusual assortments of these foreigners find and fuck each other so I can eventually fuck their daughters (after they reach the age of consent, of course, but not too long after). It's also my dream that if these parents found each other somewhere else those daughters still come here to try and make their modeling or higher education dreams come true. Without the American Dreams they're all chasing, my dream of fucking these girls—which is maybe the most quintessentially American of all— wouldn't be able to come true, which it does, so very, very often.

—— Teacher ——

Ms. Adams, or as she liked to be called, Jane, was someone I definitely wouldn't fuck now (too old), but at the time it was one of my biggest conquests. She was probably twenty-six, twenty-seven; pretty and fit, but with some laugh lines and stuff that let the world know she was a woman, not a girl. I hate girls, but I really hate women. She hated Coach Davis, so she loved me. She taught nutrition and health. It was the second semester.

The head of her department was Davis, who aside from his work with the football team seemed to pride himself on general incompetence. When out of season, he'd spend his time at school more or less lounging around in variations of sweatpants and tracksuits, leading the occasional gym class poorly. That kind of life would be great if you were Davis himself or one of his lackeys, but not if you were a young, idealistic teacher actually trying to make a difference in your students' lives.

I was doing well in her class. I did well in all my classes, getting almost straight A's since as long as I could remember, the one exception an A- in history the previous semester, which I only got because I skipped too often to drive home after lunch and have sex with Hope or Erin or whoever.

One day, after receiving a test back, a test I got 100% on, she asked me to stay after. Normally, this would have irritated me because I liked wandering the halls and being seen in between periods, but hers was my last class of the day, so it wasn't that big of a deal. All the other kids shuffled out, and I stayed, chilling in my seat, leaning back, nice and casual, like I always looked during school. I smiled with my eyes at the two hottest girls as they left, one of whom I'd fucked already, this Italian girl named Gina. When everyone was gone, Ms. Adams approached my desk, kind of leaning on the front. "You did well on that test," she said.

"I did." I smiled, nodding.

"Tell me, Frank, you're planning on going to college, right?"

"Yeah."

"Any idea what you want to do after?"

"Not really. Not anymore, anyway." I scratched my head.

"So you had something in mind?"

"Professional football." I laughed a little. "But that's not gonna happen anymore."

She chuckled, barely veiling her hatred for the guy that ruined my dreams and who I ruined physically. Then, in a turn I didn't expect, she said, "Well, if you're open to suggestion, and I hope you are, I think you have what it takes to become a doctor."

It was weird to imagine myself doing anything like that, working in a profession where selflessness is requisite. No, I was not interested in helping people or syringes. My dick was the only way I would administer medicine. Doctors only get pussy after they become doctors, well after, when they're not too busy with school and bullshit and have the money that chicks, sure, often hot, fall in love with just as much as they do them and their ideals. Don't get me wrong, doctors are great; necessary. But they don't do what

I do. I liked that she cared enough to single me out for this silly little conference, though, and smiled briefly. "Wow . . . thanks Ms. Adams. But I don't think I'm right for that. If I do more than undergrad, it'll probably be law." This was true. I was way more of a lawyer-type than a doctor, and this would be the best step to get into politics, to obtain power and celebrity—my backup plan at the time if I had to go through academics to assume a respectable alpha job. My new number one goal was to become a rock star, having been practicing the guitar secretly since Christmas break, when my frame had finally lost enough mass that I could look at myself in the mirror and see something other than a professional athlete. I knew my chords, could play some cool licks.

"Uh-ooooh. I see . . . so a lawyer? You're one of those, huh?"

"I guess. Don't really like needles. But I have other projects and goals. I play a little music." I admitted this to her because I knew she wouldn't tell anybody and would probably find it charming. She looked good and I thought about what it would be like to bend her over her desk and fuck her from behind. I thought about that at least twice each class probably, but it never seemed like an actual possibility until that moment, not that it was anywhere near that, but we *were* alone, and that was heading in the right direction. It wasn't dissimilar from the attraction ritual I knew. I had proven I was excellent, special (out of all her students, she wanted to talk to me). Now it was time to make her feel like there was a sense of intimacy between us, then special herself. "Listen—not that you would, but nobody else knows I play music, so don't tell anyone. It's a secret 'til I get really good. I can trust you, right?"

She smiled. "It's safe with me. I'll wait until we hear you on the radio."

"Thanks . . ." I smiled back. "So, if you don't mind me asking, why aren't you a doctor?"

"My first love is teaching," she said, laughing. She shifted, swayed. "Aaaaand I didn't really have the grades. That's why I get excited when I see students like you. But you're more of a law guy, I get it."

"Well . . . music guy," I said, raising my brow. Obviously she hadn't taken my music plans seriously, the bitch. I figured if there was any way I could make this work, it wouldn't be filling that niche for her, that of the promising but disappointing student, ignoring my potential as a lifesaving healer to make just a little more money as a lawyer. Not very fuckable. It would be to fill the niche every woman and most girls really want: the young, roguish lover; the devil-may-care musician with the cool car and the bad-boy streak—the guy I really was. So I corrected her. And with those three words, I started it, and soon, I was filling more than just a niche. It wasn't like I fucked her then and there or anything. I just made her laugh and told her I liked her haircut before I left. Tone set, foundation built.

In the middle of the next week, I went up to her desk after class and asked if she had a minute. She seemed pleased and wondered if I "had reconsidered my stance toward a career in medicine." I told her no, but "given her interest in me and my development," I thought maybe she would like to hear some of my music. She laughed, asked if I had a tape or CD or anything; I told her I didn't have a tape or anything, and, her finger to her temple, smiling impishly, she asked, "What do you have in mind then?"

"Well, I thought maybe I could play some songs in person for you."

"Do you play anywhere around town?"

"Not yet. That's why I need you. You're the only one outside of my family that knows I play music, and I need an unbiased opinion. You'd be like a test audience."

"Okay, then. Bring your guitar in on Friday. You can play after class."

I shook my head. "Geesh . . . yeah, I don't know. If people see me carrying it around, then they'd ask me about it, and I'd have to tell them . . . you know how it is, slippery slope."

"Well if you're gonna be a rock star, Frank, people are going to have to know you play music."

"They will, they will. In due course, Ms. Adams. But first, the test audience."

"I don't really understand what you're proposing." Her head tilted. She leaned forward and I could see down her shirt a little. She had what looked like pretty good C's. I knew from watching enough pornos that almost all chicks' titties got at least a little saggy after they turned twenty-five, that is unless they were fake. As I'd soon learn, hers weren't so bad yet. A few years earlier, though, they were probably great, or even pretty great. She was wearing a blue bra that day. Her words were friendly but formal, a safe play, in complete contrast with her body, which she moved to entice. I trusted the latter.

"That I play for you in private. Off school grounds."

She smiled, leaned back, uncrossed and recrossed her legs. She looked directly into my eyes. "I don't think that would be appropriate."

I smiled back. "It probably wouldn't be."

"That won't be happening, Frank. Let me know when you have a tape. I'll listen then."

I thought that was that; it had been worth a shot. "Thanks," I said, and started making my way to the door.

"So why am I your ideal test audience, anyway? Shouldn't you want to play for other teenagers? You're the ones who buy music."

I turned back. "Well, you were a teenager once, right? My sound's got a more tried-and-true thing going on, I think. I don't know . . . you're smart, I think you'd get it. And you've shown interest in my promise, that's really why."

She smirked. "You do have promise." We locked eyes. "Hold on . . ." She started writing something. "I have a friend. He can record you playing. Here's his phone number." She folded it. I took it and smiled, trying to hide that I was kind of pissed. I didn't want info for any weird guy's weird little bedroom recording studio or whatever. I wanted to fuck my teacher.

"Thanks." I left. I was about to crumple up the paper and throw it on the floor when I decided to read it on a lark. There was no phone number, but instead an address and a note that read "Saturday at 9:00. Park a couple of blocks away. I've seen your car. It's noticeable. – Jane." (Now, the forward tone and content of this might seem a little implausible, but, and not to beat a dead horse, I really was cool incarnate; young, hot sex on a stick. I was seventeen years old with a badass car and great fashion sense; I had an amazing body, an attractive enough face, was confident, smart, played by my own rules, and didn't give a fuck. It wasn't only the girls in the halls who looked at me with their mouths agape, women did around town, too, especially when they saw me get out of my car in a parking lot or whatever. I was a vision. Also, as you'll now learn, Ms. Adams, like all chicks, was a little crazy.)

I went over to her place that Saturday at 9:15, and carried my guitar, just for kicks, just to be funny. She lived alone, no husband or boyfriend or anything. I wouldn't have really cared if I was fucking anybody's wife, but getting caught by a guy who liked guns, which there were many of in my town, would've sucked I guess. When she opened the door I strummed a little and sang the phrase "Sweet Jaaaane" a few times over and over again like I was Lou Reed (who I'd just started listening to, getting seriously into classic rock since taking up the guitar). She laughed and then we started.

It got very intense, very quickly, beyond what I had experienced before with Cherry, Erin, Cheyenne, any of my more adventurous or aggressive partners. First, she got off by fingering herself while sucking my dick. She told me she wanted me to bruise the back of her throat. "You damn well know I will," I said. I grabbed her head and held it tightly as she moved it up and down. "Yeah, choke on that huge fucking cock." She then deep throated me for, like, five minutes. I told her to stop, that it would make me come, so instead, she started licking my asshole. I enjoyed that. I had seen it done in a lot of pornos but it hadn't yet been done to me. It was depraved and felt really weird. Then we started fucking. She had me go really fast, right from the start. I pulled her up to a sitting position so rabbit pace would be impossible—we had been going so fast I could barely feel anything but motion—and she put one of my fingers in her asshole and then tried to make me jam another one in there, too. She begged me to pull her hair, choke her. I obliged a little and she came, screaming almost, and said "Next time don't make me ask" in her authoritative teaching voice. I told her next time I'd make her beg twice as hard and that I wasn't done yet, and she came again. She told me to fuck her ass, so I did, and she embraced it like no other before, moving just as fast as she did vaginally, except the tightness of her asshole made me feel a lot more than motion. Ms. Adams was pretty fucking weird, I thought, and at first I wondered if this was the way all women fucked, if this was what girls grew into. Then she asked me to punch her in the back of the head. That freaked me out so I made myself come. I pulled out and started spraying my jizz on her ass cheeks, and when she realized what I was doing she stuffed my dick back in her mouth so that the last of my semen would drip down her throat. It was at that point I understood it was probably impossible for all girls to grow into Ms. Adams, and thought maybe there weren't any other women really like Ms. Adams in the entire world. I had assumed that kind of shit was only done in porn, as performance, for show. While I now know that there are people worse than her out there, it was an interesting little introduction to the S&M type thing and the sort of person who's into it: oftentimes, you would never know by looking at them. I fucked that goth girl, for example, who was actually kind of a cold fish (not completely her fault, as the half-men in her social circle certainly wouldn't be teaching her how to fuck properly), and I thought she'd be all into taking it hard and being tossed around and probably even anal. But she wasn't into anything like that; in fact, she made us go really, really slow. I eventually got myself to come by gradually working us up to a steady pace and going hard, but still, all that slow shit was pretty annoying. Ms. Adams, on the other hand, seemed like a mild-mannered, normal woman just going through life. But she was a fucking freak.

After we had sex, she curled up next to me and began to cry. She said not to worry, she always did this, it would pass. She told me how hard it was to be a first-year teacher at our school, how much she hated Davis and everyone else in the P.E. and Health department because they never listened to her, but how she really loved teaching and all of us students, so it made it worth it when she went home each day. She complimented me, told me how smart I was and that she knew she could trust me, could tell I "got it, life," and said I "fucked like a champ." At this point she started crying again, and said it was weird, she knew, but my arms reminded her of her father's. I realized then I should have left and never have gone back, but honestly, her strangeness and raw, crazy vulnerability got me hard again. So we fucked a second time. She cried a little afterwards then, too, said it was nothing, and showed me the back door, which she said I should use from then on. What we were doing was risky, she said.

I visited her about once a week for most of the rest of the term. She tried to incorporate more of that S&M stuff, eventually breaking out whips and bondage straps, other objects. I entertained it at first, thinking it might be fun to paddle her a little bit or whatever, make me feel more powerful, which it did somewhat I guess. Then she started lobbying to use these things on me, telling me how amazing it felt and how she knew I must be curious, but I wouldn't let her. I wasn't curious. I was the opposite. I would do the dominating, not her. The tears always came afterwards, but

again, it was her process, she assured me, and it had nothing to do with me, and she was quick about it, never taking
any longer than two or three minutes, so I would just lie
there and think about sports and whatnot while she cried
it out. It seemed like a reasonable compromise for how insane the sex was. Sometimes she would tell me about her
day, or a little story from her childhood or something,
but she never expected anything in return, in fact would
get upset if I tried to offer advice or pity or whatever,
which I did purely in a going-through-the-motions, this-is-
how-a-normal-person-would-respond-to-this-shit kind of
way, with feigned sincerity, the same way I had always pretended to care about boring stuff with my girlfriends. She
wanted none of it and it was nice. It worked.

Eventually, I realized the power I felt from using all
of the objects was artificial. It wasn't me doing the
dominating; it was a whip, a handcuff. True dominance is
achieved through will and your bare hands. Guns and
knives are for pussies. Whips, paddles, cuffs, vibrators, butt
plugs, ice cubes, and hot oils are for people who suck at
sex. I told her we would be removing these items from our
sessions, that all she needed to come was "me and my hard
dick." Then I fucked her hard, smacked her ass, choked her
some, put her in advanced, often uncomfortable-for-her
positions, and it made her come. A lot. I think also just me
putting my foot down about anything got her off.

The next time, however, I did more or less the same
thing (in varying order of positions, of course; I would
never come close to repeating a performance), even a bit
harder, and she barely got wet. It was weird. That hadn't
happened to me before. She asked me to punch her in
the stomach and I wouldn't, so she started scratching me,

slapping me. I held her arms down and gave it to her hard and she got a little wet. I eased up and she dug her nails in my back, fast and hard like a feral cat. I felt the sting of an open sore. It pissed me off. She laughed maniacally, "Punch me. Punch me, faggot!" I hit her in the stomach with a little strike, not hard at all, and it made her come. Though I guess I did that with my own hand, I wouldn't really say I did it with my will, and that made me feel shitty. I wasn't really above hurting her in some way at that point—the bitch did just make me bleed and had called me a faggot, after all—but I did it without really wanting to, without it being my idea. We had sex for literally an hour and I still couldn't come. I told her I didn't think it was gonna happen. She said, "Whatever. Already got mine," and she made like she was gonna pull me out. So I fucked her hard for a minute and it made me come. This is one of the only times a female ever really successfully manipulated me. Then she cried in my arms and talked about her parents' divorce when she was six.

The next time I came over she answered the back door wearing a large, black strap-on. "If all I need to come is you and your hard dick, then all you should need to come is me and my hard dick." I stood there for a moment kind of in disbelief and then laughed a little, anxiously. It was like me with the guitar, just a joke, I thought. But weren't we beyond that type of thing? I didn't quite know what to make of it. "I'm serious, Frank." I looked at her. She was expectant, staring at me stone-faced. She really was, the nutty bitch.

"I can't do this anymore, Jane."

"You mean you're not going to let me fuck you with this?"

I couldn't believe that shit. "You know the answer to that."

"And we can't use any of my other toys?"

"No."

"Then I can't either."

"It's been fun," I said. I tried to smile but sort of just grimaced and then looked away.

"Sometimes."

"See you in class, Ms. Adams."

"Bye, Frank." She shut the door. I left, feeling very strange. I mostly thought I had dodged a bullet; she was way too out there, and even joking about fucking me in the ass with that thing was inappropriate. But I also felt this weird form of rejection I had never known before. I mean, the only time I had really been turned away by a female was when Callie broke up with me, maybe also a few parties early sophomore year when I struck out if you could count those, but they didn't matter. Here I was being told I wasn't enough for her after having fucked her, after making her come with my big, beautiful dick. And that mattered a great deal. My dick should have been enough for any bitch, young, old, whatever, especially old, even if she was a weirdo deviant. "Sometimes" actually kinda stung, as much as anything can with me.

She gave me an A for the term, even though I skipped most of her classes after we started fucking because I knew I could. I still did well on the final, like I did on every test. I remember her fondly enough now, I guess. She was sick, to the core, and too old to fix; there was nothing my amazing dick and its amazing medicine could have done to help her. All things considered, she was a good teacher. I learned a thing or two.

———— **Dry** ————

Though, yeah, Ms. Adams was completely fucking crazy and I knew it wasn't actually my fault that she didn't want to fuck me anymore, I still ended up punishing myself over it. Since my dick had not been the answer to her prayers like it had been for everyone else, I punished it exclusively by not using lotion or even spit when I jerked off for the two weeks following the end of our arrangement. It chaffed a lot and sometimes I didn't even come, which sucked and resulted in blue balls, which really fucking sucked. Also, a few times it looked like I had broken a couple of capillaries beneath the skin of my shaft, and once I actually rubbed myself so raw that I bled a little, after a bit too much friction against a callus. That really, really fucking sucked.

The one upside to jerking off dry was that sometimes I'd do it on days where I figured I'd be having sex at some point, and my dick, all irritated, would be less sensitive to pleasurable sensations and it would take me longer to come, typically, like, around forty-five minutes, which always made me feel really good about myself, and whatever chick I was with—usually Hope—really tired and sore, and that was kind of cool, too, because they knew I was a fucking stallion and that they were barely enough for me.

——— Short Freshman Asian ———

I also fucked that skater chick, Lucy, that spring. There were a few interesting things about her. One: she was a freshman. Everybody says freshman girls don't have sex, and what that really means is freshman preps don't have sex. What I thought it meant when I was a freshman was "only the few thugs that made it to the ninth grade have sex." I was wrong. I didn't regret, say, not becoming a skater or artsy kid or whatever when I was a freshman just so I could fuck the hotter chicks in those circles a little earlier. I regretted nothing. Had I not remained a prep for as long as I had, I wouldn't have had half the power or respect I enjoyed later on; I wouldn't have fucked so many ridiculously good-looking girls, including Lucy; nor would I have been able to do so in any other social circle but my own. Two: she was Asian. Before her, I had never really fucked an ethnic girl before. I had had sex with a few half and quarter breeds, mostly infused with Mexican blood or whatever, Moses Lake being a farming and migrant work hub. And of course there was Cher, who had American Indian in her before I got in her. But all of them pretty much had Caucasian features, except with better lips and asses due to their heritage. Unlike them, Lucy was 100% non-white, purebred Chinese. Three: she was short. She was, like, 4'10", maybe 4'11".

Even though I had had sex with over twenty girls at that point, none of them had been close to that short. They were usually at least 5'4". I think it's because they were mostly preps, and preps are generally the children of two people that were also preps, or one prep and one nerd; that is to say, two like-minded and like-bodied winners or one smart guy who got rich and was able to get a hot wife because of that. Three of these four are typically tall, and sure, there are tall nerds, too, I guess, but really, if you're tall enough, there's no good reason you should be a nerd. Unless you're a nerd that's kind of a dick, and you start your own company like Bill Gates or the Facebook guy or something, odds are you have a shitty job where you do most of the work and don't make anything, while a tall former prep is an executive or in sales, which are both easy and primarily just involve taking credit for a nerd's work, and also make a shitload more money.

Her shortness made her very, very tight. At first I thought it was because I went in wrong or something. I had heard that Asian girls' vaginas were supposed to be sideways or whatever, but in the Asian porn I'd seen it didn't really look that way (the one interesting find was that their nipples sometimes seemed to point in different directions), so I thought maybe it was only some of them and that she was one of them. Then, as we kept going, I realized that everything was in its right place; it was all just really, really, super fucking tight. I was wearing a condom but could still feel a ridiculous amount—not just warmth and moisture and the walls of her vaginal canal at certain angles, but the walls of her canal at every angle; it surrounded, choked my dick the entire time. Her pussy felt as tight as the asses I had fucked, except it was a pussy so it felt better. What's more, she could take a dick. I'm not sure how long she had been sexually active (while curious because of her ability, it would have seemed insecure to ask) but she was either a natural talent or had been at it for a year, six months at least. She would move, gyrate, all while looking like she was having the time of her life. We fucked in my car down by these railroad tracks that cut across a part of the lake, and she used the car to full effect—riding me while I sat in the driver's seat, laying out over the seats in various positions, holding onto the ceiling as she did weird Chinese acrobatic twists and shit. It was great.

While I was certainly over fetishes at that point, I wasn't above preferences, and decided that short girls would join those that loved to suck a dick, ones that would let me do anal, and ones with big, rockin' tits as my favorite types of girls. The sad thing is that being really short and having nice boobs tend to be mutually exclusive, though by now I've met some girls who fall into both categories, a few even with boobs that weren't fake.

I'd fuck another short girl that summer, since I was actively seeking them out then, and it wasn't half as fun. She was from one of the next towns over, this shithole called Othello, and was an incoming junior over there or something, don't remember her name. She was a rare combination of being a hot prep and short, which I chalked up to the fact that she was from a smaller town with a more limited gene pool, and it would only be natural that their preps would, by normal standards, excluding my newfound penchant for short girls, be genetically inferior. Anyhow, she would barely let me move, like, at all, because she was so tight and I felt so big in there. It kind of defeated the purpose.

It brought me back to Lucy. I rarely thought about a girl when I wasn't trying to fuck or fucking her, and that must've meant something. I wondered if there was a way to screen for this type of thing. I knew, really, that anyone was capable of aggression in the sack, including the mild-mannered and meek, and vice-versa with chicks that seemed kinda hardcore. So it probably had less to do with her being a skater and more to do with her being Asian. They have a tremendous work ethic and those perfectionist tendencies; it would only make sense that these would extend to the bedroom. They're also sort of gluttons for punishment, many Japanese people being into those weird game shows that embarrass or hurt their contestants some-how; a lot of people in their culture kill themselves with harakiri or whatever instead of suffering dishonor. Even though Lucy was Chinese that made sense to me in some way. It boils down to pride, and if enough of that is at stake, what is happening physically is of little consequence. Mind over matter. This isn't to say that I thought our sex was painful for her or anything—again, she seemed to love it, and we actually did fuck a few more times that spring and early summer (always by the railroad tracks, once even on them) before she started to seem clingy and I stopped calling her. But I know a lot of that pleasure had to come from a mental place. She was just so fucking tight.

This other girl actually made me fucking stop, and I had to ask her to give me a blowjob so I could come, which, really, she should have just offered, the selfish, born-in-a-barn bitch. It was mediocre at best and I had to imagine scenes from this hot porno I had watched the day before to actually get myself there. I couldn't believe it. I wasn't about to create a sub-preference for short Chinese or Asian girls, though; that would be way too specific, Lucy actually being the only one in town that was also hot. No, I decided short girls would be a crapshoot, but ones worth it, ultimately, and thought I should just look for some signs of abandon, perfectionism, or just take the easy route and try to pick up on some masochistic tendencies . . . signs they currently or once had an eating disorder, if it seemed like they enjoyed drinking for the wrong reasons; maybe ask them about their parents, see how much they liked their dads, if their families were broken, those kinds of things.

Less Prom King, More Porn Star

Nothing really happened that hadn't happened before for the rest of that summer or, really, my entire senior year. I fucked a lot of chicks (including Cherry again on the Fourth of July, the last and best installment of The Quarter Squaw Chronicles) and was generally super cool and badass and having a pretty good time with life, albeit with a few challenges to overcome, but none really worth describing in detail. Though we were never a public couple, Hope thought she was my girlfriend and I had sex with her whenever I wanted. The only thing sort of interesting was that I fucked a girl I went to school with who had done some modeling, but she wasn't very good. No news is good news. In my memory, it was mostly a time marked by figuring out everything for college and practicing music. I was the coolest guy in school, not really the Football Hero or charismatic guy that everyone looked up to, the guy I had always thought I'd be, but I was happier with my lot—less prom king, more porn star—a better place to be if you've really figured life out.

I had the grades, SATs, AP credits, and so on to get into an Ivy, and a parent with a low enough income that I should have been able to attend any one of them for cheap with need and merit-based scholarships, but I didn't even try. Wasn't interested. No, I figured I'd only attend one in grad school, only if Plan A didn't work out, when that type of pedigree would be useful for a career in law and politics, still my back up. I thought they'd be kind of tough or, whatever, time-consuming I guess, and I wouldn't be able to go out and fuck as many chicks as I could at an easier school. Also, the chicks at the Ivies, all smart, would probably be a little less attractive and a lot crazier.

Easy, quality pussy was my principal concern going into college. I planned during that time to bring my fuck tally into the triple digits, so naturally I wanted to go to a state school. I applied to the largest and best one around, the University of Washington, and got in very easily with a full-ride scholarship. I also applied for and won a number of external scholarships. Due to the full ride, these would be kicked back to me as cash, which was then mine for, you know, incidentals and whatnot. The one blemish on my record, beating up the coaching staff, didn't matter at all to good ol' U-Dub, and they seemed more than happy to have someone with my numbers to add to the incoming freshman class and brag about to the next freshman classes and anyone who gave them money—I did, after all, have the numbers for an Ivy.

I spent a little bit of time that year reading outside of class, listening to music I wouldn't normally like, learning more about art and weird shit, stuff that gets college chicks wet. I knew that I was the kind of guy their dreams were made of at my core, but I figured my surface game would need to be switched up a little, refined with some culture or whatever. This later proved to be sort of a waste of time, as most college girls were just as susceptible to easy flattery (beautiful eyes, nice smile, etc.) as high school girls, and usually that's all I really needed, but whatever, it's good to be well-rounded. And it did help with some types of girls, I guess, but we'll get there.

I enlisted the help of this guy I had met when I was a junior, Dennis, to guide me through some of this. Dennis was kind of a weirdo, a delta nerd and art fag, really, with a few friends in the prep circle, mostly college-bound girls. He knew a shit-ton about books and films and music and everything, from the classics to what was new and trendy, and I used him for that, while he used me to learn about sex. While obviously I gave him the better end of the deal, it was still a friendship that worked. I liked Dennis. He was one of the only interesting people I knew, capable of stimulating conversation, which nobody else around actually was. That wasn't anything I really needed, but it was nice for a change I guess. Leon and Cole, while invaluable in other ways, were shitty conversationalists, especially at that point, since they stopped asking about my conquests and pretended to be disinterested if I ever offered anything, due to jealousy, I was sure. Besides them, I mostly just talked to the girls I fucked, and I think it goes without saying how terrible they were to talk to.

When I first started regularly hanging out with him, we would meet mostly at diners and coffee shops and stuff, where we'd drink coffee (a thing college kids do) and he'd bring music and movies I could borrow and I'd tell him fucktales. I'd add tidbits on technique, how to really work a clit, how to play with nipples if you're eating a girl out, those kinds of things. He said he knew it was nothing he couldn't look up on the Internet or see in porn, but he considered a lot of that "unreliable" and knew that "there's nothing like firsthand knowledge." I was happy to oblige him—he was right; there really is nothing like firsthand knowledge if it's mine. Dennis was gearing up for college. He told me about his sexual experiences, which were laughable: throughout all of high school, he had made out with two deltas in our grade, also artsy nerds, and got a handjob from a girl at some art camp and felt her boobs a little too or something, shit I was doing at, like, thirteen. But he saw himself as the type of guy that could get laid in college, so he wanted to know how to do it. I respected his confidence and also the realism with which he looked back on the past four years. Dennis wasn't really fuckable as a high schooler. He was short, with a weak chin, and had strawberry hair verging on red that he let grow too long because I think he thought it made him look cooler or more bohemian or whatever, but actually it just looked stupid. He wasn't grotesque or ugly, just kind of comical-looking. I can't imagine how terrible it must be to have a weak chin. You would just look so nice, so ineffective. The only way you wouldn't is if you just scowled at everybody all the time, and nobody wants to fuck a downer. But nobody wants to fuck a clown, either. Quite the dilemma. If I had a weak chin, I might have killed myself. Anyway, he looked like that. He needed a beard or something, but I don't think could grow one yet. Also, he didn't really speak with confidence about anything, unless it was something he knew a lot about, and then he did it with this intensity that would make most people uncomfortable rather than interested. Dennis was like a college guy before he was a college guy, and while high school girls would probably say they wanted that, they didn't. They just wanted a fun young stud with a hard body, a guy like me. He was smart, knew all of this, would be the first to point it out, and knew it was why he never got laid, but also, for whatever reason, felt there wasn't a whole lot he could do about it. Sometimes I'd give him advice, and by merely hanging out with me he seemed to relax his speech a little and become more assertive, a little cooler generally, and I thought it would be fun to try to get him laid before college.

I started bringing him to parties with me and stuff, which pissed Leon and Cole off (they hated him and thought he was a fag, Cole especially—"That little bitch is gayer than shit on a faggot's dick," he told me after the first party). I was at the point where really, really minimal effort was required to get a girl to fuck me while out; basically I could just do what I wanted until around 11:30 or midnight and then take my pick, so I liked to just chill, learn about weird shit from him, tell him stories. I was above needing a sidekick that was cool. I could just do what I wanted and people respected me even more for it *because* I was doing exactly what I wanted. It made him 1,000 times cooler, though, to be seen with me—going from delta to beta overnight.

He was so much cooler, in fact, that he got laid at the third party I brought him to. She was a junior beta, Michelle, a girl I had fucked the year before. Nice ass, not bad in the sack, either, if I remember right. Afterwards, he told me she let him fuck her on her side. He was pretty drunk, so it took him a while to come, too. I knew that probably made his little life, losing his virginity not as a minute-man, in more than one position like that to a girl with a good ass. I was proud of him. I felt the sort of satisfaction an older brother must feel all the time—mostly happiness for my own success as a teacher, but sure, some for his success. That was a little weird for me, actually, to care about someone else's achievement in any way, to actually feel empathy, but there it was. I think it was because his chin was so fucking weak. Sometimes you can't help but root for the underdog. Most underdogs are complete losers, though.

I didn't go to my prom. Prom is what most guys go to so they can try to fuck the girl they've liked for the past four years or whatever. To me, that was just called Saturday. The only difference was I wouldn't be trying to fuck the girl I had liked for the last four years—that wouldn't exist—I would fuck the girl *they* liked for the last four years, way before they got to her. It pissed Hope off, since it was her prom too, but whatever; she got over it and probably loved me even more in the end for treating her so poorly. I did go to a prom party, though, where I had sex with someone else's date, this girl named Rebecca. That was fun.

Graduation happened. It was fine. Everyone in my class had that communal spirit. I didn't really feel it, probably because I had spent so much of my K-12 years so high above them. It's lonely at the top. I wouldn't really miss Dennis or even Leon or Cole. I had a few fuck buddies at the time, all of them damn good, but knew I wouldn't miss any of them, either (not as people—I would never miss a girl as a person, obviously—as partners in fun); they were of Moses Lake and I already felt beyond Moses Lake. I had tapped it and pretty much the entire county dry, fucked all there was to fuck, filled those wide open spaces like they were wide open legs: with the greatness that was my dick. I conquered it the way the settlers before me had, my own Manifest Destiny. It was a time for change, time to graduate to the big leagues—sorority girls and college bars, that kind of shit. I wasn't completely devoid of nostalgia, though . . . to pay homage to my high school experience, after the ceremony I got kind of drunk and had sex with three different girls at two different parties. It was a good night I guess.

I broke up with Hopi, the sweet, slight thing, about four days before I left for college. I knew those four days would be pretty busy for me and I wanted to ride the condomless sex thing out as long as I could. The idiotic little lamb had actually thought she could maintain something of a long distance relationship with me, that we'd still be together while I was at U-Dub and she was at Wazzu, this far lesser state school near the Idaho border she settled on going to after she couldn't get into mine. She cried and cried and cried afterwards, in my room, during our farewell fuck, in the car on the way home, all the way to her door, even on the phone the next day, and the one after that, and the one after that, the poor fool girl. I had a bit of a cold that last week because of the seasons changing or something, so that was my parting gift to her, and I could hear it in her nasally sobs over the phone those next few days, making her sound even more pathetic, until I finally stopped answering. She really did love me, from the bottom of her stupid little heart.

——— My Mini-Masterpiece ———

The day before the big move, Dennis came over to my house to pick up a few foreign films he had lent me. I liked a lot of that shit; other cultures seemed to have a more laxed approach to nudity, though our movies were typically more violent. A lot of it was really fucking weird, too, right down to the names of the directors, and I knew it would probably really impress college girls if I dropped some like Fellini and Kurosawa or whatever. I figured if I dropped names like those, panties wouldn't be too far behind.

I offered him a beer, keeping them on hand in my fridge that summer (my mom cared at first, but I knew she couldn't really do anything about it, so I drank at home whenever I wanted to). We were hanging out in my room, just shooting the shit, when he asked a very important question. "So, Frank," he began. "I've always wondered, now seems like an appropriate time to ask . . . How many?"

I smiled. "How many?"

"Come on . . ."

"Thirty-six."

"Thirty-six?"

"Thirty-six."

"Thirty-fucking-six?"

"Thirty-six." It wasn't the question itself, but the timing that gave it its gravity. It was a question that Leon and Cole used to ask me all the time when I was a sopho-more. But I knew Dennis, while also asking out of a form of self-interest, wasn't motivated by anything as petty or futile as competition. His interest was part motivation and part academic, for its own sake, so I shared. It was, after all, my life's work up to that point, a mini-masterpiece by an enfant terrible. It was beautiful.

"Jesus. And all attractive?" I shot him a look. He smiled. "I didn't think we had thirty-six good-looking girls around here."

"I've been sexually active for three years. In that time I've fucked girls from six graduating classes, some from out of town, too. Do the math."

"Holy shit, man." He shook his head. "Thirty-six." That was the number. And I should also mention that I did this while staying completely disease-free, getting tested near the end of my run about two weeks before this conversation took place. I know I had fucked more girls than anyone and had gotten a shit-ton of blowjobs too, and I got away scot-free. There was a bad outbreak of chlamydia going around my junior year, for example (probably fucked those girls sophomore year). People that I think didn't even have that much sex got it. Someone just fucked the wrong fucker, I guess.

"Anybody I wouldn't expect?"

"Lots, probably." I smiled slyly. "Here—" I sat down at my desk, where I had a laptop I just bought in preparation for school. "I would care less about you revealing the contents of this list than the fact that it exists. Lists are nerdy, but I don't have it memorized or anything." I opened the spreadsheet I had worked on for the last three years as he stood looking over my shoulder.

He started laughing. "You made a spreadsheet . . ." I moved away. I sat and chilled on my bed, sipping my beer, while he read.

"Whitney Cutler!" She was a junior when we were sophomores. Super hot. I fucked her against a fence at someone's party in the summer before my junior year.

I raised my brow nonchalantly and took a sip. "Yeah, she was all right."

He laughed. "Ephrata girl two! Pure poetry!" He continued, "Oh, shit. Beth Morris. Her tits are so . . . arresting."

"Meh. Her pussy looked like a pig's foot."

He cracked up. "A pig's foot! Hahaha!"

"She's kind of a curvy girl, ya know?" The hot kind; curves in the right places. Not fat at all. But her pussy *did* look like a pig's foot. And I think she was the first girl that queefed while I fucked her, which was sort of funny but also a bit of a turn off.

"I know guys that would give their left nut to fuck her and all you say is 'pig's foot.' " Yup. He continued. "Whoa, whoa, whoa . . . Kristi Young? She's Mormon!"

"You'd be surprised."

"You fucked a *Mormon*? Wait . . . you fucked *Mormons*! Holy shit, man."

"A few." I took another drink.

"I knew they were freaks under all that goodie two-shoes shit."

"Don't say things like 'goodie two-shoes.' It's emasculating."

He kept going. "Lucy Chen . . . nice. She's pretty hot for a little skater chick. Is it true what they say?"

"What's that?"

"Sideways?"

I took a sip. "Only after I got through with her." He exploded. Fuck, I was funny.

"Rose Fallon? Oh, my god. I was in love with that girl."

"That foul-faced fuck-sleeve? Fuck her . . ." Of course her face itself wasn't ugly, I wouldn't fuck someone like that, obviously; she just scowled all the time. She was the one that did a little modeling, so she was probably always hungry.

"Oh, whatever. She's beautiful. She was in fucking *Seventeen*, dude."

"Just another fuck-sleeve, man." It was fun to fuck Rose Fallon because I knew she was a model (she had an agent in Seattle or maybe even L.A. or New York that would fly her out for shit sometimes or whatever) and also because she was about as tall as me. I wondered if her pussy would be all big and loose and stuff on account of her height, but it wasn't, probably because she was so skinny. All the same, she didn't move very well.

"You're trying too hard now. That girl's a vision."

"I'm not trying anything. She can't fuck. She mostly just laid there. I like going all-out, man. That might fly with some old, half-a-fag photographer in France or something, but not me. I'm sure she's better now from being with me, though."

He shook his head and smiled. "Jesus." He read. "Whoa, whoa, whoa, whoa. Holy fucking shit. What? What?!? Jane Adams. Like Ms. Adams? What?!?"

"Yeah . . . that happened."

"How?"

"Like all the rest, really, man. Chicks are chicks. I showed her how great I was, made a play, and she took it.

She was fucking nuts though. I guess don't tell anybody about that one. She'd probably track me down and murder me. Seriously. Into S&M, all this weird shit."

Another explosion. "She likes the paddle? What?!?" I shrugged. He shook his head and continued. "And you did actually fuck Callie. I always wondered."

"Yeah, summer after sophomore year. No biggie."

He laughed and shook his head. "No biggie. Hottest girl ever. I thought you guys didn't since you were so young when you dated." I hadn't really been aware that Dennis existed before the previous year, but of course he had known all about me and Callie in junior high. Everyone had, even at the other school, where he went. We were that important.

"Well, it wasn't while we were dating, but still, yeah, no biggie."

"Wow." He closed out the spreadsheet. "I knew it was a lot, but that just blew my mind, Frank. Damn."

"Yeah," I said. "I did all right here."

And then I went off to college.

Part II

WINGS

———— Why I Joined a Frat ————

I moved to Seattle about a week before classes started, to a fraternity house on U-Dub's thriving Greek Row. Earlier that summer I visited the campus a few times and rushed the frat, which I won't name, but will say had a reputation as being the best and most exclusive, and had gotten asked to join pretty quickly and easily enough.

Admittedly, at first they seemed sort of weary of me, this one blond fat kid named Paulsen in particular, as the guys that lived there were from wealthy families, not just rich. I wasn't really much like them, not only in background but also in presentation. Many proudly wore the preppy labels I long ago forsook, or more expensive variations of the general style. When that chubby fuck first saw me, he snickered to another guy, who also looked lame, "Is that a rushee or a gardener? Jesus Christ." He said it loud enough that I could hear it, but only just. It sounded stupid, since the house didn't have much of a yard, so I didn't think about it too much. I would later destroy him, though not for this, but we'll get there. At the time, I just kept walking and chatting with the rush chair, this guy named Britton, who was cool and I could tell liked me.

Coming from wealth and going to a public university is a bit of an oxymoron, so I wondered if my soon-to-be frat brothers had chosen our school for fun times and easy pussy like me or if they were just kind of stupid (before long I'd learn it was a combination of both). I demonstrated my worth with a conversation about my SATs and by making out with a really hot girl at a rush party my second time visiting. That all elusive mix of a guy who'll raise our house GPA and pull in choice ass? What a find! We don't care that you're kinda poor. You're in!

I planned on living a double life of sorts, with the frat as my home base. My other life would be spent pursuing a music career. The two weren't very congruent.

Fraternities aren't cool at all, not in the real, rock-and-roll sense, the one I now knew. They have a reputation of housing douchebags that pay for friends and try to seem better than everyone else, and actually smart, cool people shouldn't want to be a part of anything like that.

Here's the thing, though: Trying to seem exclusive and better than everyone is the only thing an attractive girl really knows. They respond to it from guys because it's what they use themselves. Outside of their looks, it's what makes them sought-after (though it also goes hand-in-hand with their looks—makeup, high heels, all that, are just a part of the chase, just a girl trying to look less attainable and better than others (as well as herself)). If I seem better than you, you like me more. If you feel you have no chance with me, you like me more. These are some of the most basic tenets of attraction, used by everyone, really, but they are also fundamentally feminine. Yes, I've made myself look as good as possible or whatever, *but* there was a difference in that I pretty much *was* actually way cooler and better than everyone I ever knew to begin with—even when I was just a prep, I was king prep for my grade or whatever—that extra effort appearance-wise was just icing on the cake, unnecessary but attractive. But caring too much about what you wear is girly, obsessing over your hair or whatever is girly. And, in the same way, paying dues to associate yourself with a collective that gets off on being publicly exclusive is super fucking girly.

That's why hot girls go to sororities like moths to the flame. The fraternity system is basically just there to provide them mates, which is a fucking shame, since the real Greeks were so strong and patriarchal. A typical fratboy shithead might argue the opposite, that the sororities are there to give him mates, but that would just be him trying to seem cooler and better than he actually is, like the little bitch he undoubtedly is. The Greek system works in contrast with the ideal masculine method of attraction. The actual best and easiest way to get laid is to not give a fuck. Be true to yourself, especially the more dickish parts of yourself. It makes you better than everyone because there is no "everyone," no pool to measure yourself against; no one to impress but you. Sure, it helps if you are truly excellent, but it's not necessary. Not caring is absolute freedom, and if you own it, all the way, it emits supreme confidence, the most fuckable quality there is. Do what you want to do, but don't try to do anything. Don't try to fuck a chick at a party. Know that a chick would be lucky to fuck you. Don't just believe it. Know it. It's more than a mindset. It's a way of being. The alternative, trying to seem better than everyone or yourself, only emits faux-confidence; it relies on effort, which is usually more than a little transparent and also pretty fucking unattractive for a man. Being comfortable in your own skin is the spirit of rock-and-roll and, really, the spirit of cool. (Obviously "not giving a fuck" has some limits. Everything within reason. There needs to be a modicum of effort in certain areas, like, again, grooming; you can't say, "I hate bathing and I'm going to own that." I get the devil's advocate thing, but come on. It might be a little feminine, but it's still necessary. Likewise, it is very sexy for a girl not to give a fuck in the bedroom, to just be herself, let it all out, own her body, and abandon all of the insecurities that usually mark her silly and stupid gender. Absolute effort is expected at all other times.)

At any rate, I needed to fuck these girls and the only access to them would be through a frat. U-Dub has the largest Greek system west of the Mississippi, and the hottest girls in school would naturally be there. It was as simple as that. Living in that mostly feminine world bothered me, sure, but you have to be in it to win it. And since I knew the game, I joined the one that would appeal to these girls' sensibilities the most: the one only rich or exceptional guys were supposed to get into. I aimed to operate as my own entity, the masculine hero I really was, within it, though, as soon as I could, after pledging. I knew that pledge quarter would require me to lose some sense of self, and while that was troubling of course, considering all the pussy I thought would be coming my way during and especially afterwards, it would be a sacrifice worth making.

——— Frankie Parker ———

In the meantime, there was my other life, my life as Frankie Parker, the musician, that let me stay true to myself. I had decided I'd perform as Frankie, not Frank. It had a better ring to it—more freewheeling.

This was where all my practicing, hanging out with Dennis, and cultural studies would really come in handy. At that point, I still hadn't ever performed publicly. I hadn't really performed for anybody. I'd played a few Stones and Zeppelin songs for Hope here and there in my bedroom or whatever, mainly because she wanted to hang out and I would be more interested in practicing, but that didn't really count. It was pretty productive, though, because my playing got her a little wet. She felt like she was spending time with me and that made her want to fuck, but I didn't have to talk to her and was still able to practice like I wanted. It was definitely only practice, not performance, though.

My plan was to start off playing open mikes at coffee shops kind of far away from campus, then bars, and see where it took me. I intended to play mostly original music. Throwing in a cover here and there is good to keep your audience with you when you're first starting out, but I don't understand the appeal of performing all cover sets or anything. It's sort of pathetic to just play other people's songs all the time, even if you don't feel like you have the chops to write good music. I had written about fifteen songs in the year-and-a-half I had been playing and thought all of them were pretty good. Fifteen is too many for an album, though, so I would also use the performances to gauge which ones went over best. The plan was, during my first quarter of college, I'd play these live and meet other musicians who could fill out my band—a guy or two like me and the rest more like Dennis, their fingers on the pulse of contemporary stuff, instrumentalists who could inject the songs with weird-but-not-too-weird bass and bleeps and bloops. In two years or so I'd be famous, a year after that rich, and then I would have all the power and respect I'd need for the rest of my life.

I figured since I was going to a state school, and not the Ivy I was actually capable of, that these two lives wouldn't be so hard to balance. The Greek kids wouldn't be caught dead near the part of Seattle with all the artsy coffee shops and vice-versa, so I also felt pretty confident that I could go about my business freely. Still, I proceeded with caution. I doubted my frat brothers would care too-too much if they knew I hung out at kinda gay cafés and shit, but I knew no musicians would want to associate with me if they found out I was a fratboy douchebag. They needed to see me as a rock star, a great and inspiring figure—an amazing frontman leading with my dick as we fucked our way up a mountain of glorious groupie pussy, all the way to the top, the whole world there at our feet.

—— Pledge Quarter ——

Pledging the frat was actually not that bad, not as bad as a lot of people would think, anyway. You hear horror stories (some urban legends, some rooted in truth) about hazing and all that shit—having to fuck a goat, getting branded or burned, being left in the woods, having to drink 'til you puke and then eat said puke—but I didn't deal with anything like that. There were some things that sucked, but nothing close to that shit.

I was among twelve or so others in my pledge class. The worst we had to do was basically this scavenger hunt where we ran around the city and performed kind of stupid tasks, like getting our picture taken touching a homeless person (could not be the same homeless person for all of us), buying a dildo, asking a fat girl for her phone number, those kinds of things. And also once we had to stay up all night doing a "team building exercise" where we tried to complete a jigsaw puzzle while a few of the upperclassman brothers would come and fuck it up; we didn't finish it until 7 a.m., but then we were all fed a nice breakfast. That was it.

I think this was because we were the best and most exclusive frat at the school. Most people might think that would make our pledge process the most rigorous. This is among the many reasons that most people are idiots. See, where wealth and status are concerned, shit isn't supposed to be hard. Ivies are known for "grade inflation"—though there is a lot of work, the reward for a mediocre job at completing it is still usually an A. In any given corporation, the higher the role and pay, the less that person actually does. CEOs who get fired for sucking at their jobs and losing a shit-ton of money are often given multi-million dollar "golden parachutes." It was kinda the same with this frat; we were the best, so we did the least. It was nice. Also, if any part of it were that tough, the entitled kids in my pledge class, or any other pledge class for that matter, just wouldn't have done it. They had a hard enough time doing things that were just sort of normal.

Most of the year our house would have a cleaning service, but this was suspended during the main pledge quarter to make the incoming class clean instead. A lot of people considered this worse than the scavenger hunt (except for the having to touch a homeless person part) and would bitch and moan constantly or just not do it. I hated cleaning because it's women's work, and I did a shitty job at it (and would often spit in the mop solution/dishwasher/whatever), but I did it nonetheless, most of the time, anyway. I figured, hey, I'm already living in this fundamentally feminine little world and, you know, when in Rome . . .

Once, the house's social chair, Chad, a beta plus, told this pledge brother of mine, Austin, whose father was some bigwig executive at Microsoft or Amazon or something, to mop the floors before a mixer we had with a sorority.

"No," was his reply.

"It wasn't a question. It was an order."

Austin laughed and shrugged.

"I can make your life a living hell," said Chad, in that melodramatic tone a frat brother superior might have picked up from an eighties movie or something.

"No you can't. I don't need this frat, really. I don't need anything. I'm made for life, man. I'll just call for a cleaning lady in the morning."

"No . . . you won't. This is part of your duty."

"No . . . it isn't. Don't you remember, Chad? My dad was gonna spring to have the floors heated in the upstairs bathroom."

"That was your dad?"

"Yeah."

Chad thought for a moment. "Fine. Call a cleaning lady in the morning. But do ten pushups."

"Pushups?"

"Yeah. You have to do something, dude. You can't get away with talking to me like that."

Austin shrugged again. He got down and started doing some pushups. "Gross. The floor is sticky." I think he did eight. I liked Austin.

And that was basically the tenor of the pledge-brother dynamic that quarter. Half-assed orders, open insubordination, then compromise. Our superiors didn't care because they had been the same way when they were pledges and we didn't care because most of us could afford not to. It was business as usual at the house, seemingly part of the time-honored tradition. I personally couldn't afford not to, though, and that kind of sucked I guess. All I had were the kickbacks from my scholarships to live off of. I had spent a lot of what I saved from modestly selling pharms at the end of high school to move and set up my room, and on that laptop and stuff (my mom didn't really help since she was pretty broke most of the time). So it was a little tough, what with everyone else around having a lot of money to buy whatever they felt like—expensive clothes, a constant supply of good alcohol, fancy meals at restaurants, their way out of chores. I was sort of used to that type of thing from hanging out with Leon and Cole growing up, but this was different. In both cases nothing was earned, it was family money, but here they had direct control over it, and it made me feel a little shitty to see them flaunt it on a daily basis. Still, I made the best of it, for the most part.

I didn't fuck as many girls as I'd have liked through the frat when I was a pledge, just five. This was the main downside, way worse than any of the "hazing" or feeling broke. The power structure was easy, obvious, intuitive. The juniors and seniors at the top, especially those with major titles—president, vice president, esteemed chairs, etcetera—had their pick of girls at parties and mixers. They were the alpha and top betas (actually, literally, the president was called "the alpha"—as you could expect, I decided when my time came, I would be president if the music thing hadn't worked out yet). Typically, they went for the hottest freshmen from the sororities, as they, like me when I was an upperclassman in high school, had probably already fucked most other girls worth fucking. Also, a lot of girls peak around eighteen. I knew when I was one of them, I would break all records—unless I was an actual rock star trying to break pussy-getting records set by Elvis or Mick Jagger or whoever—but in the meantime, I was left with the scraps, the girls they and the descending order of brothers didn't claim. Granted, these scraps were all incredibly attractive, hotter than most of the girls back home. They consisted of one sophomore and two freshman dormers at various parties (hot chicks who had a friend or a friend of a friend in our frat or whatever) and two freshman sorority pledges (though a little less good-looking than the pledges the upperclassmen got, they were hotter than the dormers I had sex with, as most sorority girls were, mainly because of their tireless effort and the high physical standards with which they were held to be accepted into their fine organizations).

To have sex with the pledges, I had to misrepresent myself as already being a brother, a sophomore. Telling a sorority girl I was a pledge was a turnoff—a lesson I learned quickly after our first mixer, when I got shot down by a super hot blonde with great tits that said I had "cool hair." I told her I liked hers too and asked if she was a natural blonde or not. This was the type of confusing, slightly negative compliment that I knew would drive a sorority girl crazy. It would not be the last time I'd use it. The question showed many things . . . that I didn't need or necessarily want her, that I had the balls to throw out a veiled criticism, that I was a winner. She liked me, I could tell, and started talking more. She told me where she was from, what she came to study, that she was a pledge, and since I had already demonstrated my higher value, in an attempt to make her feel special and create the sense of easy intimacy between us normally good to get a girl in bed, I told her I was a pledge too. She then wrapped up our conversation within two minutes and started talking with Sterling, our frat's treasurer and also a beta, who I think fucked her that night.

I hadn't felt that kind of rejection since I was a first-semester sophomore in high school without a cool car, and it was weird. I'm sure she was taught by her sisters that talking with guy pledges would lower her value. (Before, during the summer, when I made out with that other girl while rushing, it was because she wasn't yet a pledge—she hadn't been taught the way it worked.) This girl was too into me for it to be any case other than that. I then understood the natural order of things: Freshman sorority girls want to have sex with the best guys in the frats, not the lowly pledges. They fuck—or probably in their delusional little worlds try to enter into a relationship with—the president or social chair or whatever so they can raise their statuses. Easy. Her quick reveal of being a pledge was her direct way of showing sexual interest, an expression of vulnerability, the type of thing used to entice an elite upperclassman. You live, you learn. I figured she probably approached me in the first place because I looked unique by comparison, what with my hair and lack of preppy labels. I had the look of someone not pledging, not trying to fit in, but someone who was already there, who had figured himself out and was comfortable—someone, typically, older. So then I started lying.

Most girls I targeted believed me; the only ones who didn't were sophomores who knew better, who would know that I couldn't be a sophomore and already a brother because they would have remembered me from the year before. I asked one if she was sure she was sure, and she verified it by the lack of my presence in the previous year's fraternity composite photo, where she spent some time searching. She must have been pretty in love with me. Anyway, that sucked because it always sucks to be caught in a lie, and also because I probably would've ended up fucking three or so more girls that quarter. But it was also a little cool because some girls, most, really, deep down, like liars—I'd later fuck some of these sophomores when I became an actual brother. Other times it didn't really play because a lot of the freshman girls, known as "little sisters" if they hung out enough at the frat, who were my primary targets—they were usually the hottest and fucking them would have raised my status the most—wouldn't care about me being a sophomore. That was as high as I could sell myself; a junior or senior would've been too much of a reach, one that their older sisters would have been quick to point out (some attempts I made to fuck pledges under the sophomore rouse actually did get thwarted by nosy, cock-blocking older sisters). The two times I lucked out with pledges were when I told them I was the house manager or athletic chair or some other title that was impressive enough for a sophomore, and since they liked me a lot anyway, because of their great taste and how unique and cool I was, and there was no one around to call me out, it worked.

—— Christian Farmer's Daughter ——

The only one of these hookups that deserves some elaboration is one of the freshmen from the dorms, mostly just because that fucktale is pretty fuckin' good.

A pledge brother of mine, Will, had a friend from back home who was a dormer, and this girl was her roommate. Dorm girls loved going to frat parties because everybody loved going to frat parties, but they especially did because it made them feel special and pretty and exclusive for a night without having to do the work that sorority girls do. They fed into our system as these great one-off hookups, girls we'd likely never see again except maybe peripherally on campus or on the very off chance we'd have a class with them. Dorm girls had the potential to become little sisters or fuck buddies if they were super fucking hot, but by and large, they lived too far away (it's easier to have sex with someone all the time that lives across the street instead of across campus) and having the same one around too much might lower one's value because they were just a dormer.

His friend's roommate was named Melanie. She was very attractive, brown hair, pretty face, good ass, tits not bad, either. She had a nice smile, too, teeth big and white. She grew up as a Christian fundamentalist on a farm in Alaska, and said she was "kind of religious still, but not really." She was drinking with us and all, but said she felt like "a sinner," but that it was okay, "this was college, the time to do it." She claimed to be a virgin, which she said she would be "until the day she was married." She was very bubbly and flirty and touchy and carried on like it was one of her first times drinking. At first I couldn't tell if it was all an act or something, and I'm still not entirely sure, but I don't think it was. When I got her back to my bedroom, which didn't take long, she started kissing me, my neck, being very aggressive, and then she pulled away laughing. "Oh my God, I can't believe I'm doing this!"

"What's so hard to believe?"

"You're a boy!"

"Uh-huh . . ." She kissed me again, running her fingers through my hair, which looked really good that day. I could tell she loved it.

"And I'm kissing you!" She laughed. "Oh my God!"

"That's not hard to believe," I said, giving her one of my great, trademark kisses that never lost their touch.

"You're such a good kisser." She kissed me some more and made this weird humming noise. "And cute. You're cute, too. Oh my God." Then she pulled away and sat down on my bed.

"You all right?"

"This is bad. I'm a sinner. And I've been saying 'Oh my God' a lot. That's pretty bad. Big sin. All kinds of sins." She looked away and sad.

I moved toward her and kissed her, lightly touching her face. "It's fun to do bad things." We continued making out and I guided her down to lie on her back. I ran my hand down her face, arm, up her flank, over her boob. "Isn't it?"

She kissed me, humming again, louder this time. "It is." I reached under her shirt, undid her bra, and held her boob, grazing the nipple in one graceful, fluid sequence. "Oh my God," she said. We started fooling around and before she knew it I was fingering her while she was pulling on my dick, which she did with as much zest as she lacked skill. "Oh my God," she said. "We can't, we just can't. This is crazy, crazy." She kiss-hummed me again, louder still. "Oh my God." Her legs shook. She came. She stopped jerking me off, which I actually appreciated since it felt like she was trying with all her might to remove my dick from my body. She closed her legs and just kind of stared at me. I stared back. "Okay," she said. "That was a sin. A big sin. That was bad. Really bad. I don't know what I'm gonna do." I waited. "I think I should go," she said.

I didn't. "Hold on, relax."

"No, no, I should go."

"Stay."

"I can't."

"There's sort of an etiquette to this type of thing." While I was grateful for the reprieve from the terrible handjob, I still had a raging hardon and I intended to use it.

I didn't care how inexperienced she was; you don't just come and bounce in college. She wasn't Callie on a school bus and we weren't fourteen, though mentally she might have been. Selfish bitch. "You know, get good, give good."

"I thought I was," she said.

"I can't really come like that." I don't think anyone can come from a dry, violent jackhammer tug from uber-weird uber-Christian chicks. Maybe a self-hating Satanist, but not me, anyway.

"Well why didn't you have an orgasm? Wasn't the handy good?" Handy? The fuck? She shook her head. "Though I guess I haven't done that before. I can't believe I did that. That was bad of me."

"I can only come if you use your mouth or if we have sex."

"Well we can't have intercourse, sorry. I'm not having intercourse 'til I'm married and I don't want to marry you, no offense. I think I should go." She was something else, really. Some of the dumbest girls I ever met were in college. I was pissed off and was about to call her a bitch and stuff when I noticed she wasn't leaving. Or trying to leave. At all. She was just lying there, her eyes fixed on mine, naked and all hot-looking.

"That sin was fun wasn't it?"

She looked away. "It was bad."

"But it was good-bad, right?" She said nothing. I kissed her neck. Her eyes fluttered.

"You're bad. I'm gonna have to repent." Now, I'd fucked religious chicks before, those Mormons, but this was something different altogether. All of them got off on "how bad" I was, they were, the situation was, whatever, but the Mormons at least kept God out of it, thankfully.

She seemed determined to make it a threesome or something; it was obvious she was also getting herself off on all this weird talk, and that bothered me. I believe in God. I know I'm not moral or good, and fortunately I don't believe in Hell, especially considering what's immediately forthcoming in this episode, but I do believe in a higher power, and the Christian one kind of. In terms of the Trinity, I believe in the Father and the Holy Ghost but not really Jesus that much. Yes, Jesus was pretty badass because he stood up for what he believed in and was definitely an alpha and a man of his convictions, and all that respectable shit, and he took a hell of a beating in the end, but his message was wrong. All that turn the other cheek and love thy neighbor nonsense; be a lamb and so on. It's silly and doesn't work. The God of the Old Testament, the Father, that guy makes a lot more sense to me. He had it in him to be mean and spiteful. I get that I was made in the image of a guy who'd fuck over a nobody like Job basically for fun and to prove a point to a rival. I get that I was made in the image of a guy who'd kick two shitheads out of the Garden of Eden for disobeying Him. I get the idea of Him laying waste to entire cities with fireballs or whatever because He didn't very much like the type of people that lived there (though Sodom and Gomorrah seem like just the sort of places I'd like to hang out). If God is love, it ain't Jesus'. The Father's love, tough love, is what works. Sometimes there's difficulty distinguishing it from hate, and that's why it applies to the way I live my life. Jesus' message just makes people nice, makes them pussies, and while I'm thankful for it because it's given me the upper hand throughout my life in very Christian America, believing in it, really, would be idiotic for anyone like me, a winner. And I believe in the

Holy Ghost too mostly because I've felt Him working through me while doing really cool shit, like playing football and writing good songs or whatever. He's what people mean when they say God-given talent, which I have a lot of. The only place where I'd say He's absent would be in my biggest talent, which I believe is wholly from me, completely homegrown: fucking hot chicks. This is also why I didn't appreciate all the God talk, but whatever, my discomfort aside, it got her into it and eventually me into her. I guess that's all that should matter.

"What are you gonna repent for?"

She started kissing me, going down, kissing my neck, my nipples (kinda weird), down my abs, all the way to my dick, which she then took in her mouth, her head moving with as much enthusiasm as her hand earlier. This actually felt good, and if she sucked a dick like anyone, it was crazy Ms. Adams. I wondered then if Ms. Adams grew up super Christian or not. Maybe she told me once while I was lying there thinking about sports or whatever. Anyway, she did this for about five minutes, then popped up all of a sudden. "Oh my God, this is so sinful. Can I try?"

I squinted at her, doing my best not to grimace. She really was a selfish bitch. "That depends . . ." She waited. "I'd want to have sex if I did that to you."

"No intercourse. Can't. Not 'til I'm married."

"Well . . ." I smiled. "There's another kind, too. It's not real sex. You can still save yourself for marriage."

She thought for a minute. "Oh my God, that would be *so* bad, *so* dirty. I can't even believe you'd *want* to do that."

"Just sayin'."

"Doesn't it hurt?"

"It's supposed to feel really good." I kissed her neck.

"I don't know."

"Maybe you're right. It's something only bad girls do."

She laughed this throaty laugh. "I'll do it, but lick my front first." So I did. I started lightly eating her out and she went nuts. "Oh my God," she said. "Yeah. Lick my quinny." She moaned. "Lick the—fuck out of that quinny. Lick all my fucks out my fucking quinn—y!" I went harder. She brought my hands up to squeeze her nipples. "Bad boy, bad boy. Sinner!" I think she came again. "Now fuck me in my dirty hole!" Then I did. I put on a condom and lubed it up with the cum from her pussy and some real lube, and we took it slow. She was at least an anal virgin, that was for sure, because she had a pretty hard time taking me in at first. But once I was in, she went all-out . . . again, not unlike Ms. Adams. She moaned and groaned and kept saying, "Fuck the faith out of me!" That actually got me pretty hot for some reason, and after about fifteen minutes I felt like I was about to come so I pulled out and took the condom off and then shot my load all over her face for fun.

——— **Roommate** ———

Outside of the whole being a pledge thing, something else that sucked in the frat was that I had a roommate. His name was Brent, and he was a sophomore gamma and the son of a cancer specialist. He was my "big brother," someone that was supposed to show me the ropes during pledge quarter and, really, for the rest of our shared time in the fraternity. Obviously I wouldn't be interested in a "big brother" figure, especially a fucking gamma, as I'd always known better than anyone else about what should be done in any situation. Fortunately for me, he didn't really try. He was okay as a person I guess—I just didn't like that he existed because I didn't like having a roommate. I was used to the setup back home, where my room was my domain, and I had absolute control over everything. Here I had another guy capable of fucking it up. I'd say mine was the dominant personality in the room, and this pleased me, but it wasn't the same as it being the only personality in the room. He did get in the way sometimes, too. He had a girlfriend, who he seemed absolutely faithful to (some of my "brothers" were in similar situations, which always struck me as a bit of a waste and besides the entire fucking point, but to each his own, I guess, more for me to fuck), and when they weren't at her sorority house, where he would actually sleep a couple of nights a week (don't know how he swung that considering how tightass a lot of the sororities and their house moms were, not that I'm complaining), they were at our place, and when they would fuck, there'd be a do-not-disturb sign on our door and it would be locked. It was pretty annoying not being able to get to my shit if I wanted or needed it, but he couldn't last for that long. It wasn't like there was ever an instance where I couldn't practice the guitar or anything if I had set aside time for it that day. I used the sign sometimes, too, like with that Christian chick, or when bringing back this girl from my other life, which I did often, and which we'll get to in a second. I liked the signs, which also doubled as study aids, because they were way classier than hanging a sock on the door. Sometimes it's little fancy things like that that help girls get wet. At any rate, I missed having a place to call my own, a necessity for an alpha and someone with a clear sense of self. I considered myself the alpha pledge, if there could be such a thing, since I fucked more chicks than any of the rest of them (Austin might have fucked three or four). Some of the juniors had their own rooms, while the rest and all of the seniors lived in apartments with each other close by, and I thought I'd try to explore the latter as early as the next year. It would be in keeping with what I was sure would be a meteoric rise within the frat and would also make it easier to balance my other life, too.

<h2 style="text-align:center">—————— Coffee Shop Scene ——————</h2>

My life as Frankie Parker was going a little better by comparison. It's not like I found the perfect musicians to round out my band and I was already cutting a demo with them or anything; it's mostly because being a pledge inherently kinda sucks. I was making progress, both with my music and chicks. I guess, really, I was just getting laid more through the coffee shop scene. That would make anything better.

I knew going into college that I'd have to give up something that I loved, at least for a while: unprotected sex. The only people that have unprotected sex during their first couple of months as freshmen are A: Idiots who go to the same college as their high school girlfriends; B: Idiots who jump into a "serious" relationship with the first girl they meet in their dorm or English 101 class; and, mostly, C: Idiots who don't care about getting herpes or a girl pregnant. I thought I'd eventually sucker another chick into thinking she was my girlfriend, but understood that was something that could only happen organically and would probably take at least a quarter or two. I didn't have the cache that I did in high school, where I was the biggest fish in a pretty small pond, known and respected, when I could land two at once without really trying in, like, a week after deciding to. I figured here a lot of the girls would, like any reasonable eighteen-year-old, start college with the mission of sowing their wild oats. However, I also knew that girls were fool-romantics at heart, at any age, and with enough work, I could convince one that I would be suitable as her first college boyfriend. If the easiest of these chicks would be anywhere, it would be at places to hear music. A musician who wasn't a pussy or socially retarded or a drug addict, one that also happened to be a real man? Come on. Catnip at any age, especially eighteen to twenty. Whoever she was, she would have to be really, really hot, not only because I demanded nothing less for my own sake, but also, to gel with my other life—taking into account political considerations—there had to be a reason to have her around at the house all the time. Most of my frat brothers only had girlfriends or fuck buddies within the Greek system, exceptions made only for exceptional-looking girls. We had an image to maintain. Since I was a freshman, and freshmen don't get girlfriends or whatever within the Greek system, going outside to meet my raw pussy needs would seem reasonable if she were hot enough. Everyone would be happy, especially me.

So, while I was just anonymous at the start, not respected, not cool, not known as a good performer or local rock star, not anything, I still had that persona defined, that of the musician as a young man's man. I knew it, looked it, felt it, was it, and from all my experience in high school and studying weird music and movies and books the year before, I knew just how to talk to most of these girls. I was ready to go. It would only be a matter of time 'til I was sliding sans rubber. My first week in town I started frequenting cafés and coffee shops in the city's artsy district, Capitol Hill, basically whenever I could sneak away from frat shit. It was about twenty minutes from the University District by bus.

I didn't bring my car to college with me because Seattle is mostly a walking city and it would have been unnecessary and expensive (also, I figured it would get scratched and fucked up or something without designated parking). Growing up in Eastern Washington, we didn't really have public transportation. From seeing it on TV, I always thought it was for losers, especially busses. I could see using a subway or tram system, maybe, with a shred of dignity, sitting there in a tasteful overcoat, reading the paper or whatnot, but Seattle only had busses and nothing's worse than riding a goddam city bus. They're bumpy and stop a lot, and they would let on a bunch of gross assholes that really shouldn't have been able to breathe the same air as me. After taking it the first time, I kind of wished I had brought my car after all, but then resolved to save up and get a motorcycle or something maybe. Then I figured I'd stick it out and wait 'til I met a musician friend with a van, since a motorcycle would be impractical, even with just my guitar, and a van was something I'd probably need anyway with a full backing band. I'd just make him pick me up and drive me around. The bus would have to do for the time being, but I can't say I ever got used to it. Most of the time

I read for school and it made it go by a little faster, but still. Anyway, Capitol Hill was pretty weird. It's where all the weirdos and gay people hung out, mostly, or straight people that just looked really gay.

That first week I checked out the places, got a sense of the scene, learned where I'd fit in or wouldn't. By the next I was playing. And going home with chicks.

Like everything else about me, my stage presence exuded confidence. My first time out the gate I was a rock star. I got a five-minute-slot at an open mike. I took the stage with my acoustic guitar, didn't say anything, just started playing one of my songs. I got into it, sang with conviction, played well, owned it. I played for myself and no one else. This made me sexy and everyone in the room respect me. Then I said, "Hey, everybody. I'm Frankie Parker and this is my first time on stage." They all clapped. I went into another one, which was a bit more of a toe-tapper, one that really let me howl (I sang in a full-throated but smooth baritone somewhere between Springsteen and Bob Seger). At times I'd close my eyes to appear more emphatic, and when I'd re-open them I could see everyone was into it, nodding and stuff. I was happy I stayed true to myself; didn't play a cover my first time on stage and still won over the crowd. The girls especially seemed to like it, most smiling at me. I left only a few minutes after my turn at the mike, but before I was on my way, more than one of them had given me a right good eye-fucking.

A lot of the chicks that hung out around Capitol Hill were pretty fucking hot. Sure, there were fat ones too, and dirty ones, and ones with a bunch of dumb piercings and shit in their faces and ugly-looking tattoos, but among them were the wannabe model-types, pretty girls that just dressed weird and were into weird things because they saw pictures and read about that stuff in fashion magazines or whatever. These were the girls I'd be fucking. Many of them went to this art school Cornish close to the neighborhood. Some were just locals, girls that grew up in the city that were daughters of tech executives and didn't really have to work, so they just hung out and played in their own "bands" (chick bands are a joke), or girls from middle-class families that worked as baristas or waitresses in the artsy establishments. And a few also went to my school, including Rachel, who would eventually be the girl I'd have regular unprotected sex with, or as she liked to call herself, my "girlfriend."

——— Current Double Life ———

These days, I also live something of a double life. I suppose, really, the first time I did was with Hope and Erin in high school, but this whole Frank/Frankie Parker thing was the first time I explored a dichotomy of personas.

See, a lot of the girls I'm fucking these days—models, wannabe models, actresses, wannabe actresses, students . . . mostly exotic international-types—aren't into I-Bankers. So when I go out to a club or party, I charm them and usually say I'm an entrepreneur or in art trading or music management, something that appeals to their desperate appetite to glom onto something "cool." They all try to make up for how uninteresting they are as individuals by finding a guy that's not only different enough and fun, but also has a "cool" job. I become *that* guy. I'm not geeky like a lot of investment bankers and have been good with chicks since I was a kid, and was a fucking rock musician, after all, so I pretty much always pull this off, am always great at being *that* guy, and pretty much always fuck whoever I'm after. It's pretty great.

—————— First College "Girlfriend" ——————

I met Rachel about a month into playing. By that point, I had already fucked three other girls as Frankie Parker. It was nice telling chicks I lived in the U District, because it was too far away and they wouldn't want to come over. They wouldn't find out I was a frat guy, so they would still want to fuck me. The first two were hot and fucked pretty well. One fell in love with me during a ten-minute set when I covered Leonard Cohen's "Hallelujah" after two songs of my own (I wasn't aware at the time that he was Canadian, had I been, I wouldn't have covered him). I don't know if the next one even saw me play. The third was one of the prettiest girls I'd ever met—natural blonde, tall, great bone structure, amazing lips, tits, ass, skin, everything—but she wore glasses. That was sort of weird for me. On one hand, she was legitimately beautiful. She looked like a movie star or model (but not a foul-faced one). On the other, she wore glasses. They were thick and weird, and I wasn't sure if she even needed them, but whatever; when they came off with the rest of what she was wearing, everything was good. I added it to my list of exotic experiences, not unlike having sex with that Asian, though the idea of a girl with glasses was a much less desirable thing to add to that list. I intended at the start of college to add as many desirable variations to the list as possible, trying out girls of every race, half-breeds, short, tall, stuff like that. This was when I invented "Pussy Bingo."

So, Rachel was cool. She was hot, with long dirty blonde hair and a really great ass and good enough tits and this velvety voice that was actually sometimes pleasant to listen to. I was never terribly interested in anything she had to say, of course, but a lot of girls' voices are distractingly shrill. Easygoing for the most part, she also didn't give a fuck that I was in a frat. She thought frat guys were generally lame, but knew there were exceptions to every rule and also thought there were people in the art scene that were just as uncool and narrow-minded as the Greeks. She was right; it was sort of a joke to some of these people—the really pretentious ones too far up their own asses to ever get laid by anyone other than themselves—that someone would go to a state school, and she thought that by me being in a frat, I was at least "going all the way with it," something of a rebel within the crowd, actually, which was kind of cool in its way. I agreed with her, though insisted she not tell anybody. She was a dormer herself, with the plan of moving off campus as soon as she could, after she got a lay of the land; being from Vancouver, Canada, she hadn't really visited Seattle too much before school. (It might seem weird for me to not want to cover a Canadian but to take one on as a "girlfriend," but it's not really. To cover another artist, you need to have a lot of respect for them, enough that you want to channel them through yourself. For me to take a little piece of a Canadian's soul and present it as my own was a pretty big fucking deal. I'm an American, no thanks. But getting a hot chick to think she was my girlfriend so I could fuck her without condoms wasn't like that. There was nothing intimate about it—in fact, her being Canadian made me feel even better about using her. Also, a lot of Canadian bitches are really hot. Pam Anderson was basically the model of all-American hotness before she got old and hepatitis; that half-Asian chick from that one stupid-looking *Superman* show in the early aughts was completely fuckable; Elisha Cuthbert, too. Rachel was on their level.) Anyhow, with her I was able to straddle the frat scene and the art scene, and she was respectful and smart enough not to mention my role in either of them to the other.

We kind of eased our way into the "relationship." I met her one night before a set and thought, hey, I'd like to fuck this girl, but she was gone after my turn at the mike. When I saw her the next week at another café, she approached me and told me she liked my performance that other night, but had to get up early for class the next day, so she couldn't say "hi" after. I knew it would be cake from there. Following my set, we rode the bus back to campus together and I fucked her in her dorm room. She was good. It wasn't until after, and after I had made her come, that I revealed I lived in a frat, and this was only because I decided she had the hotness and the right type of disposition to eventually have unprotected sex with me. Also, she was a dormer, so how judgmental could she be? It wasn't really cool to live in a frat, sure, but there is absolutely *nothing* cool about a fucking dorm. Especially at U-Dub. God, their dorms are awful. She came over a couple of nights later, we fucked again. My frat brothers seemed impressed; she was about as hot as dormers get. From then on, we were fuck buddies, going at it a couple of times a week, mostly at my place, and about two months later, after several conversations about how she was getting attached, about how she never thought she would jump into a "relationship" so soon in college, but here it was, I made a successful lobby for us to both get tested (even though I had just been before school, I knew this was the smartest way to get what I wanted) and bring things to the next level. Once that was done, she went on the pill and we started fucking without condoms. This was around the tail end of pledge quarter, about three months into school. Bada bing, bada boom, done.

Starting out, my role as her "boyfriend" basically consisted of meeting her at whichever café I was performing at that night, having sex with her at the frat house afterwards, and then sending her on her merry way until the next time. Since we both had roommates, we couldn't ever stay the night with each other, which was just perfect for me, but she'd often complain about it and add it as another reason she wanted to get a place off campus as soon as possible. I'd tell her, "I know. It would be so great to sleep in each other's arms" or something ridiculous like that. I considered this the one silver lining to having a roommate. I only had to go over to her dorm a few times because the girl she shared her tiny-ass room with was there a lot, and Rachel felt like a bitch for kicking her out. Roommates were only understanding about leaving if it involved sex, so just kind of hanging out alone together was hard. Outside of my room, she didn't much like the environment at the frat house and thought most of the guys I lived with were jack-asses, having gone to one of our parties early on "for the experience" and hating it, so hanging out communally didn't really happen either. The system worked. It was great because we didn't have to do all that much talking for a "relationship," and she wasn't able to get that place off campus until the end of the year. Once she moved things got a little rougher, but we'll get there.

So, freshman year, I'd have sex with her around two or three days a week—this just accounts for days; we'd often actually do it at least twice when we saw each other—and I also had the frat parties and functions to fuck random chicks, and occasionally, when I was being very, very careful, I'd also have sex with other girls in the art scene. I didn't want to fuck things up with Rachel and cut off my supply of raw pussy, and it was the kind of place where most people knew most other people, or at least knew of them. Everyone would see us together, and while this pretty much made all the other chicks want to fuck me even more—they all basically already wanted to fuck me because I was young, cool, straight (rare in that group and neighborhood), and was proving myself to be a good performer—I only did so with those that I knew were the type that wouldn't fuck and tell, chicks that thought they were my friends and what we were doing was just being young and cool. This worked, and also let me check off a few more varieties from my Pussy Bingo, including a full Latino girl, a girl that was taller than me (pretty weird), and a girl with really small tits, which I wasn't entirely sure why I wanted to try. It was undesirable, maybe even more so than having glasses, but she had a very pretty face and a fantastic ass, and whatever, fuck it, I was just curious I guess. I had always heard college was a time for experimentation. I went for a really long time, probably because seeing her naked weirded me out a little, but she didn't complain and was actually damn good. I figured it was from an adolescence spent overcompensating for her lack of boobs. She was willing to get into all kinds of adventurous positions, in fact put us in a little less than half of them (I never let a girl decide more positions than me), which I suppose was sort of necessary to get me off because, again, it was pretty weird that her tits were as tiny as they were. It was nothing I rushed to repeat, but I did find that with any subsequent smaller-chested chicks I'd fuck—though I don't think I ever had sex with another A-cup, maybe just a borderline A/B—the itty-bittier the titty, generally the more eager they were to please.

My Worst Punishment Ever

By midterms pledge quarter, I had only fucked two girls as Frank Parker, frat guy. Such a sad and disgraceful performance called for a major punishment, so I stopped jerking off for a whole month. It was fucking horrible.

I figured it would be the right price to pay because even though I was just a pledge, I should have been fucking a lot more girls than that by then, and tying my hands down might give me an incentive or a physical imperative to get out there and do it. I mean, I was Frank Fuckin' Parker, the guy that could pull two new girls a night back home—to only pull two girls in six weeks as a frat guy was pretty pathetic. I didn't care that I was still a pledge and that I'd fucked the most chicks of any pledge. That wasn't good enough for me. Considering the loss of self I was undergoing by joining this girly fucking collective in the first place, and how sex was supposed to be the whole point of that, some drastic measure needed to be taken. It wasn't right that I should be a fratboy douchebag and not get the spoils. It defeated the purpose of the whole goddam thing.

I mean, yeah, I was still fucking enough . . . a few times a week with Rachel and with other girls in the art scene . . . probably coming on average seven to eight times during these weeks, but still, I was eighteen. This was my sexual prime. I should have been coming at least twice as often as that. All in all, it was one of the worst months of my life, and I still haven't really forgiven myself for it.

_______ Breaking into the Seattle _______ Music Scene

Musically, things continued to go pretty well. I carried the confidence and quiet but effective showmanship from my first performance to the following ones, and soon my playing caught up with it fully—not that I ever played the songs poorly, I played them well enough at first, but with just a little seasoning, I was great, like a real pro who had been at it for years. It only took about two months of performing at open mikes before I got offered a real set at one of the coffee shops.

In my time doing the more amateur stuff, I'd met some other performers, but most of them were tools. They were all pretty much singer-songwriters like me—except a lot of their shit sucked—and those that were any good were just out for themselves, also like me. I started to think it might not be as easy to get a good backing band together as I had originally anticipated. That was until my show.

I was given a twenty-minute set at this coffee shop as part of a "New Seattle Artists Showcase" that included four other acts. It was early December, a weeknight. I had played a few open mikes at the place and impressed the owner enough I guess. There was some ambivalence going in. Of course I was happy to have a show and everything, to leave the whole open mike thing behind for legitimate gigs. I would be paid a percentage of the cover, and though it didn't end up being much, only like thirty bucks, a paid gig's a paid gig. It was also good exposure. But this exposure was the cause for some concern, too. I loved my songs—they were beautiful—but I kind of wished I had that backing band to present them in all their glory, even though that glory didn't really exist yet because the songs were arranged for me alone, but whatever. If this was my one shot to make an outstanding first impression with the local industry, I didn't want to blow it. I mean Seattle, what with its tradition of musical greatness, did have some respected labels, Sub Pop and shit, and at the very least there'd be some managers there, people that could help me land more and better gigs. I saw myself as eventually filling stadiums, so, you know, a band would have been nice. But at the same time, I liked that I'd have the stage all to myself. Nobody else could fuck up my amazing songs, or make them seem like they were anything but an extension of *me*. They were great and I was great, and to play them alone seemed pure.

I played a five-song set, my five best culled from testing them out over the previous two months in front of different crowds. I had them in perfect order and everything. I started out with a good, upbeat one, then brought it to another level—faster, meaner—until the next one, where I slowed it down . . . let the people catch their breath, relax, swoon . . . before bringing it back up again with another mover and closing with a mid-tempo one, a dramatic and pretty song that would leave them thinking about me like all the girls that had ever been in love with me and, of course, obviously, wanting more.

It did. Everybody enjoyed themselves and I kicked ass for an all acoustic set. Like with my first open mike, it was very important to me during my first real show to play nothing but songs I wrote, to fill the air only with something incredible: me.

——— Early Lineup ———

Afterwards, I met the guy who would be my drummer, Phil. He approached me during the next act's set, this chick band that (obviously) sucked. Tall and lanky, he had long hair and somewhat worn-out clothes, the overall effect being that he looked a little dirty, but in a cool way that works for rock. He asked if I played a lot of these; told me he played the drums, that he thought my stuff would "sound cool with a beat." He complimented me, my "awesome" songs, and invited me to "jam." I asked him if he had a space and maybe a friend that played bass. He had both, so

I thought, hey, I guess I can give this greasy guy a try. A time was set up for that weekend. Then I got the fuck out of there because that shitty girl band, who was going for some kind of vintage punk thing, had only succeeded in being completely intolerable.

It took two busses and over an hour to get to his space, which was his family's garage, that Sunday afternoon. His house was in an outskirt of the city, this suburb, really, called Renton. He still lived with his parents, even though he was, like, twenty-one, because the only thing he had going for him since graduating high school was a shitty job delivering pizzas. While getting there was fucking terrible, when I saw that he had a van parked in the driveway, I got kind of excited. But first, I had to see if he was any good. He was, enough, and he also owned a lot of gear and continued to be as sycophantic as he was when I first met him, which were both major pluses. His friend, Julian, wasn't too bad either. It seemed he was mainly ripping off Pixies bass lines or something, but it gave my songs a weirdness I knew would be cool. They could have been a little tighter, but that aside, it felt like we were all on the same page. As for the van, it was Phil's family's (he had four siblings or something awful like that), but he said he could use it for gigs if we ever got them. He had his own car, too, the one he delivered pizzas in, and when I told him what a fucking pain it was to get to his place, he offered to pick me up from then on. I was a little worried it might have the stupid pizza sign on the top, since that would make riding in it worse than taking two busses and I would probably get kicked out of the frat if any of my brothers ever saw me in it—not that I would've gotten in, anyway—but he said the sign came off and he never drove with it when he wasn't at work; he hated it and delivering pizzas. I could tell I was his last chance, that he saw me as his ticket to becoming something other than a loser. College wasn't for a guy like Phil, but the world of stadium tours and groupies could be with my leadership. Once I knew all this, I told him I was in a frat. He thought it was a little funny at first, made some dumb joke, but really he didn't give a shit.

The one glaring thing going against them and what bothered me enough at first, music aside, I guess, was that they were both kind of ugly. In high school they were probably deltas or epsilons based on looks alone. I mean, it's a little gay to bring any of that up, but here I was, this young, robust vision, with a face that wasn't perfect, not model-like or anything, but attractive enough; nothing really too wrong with it—by eighteen, I was able to maintain decent stubble, which made me even sexier—then there they were . . . Phil, too tall and skinny with something of a hook nose, and Julian, a little pimply still, sort of pudgy. But they both dressed pretty cool. Phil had some tattoos. Julian had a beard: one of those scraggly, undecided things that looks half like pubes but still hip in a way. I knew uniformity was good for a band's look, and while I thought it would be nice if my bandmates were all relatively handsome, a consistent enough aesthetic could still be achieved through fashion. And their ugliness did have something of an upside—it made me even more attractive by comparison. It would have really sucked if one of them were, God forbid, better-looking than me. Not that it would have gotten either of them more chicks, since I would be both frontman and lead guitarist, but still. After thinking things through, I told them I thought it could work.

This was my three piece. I was a mad scientist-keyboard-electronic whiz—or two people dividing that role—away from my ideal band, and then fame, fortune, and more power and pussy than I'd know what to do with. When Phil drove me back to the frat house, we didn't even listen to music, just talked about what we had played.

——— **Going Places** ———

I spent less and less time on Capitol Hill after my real show, only going once in a while to scout for that fourth band member and just enough with Rachel to keep her happy. She needed to still think we were in a great relationship to let me fuck her without a condom.

The week after that performance, I got booked again at the same place for a show scheduled near the end of January. I'd have twenty minutes opening for this band that had been playing in the Northwest for a couple of years. The owner was a really big fan now. "Here's a kid that knows music," he'd say. He was older, sixties maybe, at least fifties. Compliments are great, and I'm sure he knew his shit, but I didn't appreciate it very much—the dude *was* old, and nobody wants to feel like their target audience is old dudes.

I devoted a lot of energy at the start of winter quarter to prepping, practicing on weekends with Phil and Julian, getting them to know the songs as well as I did. They were shaping up. I saw myself as a great sculptor, my songs these magnificent rocks, Phil and Julian my hammer and chisel, chipping-away-shards-flying until I had a bunch of beautiful statues of myself.

By the time our show hit, I was ready, we were ready, and we were amazing. Pretty much everyone was into it. The owner congratulated us. The band we opened for was impressed and thanked us while on stage, asking the crowd "How about that Frankie Parker?" to roaring applause, and in the following days, the web edition of this local counter-culture weekly called *The Stranger* named us as an act to watch. We were going places.

———— Greek Life ————

Winter quarter was also when college, as I had always thought of it—how it would be, how it should be—really began, and this is because I was no longer a pledge; I was a brother in the best fraternity at U-Dub. Earlier on, I likened individual sexual encounters to snowflakes; even though it doesn't really snow in Seattle, that quarter I felt like I was in this incredible winter wonderland. I slid around. Tumbled to and fro. I dove through the crisp air and landed on top of the biggest pile of pussy that could be found. It was like I'd died and gone to a snowy heaven. So I rolled onto my back, waved my limbs synchronously, and made a snow angel. My spirit flew. I was happier than I'd ever been.

While fraternities themselves aren't cool, they do lead to a lot of sex, which is the coolest thing there is. Sex is bet-ter than power because people use power to have sex. Sex is better than money because people use money to have power to have sex. Sex is really what motivates people; it's what makes the world work. If people stopped having sex, the world would end in about a hundred years. Think about that shit. If money and power didn't exist, people would still be fucking.

As just a freshman brother, sure, I wasn't really able to fuck freshman sorority girls that often, but that was the only limitation. Sophomores were down. A few juniors. And basically anyone from the dorms was as good as mine. My Pussy Bingo was coming along. It only took a little while before I'd had my first real threesome (it was a million times better than with Lyle and his sister; literal sex always trumps figurative half-gay sex); fucked an Indian girl (dot); a girl with really short hair (undesirable but another worthwhile experiment); more of the broad strokes. The one thing I couldn't get that I wanted was a black girl. Not too many of them were in the Greek system, and the ones that were had predominantly Caucasian facial features and skin that was on the lighter side, a bit too mocha, so they wouldn't count. More real black girls hung out in the art scene, but none of them wanted to fuck me for some reason. I did have sex with this one artsy girl who was, like, a quarter or maybe half black, though. That was cool, but her skin was even lighter than mocha and it would've been a whole lot cooler if she were full black.

I'd describe some of these experiences in more detail but that would betray them and the spirit of the time. The thrills were cheaper than they'd ever been, and that was what made it so great. Getting pussy, even somewhat exotic or interesting, had lost all sense of achievement it once had in high school. During finals week, I could see the snow begin to melt as a warm sun peeked out from behind the clouds . . . pussy wasn't cold and white anymore, it was even more blank than that. It evaporated into the air, and I inhaled it as I walked the campus knowing a nice bright spring was just around the corner. Fucking hot chicks was beyond Zen—as easy as breathing. Before, I'd describe firsts . . . my first time fucking, my first time fucking an ass, my first time fucking a Mormon or ethnic girl, whatever; but those were conquests, and I didn't know that feeling anymore. Even the threesome wouldn't benefit from an actual anecdote: it would more or less just read "I took it out of that chick and started fucking the other one" over and over until I pulled out and took the condom off and came on someone's tits or the other one's ass or whatever, you know? That quarter alone I fucked fourteen girls.

It should have been like that for everyone in our frat. I don't mean everyone should have been as successful as me—that would be preposterous—but it shouldn't have been as hard as some guys made it on themselves. Pussy was like a given for us. Many of my brothers celebrated my success, some from my pledge class even going so far as to dress a little more like me than the preppy archetype they knew so well. And then there were some, a few jealous pricks that sucked with chicks, that begrudged me for it. Paulsen, that one guy who was the weirdest about me not being super wealthy when I was a rushee, who was our frat's alumni chair and a junior omega (maybe an epsilon based on his title alone) and, what's more, clueless with girls because he had grown up a coddled, rich, spoiled shit, and not the cool kind that's entitled and ruthless, but just awkward, the kind that only knew girls in the context that they knew their own moms (he probably, actually, in all seriousness in love with his), hated me in particular. He soon became my enemy.

—— Numbers Games ——

Fucking a lot of chicks is a great numbers game. What I basically do is set a bar (a very high bar) in front of a wall that I can throw shit at, and then proceed to throw as much shit as possible against that wall to see what sticks. Eventually you get a better sense of what works, or respect and a growing reputation make things easier, and you have a better average. That's always nice, but in the end, quantity's all it's really about.

Making money is, obviously, another good numbers game. We try different things, hopefully that we enjoy, and whatever sticks is what we do for a living; I followed other elite callings on the road to investment banking, as you well know. Once you find something that works, you strive to make as much money possible with it. You throw more shit at the wall, see if you can get as many raises and promotions as you can. After you've made enough to invest—in stocks, bonds, whatever—you put it where you think it will earn the highest yield, but usually with enough of a safety net to protect your initial investment: in other words, a diverse portfolio is yet more shit thrown at a wall. In the end, your bank account is your tally and measure of success.

I'm awesome at both of these numbers games. Like I said before, people make money to have power to have sex. The easiest way to have as much sex as possible, with as

many quality chicks as possible, is through money. I make a
lot of it, I'm a winner. This is because I'm fucking smart.

They say there are eight different types of intelligence—
logical-mathematical, spatial, linguistic, bodily-kinesthetic,
musical, interpersonal, intrapersonal, and naturalistic—but
really there are only three. Most people think there are just
two, book smarts and street smarts. If you recognized the
majority of the concepts in that bloated list above, you're
probably at least a little book smart, which is one, and street
smarts is indeed the second, but then there's something
more elusive, something that's rooted where book smarts
and street smarts overlap—work smarts. Beyond knowing
what to do (book) and how to do it (street), it's about flip-
ping whatever it is you're doing so that it works for you.
Work smart, not hard, right? By understanding intelligence
in terms of these three categories, you essentially get a con-
densed and simplified version of that list of eight, which
is—in itself—a much smarter way to think of them: it's
more efficient, it serves you better. I'm book smart—was
good at school, know my shit (logical-mathematical, spatial,
linguistic); I'm street smart: I get people and my surround-
ings, how I relate to them, the best ways to interact with
them (interpersonal, intrapersonal, naturalistic); and I'm
work smart, I know how to use the aforementioned for
maximum self-gain. (The bodily-kinesthetic thing—which I
have too, of course—would be included in work smarts on
its own; athletics are fun activities that can make you rich
and respected. Musical intelligence—also me, obviously—
would be as well, since using it is another way to get paid a
lot for doing something that's really fun.)

If you're book smart, you're often held back in life because you suck with people. You went through school, you

know what you should know, but you don't have the balls or charm to make your education as profitable as it could be. You likely have a shitty job, but you think you're smarter than your boss. You're not, since he (most of the time he; men are a lot smarter and hold more management roles) had the street smarts to take advantage of whatever situation brought him to where he is.

If you're street smart, you're often held back in life because you lack the polish needed to be taken seriously. You can charm someone, but if you don't know how to act like a civilized fucking person, if you kind of speak and write like an idiot, then the best you can probably do is sell drugs or, if you're a little book smart, work in insurance or corporate sales. You might think if only you had the right education, you'd be president or something, but I don't know, in my experience really street smart people would be too lazy to become book smart since just being street smart is enough to get by and live a pretty decent life. Even becoming an inner-city corner drug dealer would probably lead to a better life than, like, working to get a masters degree in philosophy or some other highly intellectual thing and then ending up with a job as a fucking waiter or customer service representative afterwards, which happens. Those people are fucking miserable.

The geniuses, like me, have both, and also know how to get the most out of them, and that's what makes us winners. Being an investment banker is pretty much the perfect job for an all around triple-threat genius, and because I'm doing so well with it, I know I'm actually smarter than certifiable geniuses like Stephen Hawking and Einstein. My street and work smarts are as off the charts as their book smarts. I understand the things that really matter—how to get the most money and, ultimately, pussy—far better than Einstein did or Hawking does. I'll likely die considerably richer than them, probably at least their net worths combined, and having had a lot more sex, which I'm positive I've already done. This makes me a lot smarter overall, a genius light-years ahead of them. It doesn't take a rocket scientist to figure this shit out, not that one would anyway, since being a rocket scientist isn't all that smart when you could work in finance. But I digress . . . I don't think Stephen Hawking can even have sex, so I don't know why he ever wrote a book or anything—he's not that smart, when you think about it, really. Einstein I heard got laid a lot in his later years when he was cheating on his cousin-wife or whatever, and I know he probably only achieved what he did just to get the prestige, which became power, which became sex, but I think it's a pretty safe bet that now, at only twenty-five, I've fucked at least ten times more chicks than he ever did, the triple-threat, real fucking genius I am.

Enemy

Before Paulsen, I hadn't ever really had an enemy. I'd had people that hated me, but they never did anything about it, and I'd had targets—the coaches, Squanto from the seventh grade, that thug Anthony, Leon and Cole at various times, more or less any girl I'd ever had sex with—but all of those involved swift and easy battles resolved quickly enough. Paulsen seemed bent on engaging me in an all-out war.

While I prefer quick confrontations to drawn-out ones, I embraced his continued animosity as an opportunity for a new and fulfilling form of interpersonal conquest. I needed something else in my life now that it was just so goddam easy to get quality college pussy.

It began not long after the start of winter quarter, when my pledge class was officially brought in. Once we were all brothers, many of the real secrets of the frat were revealed. This didn't have much to do with fraternity tradition or history or anything like that, it had a lot more to do with partying, mainly drugs. First, we were all given fake IDs. It was nice, but I rarely used mine, since our scene was way more interesting and exclusive, with hotter chicks than any bar or club. We also had access to basically anything illicit we wanted. Anything. Except roofies. We were told nobody in our house should need roofies to get laid. And if anyone ever found out our frat used them, we'd be fucked. Our status as the elite fraternity would be lost, and there was the possibility—though remote because of our alumni and all their generosity to the university—that we'd get kicked out of the Greek system altogether. Naturally, the officers were dead serious about us not using them. I agreed. Guys who resort to that kind of shit are pretty fucking pathetic. I think they should get their dicks chopped off—not because I find what they do so immoral or whatever, just so damn unnecessary and unmanly, like twice as bad as getting a chick way too drunk in order to have sex with her. I'm really against anything to physically incapacitate someone so they can't exercise free will. A real man would never consider it. If a real man were getting a girl that was out of his league to fuck him, he'd use cunning; he'd bend her will, not debilitate it. Anyway, anything else, really, any type of prescription or hard drug, including, like, fucking *pure, No. 4 heroin,* we could get if we wanted. The caveat was if any of us ever got addicted to anything, we'd be kicked out, but none of us were supposed to get addicted to anything regardless because addiction was for weak people. We were not weak. We were the best frat on campus. I liked that the organization had this mindset; it's exactly what I thought about drug addiction before I joined it.

The first thing my mind jumped to and what I immediately started using was HGH. While I didn't have much money compared to everyone around me, my scholarship kickbacks were enough so I could afford that at least; I just had to be careful with budgeting, steal or mooch off of other people's booze, try to only eat at home, stuff like that. Finally, I would correct God's mistake—the one thing He punished me with. I would be over 6', naturally (after five months, I grew an inch-and-a-half, and didn't grow any more in the next three after that, so I figured that was it and stopped taking them; in the end I was 5'11"-and-a-half, easily over 6'1" with my hair—it still counts).

Recreationally, up 'til then, all I'd ever done was smoke a little weed. In high school, someone might pull out a joint or pipe at a party, and it was just something to make the night a little different. I liked it enough I guess. Time seemed to go by slower and some things were funnier, but aside from that it was just kind of a weird feeling, and it made me lazy. I had sex on it a couple of times and felt somewhat more sensitive to touch, and that was fun, but not enough to make weed a steady part of my life or anything. Along with getting high, potheads mostly seemed to love wasting time, and I didn't. I wasn't ever interested in taking any of the prescription drugs I'd steal, either, not only because of the whole *Scarface* thing about keeping your own supply off limits, but also there was no good reason for me to use painkillers or any of the stimulants I sold. I had no pain to kill, no void to fill, enough time in the day to get done what needed doing . . . all I ever really needed was pussy and I got a whole fucking lot of it.

However, now in college, leading two lives and trying to maintain good grades, I was admittedly stretched a little thin. The idea of some Adderall to study and a little coke to stay up at parties didn't seem so bad. So I dabbled from time to time, able to afford that stuff once in a while, too, or mooching off other people. It was fun. On coke, I talked a lot, not annoyingly a lot, like a girl, or fast or anything, but a lot. Everything I did and said seemed more interesting, so I did and said more. For an already confident guy, it brought it to a whole 'nother level. I felt like Superman. I never had a tone of arrogance or anything; I was just completely self-assured and enthusiastic about everything, all the time. Most people love a guy like that, especially chicks. Well, almost everybody. Some people get jealous when they see you having a good time and everybody around you having a good time because you're having a good time, especially if some of those around you are hot chicks that later fuck you—pussy-faggots like Paulsen.

When I was a rushee and a pledge, Paulsen was kind of a dick to me, but he was kind of a dick to everybody. I figured the "me not being super rich" thing was just whatever he designated me with to fulfill his innate need to be unpleasant. He seemed dickish to another pledge for being Hispanic, this other guy for being Jewish; he found something for all of us. He really started being an all-out asshole more or less just to me, though, in the second week after we were all brothers. The weekend before, we had a small gathering one night and an impromptu little party the next with some friends in the Greek system and random dorm girls, and I had sex both nights with different chicks. This was the first time I had done that in the frat, what with pledge quarter being what it was. Maybe he liked one of them. I didn't really know at the time. Or care. Still don't.

That week, we were all eating dinner in our dining room, which was large and had two rows of tables. Dinners were prepared by our cook, this kind of fat middle-aged woman named Linda. She was a graduate of some fancy culinary school, and I think was a sous-chef somewhere with a name in downtown Seattle before we plucked her from it, so she knew her stuff, making large and eclectic meals that tasted great and were also high in nutrients. We got along well for the most part, but sometimes she maintained eye contact a little too long with me, which made me uncomfortable because she was old and pretty fat. Usually I don't talk to someone with either of those qualities, but she fed me, and I liked to show my appreciation . . . that didn't mean she should try to flirt with me in the creepy way fat, lonely middle-aged women do, though. That job must've been a cream dream for her. She probably went home to a collection of vibrators named after all of us (mine feeling the best), all except Paulsen. So anyhow, these dinners were casual, since we were a frat, not a sorority or dysfunctional wealthy family or boarding school, which must've thrown Paulsen off, because he, like a few other pussy-shitheads, would dress like it was all fancier and stuffier than it really was, wearing button-downs or, at the very least, a polo shirt to the table at every fucking meal. Faggots. At this particular dinner, I was just wearing a gray t-shirt and some jeans, with these black Chuck Taylor low tops I liked, a standard, casual, cool-guy look.

Paulsen was sitting not across from me, but close enough. Aside from being chubby, his most distinctive feature was curly light blond hair, the curls tight and the cut a couple of inches too long. He was basically the kind of guy you'd look at and know no one could take very seriously. I think he was of German ancestry or something, and he looked like he had spent his entire life eating only sausages and chocolate. "Hey, Parker," he started. "Now that you're a brother, are you going to start dressing like one?"

"I do dress like one, Paulsen."

"That's funny. You look more like my mechanic than anyone I'd call a brother." A few of his fellow pussy-fag friends that also dressed like they never got laid, because they didn't, laughed. His main lackey was this Japanese douchebag named Hideki and he laughed the loudest in this obnoxious, over-the-top way like he was the villain on an anime cartoon or something. I hated that guy.

"What's wrong with your mechanic?" I asked.

"What's wrong with my mechanic is he's my mechanic, not my brother. I wouldn't eat with my mechanic."

That anybody actually took this "brother" shit halfway seriously astounded me. I was not his brother. You joined a frat to fuck hot chicks, not to find the playmates you missed growing up. Paulsen was so fucking lame. "There's nothing wrong with working with your hands. Or looking like you work with your hands." Obviously I had better things in mind for myself than working with my hands (at the time I was still committed to the law and politics thing if music didn't work out, though I figured it probably would), but I thought fixing shit would be a cool and manly hobby. I had actually learned a thing or two about my 'Vette during high school, it needing a little work from time to time since it was kind of old and all. I could repair some stuff. But anyway, the look was fucking cool, classic cool, and it was me.

"Yes, there is. In this house there is." His stupid friends looked at me all smug-like with these weird half-grins and their eyebrows raised in gay little contortions.

"A guy who ever got laid wouldn't say that." All of the cool people around me laughed, including the vice president, Blake, who liked me a lot, some going "Ooooooooooh!" They all knew that Paulsen didn't ever have sex because he was a flabby, bitter prick that looked like the lovechild between the Coppertone sunblock girl and Pillsbury Doughboy. He might have even been a virgin.

"You don't have to look like a fucking greaser to get laid here, brother, pardon my French. You'll never get any-thing but the type of dormer sluts you got as a pledge looking like that." Who was this guy fucking kidding? We went to a state school. A fucking state school.

"We'll see about that." I put down my fork and started eating with my hands.

——— On the Defensive ———

When I not only fucked those dormer sluts, but fucked some of the hottest of the Greek system sluts, a couple of freshmen and more upperclassmen that, when freshmen, were among those coveted by our chapter's presidents, vice presidents, social chairs, and other cool office holders in their respective times, his hatred for me grew and grew. And he chose to do something about it, the fucking fat fool. I didn't so much mind the occasional dinner remarks (I would sit close to him sometimes just to piss him off), the way he'd try to ignore me in the hallways with a complete lack of eye contact (I made it a point to find his eyes every time I saw him, showing my comfort and dominance), or the giggling with his little friends at social events, but what I did mind was his behind-the-back shit talking to people in the frat that did matter and him trying to cockblock me, which happened with increasing frequency until I destroyed him.

He had a little pull in the house because of the very same reasons he was the alumni chair: he was a legacy and, along with this, well-connected in Seattle. His father, an uncle, and maybe someone before them were members of the frat and went on to do big things throughout the greater area. Sometimes, when speaking with a visitor or someone else who probably couldn't care less, he'd go over and point out his dad in one of the old composites hanging in the living room. This is because he was a fag and not his own man.

Once, for kicks, I found the picture and was surprised to see his dad actually looked like kind of a cool guy. Not that you can really tell all you need to know about someone's personality from a photo, but he didn't have the overweight female clown thing that defined Paulsen—he was actually fit-looking, with the face of a guy who could probably get chicks, complete with this great bushy seventies moustache. His name was Otto, which also might have gotten some girls a little wet since it was sort of unique sounding. He must've knocked up the wrong one or something, or maybe he was a chubby chaser, who knows. There had to be some reason Paulsen turned out the way he turned out. Maybe his dad was such a cool guy that he was never around growing up; he was probably always out making a bunch of money and fucking other women. Paulsen then glommed onto his mother, which would account for his feminine approach to conflict resolution, love of manners and the finer things, and general fecklessness. This snowballed, and the more Paulsen became like his undoubtedly lard-assed, annoying mother, the less his father would want to be around. Ignoring him made Paulsen kind of fall in love with him (which was very confusing because he was also in love with his mother), like that does with all chicks, and that's why he went around showing people that picture all the time. Yeah, that was probably it.

Since he was this legacy and actually took the frat seriously for its own sake, most of the higher-ups had to pretend to like him somewhat, despite there being nothing at all to like. The president of the frat was just the president so he could fuck the best of the hot, young chicks, but along with the office came a sense of ownership and pride in the organization that you had to at least fake a little. His name was Russell, he was indeed the alpha, and we got along fine. He was a pretty busy guy, pre-law as well, and when we had parties we would enjoy friendly if brief chats every so often. But since Paulsen was the frat's fat cheerleader, again because he wasn't his own man and needed something else to give him an identity, he and the president were "brothers and close friends." I got along really well with that guy Blake, the VP, and a beta plus plus, who was a little more fun, a little less responsible. He was the one that told me Paulsen was talking shit about me at their meetings.

Blake liked me from the time I was a pledge. He saw what great ass I was pulling for my lowly status and said, "This is a guy that gets it." When I was brought in as a brother, he took me aside and said, "I see a big future for you here," meaning not only that I'd get tons of pussy, but I'd get even more because I'd easily have a cool office like his when the time came (except better, since I would be president).

We started doing coke together sometimes. It was on one of these occasions, in my room before a party mid-quarter, that he let me know what Paulsen had been doing. "Hey man. I wouldn't normally do this, but fuck it. Paulsen's been talking a lot of shit at our meetings," he said.

"Yeah?"

"Yeah." He did a line.

"Like what?"

"I don't know. I feel kinda like a girl talking about it. But it's pissing me off. You're a cool guy. It's fucked up." Yes, it was a girl-like thing for Blake to tell me someone was talking about me behind my back, but I appreciated him doing it. Blake was a cool guy like me, so it must've been tough. I wouldn't have ever done it. But, you know, the Greek system was a woman's world anyway so it kind of made sense.

"I am a cool guy. That's why that fat fuck doesn't like me." I did a line.

"Yeah."

"So what's he been saying?"

"Well, our first meeting after we brought you all in, we went around talking about how we thought you all were doing. You know, adjusting . . . that kind of stupid shit . . . should take three seconds, 'Everyone's fine.' Next order of business. But he stopped and said he had reservations about you." I shook my head. "He said he didn't think you were like us. He said you don't own a decent suit. That he was afraid you might embarrass us at sorority mixers. That you lacked polish."

"The fuck?"

"Yeah, man. We all looked at him like he was from fucking Mars. It was a lot all at once and just about you, and you had just had sex with some pretty hot girls at those parties. We all thought you were one of the coolest freshmen."

"My suit's nice. I mean, I only have one. But it's nice."

"Yeah. It has a good cut." He took a little bump.

"You have to look at the labels to know the difference."

"For the most part, yeah."

"That chubby asshole has nothing better to do than beat off to *GQs*. You know who buys really nice suits? Old guys. 'Cause they're ugly and that's the only way they get laid."

"Yeah . . . I don't know, man. I myself like a good suit. But I get that logic." Even cool rich kids are really into suits because they're assholes. (These days I pretend to care about suits for work, but only to the extent that I have to.)

I did a bump. I rubbed my nose. "Anyway, fucking prick."

He started laughing. "Then, at one of the next meetings, he suggested a dinner dress code." I chuckled to myself. "He goes, 'I think we should all wear collars.' And when we were like 'Nah . . .' He goes, 'Well at the very least, nobody should be able to wear tennis sneakers.' "

"Tennis sneakers?"

"I know, man. I laughed out loud. I was dying. I could tell it hurt his feelings. But anyway, he said that shit, and we were like 'Nah . . .' again, and then he goes, 'But I don't think anybody wears them but Frank Parker, in any case.' "

"What a bitch. I'm not the only guy that doesn't wear fucking oxfords or whatever to every meal."

"I know, man. I wear basketball shoes and stuff. And you saw us in September. People were wearing flip-flops to dinner. I mean, we knew he didn't like you, but that just brought it to a new level of absurdity."

"Shit . . ." I shook my head. "Anything else?"

"Well, this was the kicker. The other night, we were planning the spring philanthropy event, and he turns to Gus"—Gus, a gamma, was the philanthropy chair—"and he goes, 'Why are we even planning an event when we have a charity case like Frank Parker living under our own roof?' "

"The hell's that supposed to mean?"

"I have no fucking clue, man. Yeah, you didn't show up here in a Rolls Royce, but fuck, who cares?"

I was pissed. I started cutting up more coke. "He knows this is a state school, right? I mean it's a good school, but it's still a state school."

"Yeah. I have no idea, man."

"Calling me poor? Yeah, I'm here on a full ride, but it's because I got good grades, not 'cause I got good grades and grew up on welfare. I should punch him in the fucking mouth." I hit my palm. "Just because I didn't live in a mansion on Mercer Island or whatever. I was raised by a single mother waitress goddammit! And I can still afford this!" I did a small line. He laughed.

"I stood up for you. I was all like, 'C'mon, bro. Enough is enough. We get that you don't like Frank but these meetings are for business.' "

"Thanks, man. I'm glad you told me all this," I said.

"I thought you should know. You might want to hash it out or whatever. I'm sick of all that shit at the meetings." He dove down and did another little line, too.

"How did Russell react during all this?"

He wiped his nose. "Russell? He's Switzerland, always. That guy doesn't care. He just goes in, does what he has to do, then goes back to studying and fucking hot freshmen. He gets it."

"And everyone else?"

"I don't know. I mean, I'm the only one that actually said anything, 'cause you're my boy and all, but I can tell they're impatient with it. We all have better shit to do. But nobody's gonna outright call the guy a fag and kick him out of the meetings because of all his connects with the alumni. But if he starts in on one of his tangents again, I might. I have my own fucking connections." Blake was among the few who could make a declaration like this and mean it, and that's what Paulsen really had going for him. While the frat was mostly comprised of area wealthy kids, kids that knew people in their own right, those connections still knew Paulsen's connections, and those who didn't really have connections used him for internships and job prospects. So . . . even if people didn't like him, they were generally friendly enough, or just a little warmer than indifferent.

I would change that soon enough, though. In the meantime, we finished up our gram.

—— Eating Dollar ——

After the party that night, I ate a one-dollar bill. I tore it up into little pieces, stuffed them in my mouth, chewed hard—even though it was clear very soon that that wasn't doing anything—and swallowed.

I felt like I needed to punish myself somehow for Paulsen thinking he could get away with being a shithead to me. He should've respected me more than that, even if I was just a freshman. And I also felt a little shitty about myself for not being rich like everyone else. But that only lasted about a second. I realized my eventual success and wealth would mean even more because of my humble beginnings, and I also realized, simply . . . Fuck Paulsen.

Money wasn't everything. So I ruined some. Wasted some. Had it as a snack. It wouldn't define me. I knew this would toughen me up for the next phase of our little war. The experience was unpleasant, sure, but I'd done a lot worse. Eating a dollar was just sorta dirty, and it tasted gross . . . not a big deal. It was a nice small punishment.

In the end, I was really happy and proud of myself when the next day I took a shit and saw that a piece of one of the corner "1's" hadn't been digested. There's really nothing like seeing pieces of American currency in your shit. Sometimes, when I'm bored these days, I eat a hundred-dollar bill to see if I can achieve the same effect, but so far, no luck.

—— Tipping Point ——

Right when I swallowed the last of that dollar I started planning my vengeance. I was pissed. I was fine having our weird dynamic in the dining room and hallways and parties and whatnot, but I didn't talk shit about him when he wasn't there—again, chicks do things like that, and also, really, I never thought about him when his blubbery fucking ass wasn't obstructing my eyeline. Though I realized that's what should have been expected from someone like him, trying to turn the officers against me and calling me poor was pretty fucked up. I wanted to just go and bash his head in, but I knew that would only result in my end, not his. I'd probably get kicked out of the frat, all his shit talking would be vindicated, and, worst of all, my supply of easy Grade-A pussy would be cut off. So my brilliant brain started flirting with abstractions about how to get him kicked out. I didn't know exactly what I'd do, just that it shouldn't raise too many questions and should hit him abruptly.

While I waited for the right thing to reveal itself to me, during daily communal activities, I started playing into his bullshit a little, giving him nothing to complain about. I wore collars and nicer shoes to dinner *half* the time (I didn't want to seem too reactionary, or too much like a bitch, either), and sat far enough away that there wouldn't be any squabbling but he could still see me. When passing him in the hallways, I stopped staring. I just looked ahead like he did, but with a pleasant disposition. I mostly avoided him altogether, only being present enough to appear the model fraternity brother. This way, when it came, it wouldn't be traceable to me at all. The only place where not much changed was at parties and hanging out and stuff. I was still me, cool-guy Frank, and I was still having fun and getting laid (you don't get to bang fourteen girls in a quarter by acting kinda like a pussy). And this was enough to still bother him.

A couple of weeks after my talk with Blake, during a party, I was walking back to my room with this hot freshman from the dorms when Paulsen, a little drunk and by himself, caught us in the hallway. "Be careful with this guy," he said. "You'll wake up with syphilis."

"What?" she asked, her face all scrunched up, looking creeped out.

I couldn't believe that shit. I wanted to grab him by the throat and slam him against the wall. But I was smart enough not to, even though I was a little buzzed. Instead, I played it off the best way I could think of. "This guy, such a joker." I rubbed his greasy, curly head.

"Don't touch me. I don't want your syph. Seriously, be careful with him."

I put my arm around him. "You drunk?"

"I said don't touch me!" He shrugged me off.

"One of my best friends here."

"I hate this guy."

I took her by the hand, aggressively, and led her down the hall. "His sense of humor's a little . . . different," I said, all low, feigning comfort and intimacy.

"I'll say."

"He probably has AIDS, too!" the fat fuck called from down the hallway.

"Yeah, I got it from your dad!"

"What did you say?!" he shouted.

"Your dad!" I rounded the corner, laughing.

"Your friend's weird," she said.

"Yeah, I know. I think he's just a little drunk."

"I mean, it's not like I was going to sleep with you, anyway."

"I know, right? I just wanted to show you my guitar."

Back in my room I just showed her the guitar. She asked, "Well, aren't you going to play anything?"

"I said I'd show you. I didn't say anything about playing."

"Oh, is that how it is?" Then we started making out and after I used some hand sanitizer because I realized I touched Paulsen, I fucked her.

Following that incident, I decided it wasn't really me or what I did in the dining room or my economic background or anything like that that Paulsen actually hated—or at least what he had grown to hate me for the most—it was how great I was with chicks. That, or maybe he was in love with me and knew I wouldn't ever fuck him. The next day, I was thankful it had happened because I still fucked that chick and it was the inspiration I'd been waiting for. My revenge plot occurred to me in an instant, like a light bulb clicking on over a cartoon character. If it was me as sex on a stick that he really hated, then I would destroy him through that. I'd get him kicked out through his own shitty sexual identity, hit him where it really hurt: the balls. Everybody knew

Paulsen couldn't get laid. Everybody knew he was kind of a shit. And guys that are kind of shits that can't get laid might eventually resort to something like . . . roofies! Even his legacy family wouldn't be able to help him out then. Nobody would give a fuck about his connections. He'd, in short, be dead to us.

I was still the model brother, avoiding him, laying low, but the plan was coming together. I'd get him at the next sorority mixer. It was to take place in eleven days. A party or a gathering would be bad, but a mixer with a highly regarded sorority, which this one was, would be fucking terrible. I knew that in doing this I'd be risking our frat's reputation, so I tried to plan it to avoid as much damage as possible. That shit would affect me directly too. Worst case scenario, I knew it wouldn't ruin us completely, wouldn't get us kicked out of the Greek system or anything—the argument could be made easily enough that Paulsen was a single bad apple—but still, I needed to be careful. I devised my plan to try to make it so even the girl might not know she was roofied, but he would still be caught.

During these eleven days, the tubby asshole still found opportunities to try to fuck me. Blake told me, again while doing lines, that at the last meeting Paulsen said I was "of questionable character and had made disparaging remarks about his father, a great alum of the fraternity, having AIDS" and he wanted "some retribution" before Russell finally chimed in and said, "Paulsen, come on" and that was that. Then—and this took almost everything in me not to plow my fist through his soft, rolly gut or take him outside and curb-stomp his fat, curly head—he stopped me and Rachel in the foyer one night after I let her in and nearly jeopardized my ability to get unprotected pussy. "Hey, I don't think we've ever met," he started, extending his hand to her. I watched him. "I'm Paulsen."

Rachel smiled and shook it. "Rachel."

"Paulsen's our alumni chair," I said, waiting. She nodded.

The son of a fucking cunt then said this: "So I was wondering . . . what's it like having no self-respect?"

She cocked her head, narrowed her eyes. "Excuse me?"

"Yeah, what do you mean Paulsen?"

"You know what I mean." He smiled. "He give you gonorrhea yet?"

"I actually meant Paulsen's our alumni chair and a fat, jealous prick."

"Is he joking?"

"I'm not," he said, crossing his arms.

"What's he mean?"

"No clue," I said.

"What I mean is, I don't want either of you here. You're both bad for this organization. As for my implications, you're in college, right? Or did he pick you up off the street?"

"What the fuck? You're an asshole, man," she said.

"Yes, he is."

"I'd rather be an asshole than a poor man-whore or a dormer booty call."

"Go find a bakery, Paulsen. Eat more of your feelings. Come on," then I pulled her away and we went to my room. She asked what he meant by all that, and I explained he was just some dickhead that hated me for being younger and cooler and better liked in the frat than him, and that he probably couldn't contain his jealousy once he saw her because she was so beautiful. That seemed to put her at ease enough. Then we fucked.

—— Roofies ——

A few days later we had that mixer and I got Paulsen kicked out of the frat.

I came by some roofies through this dirtbag Phil worked with at the pizza place (I had explained my plan to Phil and only Phil, who assumed they wouldn't be for me, but still didn't really care all that much about any of it). Around fifteen minutes after the mixer started, I snuck into Paulsen's room and left a few of them in his dresser drawer inside a small bag, then carried the rest back out with me.

Mixers were okay. We mostly just stood around and met sorority girls we'd try to fuck later at parties or on our own time—working to get their numbers, get them to like us, those kinds of things (only upperclassmen with great offices could fuck a girl right after a mixer). They were pretty low-key, which would normally make it fairly difficult to drug a chick's drink unnoticed, but I had my plan on lockdown. When I returned, I got two drinks, whiskey sours I think, one of which I slipped a roofie in. We had had one of these with the same sorority before, during my pledge quarter, and I met a few girls who were cool enough to talk to for a while without making me want to shoot myself (most sorority girls were awful to talk to, obviously, especially if you knew you weren't about to have sex with them). There was one in particular, this really attractive sophomore beta minus named Sarah, that I could tell was a little in love with me. So I gave her that drink.

I was told it would take about ten to twenty minutes before the drug took effect. I talked to her for about seven in a hallway around the corner from our living room, charmed her, made her laugh, kept constant eye contact, touched her arm and back from time to time. She fell even more in love with me. I drank my drink kind of fast, all upbeat and fun, saying things like "God, this is good" and "Great drink, huh?" hoping she'd drink hers quickly too. It worked; she was that stupid and impressionable. We were talking about something dumb and boring like her hometown or whatever when I said, "Hey, can you do me a favor?"

"What?"

"See that guy over there?" I pointed back around the corner to the chubby lemon-headed goon, who was just standing against a wall with his gay little friend Hideki probably talking about the pros and cons of the Windsor vs. Half-Windsor knot. "He's a friend of mine, doesn't think he's that great with girls, and I made a ten dollar bet with him that a pretty girl would talk to him tonight. Can you ask him to get you a drink or something and then talk to him for a minute or two?"

"Sure . . ." She rocked back and forth, flirting while pretending to consider, like she wouldn't do absolutely anything I asked. Despite me not being an upperclassman with a cool office, she probably would've licked my balls in that moment if I'd asked her to. "I guess."

"Awesome. But don't tell him you were talking to me. Better yet, don't mention my name at all. I'll lose the bet if he knows I sent you."

"Okay."

"You don't have a friend you could bring, do you? He'll probably give me twenty bucks if two beautiful girls talk to him."

"I'll see what I can do," she said, blushing. "But you have to give me at least half."

I smiled. "Find me when you're done, okay? I want to continue our conversation. I like talking to you a lot." She smiled back, all teeth and sexual invitation, the slut, downed her drink, and went over to her friend, this girl Winnie, also very good-looking, a sophomore beta plus, and whispered in her ear. Then they both approached him. Sarah was hot enough for me to fuck, which means about 1,000 times hotter than any chick that would ever talk to Paulsen, Winnie too, so of course when they walked up he probably thought it was his lucky day, that God had finally answered the little prayer he made every night before jerking off and crying himself to sleep.

I slowly moved into the living room and watched from across the way, drinking by myself, briefly smiling at this or that hot girl that walked by (I didn't look like a weird anti-social loser; I was a brooding lone wolf, deep in thought and cool). Soon after their arrival, Paulsen went to the bar and they forced conversation with that little bitch Hideki. When he came back, he handed Sarah a drink. They talked for about five minutes. During this time, one of my pledge class brothers, Rob, a gamma who was among those that started dressing sort of like me, approached and I absently talked to him while looking over his shoulder and following the action. He was a good prop I guess, made me seem less conspicuous . . . not that I really looked that way, but you know, better safe than sorry. Sarah started fading, leaning on Paulsen (which I'm sure almost gave him a boner), and soon thereafter dropped, her glass doing likewise and breaking into several pieces next to her. Bada bing. Winnie was quick to freak out, going "Sweetie, what's wrong? Sweetie, what's wrong?" but Sarah wasn't really responsive, mainly just communicating in slurs and by slowly shaking her head, her eyes struggling to stay open and losing. A small crowd gathered around her. I joined it. Paulsen freaked out too and started asking, "What's with her? What's with her?" Then Winnie was like, "What did you do? What was in her drink?" Hideki slinked away through our circle at this point, the coward, leaving Paulsen there alone, this drugged chick writhing at his feet and a freaked out bitch in his face and a crowd of ever-accusatory faces all around. He was now pissed and seemed overly defensive, shaking his head and replying with "I didn't do anything. I think she's on drugs or something. What did *you* do with her before you brought her into *my* house?" all dick-like. And she shouts, "Nothing! This was only, like, her second drink! What did you do? What did you do?" Then their sorority president intervened, blah, blah, blah, an ambulance was called, blah, blah, blah, a few hours later results came back positive for Rohypnol and there wasn't even an investigation or anything, no innocent until proven guilty, the planting of roofies in his drawer completely unnecessary (though I hope when he found them he thought of me—I didn't have the satisfaction of a follow-up confrontation, playing it safe and avoiding him more or less altogether, just staring and smiling as he left). Action needed to be taken quickly and severely, as the ambulance at our frat was more than enough to threaten our image of perfection, and so he had to go. Winnie's accusations were all anyone needed as evidence. He moved out three days later. Bada boom. Done.

The real story of why the ambulance was there never spread around the Greek system, since letting it get out would have not only been bad for our fraternity but also that sorority (I think we blamed it on an asthma attack or diabetes or something). Our reputation was only mildly compromised and we were still the best frat at U-Dub. And the rest of the year was perfect—most people liked me in the house, but I had a few who didn't (Hideki plus Paulsen's one or two other friends, who I think secretly knew), which made me respected, but none of them did anything about it, so I didn't have to waste any time or energy. I fucked even more girls the next quarter (sixteen), including both Sarah and Winnie as well as some worthwhile additions to my Bingo project, among them a half-Asian, half-Latino girl and that all-black type I had been wanting for a while. Life was good.

——— Completing Band ———

I found the fourth member of my band early that spring. His name was Vlad and he was just the type of weirdo multi-instrumentalist that I knew could bring my music to the next level.

We met at a bar. Having kind of exhausted the whole café scene, musically and, more or less, pussy-wise, I started checking out artsier bars on Capitol Hill and in the nearby

Central District with the fake ID I got from the frat. He performed a DJ set and it was strange and creepy and good. He didn't use turntables or anything, just a laptop, but in addition to this, messed around with a keyboard, guitar, a drum machine, assorted pedals, and, in one bizarre turn that still completely worked, a saxophone. He had stage presence, albeit odd stage presence, moving around and twitching to what he was making. He was small, wiry, and wore cool enough clothes, and his face looked like it could get him laid, though it wasn't as good-looking as mine. Most notably, he had these light blue eyes like a Siberian Husky's, and he'd often stare out into the crowd in this way I imagined could make some weird girls a bit moist. It didn't take long to realize he could be the guy. I introduced myself after his set, and toward the end of our conversation, which he had made pretty awkward (I'd later learn he had Asperger's or something), he agreed to meet up at Phil's that Sunday.

When he showed up, my band was complete. A third-year music production major at Cornish, he knew just what to inject, just where, in all of my songs to make them modern and interesting. They still had a classic rock thing going on at heart, but from there were layered with sounds that were cutting edge, becoming richer, more dynamic. He liked my melodies, but also had some suggestions on structure, taking me away from straight up verse-chorus-verse-chorus-bridge-chorus-x2 shit into strange places that still worked. Sometimes it took a while to get—the guy was on his own planet, completely, but it was a fascinating place to be, and I knew everything would be better for the band in the end.

That first day, though, there were some personality clashes and arguments over direction. It took Phil and Julian a little time to warm to him since they were both rockers and he was mostly into making electronic music; also, because of an encyclopedic knowledge of music in general, Vlad could off the top of his head name the Pixies songs Julian was stealing from, which embarrassed him and quickly made him change the grooves to something less derivative—making my songs better, more original, instantly. But after that we were one nice, slightly dysfunctional family. We practiced once a week, rearranging and fine-tuning the songs. I was the father figure, the intermediary: reining in Vlad when he got a little too out there and reminding Phil and Julian to keep an open mind. There was quarrelling every time, but nothing ever got too serious. I'm a good, effective leader and they all knew temper tantrums of any kind would not be tolerated. If there was a problem child, however, it would have been Vlad. He was a perfectionist, and I'd constantly have to remind him that it was my songs he was perfecting, not his.

During this period, we didn't play any shows. I actually refused another offer from that coffee shop so I could iron out the songs and make them what they were always meant to be. The next time I played them, they would be finalized. People would be blown away. Managers and labels would come running, and they would fight over me, and then my life would be set. While all the pussy I was getting in college made me feel like I'd died and gone to Heaven, making it as a rock star would allow me to ascend even higher, become the ruler of my own Pussy Heaven. They call them rock gods for a reason. It was still my number one goal. There would continue to be eighteen- and nineteen-year-old girls, but so many other kinds. I longed to travel the world and expand my Pussy Bingo to nationalities (like I have now), not just races and body types. The Greek system was great, and I was still happier than I'd ever been, but I knew it couldn't give me everything I wanted or deserved, and in a year or so I might get bored. I didn't just want to have sex with a Latino girl—I wanted a Colombian, then a half Venezuelan, half Chilean, that kind of thing. It wasn't enough to fuck just Asian and half Asian chicks anymore. I wanted to fuck Vietnamese with short hair, Korean with long hair, Cambodian with big tits, Cambodian with smaller tits (within reason); half Colombian, half Cambodian—every type of hot girl imaginable. I wanted to expand my bingo board by millions of pussy combinations in every direction. I wanted to fuck the world.

———— Parker ————

About five weeks later, the songs were there and I was ready to play a couple of shows live. Soon, I knew we'd be written about on all the big music blogs, get signed, then have features done on us in magazines—*Alternative Press*, *Spin*; we'd record and release our debut and sales would go through the roof. I'd get the cover of *Rolling Stone*. I'd be rich, famous, powerful, a world-class alpha.

Before we reached out to any of our venue contacts (me the coffee shop guy, Vlad his Central District bar guy), Vlad decided it was a good time to pull something he had probably been planning for a while, the fucker. He approached me as having "a reservation on the topic of playing live." This then turned into a condition for playing any performances alongside me, followed by kind of an ultimatum for his continued involvement with the band at all. He would not play live as a part of "Frankie Parker."

When Vlad played DJ sets, which he still did from time to time, he'd perform as just "Vlad." He saw himself as his own thing, his own brand, and yeah, maybe he was—among his other idiosyncrasies, he exclusively wore red shirts or hoodies while on stage—but he was one only five people in all of Seattle cared about and nobody ever wrote about. He said, " 'Vlad' will not be absorbed by 'Frankie Parker.' 'Frankie Parker' isn't even 'Frankie Parker' anymore post-'Vlad.' " Fucking almost-autistic asshole.

I was more pissed by his insolence than anything, but I knew I had to tread lightly. I needed the little shit. He thought we should come up with an original band name. Rather than pulling me aside and going through all this, he brought it up in front of everybody, and Phil and Julian, who were usually so good, so subservient, such great kids, made it clear they didn't want to perform as just me, either. "How about Rat's Nest?" suggested Phil, the fucking idiot. Jesus Christ. "NATO sounds pretty cool," thought Julian, the pube-faced genius, just as fast.

"Hold on, hold on." I stopped them. "They're my fucking songs. We're performing them as 'Frankie Parker.' "

"Then I'm out," said Vlad. "And I'd thank you not to use any of my arrangements. Not that they'd work anyway for a three-piece."

"Two-piece," added Julian, the genius once more.

"Solo act." Et tu, Phil?

They were fucking traitors. Instead of them all being my children, here Vlad was acting like he was my fucking wife: a bitchy pain in the ass turning my kids against me, trying to destroy my beautiful family. "Those names are shit, guys."

"Hey!" Julian was offended.

"Fuck . . ." I sighed. "All right Vlad, what's your idea?"

"I don't have one. It's not my band, it's yours. But 'Frankie Parker' doesn't work." I was happier with this answer than an actual one.

"They're extensions of me, these songs, guys."

Phil crossed his arms. "Come on, Frank, I've been playing them for like four months now."

"I've been playing them for two years. And I wrote them."

"I'm just saying, they're an extension of me, too. Rat's Nest would be cool."

"How about FP 773?" suggested Vlad.

Huh? I'm a bright guy and I didn't get that shit. "What the hell is that?"

"FP are your initials and it sounds good."

"What's the 773?"

"Think about it."

I thought about it for a second. "I did. It's meaningless."

"It's an aesthetic thing."

I thought again. "Fuck you, Vlad." I hadn't ever told him "fuck you" or anything like that before; I was usually way more patient than dismissive with the weirdo and "fuck you," even as a joke, he probably wouldn't get. But he needed and deserved to be told off with that fucking "773" nonsense. He just stood there. Phil and Julian did too, waiting for me to father them. "How about Parker?" I looked at them each in the eye.

"Parker?" repeated Vlad.

"Yeah, I'm willing to lose 'Frankie.' "

"Parker? Hmmm . . ." went Julian, obviously just waiting for Vlad's reaction. I don't know why he became Vlad's little bitch all of a sudden.

I'd fill the gap, stop them before any objection. "That way, it's still true to me and my songs, but ambiguous enough. It kind of captures the spirit of the sound, you know? Like, it's rock, it's sex, you can dance to it, you know, like you're parking it in a chick." I did a little gyrating dance like I'd do sometimes while playing a great hook. Phil smiled, laughed. Julian smirked. Vlad looked at me stony-eyed, like he usually did. "But it's also contemplative, like you're parking your ass down and listening, thinking, getting through the layers, figuring out the music. Put the two together and you can groove to something that makes you think. Fuckin' Parker." They bought it, and in the end, I guess I was happier with it, too. That thing I made up on the spot made complete sense to me, should make sense to anybody. And now that the songs were different, at their full potential, it was like a rebirth of sorts. Vlad was a genius, but not as much of one as me.

Management Deal

I talked to the owner of that coffee shop I had played before and booked us a show to take place the next week. I told him to bill us as "Parker" this time. He did, and also let us headline, which was nice since I hadn't headlined anything yet. We killed it. We were amazing. Our set lasted a little over thirty minutes and every second sounded incredible. The crowd loved it and several people congratulated us afterwards and asked if we had CDs.

It worked visually, too. Vlad was as into it as he was his own gigs, dancing, darting; mesmerizing to watch as he nimbly moved from instrument to computer to instrument, often in one song, or played instruments with other instruments, like using the head of the guitar he was playing to press keyboard keys or playing the glockenspiel with some maracas as he played those. Not really worried that he'd upstage me or anything, but just knowing he was providing more energy than I'd had to compete with before from the other guys, he made me step my game up, give it my all. I'm sure he fed off of my energy too since it was so great. Our competition made us both the best we could be, and together we were a sight to be seen and, more importantly, an act to be heard.

The next show we played, at the bar Vlad deejayed at in the Central District, went even better. What was really nice about it was that it was dark, with a couple of cool lights that alternated colors, bathing us in red, green, indigo. At the coffee shop I had been playing to a well-lit room, but this was theatrical, grand, deserving of me and my sound, an environment fit for a pro. After playing there, just like when I played my first legitimate gig and abandoned open mikes, I vowed to never play a bright-ass room again.

When we finished our set, a bunch of art fags wanted to buy our music and one guy even asked if we had t-shirts. The fact that we didn't have anything made them want our stuff even more. Then I got a card from this guy claiming to be a manager. His name was Max and he seemed youngish for a manager, mid-twenties only, so I was a little skeptical at first, but I looked him and his company up online and everything checked out. He was just a young, cool guy and there was nothing wrong with that; in fact, it was ideal. I called him up the next week and then Parker had representation.

More or less everything I had wanted to happen when I moved to the city about eight months before had happened. I met the guy with the van, the experimental musician to complete my songs, the manager to get them heard. I saw myself shooting up through the clouds, about halfway there to sitting on the throne of my very own Pussy Heaven, my dick out and getting sucked and fucked by a choir of angels who otherwise spent their time joyfully singing my praises. Life was good.

——— Tour ———

That summer my band went on a regional tour. Max had us supporting another one of his bands from the area, this two-piece signed to Sub Pop or something, and we were to play ten club shows during July in Washington, Oregon, and Northern California.

We recorded a four song EP, including two of the songs that would eventually be on the album, one new one, and one of the original fifteen I wrote in high school that didn't make the cut when I started playing live. We threw those up onto Myspace, which was still relevant then, it being the mid-aughts. Then we made a few hundred CDs with cool cover art to sell at the gigs as well as some badass "Parker" t-shirts and buttons I designed. So there we were, a band with all the seeds planted, everything in order, everything in place to really make it big.

The tour itself was pretty bare bones. We basically lived in Phil's family van, driving as much as nine hours a day and staying in campgrounds or Wal-Mart parking lots between and outside the cities. I made the most of it. The experience was a way for me to sort of live the rock lifestyle I had wanted so badly and planned on living for the rest of my life; every night I could, I'd try to fuck a new chick, and often, I did. Yes, it was a far grimier variation of it, sometimes fucking a girl on a sleeping bag in the van or whatever, not in a penthouse suite, but you know, it was more or less the same thing. The guys seemed cool about it—not that I cared, it was after all the fucking point of all this hard work—and I never really put anyone out, or so I thought at the time.

The shows themselves were going extremely well. I'd do a little coke before performing to keep up with Vlad and really give 110%. Most crowds were into it, dancing and stuff, clapping loudly for us, whistling, cheering us on with "Whooos!" and "Yeahs!" We sold a good amount of EPs and merch. Some local papers wrote about us. And our Myspace page was getting more and more hits every day— mainly from people wherever we had just played, but then, inexplicably, a lot of kids from England started sending the band friend requests, too, which I thought was cool, except that most chicks in England are kind of ugly.

—————— **End of Tour** ——————

Seven dates in, everything was going great, then fucking Vlad went and fucked it all up, the fucking half-retarded piece of shit. There we were: a young, cool band, getting great press, playing great shows, making fans in fucking England, really on the cusp of making it, getting famous, then rich, then forever supplied with the highest quality pussy on the planet, and the goddam little cunt goes and quits the fucking band. He quits the motherfucking band, the fucking asshole, shithead, half-retarded art fag, dickhead-asshole, pussy-faggot, asshole-cunt.

It happened after a show in a motel near San Francisco. We had to get a room because there was a freak storm and pretty hard rain, hard enough to keep us up in the van if we tried to sleep in it. This was the third time we were forced into a room, the others because Phil had gotten us lost on the road. Having just murdered another set and sold a lot of CDs and some shirts, we were in pretty good moods. I met this girl from South Korea going to Berkeley as part of some study abroad program. The night was going well.

The chick and a friend, her roommate in their dorm, who was also hot, but less-so and just American and white, followed us to the motel. The roommate would've been a beta at her high school probably, and I don't know how this shit works in Korea, but let's just call mine an alpha. She was that fucking hot. Anyway, we got there around midnight. We all hung out in the room and drank—except

Vlad who just sat using his computer because he was a weirdo-pussy that had "no use for intoxicants"—and after a while I let Phil know that I thought mine was ready to fuck. I tested the waters with her friend for a threesome, but didn't really catch the vibe. Since all of them were over twenty-one, they just went to this bar next door. I think Phil planned on trying to get the other one in the van or something.

Phil and Julian would later give me their accounts of the following, which I used with my first-hand knowledge of the events to piece all of this shit together (doing so only for edification; none of it mattered and it was all over quickly, but I was furious and, I hate to admit it, sad, actually needing to understand . . . there isn't anything bitch-like about this . . . at the time I had a whole lot fucking riding on Vlad). So apparently after only a few minutes at the bar, after probably just sitting there silently sipping a water or Shirley Temple or something fucking stupid, Vlad decided he'd go back to the van and record the noise from the rain hitting its roof for his "Library of Sounds." He'd record weird shit like this on the road sometimes for loops and stuff to use later on. He got the keys from a reluctant Phil, who told him he may need the van in a little while, and Vlad was like "Okay, whatever" and went to it anyway. Realizing he left his laptop in the room, he then came back to the motel and, using the other keycard, which he had pocketed at check-in, and not understanding the subtleties of why they all went to the bar in the first place because he had fucking Asperger's or whatever, caught me dick-deep in this Korean chick from behind. She was all like "Oh, shit!" in Korean, freaking out, and I just kept fucking her, like "Get the fuck out, Vlad!" and he started to leave and then came back and then started to leave again, opening the door to go this time, but then he came back again instead and grabbed his computer bag real quick and then he left, finally. She wanted to stop and was embarrassed, but I convinced her to stay (wasn't hard to do, used one of my amazing kisses while lightly stroking her face), and after about ten more minutes, after she came, I came. In this time, Vlad went back to the van, where Phil was waiting with that other chick under an umbrella. Phil requested the keys, so Vlad handed them over and returned to the bar, kind of drenched from all the back and forth in the rain, where Julian was hanging out, drinking alone like a loser. Vlad sat with him and recorded the din of the room with a microphone and his computer, looking disinterested, just sort of sitting there with his hand cradling his head and sighing from time to time, Julian told me, until the bartender asked him why he was "recording anything" in his bar and told him to put his shit away. It was a little late at this point, around 1:15 or so, and we had been up since early that morning to drive to this gig, so a frustrated Vlad shouts, "Oh, what the fuck? Fuck it! This bar isn't even interesting. I just needed something to do!" and the bartender, pissed that this weird guy was "talking shit," kicked him out. Julian went with him because it wasn't like he was going to get laid anyway—nobody at this bar had seen him perform and he was too ugly—suggesting they see what was happening back at the room since enough time had passed. Vlad said that he was in there a few minutes ago and I was busy, so they just sat in the motel lobby reading tourism pamphlets, all wet, the front desk clerk scowling at them. This is when I ran into them on my way to the bar so

I could give the Korean girl back to her friend and go to sleep.

"We need to have a band meeting," said Vlad.

After Phil was done in the van (didn't take long) and the chicks got lost, there was a big, drawn-out fight back in the room too irritating to recreate, which Vlad began by telling us flat out, "I quit," and which he spent the remainder of refusing to listen to logic or reason or the idea that we were right on the verge of fame, fortune, and getting the world's best pussy, forever, with dream jobs, forever. He just brought up stupid, bitch-ass shit like me kicking them out of the van when trying to fuck chicks on the road and me always getting to sleep in a bed at the few motels we'd stayed at while he and Phil and Julian would alternate sleeping on the other bed, if there was one, and floor. He also complained a lot about how Phil had made him give up the keys to the van earlier, and ended by shouting "Music and sex aren't mutually dependent!" over and over again with increasing volume until I almost hit him. Then everyone was quiet and that was that. He agreed to play throughout the end of the tour, but this would be it for him and "Parker." Afterwards, we all brushed our teeth and pissed and washed our faces and whatever else, and I shut off the light. The storm kind of let up and instead of rain all I could hear was nothing.

—— Branding Self ——

The evening we got back into town after the tour, I locked myself in my room (which I had to myself over the summer, thankfully), took out a metal guitar pick, poked through a slit it had near the top with this little meat skewer thing I stole from a drawer in the kitchen, burned it with a lighter for a few minutes, stuffed my mouth with a sock, and, my pants down, pressed it hard into my right ass cheek. The pain was excruciating, the feeling of my skin burning so intense that well after I dropped the pick, which I did only a few seconds after making contact, it felt like I had been pressing it harder and harder into my ass for minutes afterwards. Also, because of my initial enthusiasm, I ended up poking the skewer through the pick a bit too much and puncturing the skin, too, actually going so far as to stab into my muscle a little . . . but whatever. Once I stopped hopping around, I checked myself out in the mirror. The brand was misshapen, which sucked. I guess I hadn't burned the pick evenly enough, or when the skewer poked me it lost its place, so instead of looking cool, like a pick, it looked like three fourths of a pick with a dot on top or something, which was just kind of weird.

Going into it, I wanted to hurt myself, but also give myself a little present. This had more or less been the way I would punish myself ever since that big transformation in high school after I didn't make starting halfback, when I first choked myself while jerking off. When I ate that dollar,

I gave myself the satisfaction of not giving a fuck about how much money other people had and shitting it out; when I stopped using lube while jerking off after the thing with Ms. Adams, I still, for the most part, came. The only time I didn't give myself some sort of gift was when I quit jerking off for a month, and again, it was easily the worst thing I ever did to myself, forthcoming punishments included, and that's a big reason why. Anyway, I needed to be disciplined, sure, for not being a good enough leader that Vlad wouldn't have quit my fucking band, but I knew deep down that I was a great leader and he was just a half-retarded asshole, and there was nothing I could've done. So, while painful, I also gave myself a little something to have for life, and that was a mark that meant I was a fucking rock star.

I had always been funny about tattoos and piercings. I thought my body was amazing, beautiful, perfect . . . and I didn't like the idea of modifying it. Yes, tattoos are pretty badass, and maybe a diamond stud in the ear might make some dumb chicks think you're cool and flashy, but really, I came in the world the way I want to go out. Pure and me. The only thing I was okay with were the small scars I'd given myself over the years, which I could really only detect by looking hard. A little brand seemed like a worthy addition to them. I used a pick so I'd have this nice symbolic reminder that I was fucking rock-and-roll, that I didn't need Vlad, I didn't need anybody . . . Fuck it, I'd be a rock star for life, no matter what happened. I was more rock than music even. Because even more than music, rock-and-roll is sex. That's why I branded my ass cheek. I'd know when I was moving it, using my incredible, toned ass muscles to pound into a chick, that I was a fucking rock god.

Since it didn't come out exactly as I wanted, I thought about redoing it or having it professionally corrected, but that would have gone against the spirit of the punishment, which was kind of the greater thing, despite all that other stuff, and eventually it healed for the most part, anyway. The brand is still there, but it is much smaller.

——— End of Parker ———

About a week after getting home, after getting the files of the electronic parts of my songs Vlad had created off his computer, and after persuading (and paying) him to record (over the air) us performing all the songs so I could piece them together later, Vlad was gone for good.

That little shithead had done a lot for my band, and at the time I saw it as one of the worst things that had ever happened to me. The only silver lining was that it kind of made me feel almost as bad as I'd imagined I made all the girls I'd broken up with or fucked over in my life feel, and it was nice to know I had been on the giving end of a type of pain that's supposed to be even more intense so many times.

When news got out that Vlad quit the band, everything sort of went to shit. Max didn't want us to play live again or submit to labels until we could find someone that could do what he did, especially on stage, and so I began looking for a replacement almost instantly, going to tons of weird DJ sets (occasionally I'd even run into him, which I hated; we'd avoid each other), posting ads on Craig's List, checking out showcases at Cornish, but nobody even came close. Weeks passed without a viable lead. All the momentum we gained from the tour was amounting to naught.

So, we urged Max to find us gigs to play as a three-piece, anything to get people talking again. He got us some shows in town. We'd have a friend of Phil and Julian's or someone on stage with us to cue Vlad's loops on a laptop, but without him jumping around and dancing and playing some of the parts live on the bassoon or didgeridoo or whatever, it was hardly the same. People did write about us; not press, but former fans on their personal blogs (which were starting to really break out at the time) who thought we sucked now without Vlad. Then, some of my frat brothers found out about my band and all we'd done by googling my name and reading an old show review or rising artist blurb or some shit (they all thought I was so cool and great that they fucking googled me, for Christ's sake; an alpha would never google anyone they lived with) and a bunch of guys came down to surprise and support me at this one gig, which was absofuckinglutely great for my street cred. After that, way less people would come to watch us. Months passed. Max eventually dropped us. We submitted our EP together with old press clippings to all the major labels ourselves, but never heard back from anybody. A few more months passed. I kept looking for a new Vlad. Phil and Julian kept looking. We tried a couple of people out. They sucked. More months passed. Then, eventually, as is inevitable with many young artist-types, kind of nothing happened and we went on with our lives.

It had been about a year since the tour then and I was pretty tired, disenchanted. At the time, I figured I had another six or seven years to make it as a musician, before you get too old to get signed, despite your talent, and I thought that was enough of a window to relax for a while and let success come to me when it was ready. There was no use continually stressing out about it. Technically I still have two more years to become a successful musician, but at this point I wouldn't really trade my life for anything, not even rock stardom. We'll get to how I figured out that investment banking was the perfect thing for me, my triple-threat genius aside, soon enough though. I guess all that shit was a blessing in disguise now that I think about it. Who knows how I'd feel if it had actually worked out then. Anyway, fucking Vlad.

—————— College Sophomore ——————

Sophomore year, when I wasn't looking for another weirdo musical encyclopedia to exploit, I was mostly busy living the fucking life. The whole Greek thing only got more and more amazing. I lived in the frat house again, having realized during winter quarter the previous year that I'd get more high quality pussy within the house than by trying to get girls to come back to a nearby apartment with me or whatever. Girls are lazy.

I had been made the frat's sergeant-at-arms for the year over the summer, partly due to my niche as the sort of bad-boy rebel, what with the way I dressed and my fuck 'em and leave 'em reputation with chicks (my imitators still didn't come close to capturing my super-cool persona), and

also because of a good word from Blake before he graduated. That was fun for me. I was like the muscle, with
duties that included maintaining order at meetings and
keeping the pledges in line. The latter I abused kind of, but
not to haze them or put them out just to put them out or
anything—hazing is a form of bullying and bullying is for
pussies, like I said before—I was just sort of a dick to them
in purely self-serving ways. I made them take turns doing
my laundry, had them run some errands like picking up a
sandwich for me or whatever. I got away with this because
my fellow brothers and the pledges had a lot of respect for
me (my lack of collared shirts and the fact that I had a
pompadour of sorts made some new guys who grew up all
fancy and shit look at me like I was in the Hell's Angels or
something) and also because of what happened with
Paulsen the year before, in that the higher-ups thought it
would be good to maintain a little more discipline within
the house in general. The pledges of course hated it and
some would try to bribe me by saying stuff like, "Hey, what
if instead of picking up your package at the Post Office, I
gave you fifty bucks?" which I'd respond to by acting all
insulted, and then I'd make them do pushups. I couldn't be
bought, which wasn't really in keeping with the spirit of the
frat (others still could, and insubordination was just as out
in the open as ever despite the whole new discipline initiative, but not with me), and people knew it and it made
them respect me even more.

One of the kids even dropped out because he was so
wealthy that the idea of doing anyone's laundry drove him
nuts, and even though the new president, this guy Jack (indeed an alpha), was a little pissed because I guess the kid
was going to get his parents to donate a Rothko or Warhol

painting for our study or something—which would have been a real panty-dropper—I was able to blow it off by saying something along the lines of "The type of guy that thinks he's so entitled he doesn't have to pay his dues is the type of guy who thinks he could have whatever girl he wants, too, by hook, crook, or roofie" and that was that. It was a good title for my age, still not like vice president or anything, but the cool thing was I didn't even need a good title to get the best chicks. What I had going for me was something even more valuable: a reputation as being good in bed. In college, this is the equivalent to what a reputation as a good kisser is in junior high.

Now no longer a freshman, I had free rein over the freshman sorority girls as well as the lion's share of the previous year's, since many wouldn't fuck me then. It seemed the sophomores and juniors I bagged the year before would talk about me some—there were those recognizing what it was, a good lay, an incredibly satisfying experience in the spirit of youth, who would, like the good, responsible older siblings they were, describe it, off-handedly encouraging their little sisters to give me a ride; then there were the ones that felt spurned, who were either a little crazy or loved me and my talents and amazing dick so much that when I took them away, hated me, and they would tell their sisters that I was a scumbag, to avoid me. Naturally this just made the younger ones even more curious—if I could have this kind of an effect on their venerable older sisters, I must be pretty damn good. Maybe they could fix me, maybe they would be the one I'd make my girlfriend, some of the little idiots probably thought. Either way, they came running and I had all the random sex I wanted. And by that I mean they'd actually come up to me and flirt sexually, openly; all it took on my end was not saying anything that put them out of the mood. It was that easy. A lot of these girls weren't anything special, nothing exotic to add to my Bingo project, but all things considered, there's nothing wrong with an endless supply of eighteen- and nineteen-year-old hot white girls to fuck. The malaise I feared might set in with the Greek system the previous year, when rock stardom and elusive Mongolian or Eritrean or Eskimo pussy seemed more and more possible every day, hadn't, and a little turned off by the whole rock thing in general because of everything that happened with fucking Vlad and the now frustrating search to replace him, I figured it wouldn't any time soon.

The previous year, I felt like I was happier than I'd ever been, but this made that seem like a big nothing. I had sex with fifty-seven girls sophomore year at school and an additional thirteen through the music scene. Not too far into the year I cleared a hundred partners all told since becoming sexually active, and by the end I passed 125. After this I kind of stopped filling out my spreadsheet, despite my obsession with numbers; keeping track seemed like a waste of time since it really was so easy . . . it would have been like counting how many times I'd chew when I ate. I had already accomplished exponentially more than most men do in a lifetime at age twenty. It was pretty fucking great.

—— Girl Problems ——

There was, however, one defect in my sex life sophomore year. It involved Rachel. The sex itself was great, don't get me wrong—she could fuck with the best of them—but what I had to do to sustain it was pretty damn lame. I loved unprotected sex, though; it was still my favorite thing in the world, so I did what I had to do. Really, I was more or less addicted to it—I ran off it, felt like it leveled me out in dealing with the stresses of my double life and classes and everything, and without it, I would've been fucked. Rachel called me her "boyfriend"; in my head, I called her my "little Canadian pipeline," her pussy the raw, good shit that kept my motor running.

She had managed to get herself an apartment off campus with a couple of friends before fall quarter began. Since she had been my "girlfriend" for nearly a year, and now with a private room to call her own, the expectation was that I stay at least three nights a week with her. This became a problem.

Before, I'd have unprotected sex with her usually two days a week, which was enough, hanging out in bed for as much as a half-hour afterwards if she really needed me to and then I'd make her leave because of the roommate thing, which she got. There were a few occasions that year when her roommate would be away for the weekend and she'd want me to come over to the dorms and stay with her, but I'd always be quick to find reasons not to—

fraternity commitments, I was going out of town myself (if it was a holiday weekend, for example)—and the status quo was maintained, probably because it seemed mostly reasonable on a case-by-case basis and I had made her come enough. And since she had such a cool disposition and was kind of busy herself (maybe she was involved in a drama club and theater productions? I didn't really care enough to code it to memory at the time), it never seemed like too big a deal. In fact, I figured she probably secretly thanked me for limiting our time together as much as I had then; it made getting to see me seem more special, and girls love things that feel special.

This all changed when she moved into her apartment, and I pretty much knew I was fucked. I didn't really have a compelling reason not to stay over with her, and when at first I wouldn't anyway, she started withholding sex, which was probably harder on her than it was on me—I was the only guy who'd ever made her orgasm through her G-Spot with my dick (and by withholding I mean she'd only have sex with me once whenever we got together instead of twice or three times, making me, like, hang out with her for hours before she'd fuck me and acting slightly bitchy the entire time, until it got really late and she figured I'd have to stay over, at which point she'd finally fuck me; then I would just leave anyway). I had several options. The first option, and what I really wanted to do, was to break up with her and fool another hot girl into thinking she was my girlfriend. There were a few girls I considered—different chicks I had hooked up with that I knew were completely in love with me—but most of them were in the Greek system, which would make it harder to have sex with their sisters or other random sorority girls that knew we were an item. The great thing about Rachel was even the guys in my frat just thought she was a steady fuck buddy and nothing more; this would not happen with a fellow Greek. The other girls were in the art scene and lived too far away, and probably wouldn't be too into the whole me being in a frat thing, anyway. No, Rachel was pretty much it.

The second option: actually staying over. This is what I did, and once I started, we got back into the swing of things. I hated it. Obviously the sex was still great, I mean, really great, and I was happy to come in her what was then six to eight times a week, but the worst was the subsequent pillow talk and all the time I had to spend doing nothing with her. Back in the good ol' days, after I blew a load inside her, soon I'd be practicing the guitar or watching TV, chilling. She never wanted to do anything cool like that— she didn't even own a TV, the weirdo, watching all movies and stuff on her fucking computer—the only fun thing we ever did after sex was more sex. Otherwise, she just wanted me to fucking hold her and talk. Talk talk talk. About nothing. What it was like growing up where we grew up. How we fucking felt about our parents, families. A place I'd like to eventually see in the world. Boring bullshit I guess most people associate with "intimacy" or whatever. That, or she'd just complain about things, like any other "girlfriend" I'd ever had. She'd like to do this for at least an hour, maybe two unless it was really late. I would usually pretend to fall asleep as soon as possible or was reasonable, fifteen to thirty minutes after fucking her if it was after midnight, and if she got annoyed, I'd compliment her on the incredible powers of her soothing voice or some bullshit, and that would make her smile and leave me alone. Then I would be free to think or sleep, which were infinitely more constructive activities. If it was earlier, and I'd know I was in for it, I'd usually just pretend to listen, absently giving her cues to continue to run her mouth while I tried my best to ignore her and think about cool shit—other things I could make the pledges do for me, all the world class ass I'd get on my first South American tour after I found the new Vlad, sports stuff, those kinds of things. It was just another form of multi-tasking, like playing the guitar and singing or reading while taking a shit. Her talking would be the shit in the latter. (Speaking of, once I woke up in the middle of the night and was lying there trying to fall back asleep when she farted and it grossed me out. Sure, I once literally fucked the shit out of a girl and had myself farted in front of lots of girls, including her, but this was different. Nobody had ever farted in front of me like that before. And even though I know she didn't do it on purpose because she was sleeping and all, I still should have never had to have heard or smelled any chick's fart. God, I hated sleeping next to Rachel.)

Then in the mornings, it wasn't much different. We'd just lie around for a while—talking—until I got us up to eat, which we would do without anything cool to watch, or even music to listen to, just over more fucking words. Fuck. Usually I was able to split immediately after, though, never really staying more than forty-five minutes from the time I woke up, that is unless she wanted to fuck again, of course.

This went on throughout the year, with ever-increasing pressure to stay over more often as things got more and more "serious." I guess all the blabbering on she'd do about how much she hated her parents or whatever (who seemed like perfectly decent people that gave her a pretty nice, affluent upbringing, not that it really matters) just made her love me all the more, however the fuck that's supposed to work. It's not like I offered her anything close to that from my end. I'd just nod and say "Wow, that sucks" or something and she thought I really understood her. I mean, I guess I did—there wasn't *that much* to understand—but not in the deep, connective way she thought I did. Her attempts to reach me mostly manifested in just sort of being up in my shit.

I guess because I didn't like to talk about growing up that much with her, she felt the need to try to help me work through my present and future. But there wasn't anything to work through. Aside from the whole bandmate search, my present was pretty great (from fucking so many amazing-looking chicks, but I guess she didn't know about that, so maybe it was a little understandable), and I had nothing but high hopes for my future. She had this obnoxious habit of assigning emotion to information. I'd say "I'm checking out a show tonight, some DJ that's supposed to be good" and she would turn that into something about how much I hated the whole looking for a new Vlad thing (which, yeah, I did, but it would have been useless to fucking talk about that with her, so I never did, never even let on that it bothered me). She would then try to console me, even though I'd tell her there was no need, that Vlad was a fucking half-retarded dickhead, it had all been for the best, I was excited about finding a replacement, and, mostly, there wasn't anything really to say about any of it since everything was fine. As time went on and I became more and more frustrated and disillusioned, and I stopped going out and looking as much (though she didn't know this was why), she then became concerned by my ever-waning involvement with the music scene in general. She knew how good I was, how talented, how much I had to offer, and I explained I was doing things at my own pace, that everything happens for a reason, that I couldn't rush perfection. Part of me thought she just wanted to be a cool rock star girlfriend, but most of me knew it was because I actually was as great as she said I was. So anyhow, I'd try to nip all this talk in the bud whenever it came up, and she'd back off, but then a week or two later she'd bring it all back up again as tactfully as she could, thinking she was sliding one by me, the bitch. When I'd actually get angry with her for repeatedly doing this, she'd respond with all this melodramatic shit like "You have to let me in!" (The more "serious" we got, the more prone to searching out drama she was; it was weird considering how easygoing she was before, but I guess that's just what some bitches in long-term relationships do.) Whatever. I didn't, and I know that also made her love me even more. It became a project, a challenge, and chicks like that more than they ever actually like a guy himself. It kept her on her toes, kept the sex great and aggressively tinged, and that kept me happy.

She told me she loved me a little over a year into our relationship, lying together in bed one morning. I stared at her, not smiling, just contemplative, like it was hitting me, too, all at once, and lied. "I . . ." I nodded, "I . . . love you, too." I smiled like I couldn't believe it, but knew it was there, that both of us had been feeling the same thing. I could tell she was insanely happy. She probably would've married me that day. Then I kissed her and we fucked for the first time as people that "loved" each other. I had never said that before. Hope had said it to me, too, but I knew I wouldn't have to say it back, so I didn't. I knew I had to here, or I'd risk getting cut off. Also, it was a bit more ridiculous for a sixteen- or seventeen-year-old to say they loved someone than a nineteen- or twenty-year-old I guess, for whatever reason. It wasn't that big of a deal, really; it was only a little weird to actually hear the words come out of my mouth that first time. Every time after that, I would enjoy saying it, and would sometimes even do it unprovoked (me saying it first!), laughing hard on the inside because it was just so damn funny.

Anyway, despite her push, I would only stay the minimum three nights a week, get my unprotected pussy-fill, and get out after some tedium and unpleasantness. In the end, it was worth it.

—— Reevaluating ——

I began reevaluating what I wanted to do with the rest of my life halfway through the summer between my sophomore and junior years, after the one-year anniversary marking the end of my tour. The new Vlad hadn't been found yet and, you know, the whole music thing wasn't really going anywhere, so I figured it would be smart to weigh my other options, see where else I might focus some energy. My backup had still been law, so I could eventually get into politics, but by then all of that had started rubbing me the wrong way too. Though much of my first two years in college had been devoted to required core classes, I did come in with a healthy amount of AP credits, so I was able to take some electives as well, dividing them between fun music-related shit like guitar performance and pre-law classes including Business Law, Debate, and The Sociology of Crime and Punishment. Some of these classes were okay—I liked debating because I was always good at arguing and shit, and learning about criminals was interesting since I seemed to have some stuff in common with them psychologically (I think a lot of lawyers have more in common with the bad people they represent than they'd probably care to admit)—but the more dry classes were just fucking awful. I hated legalese with every inch of my being. Sometimes, like with, say, math, you get past the barrier of the language even if it's a little difficult and unnatural and then you have fun with it. After spending enough time poring over legal documents, I realized that wouldn't happen with law. It was just too fucking dry. I mean, I could do it, sure, but it would be like sleeping next to Rachel—I would just hate it and sort of hate myself while doing it for being lame. It didn't deserve my attention and was a waste of time. I couldn't fathom studying this shit for more undergrad classes, let alone three years of reading it every day during law school, or practicing it for, like, ten or fifteen years or whatever before becoming a millionaire, and then continuing on with it God forbid for the rest of my working life if my political career wasn't ever able to gain enough traction. Fuck that.

For a while, I thought about either doing porn or becoming a reality TV personality. I knew neither one would really make me rich, but they seemed like fun ways to earn a good enough living while I was young, and I figured I could somehow parlay both into something that eventually got me rich.

Porn especially made sense, since I loved having sex, was great at it, photogenic enough—particularly while fucking (sometimes I would jerk off to the secret tapes I'd make of myself and whoever I lured into my bed)—and knew I'd be able to fuck vast numbers of chicks, many I'm sure exotic, getting me further along in my Bingo project, all while getting paid. It was almost a no-brainer. But I couldn't get past my pride . . . Being a porn star is just not a job for an alpha. It's not even really a job for a beta or gamma; it's more like one for an epsilon or omega. A guy at the end of his rope resorts to doing porn, a failed soap opera actor or someone who was molested as a kid or whatever and is too much of a fuckup to get a real job (the same generally goes for the ladies), not a cool guy like me. Yeah, there are a handful of cool porn stars I guess, your Johnny Wadds and Evan Stones, but I don't know, there's still always a bit of sadness or comedy to them, since both are a big part of what make up porn at its core. I didn't want people thinking I was in any way tragic or the type of funny you laugh at and not with, even under an assumed name (in the age of the Internet, those were arbitrary anyway). Though I had thought of myself as something of a porn star in high school, when the time came to do it for real, I just couldn't.

Then there was doing a reality show. Acting was third on my list of the best jobs to have and reality TV stars basically do the same thing that actors do without the ridiculous part, so I thought, hey, why not? I wouldn't be playing make believe all day. I would just be me, and I'd be celebrated and paid for it. This made sense. Of course the world would love to hang out with me. Maybe I'd get an endorsement deal or hosting gig or whatever afterwards, something that would make me rich. Guys on shows like

The Real World seemed to get to fuck a lot of hot chicks in whichever city they were in, too; maybe being on a show like *Survivor* would make it difficult to have as much sex still, but I figured hooking up with the hottest castmates wouldn't be so bad for a while in the desert, especially if there was a million buck prize at the end. So I sent out applications to a bunch of shows—*The Real World, Road Rules, Survivor, The Amazing Race*, stuff like that. I got a bite back from *The Real World*, and they even flew me down to Los Angeles for a casting meeting, but in the end nothing came of it. For a while, I was pretty pissed, and I thought all these shows and casting assholes didn't know what they were missing, that I'd instantly double whatever-show-I-was-on's ratings that season either by fucking a lot of chicks or just making really outrageous commentary in video confessionals and interviews, saying fucked up shit about everyone else there or whatnot. I was sure I'd make reality show history. I planned on being like one of the guys from *The Jersey Shore* years before that existed. Soon enough, though, I understood I had been ignored for a reason, that it was all a part of God's plan—all for the best.

See, later that summer, it became clear to me that fame wasn't all it was cracked up to be. It was a form of power, it led to respect and maybe money, and could get you laid, but fame is really only good or important within whatever limited circle you happen to be in, where you are also, in a way, feared. It was nice when I was a prep to be a famous prep. It was nice to be famous within my frat and kind of famous within the Greek system. Being a celebrity and dealing with the general public, though, is actually pretty shitty, mostly because nobody really fears you like they would if they regularly had to see or deal with you.

I was walking to the bus from a DJ's show in the Central District with Rachel one night (he sucked, hardly a Vlad) and we were passing this group of three Asian guys on the sidewalk when one of them, early twenties, small and darker for an Asian—if I had to guess, I'd say Vietnamese—with a stupid-looking Fu Manchu-ish goatee, stopped us. He goes, "Hey, aren't you the guy from 'Parker?'"

This hadn't ever happened to me before, being recognized on the street like that. I hadn't played in over a month at that point, and had only had like two gigs in the past three or four months, before everything more or less fizzled out, so it was even weirder. I thought this guy must be a real fan. I even momentarily forgave him for being in his twenties and wearing a goatee. I glanced over at Rachel and she was smiling. They were probably all really impressed by how hot she was, especially smiling big like that. She had great teeth and lips. "Yeah, I am Parker."

"I saw you a month or two back at some bar."

"Cool." I smiled.

"Yeah, your band really sucked, man!" What a Seattle thing to say . . . then the ugly gremlin high-fived one of his stupid friends.

"Fuck you, you fobby fuck. Why don't you and your faggy little friends go eat a dog or have a circle jerk around a bowl of pho." Sometimes I'm inspired like that. He parroted back the end of what I said to him in a high, annoying voice like a child would, trying to mock me or something, even though my voice was way deeper and cooler than his, and then they all rushed—practically running—by me and Rachel like a bunch of pussies, laughing. I yelled out "Blog about it bitch!" as they continued to scuttle away, and they didn't say anything back because they knew I could've beaten the shit out of them and put them in the hospital since they were tiny and Asian and I doubt knew karate—though even if they did, I still would've annihilated them. I really should've kicked all their asses. Rachel was all like, "Well that was weird, assholes," and we didn't mention it again, just went on our way having a good night. Frankly, I forgot about it. But then, back at her place, something strange happened . . . she wouldn't fuck me.

Granted, it was kind of late when we got back, after 2 a.m., but that had never stopped us before. She loved our sex as much as I did. In fact, earlier that night, at the show, because the guy sucked and we were sort of bored, she was pretty much all over me, kissing me, had even grabbed my dick real quick over my jeans. This wasn't uncommon while we were out in a dark place and usually preceded a night of raucous fucking, sometimes starting in a bathroom wherever we were, but always ending at home. By then, I had stayed at her place around three nights a week for almost a year, and this was the only time I was ever completely denied. She wouldn't even give me a blowjob, which she'd always at least do if she suckered me over and was on her period. I didn't know what to do. I wanted to leave, but knew we would just end up in a big fight and she might not fuck me for a week or something like that, which would probably make me break up with her, and then I'd have to start the whole "girlfriend" process over again. So I actually just stayed, just stayed over and fucking slept without having any sex. God, it was awful. But before I fell asleep, doing like I do, I made the best of it, took it as a sign of something important, knew it was time for a little introspection.

I laid there and thought about Rachel, about what she thought she was doing, and wondered how something as terrible as this could happen to me—and it didn't take long to realize it was all because of that little gook shithead and his asshole friends. They disrespected me, and of course I disrespected them right back, but the damage had already been done. Had something like "Hey man, that was a great show!" come out of his ridiculous, stringy-hair-lined and canine-and-cum-pho-encrusted mouth instead, I was sure I'd be seven minutes into the wheelbarrow right then, punching Rachel's uterus with my dick, not lying on my back with a prostrate full of backed up semen and her sleeping soundly beside me, the bitch. While yes, it's good to have a fair amount of haters, it's not good to have them on the street, where their anonymity can let them slip away without serious repercussions if they slight you, and this made me realize that fame, on its own, without fear, actually totally fucking sucks.

Fame had kept me from getting laid that night. Fame would make it so other people would bother me, follow me around with cameras, be all up in my shit, keep me from doing what I wanted to do when I wanted to do it. Fame could even potentially kill me. It killed a lot of people: John Lennon, Princess Diana, Selena. Some pussies overdosed on drugs or killed *themselves* because of it. Tupac, who was a really fucking cool guy, got killed by it. In his song *How Do U Want It*, one of the things he rapped about was just wanting money and not giving a shit about fame, and that really got me thinking. Doing reality TV would have made me more famous than rich, and that would have been awful. Even with music, I'd probably be famous for a couple of years before my wealth caught up with it. I resolved then to be as rich and un-famous as possible.

Money means power means sex. Fame means maybe power and sex or maybe disrespect and no sex and maybe death. A time would come when my persona and ability to talk to chicks well wouldn't be enough—not when I was thirty or whatever and still trying to fuck girls in their late teens and early twenties. And also, for my own sake, for pride, I wanted a great job meant only for the elite. All I needed for the rest of my life to keep fucking beautiful girls and feel awesome about myself was money and an amazing, respectable job to provide it.

I decided then, lying next to my fickle bitch of a "girl-friend," who by not fucking me had just done me the favor of a lifetime, that, about to begin my junior year, I would change my major to finance. While every moment described in this has brought me to where I am today, this was the real turning point that led to my career as an invest-ment banker.

______ Second Anniversary with ______
First College "Girlfriend"

Rachel broke up with me three months into our junior year, on what was our "second anniversary." This is because she caught me—actually walked in on me—fucking another girl. It was okay because the other girl became my new girl-friend almost instantly after that.

I met this girl, Jasmine, in one of my finance classes a few weeks earlier. She was really, really fucking hot—half Afghani, part Persian, and a mix of Eastern European nationalities making up the rest; she mostly appeared dark and sultry, but also had some striking lighter features, including bright green eyes like that famous chick on the cover of *National Geographic*. She was short, but had big, nicely-shaped tits, against thin arms, and on top of all that, she also had amazing, luscious, dick-sucking lips, which I later learned she knew how to use to full effect. I'd also learn she'd let me do anal. So there she was, a quadruple threat, all my favorite types of girls in one. And, what's more, personality-wise, she reminded me a lot of me. She was the alpha among the female finance majors. She was smart (for a chick), kind of funny (for a chick), and assertive (for a chick, which is usually just *so cute*, but she actually didn't come off as silly or dykey at all, just direct; it was refreshing since girls are normally so indecisive and flighty). She went about life with an air of quiet authority—like me—doing what she had to do and only drawing attention to herself and her excellence when necessary for personal gain. It was great because it was basically like hanging out with myself, and I fucking love myself.

We had been fucking since the week we met. Her libido was as voracious as mine, too, and we'd often have sex three or four times when we saw each other, every fuck unique, the combinations of positions always fresh and exciting. The only thing that kept it from being perfect was wearing a condom, and I actually had been considering either taking her on as a second girlfriend or breaking up with Rachel.

Our sessions were held now and again at her apartment off campus, but mostly at my fraternity house, where I still lived. She was even cooler about me being in a frat than Rachel, thinking it was really smart to be in the one I was in for all its connections. I had one of the few single rooms, which was great, a domain now entirely mine. This was the last year it was socially acceptable for me to live in the frat, and I did so because of the easier access to pussy. I didn't really care that it probably docked me ten cool points or whatever to live there as a junior; by continuing to fuck the hottest girls in the Greek system and school, I more than made up for it, earning at least one hundred cool points. Rachel had only come by a handful of times since she got her place off campus the previous year, after her bedroom replaced mine as our center of operations, so I'd been living a completely unrestrained existence there, which kept getting better and better. I was the social chair now, a pretty fucking amazing office, not that I needed it, my reputation as a good lay still spreading across campus and, most importantly, trickling down to the new freshman class. (This was also around the time Facebook started to get really popular, so that made things even easier. In high school, I didn't talk to too many girls on the Internet or anything since it was limited to the whole instant messaging thing— ICQ, AIM, that kind of shit—which was nerdy and time-consuming; also, my lack of a web presence made me even cooler and more mysterious in real life, and that made chicks want to fuck me more. Facebook was different, though, because it was quick to use and mostly about narcissism, which is attractive, so I knew I could flip it to get me laid without much effort. Tons of random girls that had heard about me would "friend" me, and I would invite the really hot ones over to the house and fuck them; then after a grace period of a couple of weeks I would usually unfriend them—just to mess with them a little, make them fall in love with me even more, for fun. This was incredibly instrumental in my Pussy Bingo project, and through it, I was able to fuck some Asian types that had been eluding me: Taiwanese, Vietnamese; half Chinese, half Japanese. I kind of went on an Asian kick for a while. The only downside to Facebook was that Rachel wanted to make us "in a relationship" with each other. I told her it was unnecessary and stupid, and that Facebook didn't matter in the scope of "our love." She bought that, but would still get a little pissed when she saw how many girls would become my friend and write on my wall or whatever, flirting, but I didn't care.)

I was as busy as I wanted to be. At the time, my room was a revolving door for the best pointless pussy at U-Dub. That, and the place where I'd spend a whole afternoon or evening, or both, fucking Jasmine, whose pussy I guess wasn't all that pointless.

It was during one of these afternoon sessions that Rachel walked in on us. There was loud music playing, either Kanye West or The Ying Yang Twins I believe. Blaring my music was standard practice whenever I fucked someone to keep my less successful fraternity brothers from jerking off to the sounds we'd make. I knew some did still, and while kind of flattering, it was also a little weird to have a live audience of sorts, dudes touching themselves. I think we were in our second or third round, and I was kneeling on the bed fucking her sideways in a variation of the Fire Hydrant. We were facing the door when Rachel walked in, and I'm pretty sure she made eye contact with both of us.

She was carrying a guitar case. It had a bow on it. She dropped it and screamed.

"Shit!" I said. I stopped fucking Jasmine, who fell to the bed and just sort of laughed.

"What the fuck?!?" shrieked Rachel, her eyes bulging out of her head.

"Hi, I'm Jasmine." She wrapped a sheet around her body. Grace under fire—what a girl. "Would you mind closing the door?"

Rachel shut off the music. "On our fucking anniversary, Frank? Our fucking anniversary, fucker?" I didn't know what that specifically had to do with anything (I of course forgot our previous anniversary), but understood why she was pissed. I mean, she caught me at my best, which she thought was all hers, with someone else. She rushed over and started hitting me—thrashing, punching, scratching. I held her arms together, restraining her.

"Stop!" I shouted.

Jasmine hopped out of the bed and grabbed her clothes off the floor. "I guess I'll get it on my way out."

Rachel turned. "Fuck you, bitch!" Jasmine was out the door, which she then shut. Rachel was digging her nails into my wrists so I'd let her go. It hurt and I did. There were red scratch marks leading up to my forearms, some skin broken. "I hate you! I hate you! I can't believe—" she started bawling. "Who was she?"

I was still naked, except for the condom I had been wearing. "What do you want me to say? Does it matter?"

"You're right. Fucking nothing matters. I—" her speech was broken by a sob. "I love you. No, I loved you. I loved you so much. I can't believe you could do that to me, to us." I just looked at her. I didn't apologize. I pulled the condom off and found my boxer-briefs. I put them on. "How long has this been going on?"

I sat back down on my bed, leaning against the wall. "That won't help you."

"I don't care about it helping me! I fucking deserve to know!" she yelled. I was glad this was happening in the middle of the day, since I figured most of the guys in the house would be in class or otherwise preoccupied, but I knew not all of them were, like the ones who had been trying to beat off to me and Jasmine. I was sure there was now a little crowd gathering outside in the hallway. (Everyone in the frat eventually did find out about it. That sucked, but in the end a lot of people thought it was kind of funny, too.)

"It won't change anything. It doesn't matter."

"It matters to me. It fucking matters."

"No."

She screamed.

"Stop," I said.

"Fucking tell me! Or I'll scream again!" She rushed over and tried hitting me. I hadn't ever seen this side of Rachel before. Even though she started being more of a pain in the ass after our "relationship" got more "serious," her demeanor had stayed pretty cool for the most part; her voice, normally so lush and mellow, was now high-pitched and screechy. We'd had some fights, sure, little spats over me leaving too early or what movie to watch or her bitching about me "not letting her in" or whatever, but never a blowout like this, nothing ever got physical. It was pretty gratifying to see how devastated she was; aside from that, though, I wasn't really a fan of the full-on tantrum, as if she were a two-year-old. She wasn't dealing with it like the mature, clear-headed adult I knew she was. Jasmine wouldn't have acted like this. I knew she had some emotional prob-lems from all the complaining she'd do about her parents and everything, but this was ridiculous—love, passion, our anniversary, all things considered, it wasn't appropriate to squeal at the top of her lungs, attack me, and make a scene like this. As I held her I noticed the claw marks, still red on my wrists. They could possibly even leave scars where the skin broke, I thought. That bitch. I decided to take control of the situation, to dominate. I'd tell her what she wanted to know, not to appease her, but to hurt her. She was em-barrassing me and had left marks on my skin. Fuck that. I was going to enjoy every little twitch, every flicker of pain across her stupid fucking face.

"Fine, I'll tell you. But sit the fuck down. And don't try to hit me again. Bad things will happen." I let go. She sat at the foot of the bed, twisting toward me. "It's been going on for a little over two weeks."

She nodded. "Thank you. Is she the only one?"

"No," I said. She shut her eyes tightly and swallowed. She was in actual physical pain. It was great.

"How many others?"

"I don't know."

"What do you mean 'you don't know?' " She parroted me, but gave my voice and its depth the gravitas and an im-pression it deserved. I appreciated that. She was shaking, furious.

"Lost count."

"Lost count?"

"Lost count."

"How long has this been going on with other people?"

I had been staring directly into her eyes the entire time, not wavering, not even for half a second. I wanted her to know I had nothing to fear or hide. I wanted her to know what she had gotten into with me and exactly what it all had meant to me: nothing. Maybe it was a bit much, but my need for retaliation aside, I also simply found her pain interesting, like when I broke up with pizza-faced Virginia in the seventh grade except 10,000 times worse since this girl was actually, really, truly, in a mature and adult way, in love with me. "Since I've known you."

"What?"

"You heard me."

"Why are you being so mean?" She was crying again. She fell on my bed in the fetal position, sobbing. She was more sad than angry now; it made me happy.

"I'm not being mean. I'm answering the questions you're asking, honestly. I know this can't be easy but I'm trying to keep it from being any harder than it has to be. Maybe you should just go. I told you it wouldn't help."

She continued lying there, crying louder and louder, but all I heard was this gorgeous little symphony. She wiped her nose and sat up. "God . . . I can't believe this. The thought of you ever being inside me right now is making me want to throw up. Fuck, I'm gonna have to get tested."

"Please don't insult me."

"I'm not insulting you. I'm serious."

"I only had unprotected sex with you."

"Ha, great for me. Asshole."

I tilted my head. "I said don't insult me."

"I'll fucking say all I want. You deserve a hell of a lot more." She was wiping tears from her face, her mascara running.

"No, I don't."

She cried for a while again, then asked, with genuine curiosity but also faux-condescension (for pride's sake), "Why am I the only one you had unprotected sex with?"

I waited a moment. "I needed someone. You were it. I would've missed it too much."

She broke out in more sobs, wailing kind of. "I don't even know who the hell you are right now! God, I can't believe this. Our fucking anniversary!" She then screamed again, just a scream on its own. At this point, I knew the damage was done, I had been adequately embarrassed in the house already. So I enjoyed it. I enjoyed the scream for the heartache it conveyed, and in addition to this, found in it something arousing. "So freshman year, that guy, that one guy who asked if I had any self-respect and if you gave me gonorrhea, he was trying to do me a favor after all. He wasn't a weirdo."

"If that's how you want to look at it. That guy was a dick. Look, I still really enjoyed and valued our time together. Most of it, anyway. And, again, I only had unprotected sex with you."

"So it was all about sex?"

"Yes."

"Everything else? Everything we've been through for the past two years?"

"Means to an end. I think it was mostly about sex for you, too, though. Be honest with yourself."

She choked on her sobs. It was hilarious. "Why did you ever tell me you loved me?"

"Come on, Rachel." I was just cocking the gun. I would still pull the trigger.

"No, what the hell was that? You don't do this to people you love."

"I lied to you. Obviously." Bang.

She cried quietly this time, lying down again. An entire minute or two passed. "Why?"

"Huh?"

"Why did you ever tell me that?"

"So you wouldn't break up with me. So I could have unprotected sex with you. I needed someone to have unprotected sex with, I told you already."

She got up. Her eyes were frenzied, her face red. "You're sick! You're sick! You're a fucking sociopath! I hope you fucking die in your sleep tonight!" She was spitting with each word. It was gross but sort of hot.

I just kept cool, leaning against the wall. "Don't be so melodramatic. You should feel honored."

She shook her head, eyes still bulging, and started leaning forward like she wanted to pounce, like she wanted to choke me. I just lowered my head and raised my eyebrows, letting her know not to even fucking think about it. She got it. Instead, she sprang toward the guitar case, opened it with a sharp pull, and started smashing the guitar, which was really nice, against the floor. For a minute I wished she had given it to me before she found me out. "How's this for melodramatic you fucking prick?" she asked between smashes. I just let her do her thing. It eventually broke at the neck.

"Are you gonna pay to fix my floor?"

She just stood there, staring at me, holding it at the neck while the body dangled like a dead goose or something. She laughed. "This stupid fucking frat's rich enough to cover it, right? You guys can pay for more than friends. Fucking douchebag."

"Look, if you think any twenty-year-old guy is capable of love, you're fooling yourself. Guys aren't in love at this age. They just get pussy-whipped, nothing more. They don't have a sense of themselves as men. So they trick themselves into thinking they're in love to justify why they'd let one girl own them. Wait for a guy in his thirties who's ready to spread his seed, put a bun in your oven, that guy might actually love you."

She dropped the guitar. "I think I'm gonna throw up." She went over to my wastebasket in the corner and pretended to dry heave over it, the silly bitch.

"Let me know when you're done."

Still crouching down, she turned back toward me and said, "You smug piece of shit. Fuck you. You're gonna rot in hell for this."

"I don't believe in hell. Neither do you, if I remember right. I still listened to you, you know." She looked at me in this very sad way, like she was remembering something good about me, like I really had cared about her after all. Nope. "Half the time."

She slowly moved to lie down on the floor, sobbing quietly. It was great. She looked like she wanted to die. I had done my job and it was fantastic. Nobody almost gives me a scar but me (thankfully, the marks faded completely in a couple of weeks). "Who the hell are you? Oh my God . . ." she whispered eventually.

I wondered if she'd go for a farewell fuck. I got off the bed and went over to her. "Come on, Rache." I touched her shoulder.

"Don't fucking touch me!" she said, jerking. She sat up. "Is it because you never knew your father?"

I laughed. "Huh?" That seemed like a really funny question to me.

"You never learned how to be a real man." Oh, whatthefuckever; like she was depending on me to feed her and our small children in the fucking Dust Bowl or something. And always with the fucking parents. What's with the fucking parents? Her and Ms. Adams. Fuckin' A, ladies. Get over it.

"I think you know what a real man I am." I moved in to try to kiss the side of her neck, her favorite spot. She grabbed my face, squishing my cheeks hard, and pushed it away. "No farewell fuck then I guess?" I smiled. She shook her head in disbelief, called me "a monster," sprang up, slapped me, and then got out of the room as fast as humanly possible, slamming the door loudly behind her. I shouted "Crazy cunt!" as she left, booming, louder than anything she had screamed, since I had nothing left to lose at that point, but still more pride and respect to gain. I wasn't going to let her completely get away with hitting me again after I told her not to and I also wanted her to remember me getting the last and loudest word. And that was the last time we ever spoke.

———— Second College "Girlfriend" ————

I fucked Jasmine without a condom about a week after that. We had the exclusivity talk; she thought she was my "girlfriend." She got a big kick out of having been "the other woman" or whatever for a time, but you know, thought we were a good match and should get together, and seemed happy that the incident with Rachel had happened so we could figure everything out. She also thought the scene itself was really, really funny, and that only included the part she was there for. When I described the rest of it, with the lying on the floor and breaking the guitar and pretending to have to throw up (naturally I omitted the part about me cheating on her with people other than herself for two years), she laughed to the point of tears and asked me to stop telling the story so she could breathe. Moving forward, she said she trusted me and knew I would have no reason to fuck anyone else because of how great our sex was. In theory, she was correct—she, like me, and to me, was sex personified—but I of course still fucked as many other hot girls as possible. That year I filled out even more of my Pussy Bingo: fucking a Palestinian chick, an Israeli chick, and a set of twins (not at the same time, unfortunately; that happened a couple of years later, though), among others. It's not "Why have hamburger when you can have steak?" It's "I'll have the filet mignon, rib eye, t-bone, and fuck it, throw a couple of burgers in there too, I guess." Alphas need variety.

At any rate, Jasmine got it. She said the one flaw in the sex we'd been having was the condoms; it always hurt a little, at first, and she frankly couldn't wait to stop using them, but otherwise it was "the best dick she'd ever had." She liked me well enough as a person or whatever too, but I think she knew off the bat that relationships at our age were mostly about sex. It's basic. She got that people of different genders come together first and foremost to fuck ("that's why guys and girls fit together so nicely"), not to hang out and talk and shit ("that's what real friends are for"). We weren't old and lame and interested in companionship; that's only functional at a certain age for child rearing or to make sure you don't die alone. Dating was fucking.

I kept in touch some with Dennis—sending emails every now and then—and he'd describe a lot of the girls at whatever fancy East Coast school he was going to as thinking in the same way. Since they were also Type A's with hectic schedules and stressful lives, guys were mostly sex objects: "It's like they pull their clits out five inches and try to fuck you with them," he once wrote. A little gay, but I got it. Jasmine would have probably done that if she could. After we started raw doggin' it, we'd have sex four to five times on the days we saw each other, and miraculously, she never got UTIs or anything. "This dick makes the old dick seem like bad dick," she said about two weeks in. She could have been a poet if she didn't want to work in mergers and acquisitions.

We never went out anywhere. We never stayed the night with each other. We never had to have forced fucking conversation over fucking breakfast, once. Basically, we would just get together, say "Hey, what's new?" and after we'd both take turns replying, usually with something short and sweet like "Not much" or "Same shit, different day," we'd fuck. Then, maybe after fucking, we might lie around, tell a few jokes or admire each other's amazing bodies, watch a good or funny TV show or movie that I'd pick out (she had pretty much the same taste in shit as me, and she would actually just sit and watch; it wouldn't be the soundtrack to her complaining or trying to have a conversation about nothing) . . . and then we'd fuck again. Or she'd come over before a class, we'd fuck, then I'd go over to her place after I was done with my classes, and we'd fuck a few more times. We pretty much always fucked a couple of times before or after the class we had together, sometimes both. We just fucked and fucked and fucked. It was phenomenal.

Once, in a twenty-four hour period, we had sex eleven times. On another occasion, she even wanted to have more sex than I did—seven times one five-hour afternoon-evening stretch (I was completely tapped out, couldn't have come if I tried; in fact, by the sixth time, I could barely stay hard, which blew my mind). I think if I believed in soulmates or anything ridiculous like that, she would have been it.

This is why she eventually made me angrier than I had ever been. This is why I actually wanted to kill her, the cunt.

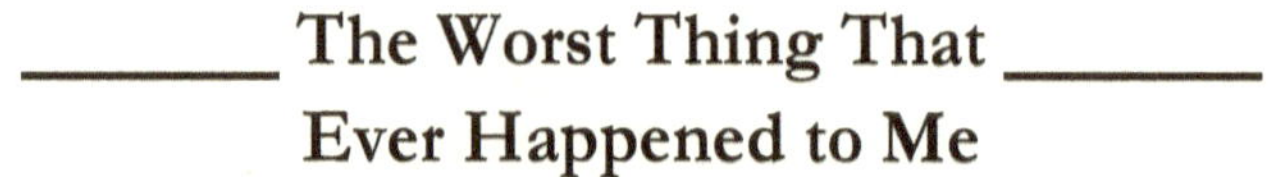

The Worst Thing That Ever Happened to Me

We were three-and-a-half months or so into our "relationship," and spring quarter had just begun. Everything was going great—she kept me happy; the other girls I'd fuck kept me happy; I was happy with my decision to study finance, all those courses were going well and a promising summer internship was on the horizon at a frat alum's hedge fund; I never really thought about Vlad and that made me happy; everyone in the house either loved or kind of feared me and that made me happy; it had recently been my birthday and on it she got me *The Kama Sutra* so we could get through it together, and on that day we made a pretty fucking decent dent in it and that made me really, really happy; it was basically the best time of my life.

Then she had to go and fuck it all up.

She cheated on me! Then fucking went and told me about it! I couldn't believe it! Somebody actually fucking cheated on me! And then fucking admitted to it?!?! (It occurred to me that, say, during high school when I had fuck buddies that knew they were just "seeing" me or whatever that, yeah, maybe once—and that's a big maybe—maybe someone might have made out with someone else or something, like at a party or out of town or whatever, and even this was doubtful considering how much they all loved me and what a good kisser I was and how most of them were all just sort of waiting for me to make them my girlfriend, but even if something only maybe happened once, none of them would have ever dreamed of taking it so far as to fuck someone else or admit any kind of infidelity to me, however loose our arrangement.)

Obviously, yeah, I cheated on her a few times a week, but I was the man and I was an alpha. It was natural. The alpha spreads his seed; any female is lucky to have been chosen by him and remains undyingly faithful. So for her to fucking cheat on me . . . and then be fucking dumb or mean-spirited enough to fucking tell me about it . . . especially, like, not that long after my birthday (even though I don't care about really *celebrating* my birthday in general, it's still *my fucking birthday*) . . . the amount of disrespect . . . I literally began plotting her murder. If we'd been back in the caveman days, I would have banished her from my cave, made her wander and soon die in the desert, alone and with dirt in her hair. The swift death I initially imagined giving her (baseball bat) seemed generous, too good by comparison. I thought maybe I could figure out a way to stick her with a needle full of AIDS blood or give her a horrible form of cancer somehow, make her die slowly and painfully. I wanted to travel back in time and punch her pregnant mother in the stomach, fuck her up so she would have spent her entire life deformed and miserable. I was that angry. I was 100,000 times angrier than when I was fucked up on roids and beating on those coaches, really the angriest I thought was possible for any living creature to be. She actually fucking cheated on me and told me about it! I still can't really believe that shit!

I won't provide the whole lengthy account of her telling me; I've tried to keep her role in this as brief as possible because she is a cunt. I will offer some broad strokes and a little backstory, though, since it's probably really hard for you to understand why anyone would ever cheat on someone like me. I'll also add, in finer detail, the part where I get her back . . . because fuck her.

It happened during spring break. She spent it in New York, cold and miserable Marchtime New York, going to parties and dinners with some finance connections she had, people she knew through a relative in the oil industry or something, trying to network. She wanted a Wall Street job because that's where all the money is, and since we went to a state school, and one way across the fucking country, they were nearly impossible for us to get. This was a smart way to spend a spring break; I supported her in it. This is mainly because I also wanted to move to New York after graduating for the very same reasons and I too wanted to utilize her connections. With our sex being as fantastic as it was, we figured we would carry our "relationship" over there after college if everything was still going well, not that we would fucking live together or anything; we'd just continue to have each other around as we started our lives there. This wasn't arrived to as a big, emotional commitment decision—it just seemed like a good business plan. If we were both busy starting demanding finance jobs, we'd hardly have the time to go out and find other people who were as great lays—not that there's anyone quite as good as me—to make our "significant others" and have unprotected sex with. So, she was in New York with my complete blessing. (I myself didn't go anywhere that year, or any year before for that matter. I didn't have career networking opportunities that would require it and I wasn't interested in the whole get-drunk-for-a-week-by-the-ocean thing. Every week was kind of like spring break for me. I mean, I got as much pussy, so there was never the need to go anywhere. Also, the type of pussy you could get would mostly just be more hot white girls. I could and did fuck them at home. It didn't require getting on a plane. If I did get on one, I'd have to be fucking Moroccans or Laotians, not more white American girls. The time spent getting to and from some beach in Mexico or fucking Florida or whatever was time I could've been fucking. I knew I wasn't missing out on anything.)

Anyhow, she met a guy from, like, Morgan Stanley; he said he could pull some strings, maybe get her a summer internship; she went back to his place, blah, blah, blah, fucked him, blah, blah, blah, but it was for her career and maybe mine too, blah, blah, blah, I should understand, blah, blah, blah, it wasn't any good and meant nothing, blah, blah, blah, and she only told me because she cared so much about me, blah, blah, blah, bullshit. It didn't matter. It couldn't be justified. It is black and white. I don't care if it was smart or meaningless or even slightly in my interests. Nobody fucking cheats on Frank Fuckin' Parker. Nobody.

Obviously I'm glad she told me. That was something I would want to know. However, I don't really see why she did. She could've gone on fucking me and getting off on my incredible dick, and I would've been none the wiser. She was enough like me to know that it wouldn't be con-structive in terms of us. I'm pretty sure it was just to see the look on my face. It's what I would've done, what I have done—all that other shit about caring about me or what-ever was probably only padding so I wouldn't hit her or something. I know I probably looked like I wanted to. Of course I didn't, just stood there and imagined killing her. Then I let her know I'd been cheating on her since we were "together."

She thought I was joking at first. I didn't smile or look defensive. "Come on," she said. "You're just upset."

"Not really. I don't care that much. I mean, obviously you and me are through, but I'm not hurt."

She knew I wasn't joking then. She flinched. Now she couldn't believe someone could actually cheat on *her*. She regained composure. "Where did you find the time?"

"We go to a state school. I have tons of free time."

She smiled. "I guess it makes sense. I was the other woman for a while, too."

I shrugged. "There hasn't been an 'other woman.' " I made air quotes. Eighteen to twenty-two-year-old girls are not women; even though when I looked at her I now saw a horrible fucking bitch, she was still not a woman, thank God. "Just countless girls."

"Countless?" she laughed.

"Countless." I smiled. She could tell I was dead serious.

"Countless . . . I see." I smirked. She swallowed, smiled, and said, "Well then."

"Bye," I said.

She stared at me. We were in my room. She was sitting at the foot of the bed, basically the same place Rachel had sat. "Isn't this a bit of a double standard? I'm willing to work through this if you are. Let's just start over."

"Of course it's a double standard, but it doesn't matter. You don't do that to a guy like me. We're done." I made sure I didn't say "cheat," not only because the phrase "cheat on me" should never come out of an alpha's mouth, ever, but also to make damn fucking well sure nobody outside of my room would know what had happened. (Nobody ever did find out. I told the guys in the frat I stopped hanging out with her because I got tired of her. My God, that would have been awful.)

She smiled. "A guy like you?"

"I don't know why you're smiling. Even if I did cheat on you the whole time, even if you're thinking, 'What, a guy that's a huge fucking hypocrite?'—do you have any idea how lucky you still were?"

She laughed. "To be in a relationship with a guy like you?"

"Absofuckinlutely."

She thought about it for a minute. She probably remembered how great I was at kissing and fucking and appreciated how fun and amazing I was as a person. She got it. "I guess you're right. Farewell fuck?" I didn't say anything back. I just ripped her clothes off and fucked her. Sex was an appropriate way to end our time together and to celebrate its spirit, despite the fact that I had just been royally fucked over by her. But soon after I started, I realized that a celebration wasn't really called for and that she should be royally fucked over by me, too. I began fucking her in positions that were more for me than her, then just ones I knew she didn't really like at all, then I went kind of crazy, all-out—I only got myself to come after over an hour, after pulling her hair and nipples harder than ever before, after choking her past erotica to alarm, after biting her so hard I drew blood, after fucking her tight little ass as hard and fast and deep and brutally as I could (without lube, when I was normally so careful and poised; graceful, even), after I could see tears stream down her face, after I was sure I made her feel like the fucked up, hopeless little whore she really was. That did the trick. She complained a little but never once actually tried to stop me, most likely because she knew she couldn't, that in those moments I wouldn't have *let* her leave, physically, but also probably because she knew she fucking deserved it.

———— Emergency Room ————

That night, to punish myself for Jasmine cheating on me, I choked myself while jerking off without lube. I used my bare hands alone in both tasks, thinking I didn't really deserve a makeshift noose, and that the entire experience should involve me and only me. I did both very intensely and with abandon—rubbing my dick so raw I was bleeding within a matter of minutes and only accepting air (and very small amounts) at intervals between thirty seconds and a full minute. I suppose the blood from my dick could have maybe counted as lube once there was enough, but it wasn't very good.

I had been at it for about a half-hour when, the next thing I knew, I was magically in the campus emergency room. I had apparently passed out. Someone had discovered me in my room, which I had left unlocked to completely own that "with abandon" angle, and since I was found whenever I was found covered in a decent amount of blood and in a pretty horrific way, a decision to get me to a hospital as soon as possible was made, and quickly. I stayed knocked out through the ride, a ride I'm positive wasn't in an ambulance because of the repercussions that would have had on our organization, and still don't really know who found or took me. The only time anything about it was ever mentioned to me was when my frat's then president, this beta minus Walker, came to my room a few days later, shut the door, and said simply, "About the other night—a lot of weird shit goes on behind closed doors in this house, but you can't do that here." He was right, and the whole thing was very hush-hush—though everybody in the frat loved and respected me so much, it probably wouldn't have mattered if they all found out about it. Maybe he was concerned I would start a trend, that a lot of other guys would've soon been discovered knocked out and with bloody dicks, rich kids being into weird fucked up experiences like that and all of them thinking I was so fucking cool. Anyway, not long after I woke up, I was released by the doctor with a "Be careful, kid." A hefty hospital bill came a few weeks afterwards. I never paid it, though. (Since it was a university hospital, the school eventually tried to keep me from registering for classes until they got their money, but I was able to argue successfully that I had been taken there against my will and also that I never received the first bill or any of their follow-ups because of a glitch in mail delivery, me living in a large-enough fraternity house, where it's easy for things to fall through the cracks, etc., etc. They wanted me to pay when I could but I never did and still graduated, the fucking idiots.)

So, yeah, it was a pretty shitty thing to do to myself, all things considered. I thought for a while in the week afterwards and decided I wouldn't do these punishments anymore. I was twenty-one, a full-grown man . . . I didn't need my fucked up version of parenting now. And even though this incident was the straw that broke the camel's back, the wakeup call I needed to realize myself as a man—a person that was above needing discipline in any form, a person that should never choke himself to the point of near death and wake up with bloody open sores all over his dick—I still feel that the time I stopped jerking off for a month was a whole lot fucking worse.

——— Post-Trauma Sex Life ———

I pretty much only had abusive and psychologically damaging sex for the rest of college. After Jasmine did what she did to me and what I then did to myself because of it, I hated girls, more than ever, and wanted to punish the very idea of them. Before, I was just selfish and inconsiderate, really only hurting their feelings and pride, incidentally; now, I'd actually put forth effort to fuck them up. Worse than in high school when I had a hard time getting off without anal, now I could only get off by directly causing pain, humiliation, and degradation. I had less sex, but it was better (even though everything was protected; during this time, my deviant mental and spiritual satisfaction far outweighed physical sensation—it was definitely mind over matter). While I was fucking less, I was still doing it often enough, and I'd just jerk off the rest of the time to make up for sex lost. I was still the best at making me come.

At first I'd try things—the Fishhook, Fish Eye, Rear Admiral, Snowmobile—with the sorority girls and dormers that normally came around. Often it wouldn't work and they would leave once I got too rough or whatever, but then I could just think about skullfucking Jasmine and easily finish the job myself. I was happy to do that, except for the clean up part, since I'd always end up coming really hard everywhere, and the fact that I was still a man on a mission. So, soon I developed kind of a litmus test. Basically, if a girl would still fuck me after I called her a slut to her face within the first two or so minutes of meeting her, I knew I could probably get away with something. And I did. The Golden Shower, Hot Lunch, Mudslide, Houdini, Surprise from Santa, Woody Woodpecker, Bullwinkle, Beetleclip, Ram, Flying Camel, Alligator Fuckhouse, Dolphin, Free Willy, Angry Dragon, Angry Pirate, Abe Lincoln, Bismarck, Chilli Dog, Purple Mushroom, Dirty Sanchez, Fire in the Hole, Rusty Trombone, and Donkey Punch, as well as a bunch of other horrible things I came up with on my own, were all executed on the burgeoning Ms. Adamses in this time, the filthy, stupid, self-hating cunts (some, like Ms. Adams, actually got off on it; a few of them even more than her, but most didn't). A number of them were U-Dub students, but the majority were just random girls I'd pick up at bars from other schools or Seattle natives; that city does have a lot of crazies. It was better to do this sort of shit as anonymously as possible, though I still did nearly all of it in my room, that giving me more control over the situation. The best part is they were all still attractive: I never once had to settle for an only okay-looking chick, since pretty girls in their early twenties are among those that hate themselves the most and are most insecure. The ensuing embarrassment was usually enough for them not to say anything to anyone, however evil the thing I did to them was. Nothing ever spread around or affected my reputation; any whispered rumors about me were just denied, denied, denied. There weren't ever any real repercussions. That is, for me. I'm sure a girl or twelve could've used some therapy after I got through with them.

I kind of suspended my Pussy Bingo project while all this was going on, this turning into its own undertaking, though I was delighted when I could kill two birds with one stone, i.e. a Lebanese girl that let me get away with giving her the Dog in the Bathtub or an Iraqi who'd perform the Blumpkin or something. I became partial to Middle-Easterners (all super hot, none hairy) in the course of all this, to some extent because of the news coverage of the wars we were having then, but mainly because that's what Jasmine was for the most part, and I equated this with how well she moved while fucking, what with belly dancing and all. I'd snap out of it after college, after moving away, leaving all the fucking baggage of getting cheated on behind me, and was able to come from regular, natural, normal enough sex again, but we'll get to why in a little bit.

———— College Job ————

I moved out of the frat house senior year because it was no longer suitable for me to live there. Seniors live in their own apartments or houses with each other because they are almost functioning adults. I knew I'd kind of miss it, considering the ultra-easy, on-site access to pussy and all, but since I was having weirder sex at the time with more and more chicks from outside of school, it wasn't that big a deal. I got a three-bedroom place with that guy Austin (beta), who was vice president then, and another brother from my pledge class, Chase (gamma), who wasn't anything interesting. I was still just the social chair, but I considered myself the alpha despite not being president since I still fucked the most chicks by far and was the biggest celebrity within the frat (similar to high school, I was just more like a porn star than prom king).

The biggest downside to the move was that it forced me to get a job. I had lived in the house as part of my scholarship, with room and board covered, but this would not extend to an independent living arrangement. Before, that summer, I had landed that internship with that hedge fund, and it was paid, which was cool (even though it was only like fifteen bucks an hour, that's still fifteen bucks more an hour than most college interns make; such is the financial industry in general), and together with the kickbacks from my external scholarships, I had a decent little nest egg saved up. It wasn't enough to carry me through the year, however, so I got a job as a barback with the intention of moving up to bartender in a few weeks time.

This did not happen. I didn't much like being a barback, and soon wasn't shy about it. I wanted to tend bar. I could tend bar. Any fucking retard can pour a beer or glass of whiskey or whatever. Most people at the bar I worked at—a college bar, close to campus, had a pub-like feel and was frequented by some assholes in my frat that didn't realize our house was better than any bar imaginable (I actually got the job because those idiots spent a lot of money there)—didn't order mixed drinks, and if they did it would be as basic as "vodka tonic" or "rum and coke." Fucking nothing to it.

But instead, a month into working there, I was still a fucking barback. Being a barback sucked. Collecting glasses, replenishing empty liquor bottles, checking beer taps, occasionally doing fucking dishes if the dishwasher was backed up or called in sick—these duties were basically just cleaning or another form of women's work. Like I was a fucking pledge again, but worse. It was hardly a job for an alpha. (Not that bartending was either—nothing in the service industry is—but bartending would have been the alpha job for my situation then, and also fun and easy: people would give you, personally, a dollar for something that took you five seconds to do. A dollar for five seconds of work isn't bad, especially if you're being paid on top of it to just kind of hang out at a party.) The fact that I once played bars as an almost-rock star made it even more intolerable. If there was one upside, it would be watching stupid douchebags, including some of the guys in my frat, buy stupid bitches drinks, seeing them piss away money on retarded shit. Lame guys buy girls drinks because, like everyone who goes to a bar, they're not actually there for a good time; they're just there to get laid (unless they're there to watch sports, which is stupid too considering it's a lot better at home). Since nothing closes a girl's legs faster than opening her purse, she'll get a bunch of free drinks she doesn't deserve (what guys don't get is it's so much easier and cheaper to never buy a girl anything while out, especially in a group, and instead act like you don't care about any of the chicks there, which makes them all really want to fuck you).

The entire time I worked there, I never washed my hands once—including after taking shits, which I'd do as often as possible, especially on busier nights, when I'd just take them quickly—and I wouldn't do any dishes that looked clean enough; I'd just put them back and touch as many of the clean ones as possible with my sort of pissed-on or shit-stinking hands. Sometimes I'd have to bring drinks over to a table, too, and would spit in them. I did these things out of spite for being a barback, and once it became clear that I wouldn't be promoted to bartender any time soon, I grew increasingly hostile to my co-workers and management, just for fun. I could have quit, just not shown up one day or something, but instead thought it would be more enjoyable to see how much I could get away with before getting fired. It didn't take long. What I did would basically get anyone fired.

I started out by looking kind of angry the entire time I was there, but this didn't make any waves since it could be confused for busy. So I began muttering things under my breath to co-workers, and I'm sure they heard at least some stuff, but not well enough to call me out on anything. They would shoot me looks afterwards, though. Then, one day, about a week after deciding to do all this, one of my frat brothers, Steven, a sophomore gamma plus, gave me the motivation I really needed to take my test to the next level. He was there and made a jab at me for still being a barback (I wasn't pissed at him; it was ridiculous for a guy as cool as me to be a fucking barback), so I decided to openly pro- voke the next co-worker to say anything to me that I didn't like. When one of the bartenders, this epsilon-at-life bitch named Kelly, who was blonde and in her late twenties and who had just all right tits, but thought she was hot shit be- cause maybe she was hot when she was eighteen, but wasn't at all anymore and had a few pock marks on her cheeks and eyes that were too close together and slanty for a white woman, who probably now just went home to a guy that hit her because she had lost her looks and knew she couldn't get anyone better, asked me to help out the dishwasher and I said "No," and she asked "What?" and I said "No, bitch," loud and clear enough for her and a customer to hear, she called me a "fratboy douchebag" and called the manager. Now we were in business. Steven thought it was hilarious. So I just sat there with him, drinking a bourbon I poured myself and refusing to work, which pissed the entire staff off since it was a Thursday night, pretty busy. The manager came down after about twenty minutes. He was this asshole named Don, somewhat built, but not as big as me, and really one of the saddest types of humans there is—sadder than the high school football coach glomming onto the glory days of his faded youth, here was an omega college dropout fuckup glomming onto his glory days of college partying and fucking up by managing a fucking bar in his late thirties and trying to act like a fun party guy most of the time, the fucking loser. He probably went home to someone like Kelly, if not her, herself (I didn't care enough to listen to any of the personal shit my co-workers talked about, including if any of them were involved with each other, but they'd make a perfect match), who he beat. Anyway, he brought me back to his office and told me he didn't like my attitude lately, asked me what happened, if I had called Kelly a bitch, and I told him Kelly was being a bitch, so I had indeed called her one, and told him he should fire her and give me her job because I'd make a better bartender, that people would like me more, would like to talk to me more and look at me more, since she was getting old and was ugly and made shitty watered-down drinks and was a giant fucking cunt who everybody hated and probably drove away over half the customers his dumbass bar could have if I were a bartender. Most of this was explained in a shouting match because Don thought he was tough shit. After getting through all that, he was like, "Get out! And don't come back! And if I see you on 'the Ave' "—the street where the bar was—"in the future, you might have a problem!" and I was all like, "Let's do this shit right now, bitch. Out back. Sad, old, stupid motherfucker!" And he pussied out because I was young and angry and bigger than him and strong and he knew I would obliterate him, and then I went home. Steven told everybody what happened back at the frat and it made me even more of a legend; nobody was really afraid it would be awkward to still drink there, and they knew it was below someone in our organization to be a fucking barback that long, especially the real alpha—some people even decided to boycott it for their complete lack of respect to me and, in turn, all of us.

Reflecting on Once Having a Shitty Job

It's hard to believe now with my amazing job that makes me so much money that I once, and not that long ago, had as shitty a job as barback. Maybe you think as a result that I might have more sympathy for people—people probably like you—the little people that still have shitty jobs. Maybe you think I shouldn't fuck with retirement funds and home mortgages and other investments made from hard-earned money in packaging and repackaging assets and selling them, or whatever the hell it is that I do, which you still probably can't figure out really. Maybe you think I should just be a human being, have a little empathy, decency. Just a little understanding . . .

Fuck that shit. Really, the definition of what makes us "human" confuses me. Showing "humanity" is like this synonym for "treating others kindly" or "like you want to be treated" or whatever, when that isn't really human at all. Whoever came up with that definition is a real scammer, and a real genius. More than anything else, humans have been terrible to each other throughout history, and this is still the way it works today and will continue to work. It's how we're wired. I have "human understanding"; that's it.

I'm a fucking alpha, and I got mine, Jack. Go get yours. Being a barback sucked, and now I don't have to do it anymore, thank God. But you do, or something enough like it, and that's not my problem. Maybe it's not fair that you play by the rules and your life is awful; that you're underemployed, bored in a lame career, or otherwise work a bullshit job you hate, and guys like me get to fuck with whatever little bit you've saved. Yes, I'm part of the rigged system that makes that suck so much for you, but you can do something about it. You just won't, or think you can't, and again, that's not my fucking problem.

I didn't make the rules, but fuck if I don't play the hell out of the game. And you know what they say—don't hate the player, hate the game. Personally, I love the game. But that's because life's overall really just another numbers game, and you know how great I am at those. If you've read this far, you should learn to love it too. All you need to know is right here; the rest boils down to whether or not you have the balls to use it. You're welcome, not that you deserve it.

Sperm Bank

After I got fired from my barback job, I had enough saved to live off campus for another three to four months max, not the rest of the year. Also, I still occasionally did coke and had little intention of giving that up, and it was expensive. Money would be needed.

At first I thought about selling my jizz to a sperm bank. It seemed like a good idea since alphas have a lot of offspring, and I knew the world would be a better place with more people like me in it. Also, because I was jerking off more at the time anyway, I figured I could make money off it, use my work smarts and be enterprising with something I was already doing—like I did in high school with going to parties and stealing pills (that itself would not work in college since most of the people I knew, those in and around my frat, already had access to all that shit). Then I found out it could take a whole six months to get paid anything, after some blood work and other dumb screening stuff and a waiting period, and only after then would they have you come in the eight times a month or whatever, I don't know. The bottom line is I couldn't wait that long.

In the end, I'm glad it worked out that way; I realized my sperm was worth a lot more than I would've been paid. Also, it bugged me that I personally wouldn't have control over who got it. Yes, alphas have a lot of kids, but they choose who to have them with. All of Gary's chicks were hot for gorillas. Here, there was a good shot some ugly woman or loser would get to carry my seed. These are the types of women that mostly go to sperm banks since they aren't hot enough to get a guy to want to marry them. The idea that the mothers of my kids could predominantly be the other type—the motivated, hot career woman that just never found the time or a guy good enough to marry—seemed a lot less likely. The more I thought about it, the more I felt I had dodged a bullet. If the child were half as smart as their genius father, they'd probably want to track me down one day when they got tired of their mother being so ugly or such a loser; realizing where all their brains and coolness came from, they'd find me and then I'd have this kid that was half ugly or half a loser in front of me trying to tell me they were mine. Fuck that. (It occurred to me at the time that perhaps the condom broke with one of the two to three hundred girls I'd fucked in my life by that point; that maybe I had gotten a girl pregnant, maybe I was already a father and never knew about it—girls are dishonest and sneaky, not that I would have liked to have known about something like that. It was weird to think that I could be a dad (and maybe I am) while not having anything to do with my seed. I am only comforted by the fact that if I do have a kid out there somewhere with some adoptive family or living with its mom or more likely its mom's parents, it's probably really attractive since I've only fucked really hot chicks.)

I couldn't get another job like the fucking barback one though, not some other menial bullshit that would make me lose respect for myself, and another finance internship couldn't be come by quickly or easily, so I decided to go to a few casinos and see what happened. I knew the odds were against me, obviously (anyone who isn't retarded knows that casinos are designed to fuck you), but I also knew I had lived kind of a charmed life. Not that everything I ever got wasn't deserved—I was smart, determined, merciless, exacting—but at the same time most things I'd ever really wanted to happen had, or if they hadn't, I realized why they hadn't eventually and knew it was for the best. My life had had no big regrets or really traumatic events except for getting cheated on that one time (and if that was karma or the universe or whatever getting me, I had since gotten it back tenfold with all the horrendous things I'd done to girls after Jasmine, so I still won), and I figured going to some casinos would probably get me where I needed to be. It did. But more in that roundabout way.

Long story short: I lost a shit-ton of money. Over the next two months, I lost everything I had made that summer, anything left from my scholarship kickbacks, and all savings from the barback job. Several thousands. Basically, I didn't have a buck to my name, nothing even for food. Fucking casinos . . . though I'm still glad I did what I did.

I briefly considered selling my car back home, but never all that seriously. Even though I still intended on moving to New York after college, where it wouldn't be needed, I couldn't let anybody else get their dirty hands on my beautiful beast, my vehicle to so much great pussy during my formative years. That car was a lot like my sperm—it was damn near priceless.

—— Back in the Frat House ——

I moved back to the frat house about four months after moving out. It was around New Years, before the start of winter quarter.

Living there again sucked at first. Had I not been the man I was, I would've punished myself for it . . . though, really, it was a pretty harsh punishment in and of itself. I was the only senior and it felt weird, especially since I had one of the three best offices and was the real alpha. I knew the only way to make it work was to own it, completely, so I did. And much like when I came in as a freshman with a different look from everyone else until people starting copying me, I was able to make it so everybody thought it was great and cool. Luckily, when I had to move back in, a junior with a single was moving out and I was able to take over his room. I don't know if my bullshit would've worked if I had to share a room with a fucking freshman or something.

See, I came back to the fraternity house because I had a dream, a revelation: as one of the oldest members with one of the highest offices, it would be better to actually be *in* the house; there at all times to offer my advice and leadership when needed. I would be doing my fellow brothers a service. More than a "big brother," I would be the biggest brother (really, more like a father), a shining example for all.

I was a visionary. I was a sage. I was a pioneer and medicine man in one. I was a messiah, but a better one than Jesus since his message is bullshit, and I would pass on tried and true wisdom about how to face the world. The frat needed this kind of presence. In fact, I created a sort of de facto role of house guru; the next year there was another one and from then on, it was official: one senior of high esteem would live in the house and provide guidance and on-call conflict resolution. I became more respected than ever.

——— Protégé ———

Around midterms I took on a protégé. He was a freshman, a delta minus when I met him, and he appreciated my teachings more than anyone else. I didn't really care about that, though. The main reason I decided to mentor him was that I realized I could use him. His name was Simon.

Simon was a good kid. He was like me before I was nine. Polite, kind, well liked in general. He was not loved and he was not feared. He was gray, beige, while someone like me would alternate between red and black. I stuck out. I mattered. He did not.

Simon had a good heart. He wanted to be a doctor.

Simon was born unbelievably wealthy. He was from New York. He was the son of an executive at Goldman Sachs. He was the baby of the family, the third of three children, with a brother and a sister in that ascending birth order.

Simon's one rebellion in his entire little life was going to school at the University of Washington, the one time he did anything as his own person. Not attending an Ivy and going somewhere all the way across the country was unheard of for someone in his family, and the only reason he got away with it was because he was able to show his dad that U-Dub actually had one of the best med schools in the country. I believe this was part of his rebellion (though he never alluded to it); he wanted to be a doctor to help people, since what his dad did was harmful to most people and really only helped himself and other rich people, incidentally. Anyhow, doing pre-med at our school gave him good odds of getting into the medical program. Even his idea of rebellion was nerdy and pussy-like.

Simon liked Seattle because it was an interesting change of scenery, he enjoyed coffee, and he thought the music coming out of the area was cool.

Simon was a virgin. He wanted to have sex. Like any reasonable person in college, he wanted to have casual sex with multiple partners.

Simon was a gift from Heaven. He was, for my intents and purposes, the new Vlad.

· · ·

I taught Simon about how the world really works, how to get chicks, how to be cool, get respect—much like I've done here, or what I did before in high school with Dennis—while he worked to get me an internship at Goldman Sachs. It wasn't like, "Hey, I will only tell you how to make a girl come if you guarantee I'll be making six figures next year," it was a lot more subtle; it grew naturally into an understanding. I made him want to help me, and I wasn't asking for all that much. I wasn't even asking for a job. Really, I just wanted an interview, just one opportunity to show them how great I was. I knew I'd be good from there.

———— Early Promise ————

After I taught Simon the basics—how to be kind of a dick while still being himself (to embrace the things in him that were more effective than nice) and how to lower his voice a few octaves (he was born a pussy and so wealthy that he never had to really compete with anyone in any meaningful way, so a pussy's voice it still was)—I taught him how to flirt with a girl at a party. Then, his first time out the gate, he made out with this sort of hot freshman dormer in his room after one of our gatherings and also played with her boobs a little. He was really happy about it, even though that's something someone should only be really happy about in the eighth grade.

I capitalized on his happiness in a conversation the next day.

"Yeah, her boobs were great, man," he said. He was in my room. "I think they were C's. Her nipples were pink, too. Not even a little brown."

"Not bad, Simon. Next time you can close."

"Yeah, damn. I better start watching some more porn!"

"Most of that's smoke and mirrors. They pull out and spit for a reason. Come back to my room some time this weekend and I'll tell you what to really do."

"Yeah, okay! Cool, thanks."

He started backing away like he was about to leave. I stopped him. "Oh, hey, I was wondering something."

"Yeah?!" He was enthusiastic, probably still thinking about playing with that girl's tits, believing my question was about that. Like I actually cared that much.

"Your dad ever talk about work? What's somebody gotta do to get an internship over there?"

"Oh . . . I don't know. He didn't really say much about it when I was growing up." He smiled earnestly, kind of shrugged.

"No?"

"All I know is it kept him really busy."

"Hmm . . . well, you think you could ask? I mean, what it takes to get an internship? Being an investment banker there is like my dream job."

"Umm . . . yeah, sure, I guess."

"Cool, man. No rush. Hey! You know what, on second thought, maybe watch a little porn, then tell me what you think you should do. That's your homework. And I'll help you cut through the bullshit and figure out how it really works."

"Okay!" he said, laughing. Then he smiled and left the room with the beautiful seed I planted in his spongy little mind.

That weekend Simon came back to deliver his report. "So, basically, you know, next time I get her shirt off, I play with her nipples, then I take her panties off and play with her clit a little bit, and then fingerfuck her a couple of times, and then I put it in."

"Something like that, those are the broad strokes I guess," I said. "But within each of those steps there's a bunch of other little steps. Also, most chicks like to put it in themselves, but that's up to you. I always stop them and put it in myself because that's more my style." I was kicking back on my bed, drinking a beer, while he sat in my desk chair.

"So what are the steps?"

"See, in porn, they don't have time to show everything that actually turns a chick on and keeps her turned on. That's why they're always pulling out and spitting or having her suck his dick in the middle of fucking, 'cause she isn't wet still. It's all kind of cut to the chase stuff like you said: put a finger in, jam it back and forth, put your dick in. Porn's mostly made for men, not women, and we don't care about what turns a chick on when we're just looking to jerk off. It's not as easy as it looks, those people are more like cartoon characters—"

"Okay . . . So what are they?" He was hanging on my every word, so excited he interrupted me, the shit.

"Relax, I heard you the first time. I was getting to it. The steps are loose and relate to principles, they're not concrete, it's not a science. It's art. The most important thing is that she feels sexy and comfortable." I laughed a little inside. While this was an integral part of foreplay, and one in which I still whole-heartedly believed, it was a pretty funny sentiment to hear coming from my mouth at a time when a lot of my own sexual practices involved shitting and punching. But it was still true, even for what I was doing, I guess. I mean, I called all of them sluts within the first few minutes of meeting them; if they were behind closed doors with me later, they obviously felt sexy enough and were comfortable in their slutdom. He nodded. "This can mean something different for every girl, though."

"This is starting to sound a lot more complicated than I thought."

"No, man. It's not. It's like anything else interpersonal, this conversation, whatever. Actually, it is its own conversation exactly. Every chick's favorite thing to do in the whole world is just talk. So talk to her physically. It's about learning the tone and running with it. Maybe she's more mellow, so you do everything nice, light, slow, but if she's aggressive, then yeah, go for it more like you were in a porno. But never just jam three fingers up there or whatever. What I mean is, make her feel good along the way, in whatever way you can tell good would be to her." I took a couple of sips. I had imparted a lot of wisdom and it made me thirsty.

"Okay. Cool."

When I was done drinking, I began again: "Obviously this is just to get and keep her in the mood. When you're actually fucking, you can just fuck as hard as you want. Go nuts. That's what it's all about and if she's a girl worth fucking again, she'll thank you for it. If not, then who cares, you already fucked her."

He laughed. "Okay."

"So that's principle number one, make her feel comfortable and sexy. What would that mean between those broad strokes you described? What would those steps be?" I was such a good teacher.

"I don't know." He fidgeted. "Touch her lightly, kiss her neck and stuff while playing with her boobs, unless she wants it rough. Then instead of kissing, suck, bite a little, stuff like that. Do this between playing with her boobs and fingering her?"

"There you go. It's not robotic, there's no set order. It's improvisation through tone. It can always change. In fact, never do anything in exactly the same way, even if the tone is the same." I took another little sip for dramatic emphasis. He waited for me, totally captivated. "You wouldn't have the same conversation twice. You'd think it was boring, and if it's with the same girl, she'd especially think it's boring."

He smiled. "Got it."

"Now principle one really only works in conjunction with principle two. You ready? That has its own steps."

"Yeah," he said, nodding.

I smiled. "Oh, hey, just a side note, because I just remembered right now, did you ever talk to your dad?"

He looked confused. I guess it was a little weird that I would be thinking about his dad while talking about sex, but whatever. I wanted to sandwich it between these principles I was making up on the spot and there wasn't really an appropriate place for a segue. If he knew how much power and respect being an investment banker would get me, though, he probably would've understood how it was a question suitable in a conversation like this. "Shit, no, not yet." Little fucker.

"It's cool. Just let me know when you do."

"Yeah, I'll call him later." Damn right you will. The advice I was dispensing was as valuable as his entire net worth, if not more so, really.

"Thanks. Anyway, so principle two actually carries over from the whole flirtation thing we were talking about the other week. You gotta tease."

"Like ask her if her nails are real or something in bed?"

"No. Fuck no." Simon was kind of stupid. It would be tough to be so naïve and stupid, even if you were set for life. "Tease her physically. Checker the romantic or aggressive touching by withholding. Kiss her and then stop. Touch her tits and then stop. Touch her clit and then circle around it. Then touch again and repeat until you know they'd kill you if you moved away. It drives them nuts. It's like when you're flirting: you are excellent, and then you offer a backhanded compliment or half-hearted insult, then you're sweet, you make sure she feels special, then you go away, then you come back and make her feel good about herself even more, then you close. It's the same with a boob or whatever. Hold it, but don't touch the tit, move away, circle around the nipple, make her want you to touch it, move away again, then touch it directly, then go away again, then touch it again, harder. Drives them fucking nuts, man—makes the floodgates open wide. Girls love to be teased. In all forms. They've loved it since they were kids on a playground, when whatever boy was calling their dress ugly and chasing them around with a stick. They've loved it since they were toddlers playing peek-a-boo with their dads." That last part actually made me down the rest of my beer I was so happy with myself, felt so deserving of a reward.

"Holy shit, man. Wow. I think I get it."

"Then, once you're in, fuck it, man. Have fun. In and out is all you really need to know I guess. Maybe play with her tits or kiss her neck or something if you think she's getting sore or isn't that into it. But otherwise, that's your time. Go all-out." I threw the bottle in the trash across the room from my spot on the bed. It made it in.

He was smiling to himself, nodding. "Thanks a lot Frank."

"You got it. Good luck."

"I'll let you know how it goes. And I'll talk to my dad soon." The plan was coming along. He smiled his childlike little smile and left the room.

—— Hiccups ——

We had a party the next weekend, not a rager, but something big enough. I watched Simon do his thing. He talked to a few girls, but all of them ended up fucking upperclassmen as far as I could tell. That night I poured a golden shower on some dormer freshman who I called a slut and told was "almost hot enough to fuck with the lights on" within the first thirty seconds of meeting her.

The next day, Simon dropped by. He was leaning against my door. "My dad said most of their interns have MBAs or are from Ivies." Bingo.

"Hmmm . . . guess that makes sense. MBAs and Ivies. A lot of those people are winners."

"Yeah."

"Hey, did you know that MBA students are the most likely type of grad students to cheat on tests and stuff?"

"Yeah?"

"You know why?"

"No, why?"

"'Cause cheaters are winners. If you ever get a girl-friend, cheat on her. It'll make you feel better about yourself."

He looked down. "Umm . . . okay."

"Come in, shut the door." He did. "Sit." He did, on the edge of my bed. I had just been studying and was sitting in my office chair. I put my hands behind my head. "So how'd it go last night, cowboy? Lose that v-card?"

"Struck out."

"Struck out?"

"Yeah." He shrugged.

"What happened?"

He hiccupped. "I don't know."

I tilted my head. "Well that's your first problem right there. You should know."

"I guess—" He hiccupped again. It was annoying. "I might have been a little nervous."

"Uh-oh. Don't do that."

"Yeah, I know. Girls like confidence."

"Girls don't *like* confidence. They *need* confidence. Game's lost before it's started without it." He sat there lis-tening and hiccupping, which continued to irritate me, but since it also made him seem so weak and me so strong, I felt like I could keep going. "It's physiological. See, a man is confident because a dick is hard, forceful. It's the aggres-sive, confident organ. A woman's supposed to be warm, nurturing, like a wet pussy. It's the receptive organ. That's why people call nervous guys pussies. They're not being men."

"I couldn't help it." He shook his head and hiccupped. "They were all really pretty." Again. "Maybe I should have drank more."

"Maybe, or maybe you need to go back to the first thing I told you. You gotta be yourself and you gotta own it. You're awesome, man. Now show them. You're smart, you're from New York, you wanna be a doctor, you're rich, you're in our frat—all of these things are panty-droppers, Simon." I got up and opened the door. "Don't come back until you at least get a blowjob."

He left the room, kind of moping like a little bitch and hiccupping still. I gave him tough love, but it was for his own good. I didn't want to press the internship thing anymore (even though he had only told me something I already knew) while he was in a down state. The dialogue was moving and that was all that mattered. I would wait until he was in a better mood for the next move. And I would get him there by getting him ass.

—— Breakthrough ——

I thought about telling whatever girl I was gonna fuck at our next party that I'd make her come four times in a row if she gave Simon a little head. In the end, I didn't have to. My brilliant advice really was all he needed.

He fucked someone for the first time during the week after I kicked him out of my room. It was that one chick whose boobs he played with or whatever from before. I guess he had her over to hang out, and maybe because he was more confident, maybe because he had already done some ground work, maybe because he went into the situation knowing exactly what to do and how to do it, he got his. He was ecstatic. He came straight to my room after she went home. "I did it, man!" He stood in my doorway with swagger, beaming.

"Did what? Got a blowjob?"

"No, the whole thing. I had sex with Gabby, that girl I told you about from the other week."

"Hey! Thatta boy." Sitting at my desk again, I reached into my mini fridge and pulled out a beer. "Have a beer." I handed it to him. I opened one too. I was proud of myself.

He opened the bottle and drank from it, exhaling with satisfaction. "Yeah, Frank. It was great. But she also gave me a little head beforehand, too, to answer your question!"

"Atta boy!!!" I slapped his hand in a big high-five. It made a loud smacking noise. "What did I tell you? What did I tell you?"

"You're a genius." He did two little bow down motions.

I was. Am. "What can I say?" I took a sip. He smiled. Then I asked, "So how was it? How'd you do?"

"It was awesome. Felt really good, even with a condom."

"Wait until you have sex without. But still. You did it, man."

"Yeah, I didn't really mind because I was able to go for longer than without, I bet. I think I lasted ten minutes. And for a while I had her in doggy!"

"Good for you, Simon. Not bad for a first time. A lot of guys are too pussy to take charge and just do missionary their whole first time."

"Naw, no way. I was in complete control."

"Make her think she's your girlfriend and start having unprotected sex. I'm telling you, it's amazing."

He laughed, "Maybe."

"Then cheat on her of course."

"Yeah, I don't know . . ."

"Or don't and just fuck somebody else this weekend!"

He smiled. "Sounds good to me!" He gave me another high-five. "Well, yeah, thanks. I appreciate all the help." He was definitely more sure of himself, more of a beta minus now, but still kind of a pussy for thanking me and all. I would've never thanked somebody for something like that.

"No worries, Simon. Let me know if you need any more coaching."

"I think I got it from here." He took a sip.

"I created a monster!" We both laughed. He was over the moon. On cloud nine. And he knew it was all because of me. I taught him how to fish—how to be cool, how to get laid. He held himself differently, moved his face differently, his voice wasn't anything like it was when I first met him. He actually seemed like someone who could get chicks, even if he was still sort of a nice guy pussy who gave heartfelt thanks for sex advice when a nod and a little bragging are all that's required. The laughter waned. "Hey . . . so I was doing some reading and apparently it *is* possible to get an internship at Goldman Sachs coming out of undergrad if you didn't go to an Ivy."

"You know what? I'm gonna talk to my dad." Then there it was. I smiled and took a drink. He nodded. "Just, ummm, send me your résumé. I'll pass it along."

"Cool, man. Thanks."

"No problem. I'll put in the good word."

"I mean, I've had a hedge fund internship. My grades are pretty damn good. I had the SATs for an Ivy."

"You don't have to sell me. My dad's such a bigwig, you're as good as in. It's all about who you know. Don't know why I didn't think of it before." I really had created a monster. Post-sex Simon not only seemed smarter and cooler, but smooth as shit. He was starting to sound like a little *me*. Fuck beta minus, this kid was the alpha freshman.

I smiled. "Yeah . . ."

"Hey, man, it's the least I can do. He's still a little pissed I'm out here, but whatever, I'll butter him up. You'll be good. Good as in."

"Cool. Thanks."

"I don't know why you'd want to move to New York, though. All the good pussy's out here!"

"I guess I'll just have to wait and see."

And I did. Simon passed my résumé along and late that spring I flew over and interviewed with Goldman Sachs, except it wasn't for an internship—it was for a New Analyst position. After meeting with me and seeing how great I was, and after taking some tests, which I passed with flying colors (I've always been awesome at taking tests), and after the word from Simon's dad, I was indeed in. I moved to New York once I graduated that June, with moving expenses covered. The pussy has been extraordinary ever since. He was very, very wrong.

———— Heroin ————

Before moving, I tried heroin. Basically I just wanted to know what it felt like and to be able to say that I did it (not that anyone's asked or I would've admitted to it in the past if accused, but you know what I mean; it's one of the most badass things a person can do). I had heard it was better than sex. It wasn't.

I just snorted it; didn't do the whole pound the vein thing (again, fuck needles—they're phallic). I felt this body high at first, and then was pretty relaxed, a little sleepy, but still feeling amazing, kind of like after really great sex . . . I don't know, maybe that part was slightly better, like nothing in the world was ever bad or wrong ever, like nobody ever cheated on me, like Vlad never existed, like I could have been a professional football player if I still felt like it . . . but then I got pretty sick and almost threw up. It sucked and I felt like shit. I hate almost throwing up. Only pussies throw up.

It was also sort of my last goodbye to the whole music thing, the rock-and-roll mythos. I let go of anything still bothering me about all that and was then officially, fully committed to working in finance. Since I moved to big, beautiful, bright, shiny New York it's been "go, go, go!" so I'm glad I got that shit out of the way first in gloomy, doomy fucking Seattle.

—— Investment Banking ——

The position began with this six-week long New Banker Training program. This was when I kind of learned how my life would be for the next few years. It sucked, but in the end I knew it would be worth it.

I worked on average ninety hours and six days per week. I understood this would be the case going in, but didn't really get it until I lived it. After the training was complete, this didn't change. It won't change any time soon; when I assume more responsibility, get a couple years as a VP under my belt, the best I can hope for ultimately is a sixty to seventy hour week (like with everything, the more you're paid, the less actual work you do). I've never worked harder than I've had to, so it's a little weird to be working this much, but right now I do feel like it's all shit I have to do. I've gotten used to it.

See, investment banking is my true calling, so I'm comfortable making sacrifices. I've basically given my life to it these past few years. It's sort of like joining the Army, except instead of going off and losing a leg in some faraway desert to make some defense contractor or oil guy rich, I get to sell things like collateralized debt obligations and credit default swaps to idiots and make myself rich. Also, I like numbers, obviously. I've always liked math because it's more masculine than writing (except this): with numbers everything is definite, hard—like a dick, like a man. I still get to bend the numbers more or less to my will, though, which makes me feel even better about working with them; it's like I'm overpowering something that's supposed to be even more manly than I am, something concrete—absolute, infallible. But I make it so it's not. I make 2+2=5, and I get to keep the remaining 1 that's not really there. I truly am a Master of the Universe. I don't just do "God's work," as our CEO once put it, it's more like I've actually become a god myself.

My first year I made 120k, consisting of an 80 grand base salary, a 10k signing bonus, and a 30k performance bonus. I brought in a little more the next, around 145. Then, I was promoted to an associate after hanging out with the right guys in the office gym (when I could get gym breaks—my body is still great, but I am not the Adonis I used to be; my physique after the roids had remained impressive enough all the way through college with weight training and whey protein, but working long hours almost every day of the week now makes it hard to maintain muscle mass, so these days I'm more trim, like I was in early high school). Last year I made a little over 200k. I'm on track to take home around 300 this year, and expect within the next two or so to be made a vice president, where the real fun will begin and I'll probably rake in around 750k to a million in my first year (as far as the young bankers are concerned, I'm definitely the alpha, a celebrity of sorts in my division and to the people that matter, which drives my co-workers up the wall since they know I didn't go to MIT or Harvard; also, with the economy still what it is, some of those Ivy-type guys have gotten fired, the losers, so my success is even more infuriating). I'm sure you see where I'm going with this. (And none of this includes my extra income from the little night trading I do, and because I'm such a fucking genius, I'm doing very, very well at that, too.) Basically, now, I'm pretty fucking loaded.

I only plan on doing this for the next five or six more years. I'll be a multi-millionaire by the time I'm thirty, probably with a quarter to mid-eight figures to my name, and I think that's all I'll need to consider my pursuit of happiness over. The allure of being a billionaire or some shit isn't enough to keep me working like this if I can still live as an alpha by the broader world's standards—again, only work as hard as you have to. In my eight or so years in the workforce, I'll still have made exponentially more than 99-or-whatever percent of Americans make in their lifetimes. I'll retire, continue to invest privately, but keep enough to live comfortably and still be considered wealthy, probably here in New York, but with another home somewhere cheap and tropical since our winters are fucking awful. Then everything will be absolutely perfect.

——— Current Sex Life ———

When I moved here, I got over all that really deviant shit. I had never deleted Jasmine as a Facebook friend, so I could track her success against mine (and I'm sure that's why she never deleted me, either—she must be fucking depressed). She's still stuck in Seattle, working for some boutique bullshit investment place, I'm sure not making any money. So, basically, she just got fucked here and thrown back out west and nothing ever became of all that, like any reasonable person would assume would happen. Her failure and the fact that I killed a portion of fifty or so girls' souls over that year-and-a-half by hitting or pissing or shitting on them or whatever were enough for me I guess. I knew I had won, and there was no use in beating a dead horse in New York, where I could have a fresh start. (Really, though, that fresh start was more like beating a dead horse's dead fetus: New York's made me more evil than I ever was before. See, like I said at the start, because I do what I do, I know I'm figuratively fucking a lot of people around the world (many of them female, thankfully, since most people in the world are female), fucking them over, fucking their lives up, doing more damage than a Donkey Punch or Jelly Doughnut ever could. And we'll always get bailed out if shit gets fucked up on our end. It's great.)

So I started having sex normally again, and by normally I mean like the pro I am. I do this with girls who only seem to get hotter and hotter, and while I grow older, they still remain on average at age eighteen-point-five. That's the beautiful thing about being a guy like me. Even in college, I'd rarely fuck seniors because a lot of them had faint age lines starting to emerge on their faces. If there was a single wrinkle on the forehead or around the mouth, or even just a hint of matured pouchiness where the cheek meets the nose—all of which I could also detect through makeup (or would just assume were underneath if it was caked on too fucking thick)—I was gone. That shit grossed me out more than, like, an outie belly button, or even too much pubic hair.

Sometimes I go out to a fancy dinner by myself, make eyes across the room, fuck an NYU or Columbia girl in the bathroom before dessert (they're always pretty grateful since so many actual fags go to their schools). And also, occasionally, when I'm really busy, maybe only have one or two free hours in a day, I get an "escort."

Now, I know it might seem weird for an alpha to get a hooker, but it's not, really. Countless politicians, actors, musicians, and athletes have done it. Charlie Sheen's fucked a lot of them; he's pretty cool. Tiger Woods, too. Paying for sex is way more honest than buying some bitch a drink at a bar. The thrill of "the conquest" ended in college, when there stopped being such things as conquests, when sex just happened. So, really, getting prostitutes here is just a matter of convenience. Alphas are busy and we know what we want. And plus, they do some pretty great sex shit more easily and better. Sometimes a pro really is a pro. I only use them for the Pussy Bingo project, making sure they aren't too far removed from remote parts of the globe (it would be absurd to buy a pretty white girl; there are so many here and they're all as desperate as the far-gone sad bitches they idolize from *Sex and the City* or whatever). They have all cost several hundred to a couple thousand dollars and have all been beautiful.

When I get a vacation, I usually go on a trip to some exotic location like Thailand or Brazil and fuck amazing-looking chicks there. Last time, I went to Shanghai and received countless massages that ended in Helicopter Blow-jobs, among other awesome, oriental sex things. I also started back up the practice of keeping a "girlfriend" or two at any given time for unprotected sex, but none of them are important enough to mention by name.

I imagine I'll live more or less like this after I retire, hopping around with the jet set and fucking gorgeous eighteen- and nineteen-year-olds everywhere until I decide it's time to settle down and actually spread the seed, raise some little-me's (once I get married, I'm still going to travel and cheat as often as possible, though). I think I can wait until my mid-forties or fifties or whatever, like Dave Letterman did (he's an alpha); I'll still be able to keep up with my kids into my sixties and seventies, especially since I'll probably live well past 100 with all the advances in medical science these days and my wealth. I know my kids will be incredible, just not as great as me.

<h2 style="text-align:center">———— Epilogue ————</h2>

Maybe this book will make me kind of famous but it's not likely since nobody really reads. If it's made into a movie, though, I might be fucked, might have to change my name and all that. At least I'd get rich enough where I could probably quit banking (while I like playing with numbers and fucking people with them, doing it for ninety hours a week can suck sometimes); I'd make sure I got back-end points and I know millions of people would go and see a movie based on me. If it doesn't get made into a movie and I still have to work, I'm not really worried about my colleagues finding out I tried heroin or shat on girls or beat myself or did any of the other shit I did, since they don't have time to read for fun, probably have done worse, and, if not, wouldn't care, anyway.

I didn't just write this for money; it was important to me to define and record my youth while still living it, when it was the freshest. I knew I had to get it published, otherwise it would just be masturbation—which is fun, don't get me wrong, but I'm much happier spreading the seed that is this story instead of just splattering it all over myself. This is how I want to be celebrated and ultimately remembered, no matter what I do with the rest of my life. There's nothing like youth. Waiting to release this posthumously would have been pretty fucking stupid; while I'm sure this will only appreciate in value throughout the years, will probably become a classic, and I'll be a major literary celebrity at some point long after I'm dead, it's obviously best to enjoy the fruits of your labor during your lifetime if you can. Still, I hope I don't get too fucking famous (though, again, as a writer, I probably won't while I'm alive). It would suck to have to wear disguises everywhere or change my name. I fucking love my name.

It's possible you're wondering how I found the time to write such a great book in between making a lot of money and fucking a bunch of super hot chicks. The short answer is: re-read this shit. You obviously didn't learn anything. I'm a fucking genius-king, that's how. But if you wanna be a bitch about it, I wrote it mostly on my iPhone to and from work or at lunch to give me something to do for a few months. People that just read newspapers or shitty new or faggy old books or that just listen to music or play Sudoku or crosswords or Angry Birds or whatever bullshit on their commute and don't ever do anything more than just pass time annoy me (it takes reminding myself I make over a grand a day and that I fuck beautiful, exotic girls all the time to feel better). Then I just cleaned it up a little bit while drinking good scotch at home in my luxury apartment, while waiting for one of my "girlfriends" or a prostitute, or sometimes both, to come over and fuck my brains out (when you're as rich as me, your "girlfriend" will be down for a threesome with a prostitute, or you will simply find another "girlfriend"). It wasn't hard. But I guess not everybody can be as great and talented and genius as me. If Gary the gorilla were a person, even *he'd* be a gamma compared to me. Yeah, you can be anything you want to be, but that doesn't mean you will be; not everyone can be an alpha; that's why I'm the best. That's why I'm me.